NO TURNING BACK

Sometimes life leads you in directions unknown to your heart. Sometimes you follow without a map and end up in exactly the place you needed to be. Sometimes there's "No turning Back".

Susan Kimmel

Library of Congress Control Number:		2016906113
ISBN:	Hardcover	978-1-5144-8545-3
	Softcover	978-1-5144-8544-6
	eBook	978-1-5144-8543-9

Print information available on the last page.

Rev. date: 05/26/2016

To order additional copies of this book, contact:
Xlibris
1-888-795-4274
www.Xlibris.com
Orders@Xlibris.com
738520

Sometimes life leads you in directions unknown to your heart. Sometimes you follow without a map and end up in exactly the place you need to be. Sometimes there's "No turning Back."

CHAPTER 1

The race is not to the swift or the battle to the strong, nor does food come to the wise or wealth to the brilliant or favor to the learned; but time and chance happen to them all.

—Ecclesiastes 9:11

Warren Oscar Wright was the owner of WOW Real Estate. He was a self-made millionaire, but at the age of thirty-two, he was still single. Physically, he was quite attractive. He was tall and rawboned with the craggy look of an unfinished sculpture. He had quite an ingenuously appealing face with smooth toned olive skin stretched over high cheekbones. He was very conscious of his towering athletic physique, which at times caused him to present a conceited aura. His dark hair, just graying at the temples, brought many second glances from women of all ages. There was no doubt about it. Not only was he a very rich and handsome man but he also boasted a certain sensuality that drove most women crazy.

Warren had served two terms in Vietnam. As a teenager, he had watched the news every night since coverage began on the war. He had listened as President Johnson advocated for peace, hoping that it would come before Uncle Sam called him to help fight. But in 1967, he was drafted at the age of nineteen and convinced himself that he was invincible. When he arrived in Vietnam, he was not prepared for the devastation he witnessed, not only with the death of human beings but also with how the war was suffocating the life out of an entire country.

He had been given the position of a gunner for the Twenty-Fifth Infantry. His job was to literally hang out of a helicopter and try to shoot human beings before they shot him. He had watched in horror as two of his buddies took hits and died right there in the stomach of the helicopter. He could do nothing but continue to shoot rounds and rounds of ammunition at targeted areas on the ground. He didn't have time to say good-bye or even the luxury of crying. There was no time for grieving in the middle of a war, no time to feel sorry for yourself or for those around you. Taking time for either meant possible death. Every minute in that helicopter was spent fighting for your life and the friends beside you.

As a soldier, Warren took his job seriously. He had no desire to be flown home in a box draped with the American flag. He wanted to be in an upright position when he got off the plane. His main motive for staying alive during the first five months was a girl named Maddie. She was the one thing that had kept him going for many days. Dear sweet Maddie—she was his high school sweetheart. They had been together for two years, almost inseparable. He could always shut his eyes and remember her exactly as she was at the train station when he left for basic training. To him, she was exquisite; a little on the fragile side, but he liked that. It meant that she needed him to take care of her. At least that was what he thought until a Dear John letter found its way to his stack of mail during October, his fifth month in Vietnam. Not only was he surrounded by physical devastation but now his heart also was feeling the same pain. The love he thought was strong between himself and Maddie had failed him. The letter caused him to lose control of his will to live. In fact, he even began to dare "Charlie" to shoot him, feeling like he had no real reason to go home. But even the Vietnamese guerillas didn't want what he was offering.

Warren survived the next eight months and returned home, only to be ridiculed and cursed as he made his way through the airport. Someone had even spit at him. His parents couldn't even take a few hours off from work to welcome him home. When he called to give them his arrival time, they told him to get a cab and that they would see him at home—not exactly the kind of homecoming one wanted after being away for twelve months. But why should he have expected any more? They had never been the kind of parents who really took an interest in any of his endeavors. Before he went to Vietnam, he was the quarterback on his high school football team and, as a senior, was being recognized as "player of the year." A banquet was being held in his honor in the high school cafeteria, but his dad couldn't get off work, and his mother wouldn't come alone. His coach, not knowing that his parents weren't there, asked them to stand and come forward. Warren never knew who was more embarrassed, him or Coach Wilson. It was that night that finalized Warren's plans to leave Millersburg as soon as he turned nineteen. Six more months, and he would go where he wanted. Little did he know that Uncle Sam already had a train ticket waiting for him. Two weeks before his nineteenth birthday, the mailman delivered the dreaded notice informing Warren that he had a place waiting for him in the U.S. Army. He was expected to arrive on the army base of Fort Hood in Texas on June 21, 1967.

Warren's dream was to be an architect, but in all reality, he knew he never would make it through another four years of school. He had not been the best student in high school.

Sports, mostly football, had taken all his time and energy. He had also enjoyed woodshop, which was an incentive for his future profession. But even before he had the opportunity to plan a career, Uncle Sam stepped in and took control of his life for two long years.

After his return from Vietnam to his hometown, his parents thought he should look for a job right away. His dad couldn't understand how a young man could stay in bed after the sun had risen. It wasn't that Warren wanted to stay in bed till noon, but lying on clean dry sheets was a luxury that he hadn't had for so long that he just couldn't make himself crawl out of bed in the morning. And really, what reason did he have to put his feet on the floor? His parents had no understanding of what he had been through in Vietnam. All they knew was that he was home and that he should pick up where he left off. And what exactly did they think that was? He wasn't in high school anymore, and he didn't want to work at Carter Construction, where half of the town worked and where everyone was over the age of forty. He didn't feel emotionally strong enough to face questions from coworkers every day about the war. Most of Carter's employees had never even been in the service, let alone combat duty. There were some who were veterans of World War II, and even though they had lived through some horrible combat, Vietnam was a totally different kind of battleground. And no matter how much a person tried to explain the surroundings in that distant country, no words ever seemed to support a real purpose for being there.

Television and newspaper reporters had played a big part in how the war was perceived. Forgetting the politics of the war, reporters allowed the world to believe that all soldiers were nothing more than drug addicts and were unnecessarily killing women and children. College and university students began protesting, swaying the American people into believing their reports. A substantial part of the public's interest seemed only to focus on the negativity of the war. But families of those being sent home in caskets had totally different perspectives. Their new reality was that the American flag not only stood for freedom but now also represented death.

Warren knew he was one of the lucky ones. He had hid in rice paddies. He knew what the words "be still" meant when lying in a foxhole. Death had passed by him many times. But what was it all for? He had come home to absolutely no support, especially from his parents. After all, he was their only son. He thought he would at least have their encouragement and maybe some compassion, but as it turned out, they seemed to believe everyone but him. His friends were either off to college or still in the army. He began to question his reason for living yet again feeling secluded as if he were the only veteran in town. He had no one to talk to or go to for emotional maintenance. No one understood the thought process of a soldier except another soldier. It was that thought that motivated him into setting his alarm clock for the next morning. He was not used to rising so early, but with this new revelation, he had wanted to be up, dressed, and ready to meet with the army recruiter.

CHAPTER 2

So do not throw away your confidence; it will be richly rewarded.

—Hebrews 10:35

As Warren walked through the door of the army office, he had given a friendly nod to two young men who were filling out applications. They returned the gesture complacently and returned to their paperwork, having no idea that signing those papers could be the same as signing their death warrants. There had been a rumor going around that coming forward to sign up before your draft notice meant you wouldn't be assigned to the front lines, so thousands were coming early for that. Little did they know that, in Vietnam, there was no front line, and Uncle Sam didn't care whether you were a volunteer or a draftee. You would go where you were ordered.

Warren thought about walking over and chatting with these boys for a minute, but what would he say? Don't sign up? That would be rather foolish advice since that was exactly what he was here to do.

As he approached the metal desk, Warren quickly looked at the man's name tag and offered his hand as he said, "Good morning, Sergeant Hill. My name is Warren Wright. If I had a brother, I could say I'm one of the Wright brothers. But since I'm an only child, I guess I can't do that."

Sergeant Hill, failing to see the humor in Warren's introduction, spoke in a commanding manner. "What can I do for you today, Mr. Wright?"

The beginning of a smile tipped the corners of Warren's mouth as he said, "I'm here to reenlist," and then he added in a courteous but patronizing voice, "Sir."

"Did you say that you want to reenlist?"

"Yes, sir, that's what I said."

"When were you discharged?"

"July 31st."

Sergeant Hill's expression stilled and grew serious before he spoke. "But that was just last month."

"Yes, sir, it was, but I would like to serve a second tour in Vietnam." He now had the full attention of not only the sergeant but the two boys at the table as well. They had laid their pens down as if waiting to hear his next announcement.

Sergeant Hill pushed himself to a standing position, pulled a form out of his file drawer, took a pen out of a homemade pencil holder, and said, "Sign here."

Expecting more questions, with no emotion, Warren asked, "That's it? No background check? Don't you even want to know if I had an honorable discharge? Don't I have to fill out some more paperwork?"

"One question at a time please," said Sergeant Hill. Smirking, he pointed to the two boys at the table. "Yes, there is a lot of paperwork to be filled out but not as much as those two over there." The sergeant sat back down at his desk, made some phone calls, and pushed more papers in front of Warren to be signed. "If you'll just sign all of these, you'll once more be property of the United States Army."

Warren's expression held a note of mockery as he saluted Sergeant Hill. He picked up the copies of his enlistment forms without speaking another word and walked proudly to his pickup, where he hurriedly leafed through the pages to find his departure date. His lips twisted into a cynical smile as he saw the yellow area that Sergeant Hill had been so kind to highlight.

Warren left home for the second time, with an unemotional departure between him and his parents. He spent three months at Fort Benning, Georgia, training to be a chief warrant officer. He then received orders to once again visit Vietnam. Arriving in Saigon the day before Thanksgiving as a replacement with the 25th Infantry Division was a difficult time to be alone, even though he was in the midst of many other soldiers. The smell of the country and the intense humidity in the air brought instant memories of his first tour. While being transported to his unit in Cho Che, he realized just how vulnerable his comrades became when talk of home developed. They were very homesick and depressed from being in the field for the past several weeks. Many had received no mail, and Thanksgiving dinner would be eaten from a can. The atmosphere surrounding the base camp was very distraught.

Warren's status was different his second time around. He was now a chief warrant officer, which meant not only a few more dollars in his pocket each month but also that he was the one in charge while out on a mission. He flew a lot of successful expeditions and organized many ground troops in pursuit of the enemy. His two-year duty was eventually over, and he found himself on a plane again returning to the United States. Stepping onto American soil, knowing that there would be no one to welcome him was not as traumatic as his first return. This time, he didn't care that no one was waiting for him. Things hadn't changed much at his parents' house. They still insisted he get a job right away.

As often as he remembered saying that he never wanted to work at Carter Construction, he now found himself in dire need of a job, and Carter's provided a better paycheck than most businesses in town, so he applied for a position. He worked long hours, saving every penny he could. He also began spending his spare time studying for the North Carolina real estate exam. He passed on the very first try and was offered a job with the only real estate office in town. He quickly accepted and wasted no time quitting the construction trade. He once again worked extended hours, learning all he could about the housing market, and became known as a most powerful but still credible agent. Within two years, he had branched out on his own and, with a small loan from the local bank, had opened up WOW Real Estate Agency.

CHAPTER 3

And do not forget to do good and to share with others,
for with such sacrifices God is pleased.

—Hebrews 13:16

Harold Snider was the janitor of WOW Real Estate. He had been there since the day Warren opened the doors. He was the most loyal employee that Warren had ever known. In the community, he was known as Hoafie; and every day, he could be seen walking to work, wearing his brown penny loafers and a Pittsburgh Steelers ball cap. When he wasn't working, he could always be seen with a cigar hanging from the corner of his mouth and his hands in his pockets, ready to pass out Tootsie Rolls. Children were convinced that his pockets had some magic powers because they never appeared empty.

No one knew exactly how old he was, but every year, he swore he was thirty-nine. His parents had died in a car accident when he was eleven. Their neighbor, who owned and operated a service station and garage, had taken him in and became his legal guardian. Hoafie, even though slightly mentally retarded, was a gentle soul. His new family, not wanting to subject him to any more ridicule at school, decided to teach him at home. He helped in the garage and became a master mechanic. Most of the townsfolk said he knew more about their cars than the manufacturers.

Warren had met Hoafie one day while attempting to change a flat tire along the side of the road. He sensed someone watching him, and when he turned around, there stood a large man—hands in his pockets—flashing a huge grin showing a few missing teeth. Warren recognized him as the man who he had seen walking along the road so many times. He stood about six feet tall with broad shoulders and arms, which seemed too short for the rest of his body. He was built like a tank and moved just about as slow. Warren stood up, held out his hand, and said, "Hi, I'm Warren Wright. You're Hoafie, aren't you?"

The big man nodded his head up and down and, with an unbelievably strong grip, shook Warren's hand. He looked toward the flat tire and said, "You need help?"

Before Warren could actually say that yes, he would appreciate some help, Hoafie was loosening the lug nuts on the wheel. Warren had never seen anyone change a tire so fast. He was very impressed and asked Hoafie if he would like a ride somewhere. Once again, Warren had no chance to answer before Hoafie had his hand on the Jaguar's handle and was sitting on the front seat. Warren laughed at the man's tenacity and promptly asked him if he needed a job. Hoafie quickly nodded his head yes and took a big puff on his cigar. Warren smiled, feeling in his gut that he had just made a good decision.

Hoafie proved Warren's gut to be right. He turned out to be a great employee. He did exactly as he was told, and he could fix anything, except plumbing issues. He was great to have around when the ladies decided that the furniture in the office needed to be rearranged. He could pick up desks and file cabinets with the strength of the Hulk. Some had even hired him to move furniture at their homes.

Hoafie wore suspenders to hold up his pants. When asked why he never wore a belt, his answer was "Why do I need a belt when I have suspenders?" No one could ever argue with that. His glasses, usually held together with tape and falling down to the middle of his nose, gave the impression that he had a nervous twitch because, every ten seconds, his hand flew to his face to push them up. He was never seen without gum in his mouth, and not only did he chew it but he cracked it as well. People remembered that sound as much as they remembered his infectious smile. It always seemed to deepen into laughter, followed by "Good morning" or "Good afternoon."

One day, one of the agents in the office, joking with Hoafie, told him that he should be draining the water from the toilets each evening and putting in clean water. So Hoafie found a shop vac, sucked out water from each of the five toilets, and replaced it with water from the spigot. Returning to the office one evening unexpected, Warren found Hoafie in the restrooms carrying water to the commodes in a gallon pitcher. After hearing Hoafie's explanation, he was barely able to keep the laughter from his voice as he explained that the water was fresh and clean every time the commode was flushed. Hoafie merely stood there with a blank expression on his face, which soon turned to confusion. Warren walked to his office and nearly doubled over with laughter. Hoafie wasn't real smart when it came to common sense, but he was the best handyman and mechanic in Millersburg, and he didn't deserve to be made fun of in such a public way. He would deal with the agent tomorrow.

Right now, Warren felt obligated to show a little compassion to this gentle giant. Maybe he could help him with his confidence if he started treating him with a little more respect. He had never been mean to Hoafie, but he knew that, unconsciously, he had never treated him with as much dignity as he treated his other employees. He was going to change that, and it was going to start tonight. As he locked his office door behind him, he called for Hoafie.

"Yes, sir?"

"Get your coat, Hoafie. We're going down to Cherry's to have some dinner."

"Sir, I don't think I should go in there with you."

"Why not, Hoafie? Don't worry about the cost. You can have anything you want to eat tonight, and I'm buying."

Hoafie's face split into a wide grin as he grabbed his coat from the hook on the door and said, "I'm ready when you are, sir."

Walking into Cherry's Steakhouse was the biggest event ever for Hoafie. He had never been in a place so big. Seeing that Hoafie was having difficulty with the menu, Warren asked if he liked steak. His smile widened in approval. "Well then, Hoafie, let me order you the finest filet mignon in town."

Warren was so proud of himself for befriending Hoafie that he decided to treat himself to a few drinks. He hadn't had a drink since he was told that he was a diabetic two years ago. He remembered the night as if it were yesterday. He had stopped at Joe's Bar for a quick drink on his way home, had passed out, and had actually fallen off the bar stool. The bartender called an ambulance because no one could wake him up. After a lot of testing, it was determined that he had type II diabetes and would have to administer a shot each day to his body. Since that day, he hadn't even had a sip of alcohol. So what could it hurt tonight if he only had one drink? He would just inject a little more insulin when he gave himself his next shot. Being sober for two years was something to celebrate.

With a click of his fingers, he motioned for the waiter to come to their table. "How about bringing me a cherry vodka with a bit of club soda, on the rocks please?"

"Yes, sir, I'll be right back."

"Could you check on our dinners? It's been a while since we ordered, and the big fellow sitting here is mighty hungry."

Within minutes, the waiter returned with Warren's drink and a huge tray of food. He placed two plates on the table, both laden with juicy filets. A baked potato, covered with foil, lay nestled alongside the steaks. The salads and two loaves of the restaurant's famous pumpernickel bread had already been devoured as they had waited.

As the vodka ran slowly over Warren's tongue and down his throat, he sat back and savored the moment. He didn't realize just how much he had missed this sweet taste. Ordering this particular drink had always caused his buddies to make a lot of jokes about what they called "sissy drinks." They had names for men who drank sugary drinks. Tonight was different. Tonight he could drink in peace—no jokesters in the crowd, only Hoafie.

Warren watched Hoafie as he cut his steak and put it in his mouth. He chewed each piece just like he walked—slowly. At this rate, he would still be chewing at closing time. So Warren decided to have some patience tonight and amuse himself with a few more drinks.

Totally relaxed and now somewhat intoxicated, Warren began moving his glass in a circular motion, swirling the ice cubes, putting himself in a trance. Inadvertently, his mind began reflecting on his life up until this point. He was the owner of a successful real estate firm, always drove a luxury car, lived in an upscale neighborhood, and had a unabridged list of women in his little black book; yet here he was, over thirty and with no one particular woman whom he would like to settle down with. There was a waitress, named Lilly, who intrigued him every time he drank his coffee in the morning, but as of yet, he hadn't asked her out.

He thought about the days before diabetes, when he was an alcoholic. It had taken many years for him to finally admit that he had a problem. Not only was he a heavy drinker but he also had a real knack for talking incessantly. Those next to him at a bar would suddenly disappear to the other end of the counter or go sit at a table because of his relentless chatter. Tonight he was with Hoafie, so it really wouldn't matter how much he talked because he knew this tenderhearted man would listen.

Hoafie had eaten more than half of his steak and was now working on the last few bites. Warren was deep into his own conversation, happy that no one was interrupting him.

Warren could hear Hoafie mumbling something about a car. Why was he explaining how a brake line worked? Warren could care less about how cars operated. He always drove a new vehicle with a warranty, so if he had a problem, he just took it back to the dealer. If he needed anything in between those times, he figured he always had Hoafie at his disposal.

"Jeez, Hoafie, why are you talking so much about cars tonight?" asked Warren, with a slur to his words.

Hoafie stammered in bewilderment. "Because, boss, don't you remember what you just said that you wished you could do?"

Warren didn't remember saying anything about cars. He had the slightest clue as to what Hoafie was talking about. He thought he had been conveying an impressive story of his days as a soldier. Just as he was about to probe a little deeper into Hoafie's version of the conversation, the waiter appeared with the check and said that the restaurant would be closing in five minutes; and if Warren would like, he could take his payment. He also told him that the valet was waiting outside with the Jaguar.

Warren reached in his pocket to pull out his credit card and noticed that they were the only people left in the dining room. Just as the waiter was ready to walk away, Warren grabbed the sleeve of his jacket and, with a thick and unsteady voice, asked, "Where is everybody?"

"Everyone has gone home, sir." The muscles of his forearms hardened beneath his sleeve as he frowned in exasperation. "It's now past our closing time, and I'm sure everyone is home in bed. May I suggest that you do the same?"

Without warning, Warren began gasping in deep and erratic breaths as he tried to push himself away from the table and stand up. However, his legs weren't working properly. His knees buckled, and he felt himself hit the floor. On the way down, he heard himself say, "Listen here, you smart young punk." Somewhere in the distance, Warren could hear a siren. Something was wrapped around his chest, keeping him from moving. It felt as if he were riding in the back of a pickup truck. What exactly was happening to him? Voices—he could hear voices. Who were they, and where were they?

"Mr. Wright, please try to be still. Can you hear me?" the paramedic asked again, and this time, his voice held some compassion. "Can you hear me, Mr. Wright?" As much as Warren tried to answer this distant voice, all he could do was let out a long inaudible sigh.

The ambulance backed in under the roof, causing the automatic double doors to open into the emergency room corridor. The paramedic flung open the vehicle's doors and called for help. Immediately, an orderly was beside him. Together, they lifted Warren's gurney and lowered its legs to the ground. The emergency room was extra crowded because of an accident, and family members—some crying, some standing in silence—lined the halls of the waiting room.

As Warren was being wheeled through the crowd, he was all too aware of the undeniable and dreadful fact that he was in a hospital and that he was being pushed as if something urgent was occurring. His destination became a tiny room already filled with an assortment of machines. As one nurse began stripping off his clothes, another one was snapping his arm, trying to find a vein. A blood pressure cuff was being wrapped around his arm by yet a third nurse as she began pumping the ball connected to the machine.

Warren's voice, rough with anxiety, whispered to the closest nurse, "What's happening to me? How did I get here, and why?" The nurse who seemed to be in charge spoke in a no-nonsense tone as she leaned down closer to Warren's ear and said, "You were brought here by ambulance from Millersburg tonight for what we think is kidney failure. The doctors aren't exactly sure what happened, but we're running blood work now. We've already done an ultrasound and a CT scan, and depending on the results of those, we'll be doing a biopsy." With a pat on Warren's shoulder, she turned and left his bedside.

Within minutes of the nurse's departure, a middle-aged doctor, carrying a clipboard and flipping through the attached papers, stood beside Warren's bed. His voice also had a degree of urgency and concern. "Mr. Wright, I'm afraid I have some good news and some bad news. We detected alcohol in your bloodstream. And normally, that would be a bad thing, given that you are a diabetic, but tonight it turned out to be a good thing. It set off a series of events that could possibly have saved your life. That makes you a lucky man. The other bad news is that we think you might have Wilson's disease. This is a rare, inherited disorder in which excessive amounts of copper accumulate in the body. The level of copper in your blood is so elevated that we can't even find charts with numbers that high. Without treatment, damage to your kidneys is most likely, and sometimes the liver is affected. Obviously, no one has been aware that you have the disease. And therefore, it has not been treated."

He removed his glasses and let them fall around his neck, dangling on a black rope. With more sincerity in his voice, he added, "To tell you the truth, Mr. Wright, we are all a bit stumped as to how you've lived this long. The kidneys seem to be damaged but nothing major. Your liver is another story. It's the most unusual case I've ever seen, but right now, we have to concentrate on how to make sure that you can continue to live a normal life. With the amount of copper that has collected in your body, you should have at least had some minor symptoms. Have you felt bad in any way, Mr. Wright?" Warren slowly shook his head, indicating that nothing had been wrong.

"The very bad news is that your liver is in such bad shape that the only thing that will save you is a transplant. In all my years of practice, I have never seen a more deteriorated liver than what I saw on that CT scan tonight. We will put you on the transplant list, but even then, there is no guarantee as to when a liver will become available. We are going to keep you for a couple of weeks and monitor your blood levels and make sure you have no side effects to the medicine. If you do, your stay will be longer. Your blood type, AB, is not a common one, so in order for you to receive a transplant, we must find a donor with the same type as you have. That may not be so easy. We'll do all we can to make you comfortable, and in a few weeks, we will discuss your returning to work, if you feel up to it. If I were in your shoes, Mr. Wright, I would get my house in order." He patted Warren on the shoulder and walked out the door.

For the past two weeks, Warren lay in a very uncomfortable bed in the hospital. His mind kept taking him back to Vietnam, where he had wanted to die, and for some reason, he had been spared. Now he lay on this hard, thin mattress not wanting to die, wondering if God would spare him again. But why should he? He wasn't a God-fearing man. He used the Lord's name in vain all the time. He wasn't always kind to folks, and he had a touch of attitude when it came to helping the poor. He was a firm believer in hard work. Unemployed people, no matter the reason, really got under his skin.

He squeezed his eyes shut, hoping all his judgments that he had just admitted to himself would disappear into the dark. But in all reality, he knew every one of them were as true as the gospel. If he was going to be lucky enough to receive a transplant and make it off the operating table alive, some things in his life were going to change. He needed to find someone who could help him with some answers. He had made so many promises to God in the foxhole and then forgot them as soon as danger had passed, but this time had to be different. He was older now, and he didn't feel as invincible. He didn't want to die. He prayed that God would allow him to live and fulfill his intentions. Exactly what intentions he wasn't sure, but he knew he was going to achieve them, and he knew they were going to be good ones. He had a friend who went to church every Sunday. He was sure that he could talk to him. His last thoughts of sitting in a pew faded into total darkness as Warren fell asleep.

The past two weeks had found Warren vulnerable to many women wearing scrubs and donning stethoscopes. He soon realized that he was becoming quite dependent on the nurses. He relied on them for his water, his food, and, of course, his much-needed medicine. All he had to do was ring a buzzer, and they were right by his side. Their concern for him seemed genuine, and he was impressed by their respect for his life. He remembered the time in Vietnam when he had actually been called upon to help some of the medics when there were a lot of casualties. Even though you could feel the soldiers' pain, there was no time for empathy. Identifying the seriousness of the wounded and getting them into a chopper became more important than being kind. He had somehow pushed those memories so far back in his mind that he hadn't thought of them until now.

Lying there, totally helpless in the hospital room under doctor's orders, brought back so many of those images. He remembered the times when he had been commanded to hold men's guts in his hands and position bandages on body parts to hold them together. For days, sometimes weeks, the smell of blood and vomit infused his nostrils and existed on his uniform until he returned to base camp for a change of clothing. He had forgotten that feeling of helplessness as he had watched men writhe in pain and sometimes die. Now he was the one dying. And the nurses, even though they had busy schedules, found time for kindness and sensitivity to his situation. They were doing their best to make him comfortable and often tried to reassure him about the possibility of a transplant, but their eyes told a different story.

CHAPTER 4

For he will command his angels concerning you to guard you in all your ways.

—Psalm 91:1

Once more, Warren awoke to the tightness of the blood pressure cuff. *How many times are they going to torture me with this thing?* he thought.

"Well, good evening, Mr. Wright. Welcome back. Did you have a nice rest?"

Warren peeked through half-open eyes and whispered, "Who are you, and where am I?"

"My name is Rita, and I will be your nurse for the rest of the night. You don't remember why you're here?"

Warren shook his head no. Why couldn't he remember? Everything seemed foggy, except the sound of beeping. That was loud and clear. He tried to talk, but his mouth felt as if someone had stuffed it full of cotton.

"Save your strength, Mr. Wright. You are going to need it. I'll give you a quick rundown of what happened, but the doctor will be in shortly, and he can give you facts much better than I can. Your liver is in pretty bad shape, and you need a transplant. That's really all I can tell you right now, but Dr. Edwards will go over all the details with you very soon. Please try to rest. I'm going to try to find you a better pillow."

"Within minutes, Dr. Edwards appeared in the doorway, looking intently at Warren. "I must say, Mr. Wright, you must be leading an extraordinary life. I'm here to tell you that the angels are definitely watching over you and obviously have plans for you. I understand from the nurse that you're not real clear on why you are here in this hospital bed. We have you on pretty high doses of a new medicine called hydramadol. Temporary memory loss is a side effect. It's still in experimental stage, but the FDA has approved it for patients in your situation. Your memory should return as soon as your body acquiesces itself to the drug. Let me try to help you remember. Two weeks ago, you were having dinner at Cherry's, and the ambulance was called because you passed out. While trying to find the reason for your collapse, we discovered that you have a very rare disease. I'm sorry to be so blunt, Mr. Wright, but there is no other way to say this. You need a liver transplant, and you need it soon. We have no other options. I mentioned angels because, by all medical reasoning, you should not even be alive. It is beyond our knowledge why you never had any symptoms of this disease."

Warren shut his eyes and opened them again, hoping that what he had just heard was part of a dream. But the man in the white coat was standing very near him, and he was very real.

Dr. Edwards patted Warren on the shoulder and apologized for being the bearer of bad news and walked out the door.

CHAPTER 5

Your thunder was heard in the whirlwind, your lightning lit up the world; the earth trembled and quaked.

—Psalm 77:18

"Why are the lights blinking? Can someone find out what's going on?" Abby's voice resonated through the dark office. The only thing she could actually see was the blinking light on the printer. The fax was beeping, and the noise coming from the computer told her that it was going into hibernation mode. She let out a groan of despair as she realized that it had been some time since she had hit the Save button. Another blink of the lights, and it was gone completely. There was a moment of silence, and then she heard expletives from the office next to her. Ironically, the bank president had just informed them at the last board meeting that a new generator was going to be installed, and power outages would be a thing of the past. Obviously, that requisition had not made it to the engineer's top priority list.

Abby's head suddenly was throbbing, and her chest felt like someone or something was standing on it. Was she having a heart attack? She told herself that people didn't have heart failure at age thirty-one. But something was definitely wrong. She had never felt this way before. It was as if someone was sucking all the air from her body, and she couldn't get it back. She moved forward and then backward in her chair, trying to expose her lungs to some fresh air. The oxygen in her office seemed to have vanished just as the lights had done a minute ago. Suddenly, she needed her husband. If she was going to die, she needed to talk to him first. She needed him to come get her.

She was afraid to move more than necessary for fear of more pain, but she knew the phone was somewhere on her desk. As she fumbled among file folders and stacks of papers, looking for it, she knocked over her coffee cup. It had been a gift from her coworkers with a note that simply said, "Try spilling this one!" Everyone had chipped in to buy Abby a coffee cup that was guaranteed not to spill if the lid was on. Right now, she didn't care how klutzy she may seem to them or how many times her coffee had been the reason for a joke; she blessed the whole gang because, even though she had knocked it over, it was true to its claim and not a drop of coffee had landed in her files.

"Linda, are you out there? Could you please get me an aspirin and tell me that everything is going to be up and running real soon?"

Within seconds, Linda appeared with a flashlight, carrying a glass of water and two aspirins. "What's wrong, Abby? Are you all right?"

Abby threw the pills down the back of her throat and drowned them with water. Realizing Linda was waiting for an answer, she took another sip of water and slowly began to describe what had happened. "It was as if I were being stepped on by an elephant. It all happened so fast that I think I just panicked. If I can just have a few minutes to sit here and relax, I think I'll be all right." She rubbed her temples to ease her throbbing head. "Do you know what caused the power outage?"

"One of the maintenance workers reported a bad accident downtown that took out a utility pole. It might be sometime before we have power again. Do you need me to stay until it's fixed?"

Abby knew Linda's Friday nights were always planned far in advance, and they were an important part of her social life. She was not going to make her stay late just because she had run into a herd of elephants. "No, Linda, I want you to go home. But before you leave, could you please find the phone, dial Jeff's number, and put it on speaker for me? I need to ask Jeff to come pick me up. I don't think I can drive."

Abby was amazed with the way Linda could handle a flashlight. It was only seconds before she heard the dial tone on the phone and the sound of ringing. Jeff wasn't answering, but he no doubt had the radio blasting loud in the car, drowning out the ring of the phone. Jeff's company had provided him with a mobile car phone. It was the newest trend in Fortune 500 companies. They seemed to be the only ones that could indulge their CEOs with such amenities. Linda was still holding the phone, as if not sure whether to hang up or not, when she softly said, "Abby, he's not answering."

"Okay, try the house phone. Maybe he actually got home early today." Linda dialed the number, but the voice on the answering machine said that no one was home.

Suddenly, Abby's office was full of electricity again, and the bright light reminded her of her splitting headache. Hoping the aspirin would kick in soon, she shut her eyes and once again leaned back in her chair as far as she could. "Linda, now that the electricity is back on, could you please try to call Jeff one more time? And then please shut everything down and go home." Abby smiled as she continued on. "I hope you have a great weekend. I'll see you on Monday. Oh, by the way, Linda, I just want you to know that you're the best secretary I've ever had."

Linda turned to leave, hesitated, and spun around, just enough for Abby to see her and said, "Thank you, Abby. You're the best boss I've ever had."

Abby smiled, motioning for Linda to leave. "Your phone is ringing, and the noise is hurting my head. Make this your last phone conversation, and then please go home."

"Thanks, Abby. You have a nice weekend too." Abby smiled in return, closed her eyes, and said a silent prayer of thanks for Linda's loyalty; but before she even had a chance to lay her head back, Linda was by her side again, shaking her arm and mumbling something Abby couldn't understand.

"Abby, I need to talk to you."

"Linda, please just give me a few minutes. I still have this excruciating headache. Actually, my whole body hurts." Abby tried to open her eyes but was again blinded by the overhead lights. As she tried to shade her eyes with her hands, Linda began shaking her arm as if trying to rip it from her body.

"Linda, what in heaven's name are you doing? Did you get in touch with Jeff or not? You don't have to hurt me just to give me the phone. I ask you to put him on speaker."

While squeezing Abby's hand, Linda spoke in a softer but still very firm voice. "Abby, I know where he is."

Abby's response was curt, delivered in a distant tone. "You're scaring me, Linda. If you know where he is, then why aren't you calling him?"

Linda knew that Abby was a woman who could handle any situation and remain unfazed, but this was going to be different. This was heart-stopping news, even for a woman of Abby's caliber. Hearing that the love of her life was involved in a serious car accident would no doubt wreak some havoc on her.

Abby looked at Linda, confused. *Jeff must be planning something and had Linda in on it.* "You don't want me to talk to him, do you? He's trying to surprise me with something, isn't he? Well, he knows that he can't ever fool me, so just tell me where he's at, and I'll be the one to surprise *him*."

The continued look of terror on Linda's face was still a bit confusing to Abby. Not knowing what else to say, she smiled and said, "Wow, Linda, I didn't know you were such a good actress."

Tears started forming in Linda's eyes, but no sound came from her lips. She tried to raise her voice to a higher decibel so that Abby could hear her but only managed an inaudible sound.

"Linda, quit being so serious. Just tell me where I can find him."

Linda tried again in a different tone. The intensity in her lowered voice caused Abby to sit back and be quiet. Abby finally understood that she was clearly shaken about something. "Okay, Linda, what's going on? Did something happen to your mother? Is that what the last phone call was about?"

"Abby, please, please just listen to me. The last phone call was the hospital."

"The hospital? Why was the hospital calling?"

Slowly, Linda explained that Jeff had been in a car accident and that Abby needed to get there as soon as possible.

Abby stood up, not even remembering her headache now. "A car accident? Is he hurt? Is he alive?"

Not waiting for an answer, Abby grabbed her purse, rushed out the door, and began running toward the parking garage when the security guard stopped her and said that he had a car waiting right outside to drive her to the hospital. As he helped her into the backseat, she realized that she was in a police car and that a large man with a huge hat had just hit the siren button, and they were flying down the crowded street. *Why would a policeman be sent to take me to the hospital? Jeff must be in really serious condition.*

Her chest went tight again, and she realized that she once again needed air. She tried the window, but it wouldn't open. She heard herself screaming at the officer to unlock the windows. She really needed some air, and the possibility of throwing up was not out of the question. Why wouldn't he put the window down, and when would they be at the hospital? She was throwing questions at this man faster than flying bullets. She could tell he was getting agitated, but his voice maintained a soft tone as he asked her to please sit back and buckle up. But instead, she leaned up over the front seat and allowed her tears to fall on the navy blue uniform, staining the top of his shoulders. He remained quiet for the next few minutes until the hospital came into view, and when they stopped, he asked her to wait for him to help her out of the car. But Abby was waiting for no one. She threw open the door and stepped onto the sidewalk, not realizing that, sometime during the ride, her legs had turned into jelly, and she couldn't find enough strength to carry herself to the hospital door. Before she knew it, someone was pushing a wheelchair under her and was whisking her down a corridor and into a room. A man in blue scrubs and a nurse were waiting for her. She heard herself demand to see Jeff.

"Mrs. Weaver, please calm down. My name is Dr. Ward, and I need to talk to you about your husband." In an affable voice, Abby heard the doctor trying to explain, in simple terms, the condition of Jeff.

"Your husband is still alive, but he has suffered a traumatic head injury." He took a deep breath, and as if delivering a speech to a room full of colleagues, the word "brain-dead" fell out of his mouth.

Abby wasn't exactly familiar with the term "brain-dead," but if it were one of those self-explanatory words, which she would have to assume it was, then she must have heard wrong. Jeff couldn't be brain-dead. He was the most intelligent man she had ever known. The mental capacity in his brain was too strong to ever give up. His brain, which was always in overdrive, might be bruised, but it couldn't be dead. He was a strong, virile man. He had just given her a big bear hug not even eight hours ago. She had thawed steaks out for dinner. He should be at home right now, preparing them for the grill while she tossed the salad and baked the potatoes. In a louder voice than she was accustomed to hearing from her mouth, she asked, "Exactly what do you mean 'brain-dead'? I want to see him. Where is he?"

Without answering, the doctor took her by the shoulders and navigated her into a small private room with couches. A nurse followed, shutting the door behind them. Once inside the room, the doctor began to talk about Jeff's injuries. "Mrs. Weaver, your husband's car collided with an oil tanker this afternoon. He sustained an injury to the brain to the extent that it is irreversible. We've done an EEG and also a radionuclide cerebral blood flow scan, and it shows complete absence of intracranial blood flow."

Abby interrupted. The medical jargon meant nothing to her. This time, she managed to squeak out in a barely audible voice, "Please tell me in simple words, Doctor. Is my husband dead or alive?"

As if reluctant to answer the question, he hesitated. Then steeling himself, in a robotic voice, he said, "His heart is still beating, and as unbelievable as it is, most of his vital organs are actually still working, but brain-dead means exactly that—his brain is dead. It has suffered such a trauma that it is not functioning. I'm afraid the scan that I just mentioned shows absolutely no electrical activity, which is necessary for a brain to function. The blow to his head caused intracranial pressure that prevents blood flow into the brain. It's called an aneurysmal subarachnoid hemorrhage. I am so sorry."

Abby wanted to believe that, as a doctor, his expression of sympathy for her held some compassion, but his callous handshake sent a different message. He stood and asked the nurse to follow him, and they both left the room.

Abby, still in shock, tried to force her body to get up from the couch, but she felt the same as she had earlier in her office during the power outage. Her chest felt as if that same elephant had returned to use her for a resting place.

Before she could analyze those thoughts, another nurse, wearing a scrub top covered with teddy bears, returned, holding a clipboard full of papers with a pen lying on top. "Mrs. Weaver, I know this is all so hard for you to digest right now, but we have some paperwork that we would like for you to sign. When you are finished, could you please bring them out to the desk? We need them *now*." As she walked out of the room, she seemed to sling the last few words over her shoulder as if she wanted Abby to hear them yet to not be responsible for actually saying them. Abby made a mental note that a more appropriate scrub top for her to wear would be covered in dragons instead of teddy bears.

As Abby looked over the papers, the very first words that she saw were "organ donor." As she scanned down through the pages, she realized that these papers were authorizing the hospital to give Jeff's body away piece by piece. Agitated, Abby walked to the nurse's desk, laid down the clipboard, and asked when she could see her husband. With a look of uncertainty, Nurse Dragon picked up the phone and summoned Dr. Ward to the ER.

Within minutes, Abby saw him walking toward her. She didn't give him time to reach the desk before she shouted, "I want to see my husband *now*!"

Almost close enough to touch her, Dr. Ward held out his hand as if he wanted a handshake and said, "Please calm down, Mrs. Weaver. Have you signed the papers yet?"

That was the last straw. Her husband was lying in a room somewhere, dying, and all they could talk about were papers. "Excuse me, did you just ask me if I signed the papers yet? That's all you can say? Did I sign the papers yet? I need to see my husband, and I'm not signing anything until you take me to him."

Before Abby could say another word, a new face with a powerful voice interrupted her breakdown, asking if there was a problem. A slightly overweight man in white introduced himself as Dr. Mongold. Compassion seemed to seep from his voice with every word he spoke, and before she knew it, he was taking her by the arm and leading her to a room at the far end of the corridor. "My apologies, Mrs. Weaver, and my condolences also. I understand your husband was an organ donor, and am I right to assume that you didn't know that?"

Abby could tell that he was looking at her, but she pretended not to notice.

"Mrs. Weaver, I can tell by the desperate look on your face that you're angry. Is it because your husband didn't share with you that he wanted to be an organ donor? Did your husband serve in the armed forces?"

Abby nodded her head as she whispered, "Vietnam."

"Well, there's your answer. Most men who have fought in a war have a check mark beside organ donor on their driver's license. They don't see it as an act of heroism but an act of duty." He ended by saying, "And most have never even thought about telling their wives."

As they reached the far door, he pushed it open and allowed her to step inside alone. She was not prepared for what she saw. On a cold, hard gray metal table lay her husband, with not even a pillow to support his head. His blood-covered toes were protruding from a thin white blanket looking large and out of place. His well-manicured hands now lay dirty and limp on top of the blanket as if they were waiting to be clean again.

Inadvertently, her eyes were drawn to a huge black-and-white clock on the wall, and she realized that only thirty minutes had passed since she had left her office. It seemed like hours. It was almost dinnertime, and she should be sitting across from her husband at a table decorated with a tablecloth and candles, not a hospital blanket and fluorescent lights. This was all so surreal, like being in the middle of a nightmare, trying desperately to wake up.

She walked closer to the metal table. She called his name, but he didn't move. She said it again but got no response. She now noticed the deep cuts covering his forehead and the blood and dirt mingled together in his hair. Someone must have tried to wash the blood from his face but had only caused it to smear. Jeff would be so upset if he knew that people in the emergency room were seeing him in such disarray. He had befriended so many people from all walks of life in this hospital through his managing of fund-raiser campaigns. He made people feel comfortable with the subject of money and helped stimulate many donations. He worked hard to reach campaign goals by finding grants and private donors. As diligently as he volunteered for the hospital, he also brought unity to the staff and other volunteers through his humble and caring ways. A lot of his spare time was spent looking for ways to improve work ethics and attitude. Not only was he in everyone's eyes the most thoughtful and noble guy but he also was known for his meticulous way of dressing. The collars on his shirts were starched, his jeans were creased, and his hands were always manicured. Abby felt compelled to lean down and whisper in his ear, "I won't let anyone else see you until you are cleaned up."

She reached for his left hand and turned his wedding ring around so that the diamond was on top. She remembered their wedding day and the feeling of contentment when she had pushed that ring on his finger. Watching his chest move up and down reassured her that he was still alive. The doctor had used the word "dead," but he wasn't dead. He was breathing, and he was breathing on his own. There were no machines attached keeping him alive. Other than those few cuts, he looked as if he were just sleeping soundly. Abby decided to touch him again, to hold his hand, to talk to him, all to which she was still sure he would respond. He always responded to her touch, and today would be no different. She asked him to squeeze her hand if he could hear her, but his hands remained still, and his lips remained silent. He was void of all movement, just like the air in this tiny room—still and cold.

She begged him to open his eyes. She begged him to talk to her so that they could go home, but with each rise and fall of his chest, she realized how much of a struggle it was for him to breathe. Without the companionship of his brain, his heart would soon quit beating, and then even his chest would be still. Without warning, her tears fell to the floor like meteors weighted with the heaviness of her heart.

Suddenly, someone had her by the shoulders again and was nudging her into a wheelchair. Before she had time to protest, she was being wheeled through the corridor as if she were trying to win the Indy 500.

Dr. Ward was waiting for her at the nurse's station, looking angry and impatient. "Mrs. Weaver, we really need you to sign these papers. Time is of the essence if we can help other patients with contributions from your husband." His facial features softened a bit, and he added, "It's what he wanted, and you must think of it as a gift to those in need."

He lowered his head as if he were preparing to pray but then quickly stood and said, "I understand how you feel. I really do, but you will be helping a lot of people by giving your consent, and we can't proceed without your signature."

Abby tried to speak but instead picked up the pen and laid it back down three times before she could make it actually connect with the papers in front of her. When she had finally signed her name for the last time, she demanded to be taken back down the hall to see Jeff one more time. She needed to physically touch him once again, tell him that she loved him and that she would always love him. She needed to feel his lips against hers, just one more time, even if they didn't respond. She needed to say out loud that she was sorry that she signed the papers giving permission for his body to be carved into gifts and handed out to total strangers.

As she turned the doorknob, the cold harshness of the metal brought an immediate image of her beloved Jeff lying helpless on the cold, glacierlike table inside this room. Only minutes ago, he had been a dedicated husband, son, friend, employee. Now he just lay there, void of those identities, just a body that soon would be shared with strangers—shared because he was a generous man, a man who gave much of himself while he was alive and now even in death was relinquishing every part of his body to those who needed it. And because of his compassion, how many lives would now be saved? How many families would be spared the heartache that Abby was now experiencing? Deep down, she knew that Jeff would be happy to know that his final contribution to the world was giving life to another person. The selfless act exemplified his character.

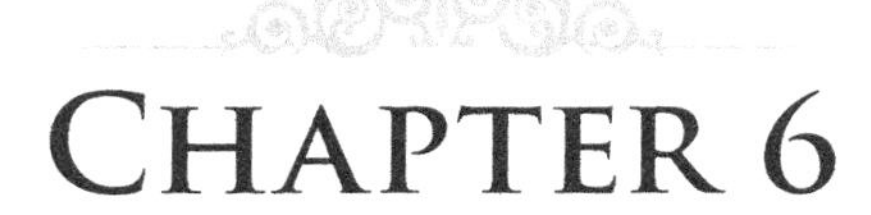

CHAPTER 6

Blessed are those who mourn, for they will be comforted.

—Matthew 5:4

For the next few days, Abby was breathing, but her will to live seemed nonexistent. Visits and phone calls from friends and neighbors brought constant reminders of her loss, though she was touched by the passable effort that so many people were making on her behalf.

As the doorbell rang yet one more time, Abby, exhausted from lack of sleep, took her time raising her head from the pillow. Before she could even put her feet on the floor, she heard the squeak of the front door as it opened. "Anybody home? My dear, you should really keep your door locked," said a voice in a high-pitched southern drawl. Abby couldn't believe her ears. Was it really Aunt Marie, her only living relative? Abby couldn't remember the last time her globe-trotting aunt had come to visit. How she found out about Jeff she didn't know, but she loved this woman and was elated with the fact that she was here to take care of her.

Aunt Marie strutted into the living room, and before Abby knew what was happening, this small wisp of a woman was gently stroking the damp curls away from her face and kissing the top of her head. With both hands, she cupped Abby's face and, without hesitation, spoke in a strong, velvety voice that overflowed with compassion. "Abby, darling, I am so happy to see you, although I would rather it not be under these circumstances. You've been handed one of the hardest things in life to handle. The sudden loss of a spouse is an atrocious heartache. But I know you, and I'm sure you will find that inner strength that is needed for you to heal. I will be right beside you for as long as you need me."

As Abby remembered, Aunt Marie never minced words. She usually got to the nucleus of the situation and dealt with it. That was how she lived her life too. In fact, she was at this instant snapping her fingers in front of Abby's face, trying to get her undivided attention.

"I'm sorry, Aunt Marie. What were you saying?"

"I was reminding you that I have lost two husbands, both to cancer, and I could have propped my butt in front of the TV all day and became depressed, but I discovered a long time ago that life goes on all around you, whether you want it to or not. Unless suicide is your plan, you're probably going to live. Life without Jeff is going to be hell. It will be like trying to complete a puzzle with a piece missing. You can still put the puzzle together. You'll just have to work around the empty space and hope that someday you will find a piece that will fit. Your life may go in a totally different direction now than you ever thought possible, and you may never be able to find the original piece in exactly the same size or color, but someday you'll be able to make a proper match."

As Abby sat there, desperately trying to absorb every word, she took in the face of her aunt. She had missed seeing her oval-shaped face, her complexion fair and rather delicate, even though wrinkles were beginning to form lines under her cheekbones. Her nose was straight but small, and her lipstick-laden lips were full and rounded over beautiful white teeth. She had a wealth of black hair, which always seemed styled to perfection. She was the kind of woman who, even at the age of sixty-five, caused men to turn and take a second look. Even though Abby had spent many, many hours with Aunt Marie, she had never seen her look more beautiful than today.

All at once, Abby noticed Aunt Marie's brow furrow, and she watched as tears began trickling slowly down her cheeks as she motioned for Abby to lean toward her. She cradled her in her arms as a mother with a newborn baby, and together, they yielded to the compulsive sobs that shook them both.

As their tears subsided, Abby could hardly lift her voice above a whisper but managed to ask, "Aunt Marie, how did you know about Jeff? I didn't even know how to reach you."

In a voice that seemed to come from a long way off, Aunt Marie related the story of how she had been home for a few days, in between Paris and Hawaii. One of Abby's colleagues had called to tell her about Jeff. She had found Aunt Marie's name listed as next of kin in Abby's personnel file. "It was only by the grace of God that I happened to be home at that precise moment," said Aunt Marie. "I was walking out the door when the phone rang, and I almost didn't answer it because the only people who call me are trying to sell me something. Thank God I picked up that receiver and found out that you needed me. I wish I were here under happier conditions, but we'll get through this together."

"But what about your Hawaii trip? Since you didn't go, will the company give you a refund?"

"Don't you worry about me, honey. There will be lots of other trips. The important thing now is that I'm here to help. Bad things happen in this world, and a lot of them are out of our control, and this is definitely one of them. We will have to rely on God to give you the tenacity that you will need to deal with your grief during this time." Lines of concentration deepened along her brows and under her eyes. When she spoke again, her voice was tender, almost a whisper. "*Your* strength and *my* willingness will help get you through these next few months, and eventually, you will look forward to a bright new future."

Abby, still barely able to talk, said, "The only way my future can be bright again is if you can figure out how to bring Jeff back to me. He was supposed to be my future."

Aunt Marie picked up Abby's hands and began rubbing them. It reminded Abby of rubbing a bottle and having a genie appear. If only that were possible, and she could be granted a wish. "Abby, look at me. I know you don't believe me right now, but please have faith in my wisdom. I know it's not something that you want to think about, and you don't have to right now, but don't give up on life so soon. Jeff would not want you to do that. He would want you to be happy. Right now, I know it's hard for you to see how that's possible without him, but time has a way of gliding over the rough spots and covering the wound with an ointment called love."

As quickly as she had sat down, Aunt Marie was once again on her feet, asking Abby for the phone book. As she pulled it from the drawer, she turned and spoke as if she were the expert on the subject of love. "Abby, I know I have said this before, but I need you to trust me on this. You *will* find peace and love someday when you are least expecting it. Just don't be in a hurry."

Abby sat still, barely even blinking, trying to convince herself that Aunt Marie knew what she was talking about and that she should believe her. She recognized the "take charge" mode as she watched Aunt Marie position the phone under her ear, allowing the long phone cord to dangle to the floor. She didn't know exactly who she was calling, but she knew it had something to do with Jeff as she watched her aunt walk into the kitchen and out of hearing range. She didn't hear the continued conversation.

"Is this the Weller Funeral Parlor? I'm calling about the body of Jeff Weaver. You should have received it yesterday. Yes, that's right. It was a car accident."

Aunt Marie's mouth took on an unpleasant twist as she continued. "Why would we want an autopsy? Do you suspect foul play? Drugs? I guarantee that you will not find any drugs in that man's body. He was an advocate for a lot of drug treatment centers. You do your drug test so that everyone's on the same page—the page where it says that Jeff Weaver is spic-and-span clean. Listen, honey, you get on that right away, and I expect a phone call by this evening, or I'll be paying you a visit, and trust me, you don't want a visit from me."

Though she missed the details, Abby could tell from her tone of voice that Aunt Marie wasn't happy and obviously didn't want her to hear. What exactly would she be trying to hide from her? Abby was so tired that she really didn't want to know or get into anything very heavy right now. If Aunt Marie thought it was of any importance, she would talk to her about it. She was just so grateful that her aunt was taking care of everything that she would trust her completely. She smiled as she thought about how Aunt Marie had magically made the doorbell and the phone cease their ringing. She made sure that a pot of hot tea stayed on the coffee table, along with a plate of tiny sandwiches, which looked too pretty to actually eat. Abby silently thanked God for sending this amazing woman to take care of her.

Aunt Marie, looking as if she might break down and cry again, came back into the room, walked closer to Abby, and pulled her from the couch. "It's time that you get a shower and put on some clothes. We are going for a ride."

Abby recognized the tone and knew to argue would be fruitless. Aunt Marie helped her up the steps and into a nice hot shower. She then crossed the room to the closet, and finding a simple but stunning chestnut-colored sundress hanging there, she laid it out on the bed. She turned on the light at the vanity and set out Abby's makeup tray. She was going to help her niece realize that Jeff may be gone, but she was still alive.

Assuming that Abby would be in the shower for a while, Aunt Marie went back downstairs to make yet another phone call. This one was to the state police. As she explained her reason for calling, the desk clerk put her through to Chief Timothy McDonald. She was told that he was in charge of this investigation.

Chief McDonald had been dreading this phone call. In cases like this, he was never exactly sure what to say to the family of the deceased. He picked up the phone and said, "Mrs. Forester, how are you today?"

"I'm sure I'll be better when you tell me exactly what's going on with my niece's husband, Jeff Weaver. I need to know why his accident is under investigation. I was told that it might have something to do with drugs."

There was a faint tremor in his voice as though some emotion had touched him. He asked, "Is it possible for Abagail Weaver to come down to the station any time soon? There are some routine questions that we would like to ask."

Suspicion lacing her voice, Aunt Marie asked, "Why? Is she some kind of suspect concerning Jeff's accident? Because if that's what you boys think, well, you better put on another thinking cap. There is no way my niece had anything to do with the accident." She heard a deep sigh come from the other end of the phone.

"Mrs. Forester, I understand that you're upset, and you have every right to be, but the fact of the matter is that someone cut the brake line on Mr. Weaver's car as he was coming down the ramp of I-80. He had no brakes and drove right into the path of an oil tanker. There was nothing he could do."

Before he could finish, Marie spoke in a suffocated whisper. "Who would want to hurt Jeff?" A few seconds of silence, and Marie spoke again. "Then it has nothing to do with a drug investigation. I was told that an autopsy was being done to examine Jeff for drug use. I told them they were crazy, but to think that someone cut his brake line is even more bizarre. If this is a fact, what are you doing about it?"

Chief McDonald hesitated, looking for the right words, when he heard the all-too-familiar sound of silence. Obviously, Marie Forester didn't want to wait for his answer.

CHAPTER 7

Come to me, all you who are weary and burdened, and I will give you rest.

—Matthew 11:28

Aunt Marie finally convinced Abby to put on the dress and even a smidgen of makeup. It had taken her a bit longer to get her to agree to go for a ride, especially when Abby found out that their destination was the mortuary. Abby was not going to argue about the ride, but she wasn't ready for the funeral parlor just yet.

But in the end, Aunt Marie won. With a trace of firmness in her voice, balanced with much compassion and understanding, she explained that arrangements had to be made today. A casket had to be chosen, memorials had to be written and printed, flowers had to be ordered, and a date had to be set for the service. Aunt Marie knew that Abby was in no shape emotionally to choose clothing for Jeff, so before they left, she went into Jeff's closet and decided on a charcoal gray suit, a white shirt, and a gray striped tie—a very conservative choice for a very conservative man. She hoped it was to Abby's liking.

As they pulled up to the curb of the red brick building, a young gentleman was waiting to open the car door. As he did, he extended his hand to Abby to help her exit the car. As she stepped inside the front room of the parlor, with the help of Aunt Marie on one side and the young mortician on the other, she was ushered into an adjoining room that was full of caskets. She turned away, not wanting to be amid the contents of this room. It was so morbid. *Why didn't they just have the same burial box for everyone? Then this wouldn't be necessary.* She stood motionless in the middle of the room, surrounded by velvet-lined boxes. One of them was just waiting to take Jeff away from her forever. She wasn't sure she had the intestinal fortitude to make such a permanent decision.

The young mortician noticed Abby's hesitance and walked toward her with a determined stride. Very gently, he guided her by the elbow to the next room, which was his office. "Mrs. Weaver, you have my deepest sympathy for the loss of your husband, and I understand how hard this is, but it is one of those necessary evils." Motioning toward the casket room, he said, "I noticed your eyes lingering on the gold silk-lined casket with the tiny stars on the lining. The expression on your face changed from uneasiness to serenity. I think that might be the one you should settle on."

Where was Aunt Marie? She would put this young man in his place. Who did he think he was, telling her which box she should bury her husband in? She was ready to come back with some fighting words when Aunt Marie stepped into the room. Sensing some tension, she asked if everything was okay.

The young man spoke first. "I was trying to help Mrs. Weaver pick out a casket." He then added, "Which, though a difficult process, is something that has to be done, and I am just here to help. I'll leave you two alone. Please let me know when you've made a decision."

A deluge of tears erupted as Abby found her way to the nearest chair. As she collapsed into the soft blue velvet, she unconsciously curled into a fetal shape, sobbing uncontrollably.

How had her life spiraled so out of control in such a short time? It was only a few days ago when she had been a happy, content young woman with the world at her fingertips. She loved her job, was financially comfortable, and had a wonderful husband. It was as if a bomb had landed right smack in the middle of her heart, retaining the perimeter—just blowing apart the inside. It left no core to her being.

Aunt Marie was nudging Abby's arm, trying to shove multiple tissues into her hands. Abby opened her eyes long enough to be reminded again that she was not in the middle of a dream. She took the tissues and wiped her nose but couldn't rid her nostrils of the sweet, nauseating smell of funeral parlor flowers—the smell of death. She closed her eyes again, hoping that maybe, when she opened them again, some miraculous change might have taken place. But the strain she heard in Aunt Marie's voice was not of the harmony usually involved in a miracle. As thankful as she was for this precious woman standing beside her, she knew that even Aunt Marie couldn't take away this excruciating ache that seemed to be tormenting every part of her body.

Finally, Abby managed slowly and faintly to speak a few words. "I'm sorry, Aunt Marie. I shouldn't be so ready to fight, but this is all so final, and I'm not ready to let someone put my husband in a box. Jeff loved to stargaze, and many nights, we would lie on the deck just staring at the sky. We didn't even have to talk, but if we did, we would often talk about the bed-and-breakfast that we wanted to open someday, a place that would have a big yard and huge decks with telescopes and binoculars so that everyone who visited could also have the pleasure of witnessing the magnitude of the solar system. We dreamed about our children and what they would be like. We would just drift off into our own little worlds. We felt like it was enough just to be together. When I saw the stars in that casket, it reminded me of those nights."

After a moment of hesitation, Abby spoke again in a weak and tremulous whisper. "Yes, the one with the stars is the one he would want."

As they left the room, Aunt Marie stayed by her side and then sat with her in the funeral director's office until she found the strength to plan the service. She had only three days before Jeff would be gone forever.

Before she knew it, two days had passed in a vague dullness. But the third day was different. As the sun rose and found its way through the blinds in her bedroom, it caused tiny glints of silver to shine on her wall. A small breeze through the open window allowed the sparkly dots to look as if they were dancing. For the first time in what seemed like years, Abby smiled. Jeff would have loved her concept of the images on the wall. It reminded her once again of the nights when they would lie on the deck watching the stars. Jeff was good at telling humorous, romantic folk stories that had some connection with the group of stars they were seeing that night. If the Big Dipper was visible, it was always a story about ice cream; and if they could see only the Little Dipper, he would tell her a story about soup. With a smile on his face, he would always say that it only made sense that you should have more ice cream than soup.

Thinking of Jeff brought tears again. Could she ever think about him without crying? How could she ever function in life, knowing that he would never stand beside her again or lie beside her on the deck and share their dreams or talk about the children whom they so much wanted? All their plans, all their dreams would soon be under six feet of God's green earth. But where exactly was God during Jeff's accident? Where was He when Jeff lay dying on that awful metal table? She was angry at God and totally confused. Had He not helped Jeff because they didn't attend church?

She didn't think that God would hold grudges, but why would he allow a good man like Jeff to die instead of some serial killer or some evil person who molested children? These were questions that Abby had never thought of, but now that they had entered her mind, she would have to find someone who could give her some answers. She was jolted out of her deep thinking by a loud knock at her door. There was no mistaking that sweet but commanding voice on the other side.

"Abby, I hung your black dress on the bathroom door. I took the liberty of picking it out for you. I hope it's okay."

"I'll be down shortly, Aunt Marie. And the dress will be fine."

As Abby made her way down the porch steps, she saw Aunt Marie, already waiting in the limo, motioning for her to hurry. Even before Abby had the huge car door completely shut, Marie was instructing the driver to pull away from the curb. They arrived at the funeral parlor within ten minutes and was once again greeted by the young mortician. He guided Abby and Aunt Marie through the side door intersecting several guests who were already waiting to pay their respects. Soon there were hundreds of compassionate, well-wishing people filing past her and her beloved Jeff. She recognized most, but there were a few whom she had never seen before. She assumed they were from Jeff's office building.

Abby spoke very little, unconscious of what she did say or tried to say. Each time someone hugged her or held her hand, she broke down in tears. She saw grown men wiping away tears and turning away as if their manhood would suffer if they were seen crying. She stood in a robotic position and listened as people expressed their sympathies and offered to help her if she ever needed them. What exactly did they think they could do for her? Bring Jeff back to her? That was the *only* thing she needed. What she knew she *didn't* need was this feeling of cynicism that seemed to be seeping into every portion of her existence.

Abby felt someone guide her to a chair in the front row of the chapel. Pastor Bill was asking that everyone be seated, and Donna Johnson, a colleague of Jeff's, began singing "Amazing Grace." It was one of Jeff's favorite old songs. An instant net of silence seemed to cover the entire room. By the end of the song, there wasn't a male or female who didn't have tears running down their cheeks, even the ones who had ridden their Harleys to the service and were covered in tattoos and piercings. They looked a bit out of place, sitting here among the men and women dressed in business suits. But on this day, it didn't seem to matter because they were all here for one thing: to honor their friend, Jeff Weaver.

Jeff had shown great respect for his Harley friends and had no difficulty befriending them. He often ate lunch with them, as they worked on nearby construction sites. People who passed by always smiled at the white shirt and tie sharing the tailgate of a pickup truck with men in sweaty T-shirts. Even though he had always wanted a Harley, it seemed enough for him just to be friends with Harley owners and listen to their stories.

Occasionally, someone would force a helmet on his head and prod him until he took one of the bikes for a spin around the block. He loved the speed and the noise. His dream was to someday own a black Harley Sportster. Smaller and lighter than other models, it seemed like it would be the best fit for him. Abby now wished that she had encouraged him more to fulfill that dream.

Realizing that the pastor was in the middle of a prayer, she bowed her head and closed her eyes. Immediately after the "amen," he began talking about Jeff and his authentic respect for life. He was saying that every one of us should live life to the fullest, just as Jeff had done, because we would never know when the oil tanker in our life would strike. Pastor Bill drew his brows together in an agonized expression as if he too were questioning God's decision to take this man away from his family at such a young age. He recovered quickly and went on to relate a few stories about Jeff. One of them was concerning the "Harley friends." A few audible chuckles were heard, followed by sniffles.

Donna was now singing another song. This one was unfamiliar, but it signified the end of the service. Time to say good-bye. But Abby wasn't going to leave, not in a million years.

Someone was touching Abby's elbow, indicating for her to stand. Pastor Bill leaned down and whispered that she could have one last look at her husband. As she stepped up to the casket, she could feel her legs begin to crumble. She reached for the casket to steady herself. She picked up Jeff's hand and noticed a small mole, wondering why she had never seen it before. Was life so busy that she hadn't taken time to really look at her husband every day? It was too late now. She also noticed tiny bits of hair casting shadows of silver near his temples. How had she been too busy to notice, and how could she go on without him? The need to suddenly hold him and tell him that she loved him and that she would always love him became so overwhelming that she lost all sense. She felt an overwhelming urge to crawl into the casket. She wanted to be in there with him. She wanted them to shut the lid. It was where she wanted to be. She grabbed hold of the casket, with a look in her eyes that scared her aunt.

Aunt Marie began crying, trying to pull Abby away. The funeral director, not exactly sure what to do, summoned Tom—the young man who had helped Abby out of the car—to come help with the situation. But he found resistance when he took an abrupt step toward her. A savage inner fire was glowing in her eyes that told him she was not leaving there without a fight.

Tom spoke softly but with authority. Abby physically paused and allowed her ears to listen. He sounded so sincere as he asked her to be careful so as not to disturb Jeff. He touched her shoulders gently, with no restraints on her arms, allowing her fingers to stay in contact with her husband's hands.

Abby heard another voice but quickly realized that it was her own, stifled and unnatural. She wanted to answer quickly, to drown the deafening sound of her thumping heart, but she only managed to whisper between gut-wrenching sobs. "Please leave me alone. I need to be with him just a little while longer. I can't leave him."

Without removing his hands from her shoulders, he allowed her a little more freedom to bend over the casket and give her husband one last kiss. When she finally raised her lips from the cold sensation of death, Tom delicately guided her out the side door and into the limousine once more.

CHAPTER 8

There is a time for everything, and a season for every activity under the heavens.

—Ecclesiastes 3:1

Abby returned to her office on the three-week anniversary of Jeff's death, but it was hard to concentrate on her work. She found herself staring at the phone, willing it to ring, hoping it would be Jeff's voice on the other end. She kept reliving the past weeks and wondering how she ever would have managed without Aunt Marie. She had been by her side when she met with the local agent about Jeff's life insurance policy and had been kind enough to order more death certificates. She had pretty much taken over Abby's checkbook, making sure all her bills were paid, especially those related to the funeral. There was a part of her that felt as if paying the funeral home was the final chapter of her life with Jeff before she would be forced to move into the future.

It was almost lunchtime, and she realized that she had accomplished nothing so far today. Maybe she had returned to work too soon, but staying at home all day was just too painful. The days were long and filled with reminders of Jeff. The air in the house seemed permeated with his familiar musk scent. At times, she clung to one of his shirts just so she could inhale the fragrance deep into her lungs. At night, it lingered like poison on her sheets. A clothing bank from downtown had come to the house to pick up the contents of his closet following a phone call from Aunt Marie. They were overwhelmed with gratefulness for the donation, but it had caused Abby a major meltdown as she watched them carry his clothes out the door. Getting rid of his clothing so soon was not easy, but she couldn't seem to get a grip on her emotions. Every time she opened the closet door and saw his shirts hanging side by side, it was too much of a reminder that he would never wear them again. She felt as if her only solution was just to remove them.

She needed to concentrate on the rental application laying in front of her on her desk, but her mind kept revisiting the long list of things that needed to be done according to Aunt Marie. Cleaning out Jeff's office at home wasn't going to be easy either, but the constant reminders were more than she could bear. The first thing she needed to do would be to start packing up Jeff's beloved collection of ceramic flowers. He had endured many jokes from his buddies concerning those flowers. Every time one of his friends made a joke about the delicate collection, he always responded the same. "Maybe your manhood isn't strong enough to support a little bit of femininity, but I know that mine is. Besides, these flowers are easier to take care of than real ones." He would throw back his head and roar with laughter, marking the end of the conversation. She thought about the set of golf clubs he had inherited from his father, which leaned against the open-arm brown leather chair in the room. He and his father had spent many hours on the golf course together, so each time he walked into the room, he made sure that his golf bag and his father's chair were touching. This was his way of keeping his father's memory alive.

He also had inherited the love of stories about the Old West from his father and spent many hours in the brown chair reading about fearless mountain men and their encounters with Indians. The rows of poetry books intermingled with his cowboy collection reflected the diversity that made up his life. He loved excitement, but it was this poetic, softer side of Jeff that had attracted Abby. She was brought back to the present as she realized Mr. Jones, from company headquarters, was standing in the doorway of her office.

"I'm sorry to disturb you, Abby, but may I come in and talk to you for a minute?"

"Yes, Mr. Jones. I didn't realize you were in town. Please come in."

"I want to say that I was so sorry to hear of your loss. I hope you haven't come back to work so soon because you were afraid of losing your job. You're one of our best agents, and you take as long as you need to grieve."

As if not really sure what to say next, he bent his head slightly forward and spoke in a soft voice. "If I may have a few more minutes of your time, Abby, I would like to tell you a story, one that I haven't talked about for some time, but I think it would be appropriate for me to tell you now." Abby said nothing, just gave a forced smile and a nod of consent.

Mr. Jones related the story of his marriage to Maggie and how great life had been. He told Abby of the accident and how devastated he had been when he received word of her death. He was convinced that life was over for him. "But as you can see, Abby, I'm alive and well. Life did continue for me. I may never find another Maggie, but I feel privileged to have experienced such happiness at least once in my lifetime. You need to hold on to that also. And who knows, someday you may fall in love again and feel fortunate that you were blessed twice."

Again, Abby was at a loss for words. She was so afraid to speak for fear that her voice would echo her grief and embarrass her in front of a somewhat stranger. She smiled, still not answering.

"I just want you to know that life does go on, and I wanted you to hear my story so that you know you aren't the only one who has had to survive a crisis. It's hard, and it's unfair, but it's also totally out of our hands. I'll keep you in my prayers."

He held out his hands, offering his condolences again. He walked toward the door but stopped in midstride, turned, and spoke one final sentence. "God will take care of you, Abby Weaver. Just let him."

Abby shut the door and returned to her desk. There, she yielded to the uncompromising sobs that racked her body and her soul. In a soft, almost inaudible voice, she asked, "Why would God want to take care of me?"

Abby's life became very robotic for the next few months. She got up in the morning, went to work, stayed late, came home, went to bed, and did it all over again the next day. She was grateful, though, for the routine of having a job. It gave her less time to think about Jeff. It was not that she didn't think about him every day, but it just helped to have something else to occupy her mind. Coming home in the evening to an empty house was worse than she would ever have imagined. There was no dinner to cook, no newspapers to remove from the kitchen counter, no dishes in the sink waiting to be put in the dishwasher. Nothing was ever out of place. It was as if she lived in a museum. Aunt Marie had called Abby almost every day, checking to make sure that she was getting enough sleep and not exhausting herself with long hours at work. Abby always assured her that she was fine and determined to pick up where she had left off.

One day, while sitting silently in front of her office window, she watched mothers with their children in the small park across the street. She had often looked through these panes and imagined her and Jeff pushing their children high on the swings. She now realized that she had never quite comprehended the idea of motherhood and how important it could be in a woman's life. She and Jeff had both chosen their careers over parenthood, thinking that they needed to build up their bank account before they would have time for a family. It felt strange sitting there, in the middle of a career that she thought she wanted so badly, and pondering thoughts that had nothing to do with answering the phone and filling out applications. They suddenly didn't seem so important. She had the feeling that someone could fill her shoes in a matter of minutes, and she could put on new shoes and try walking somewhere different. Maybe she should move to a new house or try a new career. Living on her own, without Jeff, was not something she had planned for in life, but she was now faced with a choice: become depressed and reminisce about the past or face the future with the prospect of making new memories. Aunt Marie had sent her a book with those exact words written on the very first page. To serve as a reminder, she had copied them down and attached them to the front of her refrigerator.

Chapter 9

Suppose one of you wants to build a tower. Will he not first sit down and estimate the cost to see if he has enough money to complete it?

—Luke 14:28

Abby looked up as she heard the sound of her door opening. Linda, carrying a brightly colored book, was already halfway to her desk. "I'm sorry to disturb you, Abby, but the new Homes Directory just came in, and I thought you might like to look through it."

"Thank you, Linda. I haven't seen one of those for a while, and I appreciate you thinking of me." Linda smiled but didn't answer as she slowly exited Abby's office, giving Abby the feeling that bringing the book was just an excuse to open the door and check on her. Whatever the reason, Abby was glad for Linda's friendship and concern.

As she leafed through the book, a full-page ad caught her attention. A beautiful sprawling, two-story white colonial house was pictured for sale in Carroll County. *Why does that interest me, she thought.*

The ad was in full color, and the property looked very statuesque surrounded with beautiful gardens. Her first thought was how much Jeff would have loved this piece of real estate. Instant tears clouded her eyes. It was like an answer to a prayer that she hadn't even prayed yet. Did God really work that fast?

It was only minutes ago when changing her lifestyle seemed impossible. She hadn't even had time to think about what she might want to do, and now a picture of a big white house literally was dropped in front of her, giving her the answer. It was the perfect setting for a bed-and-breakfast. It was uncanny how Jeff's description of his B&B vision was so close to what she was looking at on the page of this magazine. Without any hesitation, she picked up the phone and called the listing agency. The property was located near the little town of New Hope. The listing agent was none other than the infamous Warren Wright, owner of WOW Real Estate Agency. As an agent, he was pretty well-known throughout the state as quite a hustler. Even so, Abby decided to call about this one. She felt as if she needed to see more than just a picture, and for some strange reason, she sensed that this house had something to do with her future.

When she called the WOW office, Warren himself answered the phone. "Good afternoon, you've reached the office of WOW Real Estate. This is Warren Wright. May I help you?"

"Good afternoon, Mr. Wright. My name is Abby Weaver. I saw a house listed in the homes directory, and I was wondering if I might make an appointment to see it. The address is 604 Willow Road, and I see that you are actually the listing agent, so I'm assuming that you know which one I'm talking about."

"Yes, Ms. Weaver, I know exactly which one you are talking about, and it's a real beauty. This is quite a coincidence, but I am actually heading over that way this afternoon. I have a showing at one o'clock, and I expect to be done by three. Could you come by then and I can walk you through?"

Well, so far, he was living up to his reputation of stretching the truth and being conniving. A gut feeling told her that there was no other showing and that he was lying, and she hadn't even been on the phone two minutes with him. This man was really good.

Abby answered, perhaps a bit too sarcastically, "Why, Mr. Wright, that sure is a coincidence. I think I just might be able to rearrange my schedule so that I can meet you there." She assumed that he wanted her to believe that she wasn't the only one interested in the property. Real estate agents were known for dramatizing a showing. Knowing someone else liked a property was like adding color to old black-and-white photographs; things suddenly looked better and more interesting. But right now, she didn't really care how this man justified his behavior; she just wanted to see this big white house.

As she drove over to Carroll County on Highway 6, she was overwhelmed with the surroundings that she saw from her car window. She had driven this road many times before, but today it seemed different. A year ago, she never would have noticed all the beautiful trees or the flowers growing along the side of the road. At the mere mention of flowers, her thoughts shifted to Jeff's beloved flower collection. Months had passed, allowing dust to settle on the delicate edges of the petals, before she could will herself to take them down from the shelves and wipe them clean. She had then tenderly laid each flower into a special cardboard box and marked "Delicate" on the outside with a heavy marker. She felt disloyal by removing them from the shelf that Jeff had so meticulously placed them on, but she knew they were safe, and they would always stay in her possession.

As if to mirror her melancholy thoughts out of nowhere, clouds became visible, turning the sky a dark shade of gray. A strong wind forced the trees to sway, their branches bending and twisting. It was even beginning to hail. Her silent thoughts now interrupted, she switched on the windshield wipers. The whoosh-whoosh sound brought her back to reality, and for a fleeting moment, pain thundered through her head. It was almost like a brain freeze. As quickly as it developed, it was gone. But then she realized that her back ached between her shoulder blades, and even though her head no longer had the sharp pains, she seemed to be feeling sluggish. She pulled the sun visor mirror down in front of her and noticed that fatigue had settled in the pockets under her eyes. The sleepless nights were beginning to take a toll on her. But why had this feeling of emptiness come on her so quickly? Was it simply because she was thinking so much about Jeff? She was traveling, right at this moment, toward what could be a new life for her.

Suddenly, it hit her—a new life without Jeff. The idea of a bed-and-breakfast was a dream that she and Jeff envisioned together, so how could she even be the least bit excited now about seeing a house that she could never share with her husband? A hot tear of shame began trickling down her cheek. She was certain this feeling of emptiness was influenced by a wave of guilt and felt like it was going to swallow her alive. It was like a bird of prey hovering over her, just waiting to strike every time her memory ricocheted back to Jeff. Was it going to be like this every time she allowed self-pity and remorse to creep in?

She found a wide spot on the side of the road and parked her car, hoping to pull herself together. She didn't want to be late for her appointment with Mr. Wright, but she also didn't want him to see her in this state. She pushed some things around in her purse until she found her compact with some blush and eyeliner. As quickly and flawlessly as she could, she brushed her cheeks and lined her eyes with her favorite Avon products and pushed the mirror back into its groove. She would love to turn around, go home, and curl up on the sofa; but Mr. Wright was expecting her, and she would not keep him waiting. Plus, despite it all, she did really want to see this house.

As she turned on to Willow Road, she saw it. Even through the pouring rain, it was absolutely beautiful, and it looked exactly like the picture in the directory. Rocking chairs were lined up on the wraparound porch. Blooming flowers of all kinds were spilling out over the edges of planters as they hung from the ceiling between each white column that graced the front of the house. Abby felt like she was Scarlett O'Hara coming home to Tara. The only difference was that there was no Rhett Butler to carry her up the stairs. But there *was* an attractive man sitting on the porch in the rocker closest to the front door. Abby assumed that he was Mr. Wright and that the dark green car that she was parking beside belonged to him.

As she got out of her Honda Accord, she felt an unusual feeling—intimidation. So what if he drove a Jaguar? The bank probably owned more of it than he did. Her car may not be as new or expensive, but at least she possessed the title.

Warren was out of the rocker and hurrying down the steps toward Abby. He walked with a bit of stiff dignity shaded with an air of conceit. As he approached Abby, he reached out and caught her hand in his. In a deep and sensual voice that sent a ripple of awareness through her, he said eagerly, "I'm Warren Wright. It's nice to meet you, Ms. Weaver. Or is it Mrs. Weaver?" His dark eyes never left hers as Abby blinked, feeling lightheaded again.

She offered him a shy small smile and replied, "Actually, I would appreciate it if you would just call me Abby."

"Well, that's a simple enough request. Are you ready to fall in love with this house?"

Not wanting to give him the satisfaction of an easy sale, Abby took a deep breath and adjusted her smile. All she could think of for an answer was "Yes, I'm ready. I hope it's all you say it is."

Not waiting for Mr. Wright, she walked straight ahead to a large room that was bathed in sunlight from the many floor-length windows. A pearl-colored grand piano was poised in the middle of the room as if waiting for someone in a ballroom gown to possess its keys. She recognized the carpet underneath as a French Aubusson–style. Its rich blues and ivories were a trademark of that particular Indian company. Plants of all kinds were placed methodically around the room. Its hardwood floors shone as if they had just been buffed. This room alone, without viewing the rest of the house, was enough to convince her that this was where she belonged. This just might be the therapy that could transition her from grief to happiness.

Mr. Wright finished giving her the tour and asked if they could sit down at the kitchen table, review all the details, and give him a chance to answer any questions that she might have. She could already see him calculating the numbers in his mind. He excused himself and walked to the wall phone and dialed a number. While waiting for the person on the other end to answer, he leaned against the kitchen counter, giving Abby time to notice his attractive physique. The rich outlines of his shoulders seemed to strain against the fabric of his baby blue shirt. It was open at the neck and revealed a muscular chest covered with crisp dark hair. His profile was sharp and confident, and the shadow of his beard gave him a very manly aura. She noticed age lines around his mouth and eyes. She presumed him to be in his midthirties and wondered if he was single, married, or divorced. *Whatever his marital status, he was one fine physical specimen of a man.*

"Abby, are you okay? You seem to be lost in space. I'm sorry for the interruption, but I check in with my office every day around this time, just to make sure that everything is running on schedule. I like to run a tight ship."

Warren sat back down at the table, opened the folder again, and folded his hands together in a comfortable position as if he already knew her answer. He said in a most composed voice, "Let's go over the major details for now, and I'll call you tomorrow and see what you think."

Taking his business card out of his pants pocket, he held it out for her and said, "Here's my card with my direct line at the office. Please feel free to call me if you have any more questions or to set up another appointment." He glanced at her for a sign of objection but found none, so when he spoke again, his voice was warm. "Call me anytime."

Abby regarded him with a speculative gaze and asked, "I have one question for you right now. Or rather, I guess you would call it a favor. I would like to have the name and phone number of the owner."

"May I ask why?"

"I just get the feeling that this place has a lot of history, and I would like to hear it from someone who obviously loves this house. It's been very well taken care of, and a lot of concern has been put into the design and decor. I'm a story lover myself, and I have an interest in local history."

He studied her thoughtfully for a moment and then said, "I'll see what I can do."

As they walked out the front door, Warren extended his hand to Abby and said, "It's been a pleasure meeting you, Abby. I'll call the owner when I get back to the office, and then I'll let you know her answer."

Warren opened the car door for Abby, and she said softly but firmly, "Thank you, Mr. Wright. I appreciate your help, and I'll be waiting to hear from you."

CHAPTER 10

Do not lust in your heart after her beauty or let her captivate you with her eyes.

—Proverbs 6:25

Meeting Ms. Weaver today turned Warren's ordinary day into a rather exciting one. He felt a strange sensation when he was near her as if they had met before. That was impossible. There was no way Warren would forget a woman who looked like her. He was glad that she had been so absorbed in the excitement of seeing the house that his hungry eyes went unnoticed. She was a very attractive woman, and during the house tour, she had revealed that she was a widow. That was a green light for asking her out to dinner. There was something about her that caused a deep surge of desire to well up inside of him. It was a very disturbing feeling, and he wasn't sure what to do with it.

Thinking of dinner reminded him of Lilly. It had been two years since the pretty waitress had served him his coffee at George's Diner and had captivated his heart. He had gotten to know her with his daily visits and became more infatuated with her every day. The fact that she was a waitress connected her to a different social class than his, and for that reason, even though he knew he was being egotistical, he had followed his head instead of his heart. After all, he had built a successful business and was the kingpin of real estate in the entire county. *How would it look to my colleagues and friends if I dated a waitress?*

He sat down for a minute on one of the rocking chairs on the porch and pondered his confusion. He really didn't know Lilly all that well, but he knew Ms. Weaver even less, yet he was thinking of asking Ms. Weaver to dinner before Lilly. *What in the world is going on in my brain?* He had always been an in-control sort of guy, and now here he was, slowly losing his grip on it. For all these years, he had been satisfied with one-night stands, no commitments, but this—this was different somehow. His attraction to Abby wasn't like his feelings for Lilly. If he was really ready to settle down with Lilly, like he had thought, then why was he being drawn to this woman?

Still puzzled, Warren watched as Abby drove down the driveway and turned toward town. Nothing left to do now except call Mrs. Black as he promised. As he turned the key in the Jaguar's ignition, he realized that he was having heart palpitations, and he was sweating. He didn't remember the doctor telling him to expect anything like this after surgery. Maybe he had gone back to work too soon, but he wasn't used to a lethargic lifestyle. The two weeks in the hospital bed was enough relaxation to last him a lifetime. He really *was* trying to take things slow at work. He leaned back again, took a deep breath, and noticed just how much he was sweating.

Debating as to whether or not he should call the doctor, he had a sudden realization and started laughing. This was nothing more than a case of pure lust. He couldn't remember a time when a woman had caused a reaction like this. Abby was a drop-dead gorgeous woman who was soft but yet very firm with her responses. She didn't talk a lot, a quality in women that Warren preferred. She was classy and very confident, yet deep down, he had this feeling that there was something very special about her—something that maybe he would find out, if he got to know her. But for some reason, alarms were going off in his head, telling him to keep his distance.

He realized he was smiling as he dialed the number for Mrs. Black.

"Hello."

"Hello, Mrs. Black?"

"Yes, this is she speaking."

"This is Warren Wright from WOW Real Estate. How are you today?"

"I'm fine, Mr. Wright. I hope you're calling to say you have a buyer for my property."

Warren's voice rose an octave as he spoke. "Well, actually, I do have a potential buyer, but she had a specific request. I'm calling to ask if we could arrange an appointment with the two of you together."

"Well, Mr. Wright, I think I need a tad more information. I don't usually make it a habit to meet strangers alone. What exactly does this woman want?"

"I assure you, Mrs. Black, that Abby Weaver is most harmless. She has an interest in history, and since your house is on the historical register, she would like to know some intimate details about the property. I promised that I would ask if you would give her the opportunity to talk with you, but the decision is totally up to you."

"Because you asked me, I have to assume that you think it's okay, *and* it would be nice to have someone to talk to. So yes, please have Ms. Weaver meet me at the house at ten o'clock tomorrow morning. Thank you, Mr. Wright, for calling."

Typical Mrs. Black, he thought. Right to the point. For an old lady, she was sharp as a tack. As he heard the click of the receiver on the other end, he chuckled as he thought about the two women meeting tomorrow: Abby, young and chic, and Mrs. Black, aged and gifted with not only sophistication but with a flair for mixing contemporary with vintage. She loved antiques and, over the years, had acquired quite a collection. Warren had done his homework and had found more information about Shirley Black than he anticipated. She had been brought up under the strict thumb of a Baptist minister, and her childhood roots went very deep. Even though she was a wealthy widow, she remained extremely conservative. She was well respected in the town of New Hope and had even been elected to the town council. Warren wasn't quite sure how these two ladies would hit it off, but he could only hope for the best. He was just glad that Mrs. Black had been so willing to cooperate.

As he dialed Abby's number, he hesitated for a moment, giving himself enough time to contemplate on the exact words that he wanted to say. What he really wanted to do was ask her out, but he heard the same alarms again and decided not to be stupid. He needed to execute this business deal, and if he had learned anything from his past experiences of trying to pursue women, he knew not to rush things. He would keep their conversations strictly about business, and if and when the deal was completed, he would ask to take her out to dinner to celebrate. With that in mind, he continued dialing and waited. When she didn't answer, he simply left her a message concerning the meeting with Mrs. Black.

When Abby checked her messages that afternoon, she noticed one from WOW Real Estate. She wasn't expecting an answer so soon. Mr. Wright was obviously a prompt man of his word. *I like that in a man.* She shook her head as if to dislodge the thoughts from her mind. Abby couldn't believe that she was, in fact, looking at this man in a romantic kind of way. She really had no interest in any man right now. Would she always compare every man to Jeff? Could this be one of those unconscious emotions that a person going through grief had to deal with? Aunt Marie had not only quoted some bits and pieces from a book about taking steps to restoration but she also wanted Abby to join a grief support group. Abby had refused, insisting that she could make it on her own. To tell the truth, she really didn't want to recover fully, not yet anyway. Being in this state of mind meant that she could stay faithful to Jeff's memory. That was why she couldn't understand why she was thinking so much about Mr. Wright. *What was it about him that was so beguiling?*

Abby retrieved her message from the answering machine and listened as Mr. Wright quoted the time for her to meet with Mrs. Black. She couldn't wait to come face to face with the person who had such exquisite taste in decorating and had all the information that she needed to know about her venture into a new and unfamiliar world.

Even after taking her sleeping pill that evening, Abby couldn't seem to keep her eyes shut. She couldn't even lie still in bed. She leaned over toward her nightstand drawer and found a pencil and some paper. She began writing down some figures, erased those, and wrote the same ones again. Each time she wrote them, they seemed a little more impossible. In order for her to afford this adventure, she would have to pay a visit to a loan officer at the bank.

Satisfied with her decision, she rolled over toward Jeff's side of the bed and felt another pang of guilt. This time, she shut her eyes and kept them closed. Visions of beautiful rooms leaped on to a canvas, each one decorated in a southern-style charm of blues, yellows, and ivories. The rooms seemed familiar, yet there was no suggestion that they belonged to her.

The alarm clock interrupted her sleep, leaving her wondering what had happened to the night. It seemed as if only ten minutes had passed since her restlessness at bedtime and her vivid dreams of painted walls. It was time to face another day of loneliness.

CHAPTER 11

Listen to advice and accept instruction, that you may gain wisdom in the future.

—Proverbs 19:20

Abby rang the doorbell and suddenly felt very nervous. She was about to make the decision of a lifetime emotionally and financially. She was knocking on the door of opportunity literally, and as soon as Mrs. Black unlocked that door and she stepped inside, she knew she would once again be ambushed by the surroundings. Each piece of furniture, every lamp, every picture on the wall would seize her inner desire to live there and begin a new life. Somehow she had to convince Mrs. Black that her heart and soul had become obsessed with this house from the very first time she saw it. She needed to convince her that relinquishing this house to someone with a passion for taking care of it was more beneficial than having an extralarge bank account: she needed to persuade her to sell it for less than the asking price. Now was when she needed Jeff's expertise, but in her heart, she knew he would just tell her to make an honest deal.

Suddenly, the door was opened by a slender, willowy lady with black hair and long turquoise earrings, which seemed too heavy for her earlobes. A gaudy matching necklace hung around her neck, defining its smallness. She was definitely nothing like Abby had envisioned.

Abby held out her hand and, with a trace of excitement in her voice, said, "Hi, I'm Abby Weaver. Are you Mrs. Black?"

In a low but very composed voice, the woman answered, "Yes, Ms. Weaver, I am. I've been expecting you, and you're right on time. I really don't like people who are late. Come in please." With a sweeping motion of one arm, she invited her to step into the foyer. "Would you like a cup of tea? I hope you don't mind, but I didn't have time to bake anything, so I just bought some doughnuts at the local bakery."

Mrs. Black swiveled quickly, turned her back to Abby, and proceeded to the kitchen. Not knowing what else to do, Abby followed her.

The kitchen table, now covered with a yellow tablecloth, sat near the big bay window. The teacups and saucers, already in place, were covered with tiny blue and yellow primroses, the exact shade to match the tablecloth. Surrounded by napkins that mirrored its steel blue color, a vase sitting in the middle of the table held four large yellow roses. It was like looking at a picture in a *Southern Living* magazine. Abby was awestruck. Not only was it perfect but the china also was almost identical to her childhood tea set, which she had filled so many times with make-believe tea for her dolls. It was very uncanny looking at this spread of dishes. It brought goose bumps to her arms.

Mrs. Black was walking toward the table, balancing two platters in her hands—one with an assortment of tea bags and the other laden with the doughnuts. As she sat them on the table, she spoke very candidly. "Abby, may I call you Abby?" Recognizing that it wasn't her turn to speak, Abby just nodded her head in agreement.

There was a faint glimmer of worry in Mrs. Black's eyes as she looked at Abby. But when she spoke, her voice was kind. "What exactly do you want from me today, Abby? Could you tell me a little bit about yourself and why you are interested in the history of this house?" Mrs. Black pushed back a wayward strand of dark hair and said, "I sensed some urgency in the request from Mr. Wright. I must say, though, it is rather nice to have someone else in this house besides myself. Most days are very lonely, especially in the winter."

Her expression changed and became much more unguarded as she said, "Out with it. I'm ready to listen now."

Being intimated by Mrs. Black didn't help Abby's ability to express herself exactly as she was feeling. She was used to being the one in charge. Fortunately, Mrs. Black didn't notice the tremor in Abby's voice as she spoke. "I need a new beginning in my life. I recently lost my husband. Being a widow yourself, I know you understand my pain." Abby took a deep breath and continued. "When I saw the picture of this house in the directory, a feeling came over me that I can't explain, but I knew at that moment that I just had to have this house. It was as if all rationality was being sucked right out of my brain and transported to my heart. I have always prided myself on my ability to handle life, no matter what came along, but when my husband died, it was a quandary like I never imagined. It developed into a total transformation of my life that I was not prepared for."

Mrs. Black seemed to be listening very attentively to every word that Abby spoke, yet she said nothing. She only repositioned herself on the chair and waited.

So Abby continued, finding renewed strength to tell a stranger her most intimate feelings. "Coming here to meet you today is way out of my comfort zone, yet I couldn't wait to get here. It's as if everything that I do these days is so out of character for me. I'm very conservative and definitely am not a risk-taker. I feel like someone has me by the hand and is leading me right through this process."

Mrs. Black smiled as if in total understanding and nodded for Abby to go on. "To be honest with you, Mrs. Black, I came here today because I need to own this house, and I was hoping that we could come to some financial terms. I am not a rich woman. I do have my husband's life insurance policy, but it's not quite enough. I said earlier that I need a new beginning. My husband would not want me to sit around grieving for him, even though I find it hard not to do anything else, and that's why I feel so strong about this property. I feel as if Jeff has given me his stamp of approval. From the minute I stepped inside the front door, it felt like I was at home. I had a dream the other night about color swatches and painted walls, and it all looked so familiar, yet I couldn't recognize the location. It was this house. Everything about this place is exactly the way Jeff and I talked about our future home." Trying not to ramble, Abby took a deep breath and exhaled slowly. "Mrs. Black, not only do I want to buy the house but I would like to buy the furnishings too. Mr. Wright told me that you are planning to move into a retirement home and are allowed mostly only personal items, so this would save you from seeing them being sold at an auction. Plus, you could visit as often as you would like, and you'd still be able to sit at this table or play the piano. I assume you are the reason for the piano?"

Mrs. Black, seemingly mesmerized by Abby's bold request, sat silently for what seemed like an eternity and finally spoke in a matter-of-fact yet compassionate voice. "Abby, I do feel your pain. Losing a loved one leaves you with a never-ending ache, but I admire your determination to move on in life. I have prayed that God would send someone to buy this house that would love it and care for it as I have, and once again, He has answered a prayer. I feel that you truly do need this house and vice versa. What exactly do you plan to do with all of this space?"

A smile formed on Abby's face, and with more excitement, she answered, "I want to open a bed-and-breakfast, a place that people with small paychecks can come to enjoy a night of luxury. I could serve them and make them feel special. A place of renewal for couples and a place of solace for those who are hurting. I have been taking from the world for quite a while now, and I would like to be able to give something back. It has always been a secret dream of mine, a private dream that not even Jeff knew about. We always talked about the bed-and-breakfast, but I never told him my real reason for wanting to make it happen." She felt like she was talking too much, but Mrs. Black seemed like she was waiting for the finale, so even though her voice was still quivering, she continued. "When I was a child, I used to go to Sunday school. Missionaries who had served in all parts of the world would visit the church and show us slides of all the 'poor people' as we childishly named them. I always thought the missionaries' lives seemed so full of excitement and compassion—two things my family always appeared to be lacking, so it appealed to me. I truly believed that, after high school, I would find myself in some remote village teaching people about the very same things that I took for granted. But like most everything else in my childhood, it became an unfulfilled figment of my imagination. Wanting to serve those less fortunate than myself became my secret dream. I'm sorry that I never shared such an essential passion of mine with my husband. But saying this out loud to you now actually makes me feel as if my desire might come true."

Abby raised her eyes to look at Mrs. Black and realized that she wasn't the only one in tears. This dear old woman was on the verge of sobbing out loud. Instinctively, they reached for each other, unmindful of the union that was already forming.

As the tears began to subside, Abby regained her composure and said, "I have one more thing to say, and then I'll be on my way. I never intended to stay so long or sound so needy. Before I go, we do need to talk some business. I love the way it is decorated, and I would like to be able to make a deal, with furnishings included. I've thought a lot about this, and I think I've found a way to make my dream come true. Even though it will be a bed-and-breakfast, I want this house to serve as a modern missionary field. I may not be the typical missionary that I hear about on television, but I'm sure there are plenty of people in our little town that I could help in some way. I feel so close to making my dream a reality. I need to find purpose in my life now and try to honor Jeff's death. He loved people, and he would want me to do as much as I can for those in need. He was an anonymous donor to a lot of organizations and was a firm believer in philanthropy."

Abby swallowed hard and squared her shoulders in one last attempt to persuade Mrs. Black to at least consider her request. Her voice was full of entreaty as she said, "If you and I can work out a deal, this can become not just an inn but also a safe haven for some or just a place of peace for others. It could serve as a new beginning for couples who need their marriage restored or a place of comfort for those who have suffered a loss."

Tears of delight found their way to Mrs. Black's eyes as she rose to her feet and motioned for Abby to stand also. Before Abby knew what was happening, Mrs. Black had gathered her into her arms and was holding her tightly. Abby returned the embrace, wondering exactly what this show of affection meant. *Is she going to help me, or is it just a nice send-off?*

Mrs. Black released Abby and held her at arm's length. "Ms. Weaver, you've got a deal—on one condition."

Abby's face drained of color, wondering what the "condition" was going to be and if she could fulfill it and still see her dream come true. Before she could inquire further, Mrs. Black, smiling from ear to ear, spoke with a possessive desperation in her voice. "How would you feel about me occupying the far room on the west side of the house? I'll give you the deal of a lifetime if you allow me life interest. Of course, I would only refer to the smaller master suite as mine."

Abby was caught off guard by this very unpredictable, wonderful tiny woman. She was so surprised by Mrs. Black's proposal that she was momentarily speechless. Mrs. Black took advantage of Abby's silence and continued on with her persuasive words. "Everything would remain as it is, furniture included. I wouldn't have to move, and I could continue to enjoy this house." As if expecting Abby to argue, she continued. "I could even help you with the chores around here. I could register guests and do laundry, and if I must say so myself, I make a pretty mean omelet." Assuming that Abby needed more convincing, she added, "I wouldn't interfere with your personal life, and I'll even pay rent."

There was something so warm and enchanting about this woman that Abby found it impossible not to return her contagious smile. Suddenly, she felt in charge again. She guided Mrs. Black back to her chair and then pulled out a chair for herself, slid it up to the table, and sat down. She needed time to think this through. She didn't even know this woman, and she was asking if she could live with her. *What if she got sick?* This was supposed to be a bed-and-breakfast, not a nursing home. The deal that Mrs. Black had just put together sounded wonderful, but would it be worth it in the long run, or would she regret it?

Very gently, Abby said, "Mrs. Black, this is quite an offer you just made me, but I really don't know you, and you really don't know me. I really want to say yes. My heart is telling me to jump for joy, but the logical side of my brain is saying, 'Slow down.' I'm not one to make hasty decisions. I love everything that you've done with the house, but if I did make a few changes, would you be upset?"

Mrs. Black excitingly jumped in. "Ms. Weaver, I haven't felt this right about anything since the day I married David. When he proposed to me, I had the same gut reaction as I'm having right now. Please say you'll take me up on my offer."

Then Abby decided to do something that she had only done a few times in her life—make a decision based on her emotions. And as she touched the warmth of Mrs. Black's outstretched hand, she knew without a shadow of a doubt that she was doing the right thing.

Mrs. Black rose from her chair and walked to an adjoining room that she used for an office, found a pen and some paper, and returned to the kitchen table. She began putting some of her accounting knowledge to work. There was just something about this young lady that intrigued her, and the sooner she put together this deal, the sooner a new chapter in her life would begin. She couldn't wait to see the look on Mr. Wright's face when she and Abby presented their sales agreement to him. He didn't seem like the kind of guy who allowed himself to be swindled out of commission, but there was nothing he could do to alter this arrangement. It was going to be a perfectly legal deal.

Chapter 12

Who of you by worrying can add a single hour to his life?

—Matthew 6:27

Warren opened the door to his office and was greeted by the flashing light on his answering machine. It was Saturday, and the only reason he had stopped at the office was to grab his Day-Timer, which he had left in his desk drawer. Should he retrieve his messages or let them till Monday morning? He decided to push the button and see what was so important that clients had to call him on Saturday. The first one, Mrs. Miller needed a copy of a rental application. The second one was old Mrs. Hoover, who called almost every day to inform him that she was ready to put a For Sale sign in her front yard, yet every time he drove the ten miles to her home, she changed her mind and wanted to wait awhile. But the third one was worth listening to. He recognized the voice even before she identified herself. It was Shirley Black.

"Hello, Mr. Wright, this is Shirley Black. You have my property listed over on Willow Road. I'm calling to say thank you for sending Ms. Weaver to visit me. She is a delightful young lady, and we have come up with a sales agreement. I was hoping that you could meet us on Monday morning, say, around ten o'clock, at my house. If I don't hear from you, I will assume that we will see you there."

Warren smiled as he looked in the mirror that hung on the wall across from his desk. He began talking to it as if it were going to answer. "Typical old rich lady. Thinks she can call here and rearrange my schedule." He ran his fingers through his hair as if defeated, and his expression became tight with concern. Exactly what had these two ladies found in common so fast, and what kind of deal had they prepared? He had a feeling that he wasn't going to like it.

CHAPTER 13

The righteous cry out, and the Lord hears them;
he delivers them from all their troubles.

—Psalm 34:17

As exciting as it had been to walk through the big white house and know that she would soon be the new owner, as a result, Abby's heart was split right down the middle. One side was jumping up and down, shouting to the world about her new adventure, and the other side was bleeding from guilt. She was happy because she felt she had a future and sad because Jeff wasn't there to share this part of her life. She thought of Mrs. Black's words, that this was an "answer to prayer," and wished she had a connection to God like that. It would make things so much easier if she could hear a big booming voice speak to her and give her the answers and the peace that she needed.

She considered herself an independent woman, but as of late, she had found herself crying out to God. She had ignored him for so many years that she couldn't imagine why he would want to help her now. She *did* believe in God and always thought that someday she would go back to church and start reading the Bible, but something always got in the way and seemed more important. Before Jeff's death, she questioned herself as to whether she would give up a Sunday morning just to sit in a pew with hypocrites. It was true that her grandmother made it a point to take her to Sunday school when she was a child, but it also had confused her. She loved her grandmother and wanted to be just like her, yet she was being taught at church the exact opposite of what she witnessed with her grandmother's friends as they smoked and drank many bottles of vodka. She played near them and listened as they made fun of someone's clothing or made inappropriate comments about the men in the congregation. They talked about everybody they knew, but at the end of every "get-together," they prayed for the same people that they had just trashed. So many people whom she knew who went to church every Sunday proclaimed to be Christians and then lived a whole different lifestyle during the week.

She saw something different in Mrs. Black. Abby sometimes listened as Mrs. Black talked to her friends on the phone. If some form of gossip was being told, she was quick to silence the rumor. Abby had watched many times as Mrs. Black cooked meals and delivered them to someone in need. Devotions were an important part of her day, and she insisted on having no interruptions. The checks that she wrote for her weekly tithing and for various charities were quite generous. Abby was convinced that Mrs. Black was the real deal. She had never known anyone like this woman. She not only professed her faith but she lived it as well, a woman who truly believed in God and lived her faith from Sunday to Sunday. No matter what happened during the day, she somehow always managed to bring God into the picture. Among wads of tissue, a cold cup of tea, and an empty bag of Oreos, Abby bowed her head and in a quiet voice said, "Lord, you already know how I feel, and you also know that I'm not very good at this. I guess you already know what I want. I know there's a verse in the Bible that says, 'Ask and you shall receive,' so I'm asking for you to guide me the way I'm supposed to go. I haven't signed final papers yet, so if this is not the direction I'm intended to go, please give me some kind of sign. Mrs. Black says that buying this house is just the first step in accomplishing your plan, and I want to believe that you will allow my eyes to be open enough to acknowledge the next step and to find my way to the top of the staircase, if that's where you want me. Please allow me to be a servant to whoever comes into my house."

Before rising from the sofa, she closed her eyes and softly said, "Amen."

As she walked slowly to the kitchen to fix another cup of herbal tea, she straightened her body to relieve the ache in her shoulders and tilted her head from side to side, trying to release any tension, but abruptly recognized that she had no more aches or pains. In fact, an unfamiliar and unexpected warmth surged through her that left her feeling very peaceful.

Just as she sat down to drink her tea, the telephone rang. She really didn't feel like talking to anyone right now, but she hit the Talk button and said, "Hello."

"Hello, Ms. Weaver. This is Shirley Black. How are you?"

"I'm fine, Mrs. Black. How are you?"

Mrs. Black's voice held a rasp of excitement as she said, "I'm fit as a fiddle, but you, dear, sound as if you're getting a cold. I have the perfect cure. Give me a minute and—"

In midsentence Abby interrupted. "No, Mrs. Black, I do not have a cold. I just didn't sleep very well last night. I guess I'm having some doubts and feelings of guilt about starting a new life and being excited about it." Not wanting to continue on this subject, Abby asked, "Is there something I can help you with?"

"Well, actually, I was hoping I could help you. In seventy-nine years, this old body has never had such an exhilarating sensation in my bones as I just had a few minutes ago. It was as if the Lord Almighty himself came down, tapped me on the shoulders, and swung me around till I was in the circle of his arms. I know it had something to do with you because, right away, your face came to my mind. I just had to call you and make sure you were okay." The intensity in her voice softened as she asked, "Are you sure you're okay?"

To Abby's dismay, her voice broke slightly as she tried to speak. "I'm fine, Mrs. Black. I just had some tea, and I'm going to lie down and take a short nap. I'm sure I'll feel better when I wake up. Thank you for calling and checking on me. I appreciate that."

Searching for the perfect words, Mrs. Black responded in almost a whisper, "Remember, Abby, you and I were meant to meet each other, and even though this house was built many years ago, I believe God's intention was for you to someday be the owner. God has great plans for you, Abby Weaver. You are one lucky woman. I'll see you Monday morning at ten o'clock."

Abby heard a click and realized that Mrs. Black had hung up the receiver. She curled up on the bed and within minutes was sound asleep. Before long, she began tossing and turning, changing positions as if each new movement would rid her of the questions and doubts that kept hammering in her mind. Each time she felt herself remotely begin to relax and drift off to sleep, she found herself in the middle of a dream that seemed more like a memory. She was standing in front of a cardboard box with holes cut out for windows and a swinging door held together with duct tape. Its tenant's profile, dark against the moonlight, was handsome with blue eyes, which were deep, dark, and mysterious as they gazed into hers. His teeth, even and white, contrasted pleasingly with his tanned skin. His hair was black with just a splash of gray coming in next to his temples. He looked lean and tough. Even inside the box, his presence was compelling. But who was he? Why was he causing her to lose sleep? She rolled over once more, but this time, she sat up and leaned against her pillow, realizing that she was breathing in quick, shallow gasps and her chest feeling as if it would burst. She swung her legs off the bed until she found the floor and let them carry her impatiently to the bathroom. She took a long swallow of water and stood leaning against the counter until she could find her balance. She walked slowly back to the bed, and as she snuggled under the covers and formed her pillow to the contour of her head, images of the homeless man once again seized her imagination. An annoyed inner voice cut through her thoughts, demanding who this man was and why he was interrupting her much-needed sleep. Having no rational explanation or answers, she picked up the pillow and, with some force, threw it to the other side of the room. Determined to shake this overwhelming sensation of uncertainty, she once again crawled out of bed and walked down the hall. She was so exhausted, but knowing that sleep wasn't going to happen, she decided to step into the spare bedroom that was full of boxes. With a new cup of tea in hand, she sat down on the floor to begin the process of deciding what she wanted to take with her and what she needed to get rid of. Since the house on Willow Road was furnished with so much, she really wasn't going to need many of her things. There was so much of her life in these boxes that she wasn't going to need anymore. If she were going to start a new life, then she needed to leave the past behind, but she would definitely take some personal reminders of Jeff with her and keep them forever. Thinking of all her personal possessions brought an idea to mind—surely, there would be someone in her new community that would be in need of furniture and household items. Once she moved and got to know the people in New Hope, she was sure that she could help someone less fortunate than she was.

She loved it when decisions seemed to just pour into her mind like concrete in a foundation. There should be no hours of fretting and worrying if she was doing the right thing. Her acquaintance with Mrs. Black seemed to be sparking more and more thoughts about God. For a moment like this to occur, she assumed it was God tossing ideas in her direction, and she felt that it was her obligation to act upon them. She would put all the things in storage, and when the right time came to give them away, she would know exactly who was supposed to receive them. Without another thought, she added "Call storage unit" to her to-do list for tomorrow.

Sorting household items into boxes was easier now that she had a solid plan to follow. There seemed to be more containers in this room than she remembered. She didn't even recognize a lot of the contents. She had no idea just how much of a pack rat Jeff had been. She decided to start with the boxes on the floor and work her way up to the top. She placed three boxes on the floor and marked them appropriately with "Shredder," "Trash," and a question mark. She found it hard to believe that the shredded box was almost full and that the trash box was overflowing. There seemed to be so much unneeded paperwork.

When she opened the lid on a round hatbox, she was surprised to find it full of cards and letters. Dear old organized Aunt Marie had saved every piece of correspondence that had come through the mail during the weeks following Jeff's death. Not exactly sure what she wanted to do with them, Abby leaned back against the wall and allowed herself a minute to wonder about the sadness she felt now when she thought of Jeff. She had only good memories of her life with him, and she wanted to feel happy when she remembered them. It was times like this that brought an ache to her heart. She missed him even more than tears could convey.

Her fingers began shaking as she opened the envelopes, curious as to who sent them and what they said. *Do I really want to read all the sympathy poems and the little notations that people wrote inside the cards? Do I want to sit here and be reminded of that awful day?* Maybe she should return them to the box and pretend that she had never found them, but she knew she would eventually be overcome with curiosity. Most of the envelopes were small or square, but there were a few that were business size, so she separated those from the others and laid them aside. It looked like Aunt Marie must have gotten some insurance papers mixed in with these personal cards. As she began to read each card, she was filled with pride about the things each one said about Jeff. He had been a friend to everyone, and the sentiments they had written were proof. Each time she opened a new envelope, her gaze returned again and again to the large envelopes. Were they insurance papers? She reached for them.

Her muscles tensed at the mere touch of the envelopes, and they fell from her hands, unopened. She rose from the floor as if propelled by an explosive force and leaned against the wall behind her. She froze, mind and body benumbed. What had just happened? Her skin burned with the same sensation that she had felt on the very first time Jeff had touched her. How could that feeling be transmitted through a piece of paper? Was she going crazy? She felt as if a hand had just closed around her throat, cutting off all her air. Something disturbing had just happened there. She closed her eyes, her heart aching with pain. A flash of loneliness and fear stabbed at her as she lowered herself to the floor and covered her body with a *Star Wars* blanket that she had found in a box, still carrying the strong masculine scent of her husband. As she gave vent to the agony of her loss, she also gave in to her fatigue.

The endless night finally grayed into dawn, and Abby awoke with a monstrous headache. As she stood in front of the mirror and popped aspirin into her mouth, she would have cried at such a sight if it were possible for her eyes to produce more tears. All that was left to do was laugh. So in spite of the face of the woman in the mirror, she attempted to chuckle. The hot water from the shower helped wash away the traces of tears that had stained her cheeks during the night. It also refreshed her memory of the letters in the box. Without waiting another minute, Abby followed her instincts back to the hatbox. Now that she felt more in control, it was time to do more than just touch the envelopes. It was time to find out why the contents were so electrifying.

As she opened the flap of the ivory envelope, she noticed the address in the left-hand corner read "Gary Wentz, Attorney at Law, 552 Bricker Avenue, Millersburg, NC." The letter was printed on matching paper and read as follows:

> Dear Mrs. Weaver:
>
> As representative for Mr. Warren Wright, I am writing to thank you for signing the donor permission form after the death of Mr. Jeff Weaver. Your husband indicated on his driver's license that he wanted to be an organ donor, but it was your signature that allowed us to actually authorize the procedure. Mr. Warren Wright was in need of a new liver, and by exercising today's technology, your husband's generosity has allowed Mr. Wright to now live a normal life. Mr. Wright would like to express his heartfelt sympathy for your tragedy, but he also needs to express his deepest appreciation for your unrestrained concern for others. Even though this type of transplant is medically possible, it still is contingent upon the benevolence of mankind. You and your late husband obviously are part of today's society that believes in being "Good Samaritans" and helping those less fortunate.
>
> Please accept Mr. Wright's sincere appreciation for adding days to his life.
>
> Sincerely,
> Gary Wentz, Esq.

Hands trembling again, Abby quickly tore open the other envelopes and scanned the contents. The words she saw made her sick in the stomach. There were people out there walking around with parts of Jeff sewn into their bodies—strangers with physical fractions of Jeff attached to them. They didn't even know him. She was the one who loved him. She should be the one to have a part of his body attached to hers. The letters said that she had signed forms, giving permission to donate parts of her husband's body, but she didn't remember. *How could I forget something so significant?* she thought.

How could she go through life wondering if she was looking in Jeff's eyes each time she came face to face with a stranger? Would they still be the same tint of blue, or would they look totally different? What about his liver and his kidneys? What about his heart?

The answers could all be in the letters that she had just seen. They were all within her reach. The name of each individual who was alive today because of Jeff was in the hatbox.

As her body tried to absorb this new information, it reacted with spasms. As she began heaving, she ran to the bathroom; and while on her knees, embracing the toilet, she pleaded with God for strength—not only physical but emotional as well. She wanted to read the recipients' letters, hoping that they might shed some light on the importance of being a donor. What she couldn't understand was why God had taken *her* husband. This was a god she said she believed in and wanted to follow, yet somewhere deep inside, she was still very angry. When and how would she overcome this turbulence that she felt and could become secure in her faith, just like Mrs. Black?

She felt her stomach rolling, implying that it was empty and asking for food. She walked slowly down the stairs, thinking about what she had just discovered. She didn't feel ready to take on the task of sitting down and revisiting the letters, but it seemed inevitable. The shock was over, and the turmoil in her mind had calmed somewhat, and she knew that focusing on the substance of those letters was something that she was going to have to do.

Ten minutes after filling her bowl with oatmeal, she had all the letters spread out on the kitchen table. Reading each one with a renewed sense of unbiased reasoning, she was taken aback by the sincerity of each letter. A mother had written to express her deepest gratitude for the gift of Jeff's eyes. Her son could now see her for the first time in ten years. A daughter appreciated having her mother for a few more years with the donation of Jeff's kidneys. And a young man who had been suffering from heart disease since infancy was finally able to play baseball with his friends. The final letter was the same one that she had read the night before. As she reread it, the name Warren Wright became stuck in her memory like a record, repeating the name over and over. She knew a man with this name. Could it be the real estate agent? With a sick feeling in the pit of her stomach, she went to the file cabinet, pulled out the file for Willow Road, and checked the name on the bottom of the contract. Sure enough, Mr. Wright's first name was Warren. Could it have been Jeff's liver that was transplanted into this man's body? No wonder she had felt such an attraction to a complete stranger. Was it possible to feel such a connection, or was it just her tired mind playing tricks?

If Mr. Wright had hired his lawyer to write the letter, then he must surely know the name of his donor. And if he knew the name of his donor, then he should know that Jeff was her husband. But why hadn't he said anything? Was he waiting for the right time, or was he just being cruel? The only way she knew how to find out would be to come right out and ask him, but she didn't want to do that. She didn't want him to view her as a resentful widow trying to be seen as the victim. She *was* angry at Mr. Wright but not for receiving the transplant. She had taken offense to the fact that he hadn't even mentioned his recent surgery to her. Not that he needed to tell her about his personal life, but after all, she was the one who had signed on the dotted line, giving permission for him to receive a new liver. How could he have acted so indifferent toward her during their meetings? Did he think everything was taken care of just because his lawyer had sent her a thank-you letter? Once the final papers from the real estate office were drawn up and she gave her final signature on the house purchase, she would have no reason to see him again. But in the meantime, would he assume that she already knew and say nothing, or would he relinquish the information to her? Should she give him the benefit of the doubt, assuming that he had nothing to tell her because he was not the Warren Wright with Jeff's liver, or should she confront him and find out the truth immediately? She really hated confrontation. And what if he were the wrong Mr. Wright? What if she accused him of something that he knew nothing about? But did she care what Warren Wright thought about her? As much as she didn't want to admit it, for some reason, she did care, and that scared her. The only thing she could do would be to have some patience and observe Mr. Wright for the next few weeks. She would have to make time to do a little bit of investigation on her own.

CHAPTER 14

Like a lily among thorns is my darling among the maidens.

—Song of Songs 2:2

"Good morning, Mr. Wright. Having your usual? Our special this morning is blueberry pancakes. How 'bout I put a stack in front of you?" Lilly's infectious smile set the tone for the make-believe sparring between waitress and customer.

"Always the chipper little jokester, aren't you, Miss Lilly? When did the coffee house start serving real food?"

"Aw c'mon now, Mr. Real Estate Man. We always serve authentic food to our customers, especially our good-lookin' ones."

Warren spoke to Lilly in his casual, jesting way. "Authentic to what country?"

Lilly loved his playful camaraderie, his subtle wit. In fact, Lilly just flat-out loved this man. She had loved him from the moment she set eyes on him, and that was two years ago. She had done everything except come right out and ask him for a date. She wondered how he could be so blind as not to notice how her eyes shone each time he looked at her. Was he so out of touch with women that he didn't know when one was head over heels in love with him?

"What's the matter, honey? No comeback this morning?"

Warren smiled as he watched Lilly pour his coffee and carry it back to his table. She was the reason he drank so much of the horrible-tasting liquid. Two years ago, a business meeting had brought him to this little out-of-the-way café one day, and it was then that he had laid eyes on Lilly. But she was young. *Too young for my taste*, he thought. He usually liked them a little more seasoned, but as he had gotten to know her, he found that she could be as playful as a little girl or as composed as a prudent woman. The animation of her character was quite enchanting.

As he watched her walk toward him, carrying a mug of coffee, he couldn't help but notice her natural beauty again. She was slender, petite, and flowerlike, with hips tapering into long straight legs. She had a wild beauty about her that did seem to mature her a bit. Her delicately carved facial bones and her full mouth caused Warren to fantasize about how it would feel to claim those lips. Wisps of hair framed her face, giving texture to her everyday ponytail. One of these days, he was going to ask her on a date. He just hadn't gotten around to it. He really didn't have room in his life right now for a romance, and he thought that she was worth more than a one-night stand. Besides, he was still thinking about Abby Weaver. He didn't see her as a lifelong commitment but more of a challenge and possibly an accomplishment. Lilly, on the other hand, had become a daily craving. His need to see her every morning had become an addiction. He pretended it was the coffee he wanted, but he really just needed to be near her. He sometimes got the feeling that her flirting was not always in fun, considering the way he had seen her look at him from time to time.

He had seen that look this morning, and it had sent shivers down his spine. Maybe today was going to be the day that he asked her out. After all, he was an adult, a well-respected business man in this town; and if he wanted to take a waitress to dinner, then so be it. He wasn't asking her to marry him.

Tapping the table with her pencil, Lilly indicated her impatience. "Well, Mr. Wright, you must have a lot on your mind today. I've asked you three times what you would like to order, and so far, you've said nothing."

His gaze traveled over her face and searched her eyes. What he saw was a glimmer of mystery that was beckoning him to her. "Sorry, Lilly, I guess I was just lost in a train of thought. You can throw some of those pancakes my way if you will. And, Lilly, smother them in syrup."

Lilly caught herself glancing anxiously over her shoulder as she gave the order to the cook. She noticed he was watching her intently with a look so galvanizing that it sent a tremor through her. Something was different about Mr. Wright this morning. Something in his manner aroused her curiosity, as well as her vanity. She was undeniably flattered by the interest that he seemed to be portraying. Was it all in her imagination? Was it possible that she was responding to something that wasn't even present?

She set the pancakes on the table in front of him, and the smell of his aftershave sent her pulses spinning. As quickly as she could, she asked if there was anything else that he needed. As she turned to go, he touched her hand, sending another warm shiver through her.

"Lilly, can you take a short break and meet me outside?"

She halted, shocked. Why would he want to talk to her outside? It was hard to remain coherent when she was so close to him. Her mind became a crazy mixture of hope and fear. What did he want with her? Maybe he was going to offer her a job with his company. That would be a great opportunity, but what she really wanted was a place in his heart, not his office. Lilly tried to show no reaction as she leaned closer and said, "I'm due for a break in fifteen minutes. Will that be all right? That will give you time to enjoy your pancakes."

When she had taken care of her last customer, she gestured to Joe, the cook, that she was going on break and proceeded to follow Warren outside.

"I guess you're wondering why I asked you to come outside with me."

An unwelcome blush crept into her cheeks as she replied, "Well, yes, it set my mind to wondering."

Warren laughed as if sincerely amused. "You have a great sense of humor, Lilly. Unlike seasonal flowers, you seem to bloom all year round." His eyes were sharp and assessing as he paid her a compliment. "You look exceptionally beautiful today."

The smoldering flame she saw in his eyes startled her, leaving her riveted to the spot and speechless. Instead, she just listened helplessly.

He was making no attempt to hide the fact that he had long been aware of her and that an unquestionable magnetism had been building between them. He was explaining that today a sense of urgency had unexpectedly become a necessity. Scarcely aware of the tinge of wonder in his voice, he spoke. "I'd like to take you to dinner if you'll give me the pleasure."

Intense astonishment touched her face as the realness of his question sank in. A tumble of confused thoughts and feelings assailed her. She was totally bewildered at his behavior. *Was he on the rebound from a jilted woman, or were these bona fide feelings?* She had the opinion that he was a complex man, not easy to know intimately, and she was unnerved by his sudden interest in her. This was a victory that she never expected to celebrate. She was almost embarrassed at how happy she felt. "I'm flattered, Mr. Wright. Has something happened in your life to give you such a new outlook?"

"No, maybe I just decided to grow up today and appreciate the beautiful scenery around me. I guess I just thought it was time to stop and enjoy the roses, or in this instance, I guess it would be lilies," he joked.

"In that case, I'd love to go out to dinner with you. Oh, by the way, Mr. Wright, do you have a first name?"

Warren regarded her with amusement as he smiled and said, "That Miss Lilly will be information given to you in exchange for your full name."

He dropped a featherlight kiss on her forehead and broke into a leisurely smile. "I'll pick you up at six."

She stood there, experiencing a gamut of perplexing emotions as she watched him drive away. Her heart was refusing to believe what her ears had just heard. Even though she was in love with him, he was somewhat older than she was and much more sophisticated. She found herself wondering if she could measure up to what he was used to in women. She never expected this day to happen, and now every fiber of her body was sending warning spasms. But what was she scared of, and what could it possibly hurt to have dinner just one time?

Lilly was grateful for the absence of customers for the remaining hours of her shift. Her trembling hands could barely even pour a cup of coffee. All she could think about was what to wear. She felt like a breathless girl of sixteen who had just been asked to the prom.

With her working day finally over, Lilly rushed home to her closet, only to find what she already knew to be true—no promising dinner dress. She didn't have enough time to go to the mall, so she forced herself to examine the row of dresses one more time. The black jersey dress with a beaded V-neck was too formal. The red cotton knit looked too sporty, and the brown empire reminded her of her high school days. How was she ever going to look like a woman sophisticated enough to be out with a man like Mr. Wright?

Would he be dressed casually or just a bit casual with a tie? She wanted to avoid dressing totally inappropriately for where they were going to dinner. She needed something plain yet socially acceptable wherever they went.

The sleeveless linen jumper—it had a small jacket that she could carry with her, in case it was cool in the restaurant. The ivory color would show off her tan, and hose wouldn't be necessary. Her brown leather slides would be perfect for a summer evening, and her brown disk necklace with matching earrings would give the outfit the final touch. Satisfied with her choice, she opened a bottle of nail polish and began painting her toes.

Standing in the hallway of Lilly's apartment building, anxious about the evening, Warren was still asking himself why he had asked a waitress on a date. As intriguing as she was, he didn't consider waitresses to be his type. Before he could ponder any more about his decision, the door opened, and there in front of him stood the most exquisite female he had ever seen. Unaware of her captivating image, she spoke in a whimsical tone. "Hello, Mr. Wright, or is it Sherlock?"

Warren's eyebrows raised inquiringly as if not understanding the question. He smiled at her, and it was all she could do not to melt at his feet. "Sherlock Holmes. Get it? How did you find out where I live? You never asked for my address, so I thought maybe you did private eye work on the side."

There was a trace of laughter in his voice when he spoke. "Quite the little comedian, aren't you? For your information, I'm used to doing my homework."

Her eyes sparkled; and as if she were playing a game, she reached out, clutched his hand, and began shaking it. "Hi. My name is Lillian Noel Fisher, but my friends call me Lilly. What's your name?"

Warren's sense of humor took over, and he laughed as he answered, "Please to meet you, Lilly. My name is Warren Oscar Wright, and my friends call me Warren."

Lilly couldn't help herself as she burst out laughing. Warren was overcome with her gentle and overwhelming beauty. Her long golden hair was tumbling carelessly down her back, and her brilliant blue eyes twinkled with mischief. He had never seen her dressed in anything but black pants and white shirt, uniform of the café. Now Lilly looked like a model just waiting for a photo shoot.

Opening the car door for Lilly gave him opportunity to notice her tiny waist and the graceful way she swung her legs into his car. So far, *perfection* would be the word he chose to describe this woman.

The cuisine at the Mountain Inn was so different from anything Lilly had ever seen on a menu. She wasn't familiar with most of the listed items, so Warren accepted the responsibility of ordering for her. She was a little apprehensive when he ordered the rack of lamb with fig-port sauce, but after tasting it, she was glad that she had trusted his judgment. She knew nothing about the diversity of wines, so when Warren ordered a Dry Creek Bourdeau-style Zinfandel from the 1969 Lambert Bridge Bottling Company, she asked why he wanted that particular type and year. She sat patiently waiting for an answer.

Warren, realizing that she was truly interested, explained that a Cabernet Sauvignon was fine if having the lamb alone, but when the sauce was added, it would cause an awkward taste. If a full-bodied, high-alcohol-content Zinfandel was served, it would overpower the entire dish. "So the Zin I ordered is the best choice because it complements the delicate, gamy flavor of lamb and the jammy sweetness that goes with the fig-port sauce."

Lilly was mesmerized. Not that she had ever really been interested in wine before, but this man had made it sound like he was a renowned chef describing his menu. His voice held a rasp of excitement. His explanation made her aware of the importance of entwining just the right two commodities together, whether it be food or people. Sitting there tonight with the man of her dreams, a thought crossed her mind, and she grinned mischievously.

"Lilly, do you find this amusing? I thought you were genuinely interested."

Trying to hold back a giggle, she smiled. "I am really interested, Warren. No one has ever taken the time to explain something like this to me, and you made me feel like I was right there in the middle of a kitchen with a famous chef, preparing meals for royalty."

He was baffled by her answer. "Then why the giggle?"

"I'm so sorry, Warren. My mind gets ahead of itself sometimes. I was just thinking that, from now on, I think I'll refer to you as Zin, and you can call me Lamb Chop. It's a great combination, don't you think?" She smiled easily and then added, "You just said so."

Warren sat there staring, desperately trying to resist the modest, almost apologetic smile that was radiating from Lilly's face. Was she really this naive, or did she just like playing games? Was her wide-eyed innocence merely a smoke screen for an ulterior motive, such as "gold digging"? He needed to get off this train of suspicion and just enjoy the evening. He was always quick to assume things like that about the women he dated. He wanted to trust that she was here because she liked *him* and not his money. She was enjoying life, and maybe that was something that he should plan on doing too. Besides, his eyes had already melted into hers, and like quicksand, it was becoming impossible to find his way out.

Warren smiled, reached across the table, took Lilly's hand in his, and said, "Lilly, you're like a breath of fresh air with a vivid imagination." His dark eyebrows arched mischievously. "Are you always this quick-witted?"

Without hesitation, she answered, "Only when I'm having fun."

It was still early when they finished dinner, and Warren wasn't ready to end the evening, so he suggested that they take a walk downtown. Lilly was delighted with the thought of window shopping and seeing the latest fashions. Her work schedule didn't allow for much pleasure time.

As they strolled along, stopping occasionally to admire a window display, Lilly's hand seemed to radiate a magnetism that touched Warren until he felt his fingers lace with hers. They sat at an outside bistro table, drinking milkshakes, until Lilly accidently sucked air from the bottom of the paper cup and shocked Warren with the turbulent sound. He stared at her and then burst out laughing. To show his approval, he sucked harder on his straw until he duplicated the raw sound. As laughter gave way to hysterics, he was astonished at the sense of fulfillment he felt in the presence of this woman, just having good, plain fun together.

While walking Lilly to her door, he thought about the possibility of kissing her. Would she allow him? He couldn't believe he was even considering giving her a choice. Since when did he ever allow a woman to rule him? He was always the one in control—until tonight.

There was only one other woman who had ever caught him off guard, and that was his latest client, Ms. Weaver. There was something about her that had captivated his attention also. He was positive that some sort of vague sensation had passed between them, something that he couldn't explain. He just knew he was fighting a prodigious need to be close to her, even though she had made it quite clear during their recent meeting that she didn't want to be near him.

Why was he thinking about Ms. Weaver *now*? He was hand in hand with a spectacular woman, and he was thinking of someone else. Was he crazy?

"Warren, are you okay? You seem like you're a million miles away. Was I that boring that you're trying to escape already?"

"Lilly, I'm sorry. Actually, I was sort of lost in thought about you. I've had a really good time tonight, and I hope we can do it again real soon." With an irresistible smile, he asked, "What do ya think?"

She looked up at him with dreamy eyes and in a silky voice said, "I'm glad you had a good time tonight, and thank you for a wonderful evening. Yes, I would love to go out with you again."

Warren leaned forward and, in one smooth movement, covered her mouth with his own. The touch of his lips sent a shock wave through Lilly's entire body, and she returned his kiss with reckless abandon. It was a kiss for her tired soul to melt into. As he aroused her passion, his own grew stronger, but he forced himself to pull away and, with gentle hands, held her at arm's length. As he already told her, he wanted to move slowly. But his kiss had sent new spirals of ecstasy through her, and she wanted more. She reached up and drew his face to hers in a renewed embrace. Shocked at Lilly's response, he reacted like any red-blooded male would do and drank in the sweetness of her kiss. But then he remembered what he had just told her about taking things slow and reluctantly persuaded her to step back. "Lilly, please listen to me. When it comes to women, I'm usually a fast-paced guy. But with you, I don't want to move like that. I'd really like to take it slow and get to know you and for you to get to know me. They say there are angels around us, and I never really believed that until right now. I think you're the angel that's been sent to help get my life in order."

"An angel? You think I'm an angel sent by God?"

Smiling and lightly fingering a loose strand of hair on her cheek, he replied, "I've never actually seen an angel, but you fit the description, and who but an angel could have a name like Lamb Chop?"

Lilly burst out laughing. "And, Zin, you do remind me of a bottle of wine—strong and aged."

Warren kissed the tip of her nose, smiled, and walked down the hallway toward the elevator, feeling younger than he had felt in years. As he drove away, he echoed the entire evening in his mind and smiled as he recalled how Lilly had made him laugh and how she had made him think about his ambitions in life. He was reminded of the promises that he had made to himself and to God as he lay on the operating table not long ago. Only two promises, and he hadn't even made an attempt to keep either one of them yet. He quickly made a note in his Day-Timer to remind himself to call his attorney. He needed to compose a will. He also made a note that he needed to find someone to answer his questions about eternity. Did he really have a purpose on this earth, and if so, what was it? Did God really allow angels to impersonate people in order to get their attention? Why was he suddenly thinking about angels and sinners? He had his suspicions about God but had never really been interested. The few times that he had gone with his grandmother to church, the only thing he remembered was hearing that everyone was a sinner. He always wondered why people went to church Sunday after Sunday just so they could listen to someone update them about their immoral ways. There must be more to it, but he never had the desire to find any answers—until now.

In Vietnam, many times, he had called out to God; but as soon as he was free of the danger and his life was spared, his mind had a way of forgetting that his pleas for help had been acknowledged. He had finally understood the old saying "There are no atheists in a foxhole." He had shrugged off the meaning of that because he didn't consider himself an atheist, but he didn't really consider himself a believer either. So what would he be? An agnostic? It was hard for him to comprehend a superior being that could be everywhere all the time with millions of people asking for favors every second. How could that be possible? It was like something from a science fiction movie. How could people really believe in a supernatural being?

The closer he got to home, the heavier his eyelids became. Not only was he ready to get some sleep but he also needed to put all these questions to rest. He had put this task off long enough. Tomorrow he would make some phone calls and pursue the answers. In the meantime, he was going to concentrate on his "angel."

Chapter 15

f any of you lacks wisdom, let him ask God, who gives generously to all without reproach, and it will be given him.

—James 1:5

Lilly closed her door and leaned back against the frame, allowing her fingers to touch her lips, which were still warm and moist from Warren's kiss. Tonight had been like a fairy tale, a treat she never allowed herself to believe in. This man was everything she could ever imagine. A real gentleman—something she wasn't used to. He appeared to be so sophisticated, yet tonight when they went window shopping, he showed no sign of being an aristocrat. Except for his expensive taste in cars, he seemed to be very down-to-earth. He obviously appreciated fine food but also enjoyed a good old milkshake. He spoke with a substantial vocabulary, but she had heard in his voice tonight a touch of homespun slang that he unconsciously weaved into his speech.

He had kissed her gently and then went home. Most men wanted to stay. Most men wanted her for one thing, and when she refused, they either became angry or just discarded her. She was aware of the fact that she usually turned heads, and she did occasionally dress a little bit provocatively, but she liked the new styles and felt that she had every right to add them to her wardrobe. What people thought when they looked at her was not something that she could control. Everyone was entitled to their opinion, and she felt free to dress in her own style. The dress she chose for tonight had been very conservative yet charming enough to assure that she would be noticed in a crowd. The funny thing was she hadn't even cared about anyone else tonight. The only thing that mattered was Warren's opinion.

She couldn't believe he called her an angel. No one had ever come close to that term when describing her. Her mother used to have a lot of names for her, but *angel* wasn't one of them. She was used to hard work, and she was used to being alone. Her mother had worked two jobs just so she could pay the rent, as there was no financial support from Lilly's father. According to her mother, she had no idea who he was. She remembered a man who used to visit quite often, and he insisted that she call him Daddy, but she soon learned that his idea of fatherhood was not to love her but to use her. He had assaulted her once, but the mailman, trying to deliver a letter, rang the doorbell and shouted through the screen door that he needed a signature. "Daddy," so surprised at the interruption, left the bedroom to respond to the voice. Lilly escaped through the back door and made a vow that no man would ever touch her again against her will.

By the age of five, Lilly was quite proficient with laundry, the stove, and even a mop. She went to bed many nights without any supper so that her mother's friends would be sure to have something to eat when they came over. Lilly soon learned how to be creative with the ingredients in her cooking, and the friends eventually stopped coming because of frequent digestion problems.

It was hard for men not to be attracted to Lilly because of her beauty. She found herself in many situations that caused her an abundance of heartaches, so in order to avoid the insensitive and selfish male gender, she simply cut herself off from all masculine company. She had become like an elusive butterfly—untouchable, until tonight. She had allowed herself to become vulnerable with Warren. She had also shattered her vow—the one thing that kept her from inevitable heartache. Did this mean that maybe Warren was "the one"? From the very first time he came into the diner, she had been smitten. Even though he was a bit older, his age didn't seem to matter to her. She had never met anyone like him before. Each time he came into the diner, it had become a habit to say a small prayer, hoping for him to notice her; and now that he had, questions were popping into her mind. She didn't even attend church, so why these sudden thoughts of prayer and God? What was happening to her? Why would God be interested in her after all these years? Did it have something to do with Warren? As far as she knew, he never darkened a church door either. Maybe it wasn't God; maybe it was the devil himself. But how was she supposed to know the difference?

Chapter 16

Share with God's people who are in need; practice hospitality.

—Romans 12:3

Even though Abby was soon to be the new owner of the most magnificent house in the little town of New Hope, she had never driven on its streets. Today was going to be that day. The name of the town had always intrigued her, wondering if people really came here for that reason. When she saw the ad for the house in the Homes Directory, she questioned if the words "New Hope" had been a subliminal message.

The first building she saw when she entered town was the Morning Son New Hope Bible Church. The sidewalk leading to the snow-white door was bordered with red and white impatiens and petunias. The rest of the landscaping was also very well manicured. It actually looked quite inviting.

For the next three hundred yards, the street was lined with houses—old houses but cared for very well. Abby assumed that, at one time, these had been the homes of wealthy families. She was now into the business part of town and noticed a small coffee shop, a quilt shop, and the local laundromat; and of course, no town would be complete without a dollar store. The other side of the street was occupied by a gift shop, a photography studio, a small diner, and an antique shop. There were some empty spaces with a For Rent sign in the windows, and Abby sadly thought about the owners who had been forced to close their shops. The streets were tree lined, like those in *Leave It to Beaver.* It was almost like going back in time. Most people in her hometown of Millersburg didn't even know a place like this existed. Even if they did, most were too busy to appreciate the more simple life, herself included. But she was going to change that.

The town square was directly in front of her. She never understood how it got to be called square when it was really a circle. Nonetheless, she drove around it and was headed west on Route 23. Deciding that it was time to go home, she began looking for a place to turn around. She saw the sign for the local supermarket and put on her blinker to turn right. As she pulled into the parking lot, she noticed a man sitting alone up against the brick building.

She watched as people walked by and chatted with him as if they were friends. He had a small bucket sitting in front of him where money could be dropped, but Abby saw no one making a deposit. The man's clothes were a bit on the old side, but they seemed to be freshly washed. His long hair protruded from underneath a baseball cap, and it too looked clean enough. He was reading a book. At a second glance, she noticed that it was a Bible. He also had a pencil and a tablet as if he were taking notes.

She heard the honk of a horn and turned toward the sound, realizing that she was sitting in the middle of the parking lot, blocking a man who was trying to back out of his parking space. She waved to the man as an apology and, for some unknown reason, pointed her car toward the man with the can. She found a parking space, opened her door, and walked over to him.

She was not in the habit of speaking to what she assumed was a homeless man and was quite shocked at her boldness. He looked to be about her age, and when he raised his head, he captured her eyes with his. It was as if they were searching her face, reaching into her thoughts. For a long moment, she stared back at him. Who was this man, and why was he watching her?

In an awkward voice, Abby finally spoke. "Excuse me, but I saw you sitting here when I pulled into the parking lot, and I thought maybe you were hungry. Could I buy you some food?"

His voice had a velvety tone yet was edged with steel. "Why? Do I look hungry? Are you taking pity on the town outcast? Can't you tell? I just enjoy sitting on cement in front of a grocery store." He made a sweeping gesture with his hand. "Doesn't it look like fun to you? Who are you anyway? I've never seen you here before, and trust me, I know everyone in this town."

Taken aback by his sarcasm, Abby leaned closer to his ear and lowered her voice; and in a purposefully mysterious tone, she said, "For your information, I was feeling some empathy for you, not pity. I'm the new girl in town, and I hope not everyone is as friendly as you are."

Not waiting for an answer, Abby turned her back to him and walked quickly to her car, got in, and drove away. As she gripped the steering wheel, her hands were shaking. How dare that man be so ungrateful? Now she understood why no one was giving him money. As she drove back out of town, the homeless man's face kept getting interwoven with her more important thoughts—thoughts about her future in New Hope. Why would a man, who obviously was down on his luck, sit in a parking lot candidly asking for money and then refuse her offer for food?

CHAPTER 17

In great endurance; in troubles, hardships and distresses.

—2 Corinthians 6:4

Monday morning brought clear blue skies with temperatures in the low eighties. A delicate breeze rustled the tree leaves just enough to be noticed. With no humidity in the air, it was a perfect day to enjoy the outdoors. Drawing in a deep breath, Abby's thoughts leaped feverishly. *Why not have Mr. Wright and Mrs. Black meet her in the rose garden?* It would be the ideal place to merge the finishing touches and bind the contract. She picked up the phone and dialed Mr. Wright's number. Of course, his office wasn't open yet, so she left a message on his answering machine.

As Abby waited for her curling iron to heat, her mind wandered forward, and she imagined the three of them having tea and signing papers. She could see them all sitting in the garden, surrounded by green bushes laden with rosebuds of rich bright reds and yellows, just waiting to puncture the air with their fragrance. She could almost see the tiny buds taking turns to open wide, revealing their delicate petals. At the thought of flowers, old feelings and memories flooded her, catching her off guard. Her knees buckled, and she sank into her vanity chair. Maybe she wasn't ready for this transaction. Maybe things were happening too fast. Since losing Jeff, her whole thought process seemed to have been tampered with. There were ideas and words flying around inside her head that made her wonder if somehow she had been given a brain transplant. It was as if she were a whole new person. Her mind was congested with doubts and fears, yet she couldn't stop thinking about the bed-and-breakfast and what she could do with it. Were these subconscious emotions that were coming to the surface, and if so, why were they emerging now? She had tucked all her missionary visions so far back in to the secret room of her brain that she didn't think they could ever find their way out. In fact, she was sure that she had thrown away the key.

As she stood staring into the mirror at the face looking back at her, disquieting thoughts began racing through her mind. Loneliness and confusion had piled into one upsurge of devouring retaliation. She wanted to cause Warren Wright some pain. But why? Hadn't she just decided to have some patience and play along for a while? But if he was the same man who was named in the letter from the lawyer, didn't she deserve some sort of retribution? This man was walking around with a portion of her husband attached to him, and he didn't even have the decency to come to her in person and express his gratefulness, not even after actually meeting her. She had to wonder if, under all those Brooks Brothers suits, he was a genuine coward and not the self-confident man he seemed.

Continuing to pull the hairbrush through her hair, she felt the pain of Jeff's absence, and a slight twinge in her gut told her that the face in the mirror was not the face of a woman with vengeance on her mind. It was merely sadness and uncertainty. She closed her eyes just as the chimes of the grandfather clock reminded her that she needed to hurry. She quickly picked up her purse and headed down the stairs.

As she stepped outside, she realized a fine mist of rain was falling, so she returned to the house and grabbed her umbrella. She pushed the button to open it and hurried down the sidewalk to her car. With her hand on the door, she took a moment to inhale the sweetness of the wet grass and even the repulsive smell of fishing worms, which always seemed to emerge onto the pavement after a summer rain. She wondered whether she was like the blade of grass, which when drizzled upon with rain came to life, or whether she was like the worm, which only came out from hiding when it needed nourishment. If rain in the summer brought worms out of the ground and kept grass from withering, then surely, she could allow it to do something for her. Maybe it was to serve as a reminder that she needed her spirit renewed, that life wasn't over. When worms came to the surface, they took a chance that their life wouldn't be sacrificed to man for bait. Was God sending her this message so that she would return to the surface of reality and yield to his intentions for her? Just what exactly were his plans? She was doing the best she could for right now. Her life had been uprooted, and like the worms, she was trying to survive. What was it that God wanted from her, and how would she know if it truly was him doing the requesting?

She needed to know that Jeff's death was not in vain, so she was trying to stay on the path that Mrs. Black talked about so much and that she believed was mapped out by God himself. Everything, including her, had changed that tragic day, and so she was putting forth her best effort to trust that it was God who was leading this journey, detours included. Never in a million years would she be walking this road, if not by some divine intervention.

The rain began falling harder, and Abby realized that her daydreaming was causing her to get wet, so she hurried into the car and turned the key in the ignition, and the words "summer rain" came instantly to her mind again. She had never used these two words together in the same sentence before today, and now for some reason, they kept popping into her thoughts. It did have a nice ring to it, though.

As she backed out of her driveway, the first drops of rain dotted her windshield; and within minutes, it began to pour. So much for the weatherman's clear-blue-sky forecast. By the time she reached Willow Road, the rain had subsided, and the sun was peeking from behind the clouds. She pulled into Mrs. Black's driveway, and while getting out of her car, she observed a most encouraging sign—a beautiful rainbow sketched across the sky with what appeared to be neon colors. She thought again about the effect that summer rain had on human beings and animals. It seemed to produce so many smells and beautiful colors.

She just had the most spine-tingling, inspirational idea for the bed-and-breakfast. She reached into her purse, pulled out a small notebook, and wrote "Summer Rain" on the inside page. She was already visualizing the new sign that would hang from the corner of the big white house. It would picture a panoramic view of the mountains, shadowed with raindrops as they scattered delicately on to a pond surrounded with green grass. Tiny butterflies would be flitting along a tree that housed two doves. The doves would represent the peace that Summer Rain would offer to those in need. The words "Summer Rain" would be engraved with gold lettering, and in smaller letters underneath, it would read "A Touch of Renewal."

Abby took a deep breath and made a mental note of this exact moment. It was one she wanted to remember forever, and she also believed it was an answer from God to her ever-present insecurity about her future plans. She was finding that the more she actually became aware of God in her life, the more she found her existence to be mysterious and miraculous. Noticing such things as the rainbow and even the smelly worms seemed a good indication that developing a relationship with God was becoming a major part of her life.

Abby donned her best smile and began walking toward the porch. She began silently praying for guidance during the next hour. Sitting beside a man who she believed possessed part of her husband was not going to be easy.

Just as she stepped onto the front porch, Mrs. Black opened the door and spoke quite loudly as if she thought Abby had lost some of her hearing over the weekend. "Hello, Abby, won't you come in?"

Abby barely got inside the door when Mrs. Black embraced her with a gentle bear hug and pointed out, "Your timing is perfect. The rain stopped only minutes ago."

Wasting no time and feeling very audacious, Abby spoke before Mrs. Black could say another word. "Mrs. Black, would it be all right if we had our meeting at the table in the backyard by the roses? I can't think of a better place to begin my new life."

Smiling from ear to ear, Mrs. Black could hardly contain her excitement. "That's a splendid idea. Let me get a towel so that I can dry off the table." As she hurried off to the linen closet, the doorbell rang. "Abby, dear, would you get that for me? It's probably Mr. Wright."

Warren was, of course, expecting Mrs. Black to answer the door, so when he saw Abby, he was caught off guard and at a loss for words. Neither spoke as they shared an intense physical awareness of each other. Finally, Warren asked, "May I come in?"

Abby, embarrassed by her behavior, stepped aside and motioned for Mr. Wright to enter the foyer. Before either could say another word, Mrs. Black called out to Warren from the sunroom in a voice loud enough to wake the dead. Warren smiled, not knowing the old lady had such strong vocal chords. She seemed to have a lot of enthusiasm in her voice.

"Abby, Mr. Wright, come with me. Everything is ready in the garden."

A slight hesitation in Warren's eyes told Abby that he was a bit confused about Mrs. Black's request. Abby explained about the message that she had left on his answering machine, and although he didn't answer, a shadow of annoyance crossed his face. Without another word, she turned toward the garden and began walking. Warren followed quietly behind her.

A flicker of apprehension coursed through Abby as she watched Warren wedge himself into the seat next to her and begin to shuffle papers. She watched as he removed each one from the folder and, with confidence, laid them in order.

"I can understand your anxiety and your excitement, Ms. Weaver, so we'll get right down to business." He handed a stack of papers to Mrs. Black and an identical pile to Abby. "Please look over the contract, ladies, and if you have any questions, now is the time to ask."

Warren had no idea just how different this transaction was going to be from any other business deal that he had ever put together. He was trying to concentrate on the subject matter spread out on the table before him, but Abby's presence was causing him to lose focus on the reason for being here.

Without wanting him to know that she was staring, Abby quickly poured him a cup of coffee from the pot Mrs. Black had carried in. "I'm assuming that you drink coffee, Mr. Wright?"

Lifting his head slightly, he replied, "Yes. Thank you, Ms. Weaver. I like it black." He leaned forward as if ready to speak and then quickly changed his mind. Nervously, he moistened his dry lips and raised his eyebrows questionably. His eyes caught and held hers, and for a moment, he studied her intently. Every time he was near this woman, his heart seemed to dance inside his chest with excitement. But something was different today. He could sense the barely controlled power that was coiled in her body. She not only seemed angry with him but it also was as if the whole world had sinned against her. What had happened to cause such a drastic change since their last meeting? Or was this her true character coming to life?

Taking notice of the uncomfortable situation, Mrs. Black quickly sat down and, as casually as she could manage, asked Warren what they needed to do to get this transaction on the go. "We want this as quickly as possible. Isn't that right, Abby?"

"Ladies, I'll do my best, but first, I need to know exactly what your proposal is for this contract. Mrs. Black, we have on record that the asking price for your home is $350,000. This is most unusual for all three of us to be sitting together before the contract is written up with the exact price, but since this is the way you requested it, I am trying to abide by your wishes. Have you agreed on a price?"

Leaning toward Mrs. Black, Abby encouraged her to tell Mr. Wright of their intention. With a smile wider than Texas, Mrs. Black responded matter-of-factly, "I have agreed to sell my house to Ms. Weaver for one hundred thousand dollars."

Warren suddenly developed a small twitch in his right eye, and a muscle clenched along his jaw. A momentary look of discomfort and unbelief crossed his face as his lips tried to form words, but he could only manage a cynical smile. In a barely audible voice, he finally spoke. "Very nice, ladies. You set me up real good. No one's sucked me into a joke like that for a long time."

Abby and Mrs. Black exchanged a subtle look of amusement, and looking directly at Warren, Abby spoke. "It's no joke, Mr. Wright. That's the price we've agreed upon."

Ready to argue, Warren said, "But, Mrs. Black, your property is worth three times that amount. The price you've agreed upon isn't even fair market value."

Looking eye level at Abby, his voice hardened with a touch of sarcasm. "Who are you? Some long lost relative?" Instantly realizing how unprofessional and how desperate he must sound, he immediately stumbled through an apology.

Mrs. Black was the first to say, "Apology accepted, Mr. Wright. Now will you please get to the part where we sign our names? Abby and I have an appointment with the lawyer in three hours."

Seeing no signs of altering their decision, Warren had found himself impulsively anxious to secure this deal. Trying to change their minds would only waste his energy. What exactly had joined these two together? He slowly inhaled a deep breath as if in pain. Studying both ladies diligently, he finally spoke. "Ladies, I don't quite understand what just happened here, but as soon as I fill in the correct sale price, you may sign the necessary papers, and I'll be on my way. I will call you if I need anything else."

The two women wrote their names in the appropriate spots, and with signed papers in his briefcase, Warren held out his hand to say thank you. Abby's smile was courteous as she paused, looked at his hand, and then shook it. His fingers were warm and strong as he grasped hers, but his hand seemed to linger a moment too long in its hold. Abby pulled her hand free of his and shrugged dismissively.

Warren said good-bye to Mrs. Black and walked to his car. As he drove away from the premises, he knew he was fortunate to have a signed document in hand and that he should be celebrating, but it just didn't compensate for the time and money that he was losing. He knew the prearrangement that Mrs. Black and Ms. Weaver had agreed upon was legal, and nothing he could say or do could change anything.

Before arriving today, he had pondered asking Ms. Weaver to dinner. But this meeting hadn't exactly turned out the way he had planned. Abby had been too absorbed in the excitement of buying the house to even notice that his eyes were filled with a curious, deep longing—a longing to get to know her. This strange sensation he felt, when being near her, was so disturbing to him. He had been with plenty of women who were just as beautiful, and his need for a connection was not like this. Besides, this woman had just lost him thousands of dollars because she had sweet-talked an old lady. That was reason enough for him to stay away from her.

Chapter 18

Beloved, do not be surprised at the fiery trial when it comes upon you to test you, as though something strange were happening to you.

—1 Peter 4:12

Abby leaned against the window, watching Mr. Wright as he sat in his car. He was leaning back in his seat, rubbing his forehead as if he had a headache. She probably had given it to him. She had never known herself to be so rude. But how was she supposed to act toward someone who was using Jeff's liver to sustain his life? He was still acting as if he didn't know who she was. So why did she feel this extraordinary void the moment he walked out the door? She had no connection to that vital part of Jeff anymore. It was in another man's body, a man that was so unlike her Jeff. Why was he allowed to live and Jeff had to die? Suddenly, the same raw and primitive grief that had controlled her heart when Jeff died once again overwhelmed her. She swallowed the sob that rose in her throat when she realized that Mrs. Black was standing beside her. Her aged but beautiful face was smiling warmly, her dark eyes glazed with compassion, and her mouth curved with unspoken tenderness.

Abby wasn't exactly sure what to say or do. She felt like a volcano on the verge of eruption, and as much as she wanted to pour out her problems on this sweet, caring old lady, she wasn't exactly sure how to begin. Surely, Mrs. Black didn't need a satchelful of issues carried into her house by someone who she had only known for a short time. But hadn't Mrs. Black also taken Abby under her wing and treated her as if she were one of her own? No one but Jeff had ever shown so much affection to her, not even her mother. Maybe it was time she reached to the very depths of her soul and admitted that she needed someone else's help.

Hardly able to lift her voice above a whisper, Abby ground the words out between her teeth. "Mr. Wright was the recipient of my husband's liver. I just found out. Why do you think he acted so nonchalant as if something like that wouldn't matter to me?" As if saying the words aloud released her from this inflamed emotion, she flung herself against Mrs. Black, almost knocking her to the floor. Between sobs, she managed to whisper again, "I just don't know how to handle this. Can you please help me?"

Mrs. Black, caught off guard with such a confession, wrapped her arms around Abby, patting her back as if caressing a baby to sleep. She needed a moment for her brain to find an appropriate response. Abby deserved that much.

Mrs. Black finally removed Abby's arms from around her shoulders and guided her to the nearest chair. Half in anticipation, half in dread, she spoke to Abby as a mother to a child. "Abby, you must first get control of yourself. No mysteries have ever been solved without some investigation, and that is what we are going to do. Let me get you another cup of nice herbal tea to relax you, and then we'll figure out a plan of action."

As she sat down at the table, she urged Abby to start at the beginning and disclose exactly how she found out this bit of information. At the end of Abby's explanation, Mrs. Black, already armed with pen and paper, questioned her acceptance of the real estate agent's name. "How many people in the United States are named Warren Wright?" Abby silently shrugged her shoulders.

Choosing her words carefully, Mrs. Black continued. "Maybe hundreds. Organ recipients receive their second chances from all over America. Just because you met a man named Warren Wright doesn't necessarily mean that he was the beneficiary of a transplant." A sense of inadequacy swept over her as she tried to sound like she knew what she was talking about. She continued, hoping that Abby couldn't hear the vagueness in her voice. "You cannot have ill feelings toward this man until you know the truth. We need to call the attorney who sent you that letter and get the address of the Mr. Wright in question. Until then, dry your eyes, and freshen up. You'll find everything you need in the hall bathroom."

Abby felt exhausted and drained of all life, but without question, she obeyed.

CHAPTER 19

"For I know the plans I have for you," declares the Lord, "plans to prosper you and not to harm you, plans to give you hope and a future."

—Jeremiah 29:11

When Abby came back into the kitchen, she still seemed a bit distraught, so Mrs. Black decided to find some humor in the situation. She could hardly wait until Abby sat down at the table. "Young lady, did you see the way Mr. Wright was looking at you during our meeting? I can tell that he wants to ask you out."

Sensing what Mrs. Black was trying to do, she played along. She batted her lashes and threw a southern drawl into her words as she replied, "Well, whatever do you mean, Mrs. Black?"

Amusement glimmered in Mrs. Black's eyes as she chuckled. "You were having fun with him, weren't you? You little vixen. As I was watching his body language and seeing how hard he was trying to get your attention, I was actually feeling sorry for him. I couldn't believe that you didn't acknowledge any of his quirky little gestures or remarks."

A flash of color darkened Abby's face as she apologized. "He was quite pathetic, wasn't he? How about when he tried to touch my hand? And then he asked the name of the gym I belong to because I'm in such terrific shape." Abby giggled, remembering the look on Warren's face when he realized that all the praises and flattering remarks weren't going to change the outcome of the meeting. "How did you like it when he tried to sidle up next to me at the table? I haven't seen a man grovel so hard in a long time. I guess he really thought all his accolades would somehow change our mind. I'm not sure what got into me, but I just couldn't help myself when I gave him my puppy dog look. He almost came unglued. He was actually sweating." Mrs. Black was by this time holding her stomach from laughing so hard. Abby shook her finger gently at Mrs.

Black and said, "We should not be making fun of Mr. Wright. We *did* ambush him, you know, but I must say, I actually enjoyed seeing him a bit unnerved. He was being so obvious that stringing him along seemed the right thing to do at that time. I guess it was miserable of me." Trying to suppress another giggle she continued. "But you have to admit, this was quite a diversion from the ordinary real estate transaction. It was quite an engaging conversation, don't you think?"

"You're quite the actress, and you're right. It was very entertaining. But you'll have to give him an E for effort. I have a feeling he doesn't give up too easily."

Abby wanted to speak now, but she couldn't seem to find the words that were suitable, so she remained silent. With pure confidence in her voice, Mrs. Black expressed her opinion. "Abby, I feel the Lord has led you to this house and to me. I don't think either of us have any idea why, but that's where the virtue of patience comes into play. I know you're very excited about opening up your business, and the enthusiasm I feel about being a part of this journey is beyond anything I have ever imagined. So between the two of us, the Lord has a lot of work to do concerning our patience." She hesitated, crossed one leg over the other, and then uncrossed it again, all within a minute. "I know I'm rambling, but please bear with me. Remember, we are going to be living in the same house, so I think honesty will most definitely be the best policy. I promise to be as truthful as I can be, and I hope I can expect the same from you."

Abby nodded her head in compliance as Mrs. Black maintained her unbroken flow of words. "It took a lot of praying and arguing with God about selling this property. I have so many memories here—good and not so good. David and I were married here in the garden, and a few years later, our son died while sleeping in his crib. Many years later, David had a heart attack and died while sleeping."

Through tears and a choking sound in her voice, she spoke with her hand on her chest as if she were in physical pain. "The years between those devastating events were filled with many blessings, and I just didn't know how I was going to preserve all of those memories if I moved away. I was afraid they would somehow get lost. After many conversations with God, I was no longer fearful. I knew for sure that if I put it in His hands, He would handle it. And He did. He sent you to me."

Her slender hands unconsciously twisted as she momentarily was lost in her own reveries. When she finally spoke, her voice rose an octave. "I know I'm not worthy of the time God has invested in me. Since I've met you, I've wondered why God would allow a young man like your husband to be taken from you and then allow me, an old lady, to be privileged enough to continue living in my own home. Then I scolded myself and realized that there is a greater project in the works, and you and I just haven't seen the blueprints yet."

Abby didn't know what to do except wrap her arms around Mrs. Black and together mingle their tears. As Abby released Mrs. Black from her embrace, she reminded her of their appointment with the lawyer. If they were to be on time, they would have to leave soon.

Mrs. Black answered with staid calmness. "I would really like to continue this conversation, and it has to be before we sign the papers at the attorney's office. I want a complete understanding between us before you commit to buying this house and be laden with a liability. If you think my being here will stifle your dreams in any way, then you need to be honest and straightforward right now."

The look on Mrs. Black's face was so wretched that Abby chose her words carefully. "Mrs. Black, to begin with, I see you as an asset, not a liability. I love this house, but inheriting you is the real reason I'm so excited. I can't wait to have evenings by the fireplace and listen to your past experiences and to have you trust me with some of your wisdom. I am so looking forward to hearing you play the piano. To be truthful, I'm just looking forward to having you near. As much as I don't understand why Jeff had to die, I guess it's true what people say—God doesn't make mistakes—and so I have to believe that Jeff's death wasn't one. You and I would never have met, and the plan, whatever it is, would never be able to come together." Tears slowly found their way down Abby's cheeks as she fought for self-control. She needed to be strong right now. She felt a sense of strength come to her as she watched the expression on Mrs. Black's face change from anxiety to total euphoria. Even her facial wrinkles seemed to vanish. A cry of relief broke from her glossy lips. "Abby, you're like the daughter I never had. I was so sure that I'd be a good mother, but I never had much time to prove that. My son was only six months old when he died. David and I decided never to have any more children because neither one of us thought we could survive that kind of pain again. It was a decision we regretted later in life, but at that time, it was a mutual agreement."

Mrs. Black wiped her eyes and in a lighter sounding tone said, "As I told you before, I don't understand why God is doing all of this for me. I'm an old lady who has lived a good life, but I've never really understood my purpose here on earth. I've tried to live by the golden rule but always sensed that something was missing. If God has chosen me to be the leading lady in this intriguing scheme, I'm ready to learn my lines."

"What makes you think that God is scheming something? Does He really do that?"

"God doesn't do anything without a plan. Just like you, I was put on this earth for a purpose. And even though I'm still not sure what it is, I know now that it was no coincidence about the timing of your husband's accident and my decision to sell this house. God is using me for something, and I can't wait to see what it is."

Abby met the smile and the hand that was offered as she reached out and drew Mrs. Black from her chair. "We have to get going to Attorney Johnson's office right now, or we are going to be so late. Once we get his approval for the minute details, we can move full speed ahead and seal this deal. Once that's done, we can concentrate on our new adventure."

Mrs. Black leaned closer to Abby and in somewhat of a little girl voice said, "I get so excited every time I think about it that I pee my pants."

Caught off guard by her remark, Abby gasped and instantly erupted in laughter. "Mrs. Black, you never cease to amaze me. Is that true, or did you know that would make me laugh?"

"Unfortunately, honey, that's true. When you get as old as I am, things just aren't as waterproof as they used to be. Sort of like an old roof. Leaks a little now and then."

Once again, Abby didn't know what to say or do, so she just gave Mrs. Black a hug and whispered, "You sure are a character. I'm looking forward to this next chapter in my life as long as you are going to be in it."

Abby touched Mrs. Black's elbow lightly as she helped her down the front porch steps to the car. No words were spoken during the entire trip to town as Abby wrestled with her new convictions. Perhaps it was simply her own lack of knowledge concerning God that made the need of silence so important right now. Mrs. Black talked about God as if he were a real person who was writing a Broadway production. Abby couldn't help wondering, if she tried out for an audition, if she would get picked for the part.

Abby couldn't have been happier that her newfound friend was so elated by her new purpose in life. She just wasn't quite convinced that what Mrs. Black so sincerely believed was likely to be validated. Was it really God who had a long-term plan in mind, or was it just fate and coincidence? Abby hoped it wasn't the latter, for she wanted to believe and have faith like Mrs. Black. She wanted it to be God's hands that were causing things to happen. She had the feeling as if something or someone was tugging at the center of her heart, pulling her closer and closer into a life where she had no training, no skills. She had been a significant yet menial body in the corporate world, far from the simple country life, and now she was leaning into a 180-degree turn, pursuing a saintly endeavor. The two worlds were definitely light years apart. If anyone would have told her a year ago that she would be in this position, she would have been hysterical with laughter. All the more reason for her to believe it was a greater power that had compelled her to call the realtor and be introduced to the rest of her life.

CHAPTER 20

Commit your work to the Lord, and your plans will be established.

—Proverbs 16:3

Abby felt like Alice in Wonderland as she pushed the attorney's office door closed behind her. She and Mrs. Black had signed the final papers, allowing her the privilege of now being the proud owner of "Summer Rain." Stepping from the corporate world into something so new and unfamiliar to her felt as if any minute the Mad Hatter would turn up and invite her to tea.

As she helped Mrs. Black into the car, she could hardly contain herself from jumping up and down and shouting to the whole world about her new adventure. Being the reserved businesswoman that she was, she only leaned down and gave Mrs. Black a big bear hug and said, "Thank you."

Taken by surprise, Mrs. Black asked, "Whatever for, my dear?"

Without answering, Abby shut the passenger door and ran around the front of the car, laughing. As she flung open the driver's door, she jumped into her seat and looked straight at Mrs. Black. "Because without you, I never could have known what my purpose on this earth is supposed to be. I'm still not sure that I know exactly, but I think that somewhere along the way, and for whatever reason, God saw me as a stepping stone for you. Listening to you reminisce these past few weeks about your life has brought me to the conclusion that you don't feel as if you've ever been challenged with the real reason for your being. I think your faith in God has sustained you all these years, and you've probably never questioned him, yet deep down, you've never really felt as if your purpose has ever been revealed. And I think God put me here, in your house, to do just that."

Smiling, Mrs. Black retorted, "Well, Abby, you forgot to tell me that you have a psychology degree. You actually sound as if you know what you're talking about."

Abby caught her breath and continued. "Well, I did have one psychology class in college. But really, Mrs. Black, haven't you ever wondered why you were born and if we all really have a purpose on this earth?"

"Yes, Abby, I feel God puts everyone on this earth for a purpose, and I guess it's up to us to try to find exactly what that purpose is. That's why he gave us free will so that we can make our own choices." Abby remained silent, sensing that Mrs. Black had more to say.

"I may not be the smartest person in this world, Abby, but what I say usually comes from the heart, and I hope that is worth something. My concept of all this is that I think some people are born just knowing what their goal in life is, and they choose to pursue it. Some people never even realize that they have a purpose, and they go through life always looking for the pot of gold. Then they choose to never venture out to the end of the rainbow. And then there are people like us who thought they had life figured out, until one day they come face to face with a roadblock and discover that life is no longer predictable, and its purpose is no longer transparent. Only then do we begin to question our purpose here on earth. I believe it's at that time in our life when God reveals his purpose for us through opportunities that he makes happen—opportunities that lead us to fulfill our destiny. I believe it's been divine intervention that has brought you and me together, and I think we're in for the journey of a lifetime. So what d'ya say we start this car and head for home?"

"You're right," said Abby. "Let's go home."

As they turned into the driveway, Mrs. Black shouted, "Look, Abby, they're putting up the sign! It's beautiful!"

There on the front lawn, for everyone to see, stood the most elegant sign in all of New Hope. People driving by were already slowing down, craning their necks to get a look at the new sign and hopefully catch sight of the new owner. Tears filled Abby's eyes as she silently thanked God for bringing her "Summer Rain."

Abby followed Mrs. Black into the kitchen and stood watching as she began running water from the faucet into the teakettle. "What kind of tea would you like, dear?"

Before Abby had a chance to answer, Mrs. Black was already reaching in the cupboard, pulling out a box of tea. "Today's event calls for celebration, so let's have a cup of Raspberry Zinger." As she began pouring the water into the cup, she smiled at Abby as if she were a small child and asked her to please go find some paper and a pen. "While we're enjoying our cup of tea, let's start making a list of things we need. And then maybe later, we can go to town and shop till we drop."

Abby smiled, thinking about how long it had been since she had been on a real shopping trip. She found it impossible not to feel excited, yet at the same time, guilt kept piercing her heart. She felt elated by thoughts of her future yet saddened because Jeff was not there to help her celebrate. How long would she be so sensitive to just the thought of him? It had been nine months now. Would there ever be a time when she could say his name without feeling guilty?

Mrs. Black's voice startled Abby, causing her to spring from her chair. "My goodness, dear, are you all right? You seem a little tired. Maybe we should postpone shopping until tomorrow. We'll get a good night's rest and start early in the morning."

"No, let's drink our tea, make our list, and drive to town. I'm sorry I got lost in thought for a few minutes, but I was thinking about my husband and feeling guilty again. It somehow doesn't feel right that I should be so happy and excited about my future when his future was ripped from him at such a young age."

Leaning forward in her chair, in a controlled voice, Mrs. Black spoke softly. "You know, Albert Einstein was considered a very smart man, and he once said, 'I never think of the future. It comes soon enough.' Let's, you and I, quit dwelling on the future and live in the present. Let's take one day at a time and live it to the best of our ability. We need to allow God to take care of tomorrow."

CHAPTER 21

He who guards his mouth and his tongue keeps himself from troubles.

—Proverbs 21:23

As Abby and Mrs. Black drove through town, Mrs. Black eloquently described each building and its proprietor. She seemed to know something about each one. She suggested that they visit the diner and enjoy the owner's specialty of stuffed peppers. Big George, as everyone called him, had owned the diner for the past twenty years and was known countywide for his culinary creations.

By the time they reached the inside of the diner, Mrs. Black had already spoken to four people. Obviously, she was a very familiar face in New Hope. With each introduction, Abby's hands were met with warm and gentle handshakes. As she pulled the chair from underneath the table, her body began to relax, and she smiled in contentment, smelling the aroma of fresh coffee.

As the waitress laid the menus on the table, Abby noticed the delicacy of her wrists and her well-manicured fingernails. She was a stunning young woman. Her blue eyes were set close to her cheekbones, and her pale ivory skin looked like it belonged on a china doll. Her makeup appeared fresh as if she had just put it on her face. She seemed to carry herself confidently, aware of the appreciative stares. Abby smiled as she glanced quickly at the young woman's name tag and said, "Good afternoon, Lilly."

Looking directly at Abby, Lilly said, "Good afternoon. May I get you something to drink?"

Before Abby could respond, Mrs. Black said, "Yes, Lilly, could you please bring two coffees? You know how I like mine, and Abby takes one sugar, two creams. Oh, and by the way, this is Abby Weaver. She just bought my house, and she's turning it into a bed-and-breakfast."

Abby noticed Lilly's smile fade fast at the mention of her name. A suggestion of annoyance hovered in her eyes, but she managed a demure smile and said, "That's wonderful, Mrs. Black. I'm so happy everything worked out for you. I'll be right back with your coffee, and then I'll take your order." With long purposeful strides, she made her way back to the coffeepot.

Abby leaned toward the table and lowered her voice. "Did I just hear some sarcasm in that young lady's tone? As soon as you mentioned my name, her face went a bit sour. Have I made that bad of a first impression?"

A muscle quivered in Shirley's jaw as she shook her head in dismay. "I've known Lilly for a long time, and she's one of the sweetest girls I know. I noticed a bit of attitude in her voice too, but I don't understand why. It's as if she has already heard of you and has formed an opinion." Reaching across the table, she patted Abby's hand and said, "Don't worry, dear, I have my sources. I'll find out exactly what has been said about you."

Abby forced a tremulous smile. She wasn't used to being the topic of conversation. She couldn't imagine what gossip was being spread around town about her, but until she actually heard some harmful words fall out of Lilly's mouth, she would give her the benefit of the doubt. Besides, she trusted Shirley to get to the bottom of Lilly's reaction.

Lilly returned with the coffee and asked if they were ready to order. Since peppers were not on the menu today, Shirley ordered the lunch special, which up until a few minutes ago sounded rather good, but Abby's stomach suddenly seemed to be reacting to Lilly's attitude. She ordered a cup of noodle soup and hoped that it could help settle her fears and anxieties. Perhaps moving here wasn't such a good idea after all. People already had an opinion, and they didn't even know her.

Abby picked up the tab, and as she was paying at the register, she noticed Lilly watching her from behind the counter. She noted a look of disgust emerging on the young lady's face, and Abby wondered what she could possibly have done to cause such unmerited feelings. As she and Shirley made their way to the antique store, a familiar-looking figure was seated on a bench across the street. It took Abby a few minutes to think about where she had seen him, but then she remembered. He was the rude man in the grocery store parking lot.

CHAPTER 22

For lack of wood the fire goes out, and where there is no whispers, contention ceases.

—Proverbs 26:20

Harley decided to walk uptown, with plans to go in the diner so that he could read the newspaper. He still considered himself a pastor, no matter the hearsay around town. He felt obligated to keep up with the local news and the obituaries. In spite of what people thought about him, he continued to pray daily for those in need.

A stone had somehow managed its way into his sandal, and as he sat down on the nearest bench to remove it, he sensed someone watching him. From the corner of his eye, he saw her. It was the woman from the parking lot. She was just about to enter the antique store when she stopped in midstride and turned her head in his direction. For a long moment, she watched him. He stared back in waiting silence. She stiffened, shot him an impatient glance, and disappeared behind the door.

What was it about this woman that was so intriguing? Exactly who was she, and why was it that, every time he saw her, he felt agitated? Last week, he felt anger toward her, and today he felt as if he was surrounded by some magnetic force, pulling his body toward her. He stood up from the bench and began walking across the street, hoping that he could get into the diner before she came out of the antique store. He opened the big glass door and made his way to his usual stool at the bar and ordered his coffee. As he was pouring his cream, he saw her walk past the diner window. He pretended not to see her, but the tensing of his jaw betrayed his contemptuous stare.

Lilly noticed the expression on his face change and become somber when she startled him by asking, "So you don't like her either?"

Nearly choking on a sip of coffee, Harley mumbled, "Don't like who?"

"C'mon, Harley, I saw you look at her, or should I say you tried not to look at her, but you couldn't help yourself."

"Well, Lilly, I'm not sure what you're talking about." He continued stirring his coffee and added, "You know I don't dislike anyone, especially someone whom I don't even know."

Lilly smiled, knowing what he said was true. He was one of the kindest men in town. What the church elders had accused him of was a terrible tragedy. The sting of being called a thief seemed to hang over him like a swarm of bees waiting to attack. Even though the busy bees of the church had no concrete evidence, they had convinced enough people to question his integrity, and that led to the deacons asking for his resignation. She always felt sorry for him and never understood why he had remained in New Hope after being ostracized by the church that he had served so faithfully for over five years.

Harley tapped the counter with a spoon and said, "Lilly, did you hear me? I asked you who you are talking about."

"I'm talking about that woman who just walked past the window. She was in here this morning with Mrs. Black. I've been hearing some 'stuff' about her, and I'm worried about Shirley being taken advantage of. They say she had her husband murdered, got all his life insurance money, and talked Shirley into selling her place really cheap. She says it's going to be a bed-and-breakfast, but some say there are drugs involved, and it will just be an asylum for dealers."

Before she could continue, Harley interrupted her by holding his hand in the air and very gently just said, "Stop. Lilly, you know better than to repeat such gossip. 'They' like to spread vicious rumors, and until you know the facts, please don't get caught up in their lies. The lady is new in town, and everyone needs to give her time to establish herself in our community before we scratch her eyes out. It's not like you to harbor such ill feelings toward anyone, especially someone whom you have just met."

Lilly opened her mouth, ready to defend herself, but Harley held up his hand again and in a voice smooth but insistent said, "Lilly, I don't need to remind you of what happened to me all because of the famous 'they committee.' I was never given a chance to defend myself and tell the truth. They convicted me, even without any evidence." Harley raised his coffee cup to finish the last few drops, realized it was empty, and gently pushed it toward Lilly. "I don't know if I ever told you, Lilly, but I always appreciated your belief in me. You always gave me the benefit of the doubt." Lilly poured more of the steaming coffee into his cup as his eyes came up to study her face. "So why are you so hard on the new face in town?"

Lilly pretended to be wiping up a spot on the counter as she spoke. "I don't really know, Harley. It might have something to do with jealousy."

"Jealousy? Why would you be jealous of her, especially considering what you just told me about her? She's a stunning woman, but so are you, Lilly. And I know you're as beautiful on the inside as you are on the outside. So what do you really know about her that you're not telling?"

Lilly's mouth turned into an unconscious smile, and her eyes, for a moment, seemed unseeing. As she began recounting her evening with Warren, a softness seemed to creep into her voice so different from a few minutes ago.

Harley, a bit confused by the sudden emotional change in her attitude, pushed his coffee cup toward her once again and said, "Spill. And I don't mean my coffee. What does Warren have to do with the mystery lady?"

"I'm not sure, but I get the feeling that he knows her somehow. I heard him talking to another real estate agent yesterday morning while they were having coffee, and when he mentioned Ms. Weaver's name, his eyes lit up like firecrackers. When I asked him about it, he tried to pretend that I was only imagining things, but curiosity was written all over his face."

"But, Lilly, it was you that he asked out on a date, wasn't it?"

"Yes, but one date doesn't guarantee a lifetime together. Between you and me, I've had a crush on Warren since the first day he came into the diner, and that was two years ago. I nearly had a heart attack when he finally asked me out. I felt like Cinderella that night. He was such a perfect gentleman. It's just that when I heard him talking about Abby—that's her name—I felt myself turning green."

As Harley sat nodding his head, offering her his genuine concern, Lilly surprised him by asking a question. "Tell me, Harley, as a pastor, what advice would you give me?"

Without hesitation and with quiet assurance, he answered, "In the book of Corinthians, it tells us that love is patient, love is kind, and it is not jealous. If you're truly in love with Warren, you'll find a way to keep the green-eyed monster out of your relationship. You can't be jealous every time he speaks to another woman or even when he talks about her. Beginning a relationship without trust is not something that you want to be a part of."

After another sip of coffee, Harley added, "I'm sorry. I guess preaching is in my blood."

Lilly smiled playfully. "As I recall, I asked for it." She reached across the counter, touched his hand, and simply said, "Thank you. I needed to hear all of that."

Harley pulled out a crumpled one-dollar bill, but Lilly gestured for him to put it away. "Since your advice was so freely given, so is the coffee."

Harley looked up as he was stuffing the money back into his pocket and flashed a smile of thanks. The even whiteness of his smile was so dazzling that, every time Lilly encountered it, she wondered how anyone could have accused this gentle man of any wrongdoing at the church. He had the most honest face in the entire town, and when he showed those pearly whites, well, it was enough to cause palpitations.

Lilly watched as Harley silently left the diner and disappeared around the corner. Her heart ached each time he sat at the counter and ordered coffee. His eyes used to be so full of life, but now they always seemed glazed with pain.

He may have denied seeing Ms. Weaver walk past the window, but the look on his face told her that he knew her somehow. She had been pleasant enough when she served lunch for her and Mrs. Black, but Lilly wasn't convinced that she was good for this town.

CHAPTER 23

I lift up mine eyes to the hills—where does my help come from?

Psalm 121:1

Abby looked around at the many boxes in her living room as she waited for the moving van to arrive and felt the tears as they ran down her cheeks. She asked herself if these were tears of joy or tears of sadness. She guessed there were some of both—sadness because she was leaving the house that she and Jeff had vowed to live in until they were old and also because she was now alone and joy because she was buying a new house that she hoped would bring with it a new purpose for her life.

One last walk through the house brought more tears but also a needed sense of closure. She had committed to memory the endless occasions during the last eight years that she and Jeff had spent together in each room, and now it was time to box them up and carry them with her. She needed to get on with life, and the help that she felt she was going to need would somehow be found at Summer Rain.

As she drove toward her new home, she remembered that the cupboards would need some restocking, so she decided to continue on into town and stop at the grocery store. Just the very thought of groceries brought to mind the man with the Bible. Abby wondered if he would be outside the building today. As she pulled into the parking lot, her eyes scanned the area, checking to see if he was around. Not seeing him, she breathed a sigh of relief, parked her car, and proceeded to go into the store.

Returning to her car with the groceries, she saw him sitting under a tree at the far end of the parking lot. He looked perfectly healthy. Why didn't this man go out and get a job like everyone else?

Sitting in her car, staring at him, her heart felt as if it was doing somersaults. Why was her heart going into an aerobic state? Why was she troubling herself about a man who spent his time in a grocery store parking lot begging for money? What unimaginable debris could this man have in his life to generate such low self-esteem? Abby vowed that, if she saw him again, she would take time to talk to him—but not today.

Abby returned home, and as she transported the groceries from the car to the kitchen, Mrs. Black began putting them away. She had just finished carrying in the last of the bags when she heard a loud horn. It was the moving van announcing that they had arrived at Summer Rain with all her belongings.

For the next three hours, Mrs. Black stood back and watched as Abby turned gruff, boisterous furniture movers into polite, docile men who couldn't seem to wait for her next command. She was amazed at Abby's graceful stamina that caused men to vie for her attention. She smiled as she thought about her future in this house with Abby. Living there was going to prove very interesting and quite entertaining. For the first time in years, she felt totally at peace, and tears of happiness found their way to her eyes.

After saying good-bye to the movers, Abby walked to the mailbox and retrieved the mail. Mrs. Black was coming slowly down the stairs as Abby came through the front door. "You got a lot of mail today, Mrs. Black. I'll lay it here by your purse."

"Abby, dear, before this living arrangement goes any further, we need to clear something up. I've been meaning to talk to you, but we've all been so busy lately." Her voice carried a distinctive energy as she said, "I want you to call me Shirley. I'm really tired of the formality."

Shocked at Mrs. Black's straightforwardness, Abby took a step back. Within seconds, a smile found its way through her mask of surprise. "I'm so glad you've told me this. I didn't want to seem disrespectful, so I never said anything."

"Nonsense. I could never use your name and the word *disrespectful* in the same sentence. And please, when you introduce me to your guests, I want to be known as Shirley, not Mrs. Black. I may be old, but I'm definitely not stuffy."

A depth to her smile that had been missing too long allowed tears of joy to flow down Abby's cheeks. God had truly blessed her by allowing Shirley to come into her life.

"Mrs.—I mean, Shirley. I have been waiting so long to call you that. I wanted to approach you about it, but as I said, out of respect, I decided to wait. Could I tell you what I really want to call you?"

Shirley bit her lip to stifle a grin and said, "Well, do I really want to know?"

Abby, realizing how that must have sounded, smiled as she whispered, her hand on her chest, "I would be so honored if you would allow me to call you Mother."

Shocked at this request, Shirley's entire face spread into a smile, her eyes brightening with pleasure. She had not expected this from Abby, but nothing could have made her happier. Her heart swelled with a familiar feeling that she never thought would be possible again since the death of her son so many years ago. Her eyelids trembled as she fought to hold back her tears of thankfulness.

"Abby, dear, you've just made me the happiest old lady on this planet. It's as if we have known each other all our lives. I'm not sure I'm worthy to be your mother, but I love the sound of it, so the answer is *yes*."

As if on cue, both women rose from their chairs and wrapped their arms around each other, savoring this special moment.

CHAPTER 24

In the day when I cried out, you answered me and made me bold with strength in my soul.

—Psalm 138:3

For the next two weeks, Abby and Shirley hung new pictures on the wall, arranged furniture, hung fresh curtains, and ordered linens to match the newly painted bedrooms and bathrooms. They spent hours deciding on breakfast menus. They even discussed the possibility of serving evening meals. Abby was fascinated with Shirley's knowledge of gourmet food preparation, and Shirley was impressed with Abby's business background, so they agreed without hesitation that each would manage the appropriate subject.

Abby's days became so filled with advertising agency appointments, photo shoots of the inn, and working with a design landscaper that keeping up with the daily household chores became almost impossible. She would never have been able to manage had it not been for Shirley. She had more energy for a woman her age than anybody Abby had ever known.

Job opportunities for a housekeeper and a gardener at Summer Rain had only been advertised in the local newspaper for one day, and Abby was already receiving calls faster than she could answer them. The inquiries were all about the housekeeping position except one. A man by the name of Harley had called, and Abby had scheduled an interview with him for the next morning at nine o'clock. She wanted this position filled as soon as possible. The grass needed cutting, and a lot of bushes were waiting to be trimmed.

Shirley walked into the kitchen just as Abby was setting up the appointment time with Harley. "I didn't mean to eavesdrop, but did I hear you say that Harley called about the gardener position?"

"Yes, do you know him?"

Drawing in a slow, steady breath, Shirley took her time answering. "Well, everyone in town knows Harley. He used to be the pastor at the Morning Son Bible Church."

Abby, scarcely aware of her own voice, blurted out, "A pastor? Why is a pastor calling for a job as a gardener?"

"I said he used to be a pastor."

"What do you mean used to be? Is he of retirement age? Because if he is, he might as well save the gas that it will take to drive out here. I need someone who is strong and can handle the work. I have a lot of plans for this yard."

"Okay, missy, cool your jets. You're getting way too excited. I'll answer a few of your questions the best I can, but you'll have to ask him to tell you the whole story when you interview him tomorrow." She glanced at Abby for a sign of objection but, seeing none, continued. "I know Harley is a good, honest man who's going through some rough times right now. This is a small town, and if you listen, you'll probably hear things that are not in Harley's favor, but don't be too quick to judge."

"Well, I must say, you have gotten my attention. This could be an exhilarating interview."

Shirley, grinning, muttered hastily, "In more ways than one."

"Did you say something more, Shirley? I couldn't hear you over the hum of the dishwasher."

"I just said it should be a good one."

The next morning, Abby was up at the crack of dawn. Her first thought when she opened her eyes was about the upcoming interview. She really shouldn't be this excited about hiring a gardener, but she was so curious. Even though she didn't know anyone by the name of Harley, his voice had sounded somehow familiar on the phone.

When the doorbell rang, Abby was just finishing her second cup of coffee. She poured the last few drops down the sink drain and walked to the door. When she opened it, there stood the man from the parking lot. They exchanged a definite look of bewilderment. Abby was the first to speak. "What are you doing here?" Inside, she wanted to ask furiously, *Didn't you insult me enough in the parking lot? You went through all the trouble of finding me. Do you have more that you need to say?*

Harley couldn't believe he had answered an ad for a possible job and then have the door open to reveal this insolent woman. His life just kept getting worse. He answered her as politely as he could manage. "I'm sorry to bother you, ma'am, but I'm answering an ad in the local newspaper for a gardener. I called and was told to come at this time. As I got closer to this address, I realized that this is Shirley Black's place. I was expecting her to answer the door. Is she at home?"

With a slight twinge of remorse in her voice and sounding one octave higher than normal, she asked, "You're Harley?"

"Yes, ma'am. I called yesterday."

Trying to lose the steely edge of her voice, she said, "Please don't call me ma'am, and it was me that you talked to on the phone." With an outstretched hand, she spoke in a softer tone. "My name is Abby Weaver. I'm pleased to meet you Harley. Please come in, and have some tea while we talk."

Harley wondered why the sudden change in attitude. Maybe Shirley had already told her of his plight, and she was again feeling sorry for him. He didn't want her pity, but he did need a job. He followed her into the kitchen and was instructed to sit in the chair by the window. She set a large glass of iced tea in front of him and said, "Okay, tell me about yourself."

"No disrespect, Ms. Weaver, but I just came here to apply for the gardener's job. I really don't see what my life history has to do with weeds and dirt. I'll be honest with you, though. I don't have a lot of experience with this type of work, but I am an avid reader and a hard worker. I think between the two, I can do whatever it is you need done."

Abby was both impressed and irritated with his obvious confidence. Just because he wasn't afraid of hard work and he liked to read didn't mean he could be a gardener. He was going to have to come up with something a little more convincing.

Abby had pen and paper in front of her now ready to continue the interview. "Harley, I need your last name and an address."

"Again, no disrespect, but if you call Shirley, she will vouch for my credibility."

Abby wasn't sure she liked the suggestive tone of his voice, but the silent sadness in his face overpowered his flippancy. The unspoken pain was alive and glowing in his eyes. He seemed to be peering at her intently, waiting for some sort of response, so as politely as she could, she looked boldly in to his eyes and said, "Harley, I am the new owner, and I need a gardener. I am opening a bed-and-breakfast, and I want the grounds to be kept impeccable. Mrs. Black is going to continue to live here, and actually, she did speak on your behalf after our phone conversation. If I'm going to have an employee, I want to know a little bit about him. It's not because I'm nosy. It's because I genuinely care and take an interest in people. Shirley told me that you used to be a pastor, but that's all I know.

Would you care to elaborate on that a little?" Abby flicked an imaginary speck of dirt from her dress, leaned back in her chair, and waited.

Harley took his time. Just how much should he tell this woman? Shirley knew the whole story. Surely, she would have told Ms. Weaver, especially if they were now living in the same house. Was she playing games? Maybe she was going to compare stories. Maybe she was testing him to see if his story matched Shirley's. It seemed that, if he wanted this job, he was going to have to bare his soul to this woman. She was a pretty lady, and something about her seemed to possess an energy that undeniably fascinated him. Even though physically she appeared very delicate, there was an unmistakable strength that was reflected in her face. Her eyes were full of life and unquenchable warmth, yet they seemed to echo the same disappointed pain he felt in himself. He didn't know about her past, but he had the feeling that she had come to New Hope for a fresh start, an indication that she was running from someone or something.

Abby's skin tingled unexpectedly as she leaned forward to lightly touch Harley's hand, hoping to jolt him from the tense silence that enveloped the room. She was suddenly anxious to escape this uncomfortable feeling and move on to the next phase of the interview.

"Harley, are you all right? You haven't said anything for the past few minutes. Do you have some questions that you feel awkward asking me? If you would like to have Shirley come into the room with us, I'll be glad to get her. But I would like to show you around outside first so that you'll know what your job description is going to entail."

"Ms. Weaver, I'm sorry I didn't answer you right away. Sometimes I'm a bit slow in processing new ideas, especially when they pertain to my life." Searching for a feasible explanation, Harley swallowed hard, trying to manage some composure. His voice sounded tired yet guarded when he said, "To start with, I want to apologize for the way I talked to you in the parking lot. You have to understand that my pride has been badly bruised, and humility doesn't always present itself at the proper time."

Before he could say another word, Abby extended her hand and pulled him from the chair. "We're going for a walk around the gardens, and while we're walking, please continue to tell me why you're applying for this job. It seems we have something in common. Both our pasts obviously have seen some rocky roads."

Harley remained silent but promptly walked beside Abby as they went out the side door and into the gardens. He was totally in awe of the sight before him. Coming to work every day in this environment might just be the therapy that he was so in need of. As they meandered on the stone paths between the tall pines and the majestic oaks, Harley took note of the tall feathery plumes from ostrich ferns as they hovered over the many varieties of hostas. There were purple and yellow flowers scattered among the mountain laurel, saturating the premises with a sweet smell and the nuance of enchantment. A man could almost forget his troubles in a place like this.

"Harley, do you want to tell me a little of your background, or are you just not interested in this job? There would be more than just gardening. I need someone who is a bit of a handyman. Are you good with a hammer and nails?"

"Yes, ma'am, I mean Ms. Weaver. I've built a few things in my life, and anyone you ask will tell you that you'll never find anyone with a better work ethic than mine." Abby didn't fail to catch the note of sarcasm in his voice as he added, "That is unless you talk to half the people in town."

Something cautioned Abby to be silent and allow him time to speak. The inflection in his voice gave the impression of embarrassing discomfort, but he continued on. "I was the pastor at the New Hope Morning Son Bible Church for five years. I was the youngest minister ever to be in charge of that congregation. I loved my job. Actually, it wasn't even like a job. It was just like being part of a big family." His cheeks burned in remembrance, and he turned his head so that Abby wouldn't see. "It's been two years since I was asked to leave. It seems like a lifetime ago." A vacant look of despair began to spread over his face as he tried to maintain his composure. "I loved those people, and I thought it was mutual, but when gossip is used like fertilizer and scattered over the entire flock, it doesn't take long for lies to grow. There are a few women who have a lot of clout in that church and who seem to have nothing else to do but gossip. They launched the inconceivable notion that I was a thief. Mrs. Black knows every one of these ladies, and I will never forget how she stood up for me and rallied against the board that wanted to dismiss me. She visited each lady and tried to convince each one that they were wrong. But as time went on, pride became more of an issue than the so-called crime itself. They were not about to admit that they were mistaken, and the word *sorry* just didn't seem to be in their vocabulary. They had no evidence. The only fact they had was that there was a large amount of money missing, and I was the last one who had access to it."

Harley unconsciously rubbed the back of his neck, and Abby could see that his emotional suffering had become so intense that it was causing physical pain.

"Abby, is it okay if I call you Abby? We are about the same age, I would guess, so I feel a little strange putting a title in front of your name. I've never really talked about this before with anyone, and even though we got off to a rocky start, you've made me feel real comfortable. If you're going to be my boss, I will continue to call you Ms. Weaver, if you want me to." He offered her a forgiving smile as he said, "I'm sorry I'm rambling. It's not really my style. I usually know what I want to say and when, but I guess I'm losing my touch."

"I'm a pretty simple woman, Mr.—I don't even know your last name. If you're going to be hanging around here in the future, I need to know a name to put on the paychecks."

"I haven't told you because I'm sure you'll have the same reaction as everyone else when I tell you." He hesitated, hoping he wouldn't have to tell her, but hearing no feedback from her, he blurted it out. "It's Davidson."

Abby started to ask what was wrong with the name *Davidson* and then brought her hand up to stifle her giggles. "I'm sorry, Harley. You just caught me off guard. Are you part of the Harley-Davidson empire?"

"No. Do you know the Johnny Cash song 'A Boy Named Sue'? Well, it's sort of the same concept. I've built a lot of character over the years because of my name. I've been teased and was even dubbed a nickname. Kids called me 'Cycle.' It was rough at first, but then I learned how to handle animosity, and I think I became a better person because of it. Maybe someday I'll tell you how I became Harley Davidson, but for now let's talk about the job and if you want to hire me."

Abby smiled, now finding it impossible not to like this man. Even his appearance totally captured her attention. The dab of gray that lay near his temples overshadowed the few tendrils of dark hair that curled around the back of his ear. It was almost identical to the silver that she had noticed in Jeff's hair as he lay in the casket.

Harley was waving his hand in the air, trying to get her attention. "Are you trying to avoid that question, Abby?"

Abby tilted her chin up, wiped her eyes, and turned away. "I'm sorry, Harley. There's something about you that reminds me of my late husband, and for a moment, I was taken back in time. Please forgive me. That was quite rude. To answer your original question, yes, I would like to hire you. Let's go back to the kitchen and work out the details for your hours and wages."

Abby turned toward the house and began walking, giving Harley the cue to follow. A sense of newly found strength came to him and his despair unexpectedly diminished. His defenses began to subside, and the weight of the chains that he had become accustomed to no longer seemed like the burdensome kind. He had needed a job and a reason to live. With this opportunity, maybe there was still a chance for him to grow whole again. Maybe God really had led him here for a purpose. He drew in a deep breath and vowed to discover exactly what that purpose was meant to be.

CHAPTER 25

And I shall give you pastors according to mine heart, which shall feed you with knowledge and understanding.

—Jeremiah 3:15

The next morning, Harley woke with a monstrous headache. He found two aspirins and downed them with a bottle of orange juice that was lying in his cooler. He knew that walking sometimes relieved the throbbing; so he threw on some shorts, a T-shirt, and his most comfortable sandals. On a beautiful day such as this one, a leisurely stroll to the park would be a great deterrent from the pain in his head and the ache in his heart. Living this kind of life was beginning to affect his trust in mankind, and his mind was becoming congested with doubts and fears. Why would God bring him to this town, involve him in people's lives, and then allow him to be accused of being a thief? Ceaseless inward questions. How long before he got some answers?

He continued on to the park, walking toward his favorite tree near the backside of the ball field. It was a weeping willow with branches hanging so close to the ground that a "secret garden" of sorts had been created underneath. It was a treat each time he visited to take off his shoes and allow his toes the privilege of sinking deep into the plushlike moss that surrounded the tree trunk. He had come to think of this spot as his own little utopia. Sitting in the same position under the canopy of green so many times to do so much thinking had caused an impression of his behind in the moss. He smiled as he sat down, conscious of the familiar shape.

He leaned his head against the tree, hoping for a few quiet moments, but instead, his mind once again wandered back to the first time he arrived in town. It was as if it were yesterday. He envisioned his map lying on the front seat of his car, with his route highlighted in yellow with a big circle drawn around his exit number off the interstate. It was at that moment when his life took on new meaning.

Entering town from the west side had brought him into the historic side of New Hope. Massive brick homes sat nestled among huge oak trees. Their stately porches and round columns reaching to the second floor balconies were distinct architectural designs of post–Civil War. The scenery was impressive. As he turned onto Main Street, he remembered being overcome with a feeling of serenity. Flower baskets hung from each light pole, and benches sat in front of many store windows as if beckoning shoppers to rest their weary feet. Large trees shadowed the sidewalks, giving them a cooler feel. It was as if everything in this town had been strategically placed or constructed to allow its residents and visitors a sense of harmony. It had hospitality written all over it.

As he turned onto High Street, he sucked in a bit of air. There sat his church. No doubt about it. It was exactly as Dr. Daniels had described it. The huge stained glass windows depicting Jesus in the garden and Jesus surrounded by little children were breathtaking, even from this distance. As he drove closer, the church sign had come into view; and for a moment, he was overcome with emotion. There for all to see, etched in gold, was the name Harley Davidson, pastor of the Morning Son Bible Church of New Hope.

As he parked the car and stepped out onto the street, he became so engrossed in admiring the church building and its canvas-worthy setting that he didn't notice the old man who was slowly making his way down the sidewalk. He had been mesmerized by the size of the oak trees that shadowed the back side of the church and was impressed at how ingeniously the hand-crafted windows had been placed so that the light from the morning sun would shine directly on them.

Harley turned around quickly as he felt someone touch his shoulder. An older gentleman, dressed as if going to a funeral, now had a hold of Harley's hand and was shaking it with all his might. "You must be Pastor Davidson. Welcome to New Hope. I'm Pastor Evans, but everyone just calls me Dave."

"Pleased to meet you, Dave. Yes, I'm Pastor Davidson, but please call me Harley. I am overwhelmed with the presence of this church. It's absolutely beautiful." In a lower voice, hoping to sound compassionate, Harley had added, "I'm sure you're sad about leaving."

"Young man, I am sad to be leaving my congregation, but my wife and I can't wait to fulfill our traveling plans. I wanted to retire three years ago, but Dr. Daniels kept urging me to stay. Said he would tell me when the time was right. Sure enough, I got a phone call saying that he has the perfect replacement for me. Obviously, God wants you here. You have my blessing, and if I can help you with anything, anything at all, you just ask." He took a deep breath, rubbed his forehead as if debating whether or not to continue, and then as if he couldn't say it fast enough blurted out, "Anything except giving you information about the parishioners. You'll have to make your own impression of them. On their behalf, I will say this. Most of them are all good people, and they are anxious to meet you and get you settled."

He once again paused as if he wanted to add something to his thoughts but was apprehensive about doing so. He looked Harley straight in the eyes and almost in a whisper said, "Have you ever heard the expression 'wolves in sheep's clothing'?" Harley nodded, not really sure if he should answer.

"Just remember that your flock is not all made up of sheep. There are other animals, such as wolves and foxes. They think they are being protective of their own by disguising themselves. They hide in the bushes, pretending to be friendly, waiting for an opportunity to jump in, supposedly to help. But they don't jump. They pounce, and when they attack, their paws are big enough to suppress an entire congregation. They have intimidation skills that should be patented." Dave massaged his chin as if rubbing would erase his last few sentences, and then in what seemed like a desperate attempt to make Harley understand, he leaned closer and, with impeccable surety in his voice, quoted a scripture verse. "'Behold, I send you forth as sheep in the midst of wolves: be you therefore wise as serpents and harmless as doves.'"

Harley thus had found himself in an awkward situation. He hadn't been exactly sure what Dave was trying to convey to him, nor did he really want to know. He was looking forward to this new challenge, and he wanted to form his own opinions about the people in his congregation. On the other hand, he didn't want the old man to think that he was too good to take his advice; so he had turned to Dave, shook his head as if genuinely concerned, and said, "Dave, I really appreciate your concern for me, and I'll take all your advice to heart. I'm not exactly sure what all that meant, but I'm sure I'll figure it out in time. Right now, I would really like to see the parsonage. Would that be possible?"

Dave then turned to Harley with a calculating expression and said, "Is that your priority? Don't you want to see the inside of the church? I thought you would be more interested in seeing our place of worship, not your place of pleasure. I thought you would be interested in what I'm saying too." Suddenly, his tone became cool and disapproving as he continued. "You're not exactly the man whom I was expecting."

Harley was not used to defending himself as if on trial and answered the pastor's accusation in a tone that was overly gracious for the situation. "Dave, I really do appreciate your concern, and I'm so grateful that you're trying to give me some inside information, but maybe we can talk about this later. Right now, I need to spend some time alone in the sanctuary. I just wanted to put my few things in the house and then be free to spend some time in prayer."

Dave had lowered his head in embarrassment. "I'm so sorry, Pastor Davidson. I guess I'm a bit more anxious about this transition than I'm willing to admit. I had no right to come back at you like that." He began walking toward the side of the church and, with his hand, gestured for Harley to walk with him. "The house is right behind the church. Follow me, and we'll take the tour." Nothing more was mentioned of the incident, but Harley made a mental note of the judicious manner in which the former pastor had tried to warn him about someone in his congregation.

The house was a one-story brick rancher with adequate room for Harley's lifestyle. He would have his own study, where he could spread his notes and books as far as he wanted without someone coming along and picking them up. There was room for his stereo and a new TV that he was going to order. And the best luxury of all was having his own bedroom; it would be a treat after sharing a dorm room for all those years.

He thanked Dave for showing him around and promised to be at work bright and early the next morning. He still had three days before Sunday morning, but he had a lot of work to do. His first sermon had to be perfect.

The doorbell had interrupted his thoughts, and as he opened the door, his nostrils were filled with an aroma that reminded him of his grandmother. An apple pie was being held out as if he should take it, so he did. The lady behind the pie was about five feet tall with slightly gray hair. She was dressed in slacks and a matching sweater. Even her shoes were the same color.

Harley thanked her for the pie and introduced himself. The little lady squinted as if she were having trouble seeing. "Are you all right, Mrs.—I'm sorry I didn't catch your name."

"That's because I didn't give it to you. My name is Edie, short for Edith. You won't forget that now, will you?"

Harley smothered a smile. "No, Edie, I won't forget. Would you like to come in? I just arrived a few minutes ago, so I haven't had time to get any food, but since you brought a pie, maybe I can find some plates, and I'd be glad to share. How does that sound?"

"Well, to begin with, if you look in your cupboards and refrigerator, you'll find that they are fully stocked. And I can't stay for pie. I just came over to see what you look like."

Harley could barely keep a straight face. "How did you know that I was here? It was only minutes ago that I met Pastor Evans."

"Honey, in this town, we know everyone and everything, so you might want to mind your p's and q's. The ladies of the Morning Son are quite famous for our knowledge of this town. We like to think of it as writing history." She wrinkled up her tiny nose as she continued. "As Napoleon Bonaparte once said, 'What is history but a fable agreed upon?'"

Harley tried to silence another chuckle as he replied, "Edie, I'll have to think about that one for a minute."

Wanting to change the subject, he said, "Are you sure you won't come in?"

"No thank you. I'm meeting Ethel and Brenda for lunch. Enjoy the pie." And with that, she was gone. Harley shut the door and broke out in laughter. He hoped everyone in this town was as straightforward and honest as Edie.

He had chosen potato salad and cold cuts from the many choices in the fridge, which were there just as Edie had promised, and decided to save the pie for later. He grabbed a soda and went out the back door, hoping it would be a more discreet access to the church. The inside of the church was as magnificent as it was on the outside. The stained glass windows took on a whole new kind of beauty. The reds were rosier, the oranges and yellows more brilliant. Even the blues surpassed the color of the sky. Harley had never seen anything more striking. It would be a shame if the doors had to be closed on this beautiful place of worship. As he stood at the pulpit and looked out across the empty pews, he raised his hands in thanks. He vowed to do the best that he could to bring it back to life. He had knelt at the altar and asked God's blessing for the congregation, the church, and himself.

CHAPTER 26

But select capable men from all the people—men who fear God, trustworthy men who hate dishonest gain—and appoint them as officials over thousands, hundreds, fifties and tens.

—Exodus 18:21

As Chief McDonald took off his jacket and hung it on the coat hook by the door, he chuckled. He would love to see the look on Stacey's face if she could see him actually hang up his coat instead of throwing it on the chair. Because of her, the office was in immaculate order. Tim had noticed, though, that for the past few months she had quit badgering him about his slovenly ways. He guessed she had just given up.

He slid gracefully into his worn leather chair and swiveled around to come face to face with a tall stack of files. Somehow, the same green folder labeled "Weaver" kept getting placed on top of the pile. It was something he didn't want to think about yet couldn't seem to get away from. Why would anyone have messed with Jeff Weaver's brake lines? As chief, Tim had assigned a few officers to investigate the accident, and they had come up with nothing. The only true fact they had was that the lines had definitely been cut on the 1982 Lincoln.

Tim had done some off-duty investigation, and it seemed as if the worst thing Jeff Weaver had ever done was get a parking ticket. Everyone he talked to had nothing but the best to say about him. He had received not only the Purple Heart in Vietnam but also the Silver Star for bravery. Jeff was highly respected among his peers, and Chief McDonald could find no enemies. Perhaps Stacey could do a little more investigating about Mr. Weaver's bravery and his wounds that he acquired in Vietnam. So far, everything seemed to lead to a dead end.

Spreading out the contents of the file on the desk, once again, Tim began leafing through the report and found a notation that he had missed. Apparently, everyone else had overlooked it too. If the media had gotten this information, it definitely would have been front-page news. There was an anonymous driver who witnessed the heroic act played out by Jeff Weaver. He happened to be sitting at the stoplight when he saw the Lincoln coming at full speed. He watched as Jeff made a split-second decision that cost him his life but saved an entire family. Jeff had been headed straight for a blue sedan filled with kids. His only other option had been to crash into the tanker.

Tim felt a wave of guilt as he thought about Jeff Weaver's heroic act. Would he have been as brave? His muscle tightened along his jaw as he envisioned the tanker, a wall of metal that had blocked Jeff's path. What was he thinking those last few seconds of his life? What exactly would a man think about right before he died? He stood up and walked to the water fountain. What he wished he could have right now wasn't water but a good cold beer. It took a lot for him to be ruffled, but every once in a while, when an incident like the Weaver tragedy occurred and there was no motive for the crime, his temperament took a hit. Life just didn't seem fair, and as chief of police, he had more opportunity than most to see firsthand the destruction that a family can encounter when dealing with a catastrophe of this magnitude. He needed to find out who had caused this accident and why. Not that finding out was going to bring Mr. Weaver back, but having the villain brought to trial sometimes brought a small amount of justice to the family.

Tim McDonald had been promoted to chief just four months ago. When asked if he would take the promotion, he hesitated and took two weeks before he gave the department his answer. There had been a total of three men who qualified for the job, but he was told that he had an air of authority about him, and to the public, he appeared to be someone who demanded instant obedience. He disagreed with that, but if the public saw him in that light and respected him for those qualities, then so be it. Those who knew him well knew that he was just a regular guy who was really quite sensitive and preferred "chick flicks" as opposed to war movies. He saw enough violence right here in the small town of Millersburg. He had no use for violence on the movie screen.

While trying to make himself comfortable in his worn-out chair, he took out his notebook and began jotting down bits of information that might have slipped by the reporters and even the investigators. What other significant facts could have been missed? There had to be something, some other clue as to who was responsible for cutting those brake lines.

Grabbing his coat, he disappeared quickly to the parking garage and headed for the police compound. Hopefully, the Lincoln was still on the lot. As he showed his badge to the attendant, he began scouting the lot for the dark gray car. He saw it sitting in the corner by the wooden fence. It didn't have much shape to it, not much more than a mangled piece of metal. The attendant gave him the okay to snoop around, and as he walked toward the pile of scrap, he thought once again about Mr. Weaver's last thoughts. He may not have had time for personal thoughts given the fact that he sacrificed his own life to save that of a family. He hoped that he could find the right words someday to tell Mrs. Weaver about her husband's courageous act.

He motioned for the attendant to join him next to the once-beautiful Lincoln and asked him to give him some insight as to how much effort it had taken to crawl under the car and slash the lines. As he inspected the car, he realized that he really didn't know why he was there. By looking at the line, it was obvious that it had been cut, but that was old news.

With a sad feeling in his bones, he returned to work and once again picked up the file marked "Weaver" and read the report one more time. He had read each page so many times that he almost had them memorized. And nothing.—Each time, he came up with nothing. Everything seemed to be in order. The investigation was still at a dead end. All they knew for sure was that Jeff Weaver's brake line had been cut by someone who knew exactly what they were doing. The question now wasn't how it was done but who would have done such a deadly deed. And if they really meant for Jeff to die, how did they know for sure that it would be a fatal crash? Did they know where he was going that day and just how long it would take till all the fluid ran out of the brake line? There was no way anyone could have known how fast or how slow he would be driving. It had to have been strictly a guessing game. The fact that Jeff lost the game was a bonus to the murderer—if that was what the game was about. Maybe it was to serve as a warning. If Jeff would have just been involved in a fender bender, the garage would have found cut lines, and he would have known that it was deliberate and that someone was out to get him. Maybe he would have been more careful. Maybe the police could have gotten involved before it became a homicide. A lot of maybes. But who would go that far and take a chance of causing a fatality just to give someone a warning? And warning for what? Tim's only hope was that someone would start crowing about their premeditated strategy and how much they got paid for the job. Many criminals found themselves behind bars after firing off about their so-called success stories.

Tim had gone as far back as Jeff's return from the army, and he couldn't even find someone to say that they had ever had cross words with him. He seemed to have an impeccable personal record. With that thought in mind, he reached again for his notepad and pen so that he could leave Stacey a message, requesting that she dig up Jeff's service records. Perhaps he could get some insight from the army.

The sound of the phone ringing brought him back to the moment. "Good afternoon, this is Carroll County Police Department. Chief McDonald speaking. May I help you?"

"Chief McDonald, just the man I'm looking for. This is Marie Forester. I'm Abby Weaver's aunt."

"Yes, Ms. Forester. How are you today?"

"I'm fine, Chief McDonald, but I have a question for you. What are you doing to find Jeff's killer? I've been waiting for a phone call from you. It's been months, and I haven't heard a thing. I think I've been quite patient, but now it's time for some answers."

"I'm really very sorry for not getting in touch with you, but I wasn't exactly sure where you were. I left a few messages, but when I didn't hear from you, I assumed you were on one of your excursions, and besides, I have no new information. It seems that every piece of evidence we think we have leads us nowhere. There are no fingerprints, no motive, and no enemy. It's as if this man was a saint. I even went down to the compound and checked out the car myself. We have nothing to go on, but I promise you I'm not giving up. As a matter of fact, I have the file in front of me right now, and for the umpteenth time, I was reviewing what we have so far."

"Chief McDonald, have you heard at all from Abby?"

"No, I haven't, and I decided not to get in touch with her again until I talked to you. I wasn't even sure if she realized that her husband's death was ruled a homicide. She was pretty upset the first time I spoke to her, so I really didn't push the issue of homicide. I promised to call you before I talked to her again, so I wanted to at least give you that courtesy."

Tim detected a tone of thawing in her voice as she said, "I'm grateful for that, but I think it's time she knew a little more about the accident. I'm not scheduled home yet for another month, so if you could meet with Abby and fill her in with the details that you know, I would appreciate it."

"I'll take care of it, Ms. Forester. Is there a number where I can reach you if I find any new evidence?"

"Please just leave a message on my home phone. I promise to check my voice mail from now on, in case you call. And, Chief McDonald, please be gentle with Abby. Jeff's death has been hard on her, and I'm not sure how she will handle this."

"I promise to treat her as if she were part of my family, and I'll do all I can to help. I'll be in touch with you as soon as I can. Thanks for calling."

"Thank you, Chief McDonald. I'll be looking forward to a phone call."

The clock on the wall struck eight o'clock. It was definitely time to go home. All of this would wait until tomorrow. It had been a long day, and his bed was calling.

CHAPTER 27

For you have girded me with strength for battle. You have subdued under me those who rose up against me.

—Psalm 18:39

The next morning, as Tim walked into his office, the first thing his eyes were drawn to was the green folder marked "Weaver." Why was this case so frustrating? What was he missing, and where should he look for more clues? Just as he was about to open the report, Stacey appeared in the doorway. "Excuse me, Tim, but I see you're staring at the green folder again. I think I might have an idea that just could get us some information about Mr. Weaver's army time."

Tim became instantly wide awake and spoke quickly as if allowing another minute to go by would change what Stacey was about to say. "Come in and tell me what's on your mind."

Stacey sat in the wicker chair in front of Tim's desk and began by saying that she just found out that a friend of hers was working for the army in the Personnel Department. She had his phone number, and if Tim wanted her to, she would call and ask for a favor—if nothing else, just to find out if there was anything out of the ordinary about Jeff Weaver. The phone call that she made before was just to a desk clerk, and possibly, something had been overlooked.

His face creased into an abrupt smile. "That's the most encouraging news I've heard yet. When can you call?"

She administered a mock salute with her hand to her forehead as she was going out the door. Tim huffed out a half laugh. He didn't have a lot of confidence in the army personnel, but Stacey had a way of getting what she wanted.

Sure enough, within the hour, she stepped inside his office and laid yet another green folder in front of him. Without looking up, Tim opened it and found a copy of a newspaper article from the *Cloverleaf Times* in Virginia, dated June 1969. Before reading the article, Tim raised his head and glanced at Stacey, waiting for her to say something. When she didn't, he said in a matter-of-fact tone, "Exactly what am I supposed to be looking at?"

"I know that you haven't been able to find anything dreadful about this guy, but if you read the article, maybe you'll understand why someone might have a grudge against him. Being that this is a newspaper article, it is, of course, public knowledge, but my friend tells me that the government has much more detail. Maybe you could subpoena the army for the complete story."

Tim could hardly believe it. The further he read into the article, the more confused he became. The story insinuated that Jeff Weaver had started a fight against his commanding warrant officer—a big no-no in the army. From everything that Tim had read about Jeff Weaver, he was one of the least likely people to initiate a conflict, especially with a higher-ranking officer. If the article was correct, why hadn't he been court-martialed?

"Stacey, I need you to find out where Mr. Weaver originated from. If not from here, then where? I need to know when he moved here and when he got married. I also need to know the exact date when he was in Vietnam and the name of his commanding officer. Get me his rank when he entered the army and his rank when he was discharged." Tim shook his head in utter disbelief as he barked out one more order. "Check the records to see if it was an honorable or dishonorable discharge. Let me know as soon as possible."

Stacey promised Tim an answer, even if it meant that she had to stay late. She knew that some cases were just harder than others to investigate, and she wasn't sure exactly why, but her boss seemed to have a personal interest in this one. Whatever his reason, she was only here to do her job, and she knew that asking personal questions wasn't in her job description. She went back to her desk, sat down, and began making the necessary phone calls.

Tim slammed one fist against his palm. If Stacey saw him, she would scold him as if he were her child. He wouldn't have allowed anyone else to address him in such a way, but in all reality, he had come to appreciate not only her office skills but also her highly sophisticated hijacking of his entire thought process. She always seemed to know what he was thinking. She could finish his sentences if she wanted to, but she was smart enough to know when not to do that. She knew his habits so well that it scared him. Was he that easy to decipher? Did he wear his emotions on his sleeve? However she figured him out, she was doing one hell of a job. No other woman had ever come to know him like Stacey.

He slammed his fist again, this time on the desk, and asked himself out loud why his county always ended up with the most bizarre investigations. He had spent so much time on this case, and every avenue he explored brought nothing but dead ends. He was pretty much convinced that this would be an unsolvable case, yet here he was, exploring again, searching for a plausible explanation—an explanation that he wasn't even sure existed. But now that he was back on the trail again and had another possible lead, the scent of a good hunt was making his blood run fast through his veins.

The possibility of new clues was exciting, and he actually had an urge to call Ms. Weaver and give her the information. Even though the urge was strong, he had made a promise to Ms. Forester, and he was a man of his word. If and when some new data appeared to be worthy of investigation, the old lady would be the first to know. Whether or not she told Abby would be entirely up to her. So for the time being, thoughts of talking to Abby Weaver would have to be put in the back of the green folder.

The noise coming from his stomach told him that it was time for lunch. He wasn't really hungry, but a quick sandwich from the deli across the street would settle the rumblings and allow him to totally focus on the pile of folders and phone messages laying on his desk.

Just as he pulled his hat from the rack, Stacey appeared in the doorway. "I see that you're going out." With a smile and a wave of another green folder, she said, "I'll just wait until you come back, and then you can take your time looking over this new information."

Tim leaned across the desk, grabbed the folder, and sat back down. Between giggles, Stacey managed to say, "Sure wish I had a video camera so you could see the look on your face."

Tim rewarded her with a larger smile of his own as he began studying the few papers in the folder. One was a copy of Jeff's honorable discharge. This was not something that was going to help his investigation. His face took on a mask of uncertainty, causing his eyes to flash impatience and his smile to turn sour as if he had just drunk curdled milk. Within seconds, an even bigger smile gained possession of his face as he noticed the form documenting a fight between a chief warrant officer named Warren Wright and S.Sgt. Jeffrey Weaver.

For some unknown reason, a court-martial that was scheduled had been postponed several times; and in the end, the paperwork had never made it to the courtroom. To Tim, that spelled *unusual* in capital letters.

His first thought started spiraling toward a payoff. It was not something that happened a lot in the army, but it was possible. He continued to read further into the report and found that Jeff had only received an Article 15—another thing out of the ordinary. Usually, when a court-martial was recommended, it was only a matter of time before a court date was set. A fight with an officer was deemed as a serious offense, and an enlisted soldier usually didn't get off so easily. Red flags began waving in front of Tim. Something definitely was off kilter there. The only thing that Tim knew about an Article 15 was that it was a nonjudicial punishment available only to commanders. This meant that a commander had the right to issue an Article 15 instead of slapping a court-martial charge against the accused and spending many days in court. This gave the authority to the commanding officer to decide the verdict, guilty or not guilty. It was up to the soldier to relay his version of the incident and convince the officer of his innocence.

Tim continued reading the recorded statement, hoping to find some insight as to how Jeff had obviously convinced the officer not to court-martial him. He continued leafing through the pages of the report, almost missing the crucial information. According to Jeff, being sworn in under oath, he was proceeding to leave the Officers Club one evening around ten o'clock when Chief Warrant Officer Warren Wright approached him, in a bit of a drunken state, and began pushing him and shouting that he didn't want him occupying a seat on his plane anymore. He said he was sick of Jeff trying to tell him how to fly a plane. If he wanted to fly close to the ground and cause the Vietcong to deplete their ammunition supply by shooting at him, then so be it. He would fly as low to the ground as he wanted. He was the commander in charge, and Jeff was nothing more than a peon waiting to take orders. The report also stated that Jeff had punched Warren so hard and so fast that he had been knocked to the ground. Bystanders kept Warren from retaliating. Another red flag went up for Tim. Hitting an officer was like signing your death warrant in the army. How did Jeff get away with only an Article 15? Tim kept reading, hoping to find some answers. The second page of the report repeated Jeff's claim of innocence, stating that Officer Wright had instigated the fight when he bestowed the first shove.

Tim was beginning to get a bit frustrated. The reason for the fight had definitely been established and reported. He was only interested in the outcome, and this report was very vague. Hitting an officer was all the more reason for a court-martial. So how did Jeff get his punishment reduced? Tim concluded that he must be missing something somewhere. He got up from his desk, poured more coffee into his mug, and sat down again. He was going to read this again and again, until he found something of significance. He was tired, but he wasn't ready to give up on this case just yet. He had to get a better feel for what had happened. Someone in the crowd that night had to have seen the initial argument. He may not be able to find one of those bystanders, but he was pretty sure he could track down Chief Warrant Officer Warren Wright.

CHAPTER 28

Above all else, guard your heart, for it is the wellspring of life.

—Proverbs 4:23

Stacey's desk was positioned in the middle of the front office so that no one came in or out of the building without her knowledge. That was where everyone expected to find her, but today she couldn't sit still. She was so elated with the information that she had given to Tim that she began prancing around the office like a cat on a hot tin roof waiting for his approval. Everything she did was for Tim. She had been trying to suppress her crush on him for quite some time, but it only seemed to get worse. He was oblivious to all the attention she gave him. She knew how he liked his women, and she did all that she could do to fit into that category. He was so convinced that he would never find anyone like his late wife that he was blind to the woman who, at the moment, not only stood in front of him but also stood beside him through all his business and personal tragedies. She implied many times about her feelings for him, but he somehow always managed to sidestep the situation and to treat her as only a secretary. She had worked long and hard to get this news for him. Maybe now he would at least acknowledge her passion for the truth. She was watching him read the report when his eyebrows shot up in surprise. Seeing the gleam of interest in his eyes, she smiled in contentment.

He stood up, beaming with satisfaction. "This calls for a celebration. Are you hungry? How 'bout grabbing a burger with me? It's my treat."

Stacey, so overwhelmed with surprise, took a deep, steady breath and stepped back. Tim repeated the question in the same cool tone, looking intently at Stacey, waiting for an answer. "Are you all right? You look like you've just seen a ghost."

"I'm not sure I've *seen* one, but I know I sure *heard* something strange. Did you just ask me out to lunch?"

"Did I commit a crime? Can't a boss ask his secretary out for a burger? What's wrong with you today?"

Stacey wanted to turn and walk out; but she whipped around to face him, blew out a breath, and threw her hands wide. "I'll tell you what's wrong with me today. I have worked for you for the past three years, and that includes a lot of overtime." She gestured a sweeping motion with one arm and said, "Why do you think I do that? Do you think I put in all these hours for the county? I don't get paid enough to do that." Tilting her head back, she peered at his face. "Are you seriously telling me that you have no idea why I stay here so much or why I was just so shocked that you asked me out for a burger? Are you that blind and oblivious to me and to my feelings?"

Before Tim could mutter an answer, Stacey was already leaning over the desk as if ready to pounce. Her eyes were compelling and a bit magnetic. He wasn't exactly sure what he should say or do. To be honest, he was a tad frightened. This was so out of character for Stacey. In all these years, she had never so much as raised her voice to him. He held up a hand to silence her, while she threw up her hands in disgust.

"Stacey, please calm down. I'm sorry if I offended you in any way. I guess I'm being an idiot, but I don't really know what you meant when you said that I've been oblivious to your feelings. What have I said or done that was so insulting to you?"

In an attempt to ease her embarrassment and his as well, Stacey smiled timidly. Tim gave her a larger smile of his own that seemed almost apologetic. As she tried to speak, her voice was fragile and shaky. "I'm so sorry, Tim. I didn't mean for you to find out how I feel about you. I thought you would figure it out on your own. I'm totally embarrassed now, and maybe I could just crawl under the desk for the rest of the day."

Tim leaned forward on his elbows and shrugged matter-of-factly. "You know, I am a detective and usually a pretty darn good one, but you slipped this one right past me. Before I stick my foot in my mouth and embarrass us both even more, why don't you define 'feelings for you' to me so that I don't make a fool of myself again?"

Biting her lip, she looked away, suddenly anxious to escape from his presence. When she tried to speak, her words wavered as if they were stuck in the middle of a tunnel, not knowing how to get out. She became more uncomfortable by the minute until Tim walked forward, stopping in front of her. There was a tingling in the pit of her stomach. She tried to throttle the dizzying current racing through her, but the prolonged anticipation for this moment was almost unbearable. He was looking at her as if he had never seen her before, yet she thought she detected a flicker in his intense eyes. She moved toward him, impelled involuntarily by her own passion, but he turned on his heel and strode to the door. "If we are going out for a burger, we need to go now. We have a lot of work to do."

His voice rang with command as Stacey picked up her purse and walked toward the door. An electrifying shudder reverberated through her as she sighed, already weary of the situation. *Now that Tim saw another side of me, would he still want to work with me, or would he think working together would no longer be feasible?* The phone rang just as she was ready to walk out the door, so she took the time to answer it. She wrote the message and followed her boss.

As Tim crossed the street to the diner, he casually looked over his shoulder to see if Stacey was following him or if she had decided to go home for the day. No sight of her, but he would get a booth, just in case she showed up. He had been truly caught off guard with Stacey's admission of her feelings. He had also been surprised to hear her words echo his own thoughts. If he had allowed his subconscious desires to surface, he may have been the first one to admit that there was a war of emotions raging within him. He seemed to be more afraid of himself than of her. Perhaps he *had* witnessed some of the little insinuations she cast his way, but he always assumed it was his imagination working overtime. She was right. He *was* an idiot. Stacey was a beautiful woman. She was a bit younger than he was, but she had a maturity about her that definitely smoke-screened her age. He shouldn't be afraid to get involved with this woman. She was a loyal, intelligent coworker, a bit like Radar on the television show *M*A*S*H*. She usually knew what he wanted or needed before he actually asked for it. Thinking about that now, he realized that part of their relationship was a bit unnerving. All in all, he knew her to be not only someone he worked with but also a very giving and trusting friend. He hadn't been with a woman in a long time, and the thought of being accountable to someone again was a major consideration. Maybe subconsciously, that was his reason for not dating. He had been on his own for so long that he was convinced that he liked it that way, although Stacey had been the one to actually get him to hang up his coat, and come to think of it, he did a lot of things in the office that she had implemented. Things were getting somewhat clearer now. She had him under her thumb, and he didn't even know it. But she *had* been patient with him, even though he had not been observant about the situation. She obviously had things under control, and somewhere along the way, she had found him lovable.

He was trying to understand her sudden personality change today at the office. She had actually scared him. He hadn't known how to react, so instinct told him to apologize. However, that came out sounding shallow. He just wasn't sure what "feelings" she had for him and how long she had felt this way. As soon as she joined him for lunch, he planned to get answers to all his questions.

Embarrassed and humiliated, Stacey walked across the street to the diner. Even before she opened the double glass doors, she knew exactly where he would be sitting. He was undoubtedly a creature of habit. As she slid into the booth, Tim raised his eyes from the menu, with an easy smile playing at the corners of his mouth as he spoke gently. "I told you I'm treating today, so order whatever you want. You don't have to have a burger."

She grinned back briefly and, with as reasonable a voice as she could manage, said, "Thank you."

Chapter 29

Beware of false prophets which come to you in sheep's clothing, but inwardly they are ravenous wolves.

—Matthew 7:15

Answering the phone had become a full-time job for Abby ever since she placed the ad in the newspaper for a housekeeper at Summer Rain. There obviously were a lot of women looking for work in New Hope. Abby's heart went out to each of them, but she could only afford to hire one. After several phone calls, she developed screening techniques, keeping the interviews to a minimum. She wasn't exactly sure why she took an interest in the latest caller by the name of Joan Martin, but she sensed a bit of adversity in this woman's voice. While talking with her, Abby felt a strange sensation come over her, compelling her to ask the woman to meet with her at Summer Rain as soon as she could get there. Why this sudden urge to see this woman? She knew, even before meeting Joan, that she was going to hire her. It was as if God himself were dictating to her, showing his authority, and expecting her to obey.

When the doorbell rang, Abby jumped, not expecting Mrs. Martin quite so soon. She wished that Shirley could be there with her, but her mother had gone to town to run some errands and wouldn't be back for a few hours. She was on her own for this one, so she did what Shirley would have done. She said a quick prayer and answered the door.

Abby's first impression of Mrs. Martin was not what she was expecting. As the tall blond woman greeted her with a very pretty smile, she also extended her obviously delicately nail-polished hands toward Abby, causing her to think that these weren't exactly the kind of hands that wash windows and scrub floors.

Abby hoped that the tensing of her jaw did not betray her shock. "Hi, I'm Abby Weaver. Won't you come in?" Abby remembered the strength of the feeling that had rocked her gut, indicating that she hire this woman, yet here she was in real life, seeming to be the total opposite of what Abby was looking for. She was dressed impeccably as if interviewing for an office position.

As if reading Abby's mind, Mrs. Martin replied, "I apologize for being so dressed up, but I was just leaving another interview at a small office, and I didn't have time to go home and change."

In a more matter-of-fact tone, she added, "I do have jeans and rubber gloves."

Abby laughed as if sincerely amused, causing a confused look to creep on Mrs. Martin's face. As soon as Abby realized that she was laughing out loud, she began apologizing. "I'm sorry, Mrs. Martin, but when I first opened the door and saw you, I must admit that I was instantly wondering why you were dressed the way you are. I thought you looked like you were dressed for an office interview, and then when you told me that was exactly the reason, I just couldn't keep myself from laughing."

Mrs. Martin indicated by a motion of her head that she was listening, so Abby continued. "This is all new for me." With a swing of her arm, she gestured toward the entire house. "I never dreamed that I would someday have the opportunity to run an establishment such as this. Please come in and sit down. Would you like a glass of tea?"

"No thank you. I'm fine."

Abby motioned for Mrs. Martin to sit over by the window that overlooked the front driveway. Through it, Abby glimpsed Mrs. Martin's car parked next to the porch. It was an older model and looked as if it needed some repairs.

Mrs. Martin began the interview by speaking with a silky voice that barely disguised a challenging tone underneath, causing Abby to wonder just why this woman was here. Was it really for the job, or was she the town gossip, ready to spread rumors? Abby remembered Lilly's attitude at the diner. Maybe this woman was here to reiterate whatever it was that was circulating about Summer Rain and its owner. She quickly dismissed those pestilent thoughts when she realized that Mrs. Martin had stopped talking, and a cast-iron look of despair had begun to spread over her face.

Abby awkwardly cleared her throat, struggling with the uncertainty that this woman was causing in her mind. "Mrs. Martin, I am in dire need of a housekeeper, and obviously, you are in dire need of a job. As I look at the way you're dressed, your long nails, and high heels, I have to ask if this is a job that you really want to do or can do. Please understand how it looks from my point of view. I need someone who is loyal and trustworthy and isn't afraid of hard work. As much as I am planning to run a successful business, I also know that a lot of that will depend on my staff." Abby looked at Mrs. Martin as she said this, only to find that her lips had twisted into an odd smile, and without warning, an air of pleasure suddenly seemed to surround this mystery lady. Abby, not exactly sure how to continue the interview, offered a smile and said, "I need to see your résumé, and I need you to tell me a little bit about you and your family. You can just tell me anything that you think is important." Abby leaned back in her chair, waiting, not knowing what to expect.

Mrs. Martin began by handing Abby a sheet of paper that looked like a résumé. As she reached across the coffee table, she spoke in a voice that sounded tired. "I have just been laid off at the bank, and I could draw unemployment, but it's just not enough to support myself and my son. He is a sophomore in college, and even though he has a job too, it's barely enough to keep things going. My husband died three years ago of cancer, and he didn't have life insurance. We still had a mortgage on our home, so I had to sell it when my son, Taylor, left for college. It was very important to his father and me that he get a college education. He was on the list for a scholarship provided by a local church camp, and even though he had the highest test scores, the grant was given to someone else." A thin chill seemed to hang on the edge of her words, and her eyes appeared to be hard and filled with dislike. Abby suspected that whoever had been responsible for that decision was one of the reasons that these steel blue eyes seemed dangerously dark.

Mrs. Martin was still talking about how she had to go to work just to survive, and because the bank had downsized, she, of course, was the first one to go. The intensity in her voice influenced Abby to be cautious, even though she was so sure of what she was about to do.

Abby stood up and moved closer to Mrs. Martin. She felt that same gut feeling that she had felt when she talked to her on the phone. Ignoring the questioning voice inside her head that kept asking why she would hire this lady, she heard herself ask Mrs. Martin when she could start work. A bit shocked at the abruptness of the question, Mrs. Martin was barely able to control her gasp of surprise. "You mean I got the job? Just like that?"

"Just like that. I'm not in the habit of making fast decisions, but something tells me that you are going to help make a difference here at Summer Rain. I'm counting on you to not make a liar out of me. But I still need an answer. When can you start?"

Mrs. Martin, girding herself with resolve, stood up and, while shaking Abby's hand, spoke without inflection. "I'll be here first thing in the morning." As an afterthought, her mouth eased into a smile and she added, "With jeans and rubber gloves." Abby returned the smile and walked with her to the front door. As she watched her newest employee back out of the driveway, she could not stop herself from wondering if her impulsive actions would come to haunt her in the following days. There was just something about this woman that touched her heart in a most unfamiliar way.

As much as she didn't want to admit it, there seemed to be some underlying mystery surrounding Joan Martin. Whatever is was, she was going to trust that Shirley would be the one to discover it. She was much better equipped emotionally to handle the situation.

CHAPTER 30

For I was hungry and you gave me food, I was thirsty and you gave me drink, I was a stranger and you welcomed me.

—Matthew 25:35

Abby answered the door at precisely eight o'clock the next morning. True to her word, Joan was dressed in jeans and carried with her a bright yellow pair of rubber gloves. Her well-worn sneakers were in need of a washing machine, and her strawberry blond hair seemed to be escaping from her ponytail in glossy strands around her face. It was quite the contrast from yesterday's business attire.

Abby, conscious that she was staring, dragged her gaze back up to Joan's face and motioned for her to step inside. As their eyes locked, Abby couldn't help but notice the thick ebony lashes. Joan's eyes then became flat and unreadable as stone when she thought she saw Abby's face show signs of doubt. Within seconds, there seemed to be an unspoken challenge in the depths of Joan's midnight eyes.

A ping of caution erupted in Abby's chest. *Was this woman here simply for the job, or did she have other ulterior motives?* Abby felt a deep sense of shame for being so skeptical. Just because the woman had a strange look on her face didn't make her a criminal.

Abby tried to speak in a jesting tone but questioned exactly how she sounded to this obviously very nervous woman. "Forgive me for staring, but I hardly recognize you."

Joan's smooth smile betrayed nothing of her annoyance. "I'm sure that I must look different, but this is really my typical style. I don't have much of a chance to dress up any more."

Abby usually spoke clearly about what she was thinking, and this time was no different. "Well, actually, I was wondering how you can look so good even in work clothes."

Joan was caught off guard, not expecting Abby to be so complimentary. "Thank you, Ms. Weaver. I appreciate that. I don't get many compliments anymore either."

"Come in, and I'm going to let Shirley show you around and let you know exactly what your responsibilities will be. Do you know Mrs. Black?"

Joan felt instantly guilty again. Mrs. Black had attended church with her. She swallowed the guilt and lied casually, "I used to see her come in and out of the bank, but I don't know her personally. I have always heard that she is a wonderful lady."

Abby let out a long sigh as she said, "Indeed she is."

Shirley's footsteps were heard coming down the stairs, and within seconds, she was hugging Joan as if she were a long lost relative. "It's nice to have you here with our family. I'm sure you're going to be a great asset to our staff." Before Joan knew what was happening, Shirley had her by the hand and was leading her toward the kitchen, chatting all the way.

CHAPTER 31

For where envying and strife is, there is confusion and every evil work.

—James 3:6

The rich earth scent of dew, damp grass, and flowering trees connected with Joan's nose as she pushed up the window in her bedroom. A breeze, a little stronger than she anticipated, caused a stack of papers to go airborne. She bent over to pick them up and saw that one of them was a copy of her résumé. She felt tears prick her eyes at the thought of what she had done and what she was about to do. She wanted to scream aloud at the injustice that had brought her to this point. It wasn't that her résumé was totally false; she just hadn't told the entire truth. Half truths and evasion seemed to come so easy for her these days. Did she really need to convey information about her volunteer work at the church? There was no changing the past, and she needed this job with Ms. Weaver, even if it did mean scrubbing floors on her hands and knees. Joan only answered the questions that Ms. Weaver had asked her, giving her limited information, hoping that she didn't delve too much into the past. Obviously, she had given the right answers because Ms. Weaver had hired her on the spot.

Joan ran the brush through her hair one more time, made sure she had a rubber band in her pocket that would allow her to pull her unruly hair into a ponytail, grabbed her purse, and went out the door, praying that her car would start. Praying—now that was a bit of a stretch. What made her think that God would help a woman who not only had violated his commandment of "Thou shalt not steal" but also had cost a man his godly calling and his virtuous standing in the community?

First turn of the key, and the motor purred. Joan smiled as she quickly embraced the thought that maybe this was a sign of how the day was going to progress. The idea of being someone's maid weaved an unsettling path through her consciousness. She suddenly felt ill-equipped to take on this job. Wrestling with guilt and constant thoughts of more revenge was taking a toll on her emotionally and physically. Antacids were now a regular staple in her diet along with sleeping pills at night. She had the same thoughts when she went to bed as when she woke up. There were questions that burned her mind like hot lava. Why had Pastor Davidson never implicated her in the crime? She wanted to tell him so many times why she had done it, even though she was sure he knew. That in itself was disturbing to her. Why would he just let her walk away after she had ruined his life? Why hadn't he come and confronted her? Why would he take the blame for something that he hadn't done? Who did he think he was? Jesus? Was he just waiting till she broke down and turned herself in? Most of all, she just wanted him to explain why he had chosen someone else for the scholarship.

Facts were facts. If the scholarship would have been given to the most deserving boy, her son, she would never have become so desperate. Her heart hadn't been able to handle this new emotion. Its mere presence in her life made her feel small and insignificant; at the same time, it yielded strength in areas that she never had before. Without desperation, she never would have blamed the pastor for the decision he made, nor would she have opened the safe and taken the money. Desperation caused a powerful rush of unfamiliar feelings. It prompted the nauseating feeling of despair, enough to shatter the last shreds of her control. It was like standing at the edge of a frigid river, not knowing if you could survive the strong current. But you jumped anyhow because you felt you had nowhere else to go. Surprisingly, you realized that the icy water was very invigorating. Then you got really cold, and that initial reaction of satisfaction turned to fear that coiled in the pit of your stomach.

Someone blew the horn, jolting her back to reality. She pushed the gas pedal and watched as an impatient motorist passed her while offering an obscene gesture. She felt the need to return the favor but offered a princess wave instead.

To her annoyance, her mind kept going back in time. It had all started when her husband died unexpectedly, leaving her with a stack of bills and no life insurance. Her son, Taylor, was a senior in high school and had great aspirations to go to college. Without his father's income, the possibility of that happening was slim to none. That was when the camp scholarship became available, and Taylor applied. It was based on scholastic achievement, family income, and community involvement, all of which Taylor qualified. Pastor Davidson was chairman of the camp board and had the final decision. Joan was so sure he would make Taylor the recipient that, when he chose someone else, both she and her son were devastated. She was appalled. She had given many hours of her time to this church, without pay, and this was the thanks she received?

Every Monday morning, the cash offering from Sunday was delivered to Harley to be placed in the safe. Joan never knew the exact amount, but it had been quite a while since any money had been withdrawn, so she knew the amount had to be substantial. What could it hurt if she borrowed a few thousand for a short time? She planned to pay it back as soon as possible. It seemed like a foolproof plan, and no one needed to know. It was essential that she pay her son's tuition for his first semester at college. After that, he would have to get a job. Besides, it was Pastor Davidson's fault that her son didn't get that scholarship. He knew how badly her son needed it.

Some of Joan's anger had slowly and unwillingly evaporated in the past two years, leaving her even more confused about the reason why Pastor Davidson had never revealed her part in the crime. She held him accountable for that too. Knowing that he had taken the rap for her offense only deepened her animosity toward him.

A deep sense of shame washed over her as her mind drifted through these thoughts. She could feel the heat stealing into her face. She pulled down the sun visor that exposed a tiny mirror and was mortified by her crimson red cheeks. She quickly found her brush and powder in the pocket of her purse and proceeded to swipe it across her face.

Nearing the driveway to Summer Rain, she saw a man dressed in somewhat shabby clothes walking along the road. He had a familiar gait to his walk, but the hood on his sweatshirt was covering his hair and face, keeping his identity secret. She looked in the rearview mirror as she passed this familiar stranger, trying to get another chance to see his face, but his head was lowered as if he were counting his steps.

As she drove into her parking spot, pulled the key from the ignition, and reached for her yellow rubber gloves, another emotion ripped through her like shards of glass cutting into her last ounce of dignity—jealously. She was bringing rubber gloves with her to work. How humiliating. Holding her tears in check, she sat staring at the stately house. She knew Ms. Weaver was a widow, just like herself, but the difference she guessed would be the actions of the late husbands. Ms. Weaver's husband obviously loved her enough to make sure she was taken care of if something happened to him, while Joan's husband had been negligent about her future. Now instead of being able to own a house, she only got to scrub floors in one. She knew, just from spending so many hours with Pastor Davidson, that coveting anything was wrong, but this just didn't seem fair. She had also heard him quote Shakespeare on this particular subject so many times that she knew the line by heart. "O, beware, my lord, of jealousy! It is the green-eyed monster which doth mock the meat it feeds on." For the first time, she actually understood its meaning.

As she stepped out of her car, she caught sight of the mystery man walking up the driveway. There was just something so familiar about him, but she still couldn't see his face. Why would he be coming to Summer Rain, and why wasn't he driving a car? Not wanting to meet face to face with this stranger, she shut the car door, hurried up the front steps, and rang the doorbell. The door opened, and she stepped inside.

CHAPTER 32

But each person is tempted when he is lured and enticed by his own desire.

—James 1:14

As soon as Shirley took charge of Joan, she seemed to relax a bit. The man outside had, for some reason, given her an eerie feeling. Shirley took her to the back of the house, where a walk-in pantry—the size of a room—became the hub of her job. Everything from toilet bowl cleaner to vinegar was on the shelves. It reminded Joan of a small convenience store.

Shirley was explaining how they kept such a precise inventory and that part of Joan's job would be keeping the shelves stocked. As they moved through the house, Shirley acquainted her with each room and what would be expected of her. She soon realized that her duties were going to include more than cleaning and changing bedsheets. She was going to have a key to the house and be in charge of a checking account for the necessary items that she would need to buy for Summer Rain. A twinge of guilt collided with her heart when Shirley handed her the checkbook. Knowing what she had done in the past with the church money made her doubt her own morality. She wanted to be an honest woman. She never meant to steal the money from the church safe, but desperation had given her strength to do something that she never would have thought of before. She had every intention of replacing it before anyone found out, but things hadn't worked out that way. If only she would have confessed right away, Pastor Davidson would still have his job and his reputation, and she wouldn't be living with so many plans for retaliation. As much as she tried to let it go, there was a small part of her that just couldn't seem to release the past. The last few years had carved a hardness to her usually cheerful nature, and she felt as if the devil himself were taking advantage of her every doubt and weakness.

Shirley asked if she would like to see the gardens, and Joan enthusiastically replied, "Yes, I would love to."

As they made their way out the back door onto the patio, Joan caught sight of the mystery man again. He was working down by the fence next to the road. His hood was no longer on his head, but his back was toward the house, and she still couldn't see his face. Shirley had obviously not seen him, or surely, she would have made a comment. Joan said nothing as she followed Shirley on the well-worn path through the trees.

CHAPTER 33

Therefore do not worry about tomorrow, for tomorrow will worry about itself. Each day has enough trouble of its own.

—Matthew 6:34

After looking at the gardens, Shirley and Joan made their way back into the house, and Joan started in the kitchen by washing the morning's breakfast dishes. As she stood at the sink, she could look out the window and observe the gardens near the garage. She almost dropped a dish when the mystery man came walking up the path. She felt the blood drain from her face. It was Pastor Davidson. No more hood covering his face. It was him, plain as day. Was he the new gardener? He had a pair of tree trimmers in his hand and was pulling a small garden cart. Why hadn't someone told her that he was going to be here every day? What was she going to do? She stepped out of view just as he stopped by the bush under the window and began to trim its branches. Until she could figure out what to do, she needed to stay out of his sight.

Joan's day ended at five o'clock. She said her good-byes to Shirley and decided to exit by the side door, hoping to have a better chance to slip into her car and drive away without being seen. She wondered if Harley had recognized her car. Did he know that she was working there? Her mind was racing in high speed, her heart hammering. A shimmering wave of pulsing fury clouded everything. She would have to make a decision: be employed and walk on eggshells every day, expecting to run into Harley, or quit a job that paid a decent salary and had good working conditions. Her mood veered sharply to anger. How could this be happening? It had been two years since she had any contact with Harley, and now without warning, she was thrust into working side by side with this man again.

She gave in to the tears as soon as she sank into her worn-out couch. It had been a long time since she yielded to uncontrollable sobs, so she allowed them to flow until they subsided to sniffles. The stress at work caused by Pastor Davidson had unleashed something within her. She was feeling anger pouring through her, boiling her blood, and clouding her brain. She was not going to let this man unnerve her just because he too was employed at Summer Rain. She needed to keep this job, but going to work every day, knowing that she might cross paths with him, was just too much tension and could possibly affect her job performance just as it had affected her driving abilities. It was essential that she come up with a plan to initiate his dismissal.

Joan's third day at work proved to be one of importance. Abby introduced her to Harley. She doubted that she could look him in the face without showing guilt, but for several surprising seconds, she stared at him. She was determined not to give way to her fears as she met his piercing eyes. Harley composed his face to be completely expressionless. His blank stare was really beginning to piss her off. Was he going to admit that they knew each other? Should she be the first one to enlighten Abby about their association?

Before she could respond, Harley answered in a tense, clipped voice that forbade any questions. "Yes, Joan and I know each other from a few years ago. She was a member of my church."

Abby smiled, thinking about how this would be a great balance of support for both of them, but her smile faded as she realized something else seemed to be happening. The air was thick with unspoken emotions. Abby had a lot questions to ask but decided against it. These were two adults who would have to work out their differences if they were to continue working for her. She would give them some time to find a solution before she became involved. Maybe Shirley would have some insight. Instead, Abby made a silent exit and returned to the front desk.

Harley and Joan were still floundering in an agonizing maelstrom. Neither wanted to be the first to speak. Joan felt guilty and selfish, yet retaliation plans kept creeping into her thoughts. Harley, on the other hand, clung to reality, praying he would not betray his agitation. An inexplicable look of withdrawal came over his face as he broke down and said, "It's nice to see you again, Joan. I'm glad things are working out for you." With that, he picked up his tools and returned to the garden.

Tossing her hair across her shoulders in a gesture of defiance, Joan turned on her heel and strode to the side door. She too had work that must be done before she went home.

CHAPTER 34

For the vision is yet for an appointed time; but at the end it will speak, though it tarries, wait for it because it will surely come.

—Habakkuk 2:3

Harley couldn't believe his eyes. How was it possible that Joan Martin could end up working in the same establishment as he did? He hadn't seen her in two years, and now it might be an everyday occurrence. He was surprised at his relatively calm reaction when Abby introduced them. It had been all he could do not to lash out at this woman who had ruined his life and jog her memory about the way she had wronged him. He hung the tree trimmers on the rack inside the shed, took a water bottle from his backpack, and retreated into the woods. He found a bench and sat down. With his head in his hands, he pleaded with God for wisdom. It wasn't the first time that he had begged the Almighty to deliver him out of his bondage. He felt a bit like Joseph, who had been thrown into a deep hole by his brothers. He had given this whole issue to God ten minutes after it happened, and he had been anticipating an answer ever since. Just how was he supposed to handle this? Maybe it was time to confront Joan. He always expected her life to be overshadowed with guilt and to confess to the church elders, but obviously, she had channeled her anger about the scholarship toward another venue. He wondered if she found revenge to be as sweet as rumored. He thought he had done a noble thing to suck up his pain and leave her alone. Now he couldn't afford to care or indulge himself in emotions that would only lead to disaster. Was it God's way of extracting patience from him by throwing another barricade his way?

CHAPTER 35

What is twisted cannot be straightened; what is lacking cannot be counted.

—Ecclesiastes 1:15

Joan wrestled with her emotions every morning when she climbed out of bed. She seemed to have acquired full custody of every memory since the day her world crumbled. Today her memory was dredging up the day when gossip took over. Once word got out that money had been stolen from the church, the chatter started. Fingers automatically pointed to the pastor, especially when the rumor declared that a considerable amount of cash was kept in the safe in his office and that he had been taking money in small amounts, thinking no one would notice.

The part about the large amount of cash was true. The benevolence fund was retained in cash for immediate use to a family in need. The only ones approved for access to the safe were board members and Pastor Davidson, but Joan had accidently come across the combination while retrieving some papers for Harley in his office and had memorized the numbers. In the five years that Harley served at Morning Son, there had only been a few times when cash had been withdrawn from the safe. A percentage of each month's offerings increased the total, allowing it to become quite large over the years.

Dennis Miller, financial trustee, appeared one morning in Harley's office, requesting cash for a local family whose house had just burned to the ground. The money was kept in a custom-made wooden chest that housed a locked safe. It sat next to the pastor's desk, supporting his small printer. When Dennis arrived, Harley offered him the use of his desk so that he could grab a quick cup of his favorite coffee at the convenient store next door. When Harley returned, he found a copy of the withdrawal slip for two thousand dollars laying on his desk. Dennis had documented the amount of cash in the safe, took it back to his office, and compared it to the amount on record. There was a missing sum of ten thousand dollars.

It had been the very next day when, without warning, the door flew open, and five board members entered the church office, looking for Pastor Davidson. Joan remembered it so well. Panic like she had never known before welled in her throat. The board members never noticed the color draining from her face or how badly her hands shook when she knocked on Harley's door. They had one thing and one thing only on their minds—a conviction. No trial, no jury, just five men who formed a posse, acting as if they were about to string up a horse thief.

Joan had held back tears as she listened as they accused Harley of stealing money, and she watched as his knees buckled and as he collapsed into his chair. He had looked up at her as she stood in the doorway; his expression of pained tolerance told her that he knew she was guilty. She waited for him to turn her over to the posse. Instead, he let out a slow, controlled breath and held up both hands in a classic gesture of innocence; and with desperation in his voice, she heard him say, "Gentlemen, I'm not exactly sure what you're talking about, but I assure you that what you are implying is not true."

Mr. Walker, the leader of the group, leaned over the desk, his black eyes impaling Harley's blue ones. The black ones were stony with anger. The blue ones darkened with emotions. "Pastor Davidson, there's an emergency board meeting scheduled for this evening at seven."

The memories of that day frequently affected her perception of life, and it seemed more confusing now than before she became the housekeeper at Summer Rain. Having an income was supposed to make her life more comfortable and financially stable. Instead, her shrewdness was affecting her common sense and her ability to discern. The more she tried to reflect on the good years with Pastor Davidson, the more her spirit became offended. She staunchly constructed a mountain around her heart with Harley and God on one side and her on the other. She wasn't sure if she could ever meet both of them on the top. Her awareness of the wrong she was judging seemed minor compared to the justification she felt she was entitled to. Her self-esteem and her trust in God had been fractured. In between the splinters of that break, evil had forced its way in, absorbing her former prudence.

As hard as it was to admit, she was actually enjoying her position at Summer Rain. Shirley and Abby had embraced her as part of their family and always made her feel like she was a vital part of their household. Now that Harley was part of that household too, she was fighting her emotions every day for some form of insight into how to go around this stumbling block or find a way to leap over it. Leaping over would mean that she was going to forgive Harley and come clean with a confession. Going around it meant that she could possibly influence another assault on Harley. She had never been so confused in her life. One minute, she was ready to run to Harley and ask him for forgiveness; and the next, she was planning more ways to make his life miserable.

She pulled the sheets out of the dryer just as Abby came into the laundry room. "Hello, Joan. How are you today?"

Joan felt irritable and unhappy with herself, and it came across in her voice. It was dripping with misery. "I'm fine, Ms. Weaver. Did you need me to do something right now?"

Seeing the change in Joan ever since her encounter with Harley in the garden made Abby curious. *What was it about these two that caused such tension?* Joan was walking around as if carrying a huge chip on her shoulder, and Harley made sure that he wasn't anywhere inside the house during Joan's working hours.

Abby found Shirley in the sunroom with a cookbook open on her lap. Her head was leaning against the chair, and her eyes were closed. Normally, she wouldn't have disturbed her, but she felt that this was important. She called her name quietly until Shirley opened her eyes. Within seconds, she was sliding her reading glasses off her nose and rubbing her temples.

"I'm sorry, Mom. I didn't want to wake you, but I need your input in a situation. It's about Harley and Joan. Do you know the reason why they don't like each other?"

"They don't like each other? Why would you say that?"

"Haven't you noticed the distance that they keep between each other?"

Shirley looked up at her and admitted, "I have no proof, only a hunch."

"A hunch about what?"

"Like I said, it's only my opinion. I think Joan had something to do with Harley's dismissal from the church. I did a little investigation, and as I said, I have no proof, but I think, in her mind, she felt that she had a valid motive to do what she did."

"A motive for what? What did she do?"

"Harley had the final say as to who received a camp scholarship from the church. Joan felt that her son, Taylor, should have been given the grant. Not only had he passed all the requirements but his mother also was a longtime volunteer who worked closely with Harley and was in desperate need of financial aid. When Harley assigned the subsidy to another student, she became very insulted. A short time after that, Harley was accused of embezzlement."

Abby was speechless. How could she have been so wrong about Joan? She had truly believed that God had sent this woman and that she was going to be part of Abby's mission at Summer Rain.

"Abby, I told you that it was only my thoughts. There was no proof, but I'm not sure anyone even thought of confronting her. I tried my best to initiate an investigation beyond Harley, but a certain quartet of women decided his fate, and heaven forbid that anyone would question their verdict."

There was no smile in Abby's voice as she questioned her mother. "So what do we do?"

"I don't think we should do anything right now. She deserves a chance to either refute my misgivings about her or validate our suspicions. We want to give her the benefit of the doubt until we witness a distinct wrongdoing."

"So how long do we wait?"

"Oh, I don't think it will be long. I've seen her watch him through a window, and her eyes are filled with a ruthless determination. What exactly she's determined to do I'm not sure, but if looks could kill, she'd need a permit for those eyes. She has the gaze of a hawk focused on prey. I hope she proves me wrong, but the nagging in the back of my mind is refusing to be stilled."

Standing abruptly to end the conversation, Shirley glanced out the window and, without saying another word, moseyed to the kitchen. Abby too decided to quietly disappear and avoid the drama. Conflict was not something she took pleasure in. That was one reason she hadn't confronted Shirley about her trusting ways with Joan. Abby thought it might have been a little too early to surrender the house checking account and the key to the safe to the newly appointed housekeeper. However, Abby had found her mother to have prodigious instincts when it came to discovering someone's intention. She totally relinquished her authority on that subject to Shirley.

CHAPTER 36

Keep your tongue from evil and your lips from speaking deceit.

—Psalm 34:13

The parking lot at the café was full as usual, but Joan found a spot near the side door just big enough for her small car. Brisk and businesslike, she swept into the diner, indicating to Lilly that she would take the booth in the back. Her body movement was evidence that she was in a big rush. A wicked gleam burned in her eyes as they made contact with Lilly. She raised her hand to her mouth as if drinking—her way of telling Lilly to hurry with the coffee.

Even though Joan Martin wasn't one of her favorite people, Lilly knew that, ever since her husband's death, things had not been good; so this morning, she would give her the benefit of the doubt and do her best to be civil. As she poured the coffee, Joan said nothing except "I need cream." Lilly pulled three packets from her apron pocket, laid it on the table along with the menu, smothered a groan, and turned toward the kitchen. She was not in the mood to coddle another pissy customer, especially this one. Out of the corner of her eye, she saw Martha Bentley, a friend of Joan's, hurriedly lower herself into the same booth.

As the two friends exchanged a polite, simultaneous smile, Joan spoke in a troubled voice. "Thanks for meeting me here."

"Sure. Anytime. You know if there's food involved, I'll be here. Did you order yet?"

"No, I was waiting for you. Do you want coffee?"

"No, actually, I think I'll have a cup of tea."

Joan was already motioning for Lilly to come back to their table to take their orders when Martha looked at Joan and said, "What's so important that you needed to see me right away?"

"I thought you should know. I got a new job."

"Wow, that's wonderful. What are you doing, and who are you working for?"

Joan felt a shudder of humiliation and was angry at herself for being embarrassed. After all, Martha was her best friend and had stood beside her for the past several years in everything that happened to her. She had helped her survive the days and months following her husband's funeral. She had felt sorry for her when Taylor was passed over for the scholarship. She had even kept her secret about the money. But Joan was about to ask her for another favor. She was going to ask her to keep another secret. Was she brazen enough to expect so much from her friend? She had no choice. She needed an alibi. She had been living in hell for the past two years, blaming the pastor for her constant anxiety, and because of it, she now had a stomach ulcer. Revenge had been pacifying itself by patiently waiting on the edge of her heart, ready to pounce at just the right moment, and now that moment had come.

Martha leaned forward and lowered her voice. "Joan, are you all right? You look as if you've seen a ghost."

"Well, in a weird sort of way, I have, only he's as real as the desert is dry."

Martha's mouth dipped into an even deeper frown as she spoke in a voice so chilling that it surprised even her. "Joan, in simple words, tell me what you have done, and who is he?"

Joan's face contorted in concentration. She had to say the perfect words to Martha, or she might not go along with the plan. "*He* is Pastor Davidson, and I haven't done anything yet, but when I have everything worked out, I know for sure that I'll need your help."

Before Joan could say anything else, Martha began shaking her head disapprovingly. "I can't be a part of anything else. Why can't you let this go? You got away with a felony. Why do you want to go down that path again?" Martha leaned back, suppressing a sigh. What was happening to her friend?

Joan was quick to respond, her face set in a vicious expression. "You may think that I'm not the victim here, but I am. My whole life changed because of that man. He was in a position to help, and he turned his back. He was always there for me when I needed help, and then he just turned on me."

Martha interrupted. "He did not turn on you, Joan. He obviously felt that the other boy needed the scholarship more than Taylor."

Joan folded her arms across her chest in a defensive gesture, and in a softer, more menacing tone of voice, she quickly spoke. "So are you saying that you won't help me this time? You're the only one who even cares a little bit about Taylor and me." With a quiet emphasis, she added, "I thought I could count on you."

Martha nervously ran her hands through her hair while her gaze came to rest on Joan's questioning eyes. She leaned across the table and lowered her voice. "I want to help you, but I don't know if I can. It's hard for me too, you know. The truth is I've actually aided and abetted a criminal, and if you get caught, so do I. You're my best friend, but I'm not sure I'm willing to go down with you just because you have the revenge bug biting you all the time. I have to know what you need from me and what you expect of me. Until I know, I can't make a commitment." She blinked, then focused her gaze, and continued. "By the way, you still haven't told me about your new job."

A nasty smile spread across Joan's lips. "I actually can't believe this is all playing out the way it is. I couldn't have planned it any better myself. Even though I'm a bit embarrassed about what I'm doing, it's a job." Martha kept her expression under stern restraint while she waited for Joan to continue.

"I'm working for Abby Weaver. She's the new owner of the bed-and-breakfast out on Willow Road." The sneer she managed not to show on her face was very present in the tone of her voice as she said, "I'm the new housekeeper. Can you believe it? I've been working for three days now, and other than wearing rubber gloves a few hours a day, it's actually not a bad job. And like I said, my attempt to revive my revenge plot just fell into my lap. The ghost I mentioned? He's the inn's gardener." Her eyes were filled with contempt when she blurted out the words.

Martha's jaw dropped open in surprise as she sucked in a shallow breath. She spat out the words contemptuously. "*You* are going to be a housekeeper? How are you getting revenge at the pastor by getting dirt under your fingernails? Are you trying to get us thrown in jail? Why do I have to get involved?"

Joan held up her hands in protest as Martha continued firing questions. "Martha, please calm down. Neither one of us are going to jail. I've only been working for three days. I need some time to fine-tune my plan. It might take a while for it to come to fruition, but when it does, you'll be real proud of me."

Martha hated the wounded-animal look in her friend's eyes as if she had just been hit by a truck and was pretending not to be hurt. She could feel herself being drawn with mesmerizing force into Joan's trap when her thoughts were abruptly interrupted by the waitress, asking if they had decided what they were having for breakfast.

Joan was quick to speak. "We'll both have the breakfast special, and could you make it quick because I have to get to work, and I can't be late? Thanks."

Lilly nodded. If these two only knew how she was counting the minutes until she saw their backsides going out the door, they would be stunned at how fast she could make eggs appear on their plate. She wasn't in the habit of tuning in to customers' conversations, but something was going on between these two. She knew they were good friends, so why was the tension between them today thicker than one of George's steaks? Even though she hadn't meant to, she had caught a few words, and one of them was "Pastor Davidson." Everyone knew him as Pastor Harley. He was an icon in the town. People looked up to him and valued his opinion.

More than 70 percent of the population of New Hope attended a church, yet less than twenty people had stood up on Harley's behalf when he had been accused of developing sticky fingers. Lilly was one of the town residents who believed in him. She had put an end to many conversations about "the preacher gone bad." Comments made about Harley usually got pommeled like hail in a summer storm from Lilly. Her words were simply spoken and right to the point. How dare these friends, these Christian friends turn on a man who had bent over backward to help with whatever problem they brought him?

Joan was waving her hand, motioning for Lilly to bring the check. Lilly gladly ripped the receipt from the pad, walked the few steps to the table, and very politely handed it to Joan. She bit her lip to stifle the questions that she wanted to ask these two ladies. She had heard enough of their conversation to know that Harley had been the main topic during their breakfast. According to their facial expressions, things were a bit strained. Lilly resolved to let her patience win. If these ladies were up to something, they no doubt would come back to their favorite booth and finish the plan. When they did, Lilly would make sure she overheard the conversation.

CHAPTER 37

A wife of noble character who can find? She is worth far more than rubies.

—Proverbs 31:10

Lilly's shift was almost over, and she had a date tonight with Warren. He was taking her to the Mountain House again, so she needed extra time to get ready. Maybe she could ask his opinion concerning Joan Martin. It would be good to get a man's view of the situation.

When she arrived as usual, Warren was captivated at the first sight of Lilly. Sitting across from her in the restaurant convinced him that his one-night stands were past chapters in his life. He found himself counting the hours until he could be with Lilly. Even though they had only been together for six months, he knew he was going to propose very soon—as soon as he acquired enough nerve. His reason for the visit to the jewelry store had been for looking only, but when he saw the princess-cut baguette-style ring, he thought about Lilly's delicate hands and purchased it. He had it in his pocket tonight, although he wasn't quite sure about asking her. He was so afraid that she would say no. He thought she was in love with him and not his money, but how could he really be sure? He hadn't known it was possible to love someone so deeply, so completely in such a short time. Lilly awakened something in him that hadn't been touched in years.

"Warren, do you feel all right tonight? You seem preoccupied about something."

"Well, I do have something on my mind tonight. I just don't know how to say it to you."

Lilly braced herself against painful news. Did he bring her out tonight just to say that he didn't want to see her again? She was so sure that Warren was different. She had even dreamed of having a future with him. What had gone wrong? She pressed her lips together in anger. Whatever his reason, she was ready to fight for him. She set her chin in a stubborn line and blurted out, "You're dumping me, just like that? And you had to bring me to a high-end restaurant to do it? Wasn't the parking lot at the diner good enough?"

Warren's tight expression relaxed into a smile. "You think I want to break up with you?

You think that's what this is about?"

Lilly shrugged, allowing some anger to fade, leaving only confusion. Warren, galvanized by her reaction, stood from his chair and within seconds was sinking to one knee beside her. He was clutching a small velvet box in his right hand and was holding it in front of Lilly. His face was turning red as if he were a teenage boy, confessing love for the first time.

Lilly's thought process changed in an instant. She couldn't believe what she was seeing, and Warren couldn't believe what he was doing. Customers had stopped eating their dinners and were watching the drama play out in front of them. Without waiting any longer, Warren spoke with as reasonable a voice as he could manage. "Lilly, will you marry me? Will you let me take care of you and love you as I've never loved anyone else? Will you let me do these things for the rest of our lives?" He rigidly held his tears in check as he waited for a reaction from Lilly. He had never felt so blissfully happy and terrified all at the same time.

Lilly stared wordlessly across at him, her heart pounding. Nothing could have prepared her for the mind-blowing intensity of this moment. This man, who could make a woman weak in the knees with just a glance, wanted her. He wanted to marry her, be with her for the rest of his life. Tears filled her eyes as light overflowed her soul. She wanted to lean into the safety of this moment, to be assured that life would always be pure and unsullied as it was right now. She pressed a kiss in his palm before replying delightedly. "Yes, I will marry you."

Warren expelled a long breath and wiped the tears from his face, stricken with the splendor that he had just witnessed. Lilly was going to be his wife, and it couldn't be soon enough.

Lilly felt as if she were being transported on a soft and wispy cloud as Warren kissed first her nose and then her eyes, and finally, he satisfyingly kissed her soft mouth.

Everyone in the room was clapping, and some of the men were whistling. Warren bowed from the waist in a courtly old-fashioned gesture, then put his arm around Lilly's waist, squeezed her affectionately, and waved his hand in a gesture of dismissal to the remaining patrons of the restaurant.

Once outside, Warren heard Lilly sigh, the sound soft as the slow fall of rain. His heart was so grateful for the opportunity to unlock and share her heart. He made no attempt to hide the fact that he was ecstatically happy. He was sure he felt his toes tingle as he spoke her name again. With a giddy sense of pleasure, she too let her happiness show. Within seconds, he swept her weightless into his arms. She relaxed, sinking into his cushioning embrace. Contentment and peace flowed between them as his lips slowly descended to meet hers.

The next morning, Lilly's eyes were clouded with tears of joy, and it was hard to concentrate on eggs and coffee. Her normal eight hours of sleep had been interrupted with visions of wedding dresses and flowers. Knowing that Warren Wright wanted to marry her was honestly more than Lilly's heart and mind could grasp. She couldn't wait to tell someone, but who? She had no close friends, and she knew telling her mother would somehow end up causing her embarrassment.

Suddenly, she knew who she could tell about her news and what she had overheard at the diner. Stuffed peppers were on the menu at the diner today, and hopefully, Shirley Black would be stopping by for Big George's specialty. Lilly had decided that, based on her gut feeling, Shirley would be the one to tell of Joan's plot. Lilly would show her the new ring and casually allure to Joan and Martha's breakfast chatter.

As luck would have it, Shirley chose to sit in the booth that had earlier cushioned Joan Martin's skinny little backside. Lilly grinned mischievously as she said hello to Mrs. Black. "My, my, Lilly, you look like someone who has a secret." Before she even finished her sentence, Lilly thrust her hand toward Mrs. Black's water glass, nearly knocking it over, and held her hand perfectly still. The generous-sized ring was so vibrant that it reflected the rays of light coming through the window, casting rainbows on the table. Lilly couldn't contain her excitement as she enlightened Mrs. Black with all the details.

After bringing Mrs. Black her meal, Lilly asked if she could occupy the opposite side of the booth while she took her break. Mrs. Black said she would be glad for the company, so Lilly took a seat. She wasn't exactly sure how to initiate the conversation, but Mrs. Black made it easy. "Is there something you want to ask me, dear? It's not that I won't enjoy your company, but I have been in here many times, and you have never asked to sit with me. Can I help you with something?"

Lilly's happy expression turned somber. "I do have something that I think you should know, but I don't want you to think I'm gossiping. I heard something the other day, and I'm 99 percent sure that it involves someone we both know and love." Lilly let out a sigh and continued. "I just found out that Joan Martin is working for you, and I heard her and her friend Martha plotting something. Pastor Harley is also working for you too. Is that right?"

Shirley nodded hesitantly, her eyes narrowing. "Now what is being said about Harley? Do people think he shouldn't have a respectable job? It was Abby's choice to hire Harley and Joan Martin. She didn't know either one of them before their interviews. I think it was divine intervention that brought those two together." Shirley muttered something unintelligible under her breath before she said, "Okay, so what did you hear?"

Lilly leaned toward the middle of the table and, in a voice that was soft but alarming, informed Mrs. Black that Joan was definitely preparing to cause Harley further trouble with the law. She mentioned that Joan had also said that she was positive that charges would be pressed this time. "Whatever she has in mind, it's going to happen at Summer Rain. I thought you would want to know. We both know Harley had nothing to do with the money at the church. I didn't know who the guilty party was, but now I do. If I hear anything else, I'll let you know."

"You do that, dear. I'll be waiting to hear from you."

Lilly promised to keep her ears open if Joan and Martha returned.

CHAPTER 38

He who covers an offense promotes love, but whoever repeats the matter separates close friends.

—Proverbs 17:9

The next day, Lilly watched Joan and Martha as they came in the diner door. As usual, Joan's mouth was moving as fast at the ceiling fan was turning. Martha was trying to disguise her annoyance in front of the diner customers, but Lilly could tell that her responses held a note of impatience. "Joan, what is so important that we meet here again?"

The cynicism of the remark grated on Joan. "I thought you were my best friend, Martha. I thought you were going to help me with my plan."

"I never said I would help you, but I did say I would listen, so that's all I'm going to do right now. Let me decide what I want to eat and then out with it."

Lilly was just bringing the menus to the table when she heard the chilling words. "This time, he's not dealing with a church. These ladies will press charges." Lilly pretended not to hear as she laid the menus on the table, and asked if they both wanted coffee. Each woodenly nodded their heads, and Lilly turned toward the kitchen but not before seeing the ice-cold look of treachery in Joan's eyes. She had been right about these two coming back to the diner to chat about their intentions concerning Harley. Obviously, they thought their cloak-and-dagger agenda could be shadowed by a plate of eggs. Who would ever believe that two friends having breakfast were really planning the framework of a scheme that would entrap and imprison an innocent man?

Lilly returned with their coffee and took their order. Then she pretended to clean the table next to theirs. Clearly, neither Joan nor Martha knew of her relationship with Harley, or they wouldn't have talked so blatantly about him around her. All Lilly could do was not to react to their opinions of him. Martha was trying to be nice and not say anything so derogatory about the former pastor and friend, but Joan was practicing no such restraint. Lilly listened to her as she spewed venom about Harley. He was a pastor, not someone who was used to getting his hands dirty. How did Ms. Weaver think she was going to rely on a guy who never had dirt under his fingernails? He had to walk to work because he didn't even own a car. Now all of a sudden, he was a gardener and a handyman who owned no tools. Joan was criticizing Ms. Weaver for hiring him, given his past record. Abby may have been new in town, but Mrs. Black knew the story precisely as the elders of the church had told her. Joan was shocked that this refined old lady would have allowed Abby to employ the fallen preacher.

As she spoke, Joan was amazed just how good it felt to expose all of these thoughts to someone out loud. It almost made them seem true. Deep down, she knew that everything she had just spilled out to Martha was a lie, but it was so long ago and so hard to remember that she and Harley had once been great friends. It was also hard to remember the kind, considerate man who was always there for anyone who needed him, except when she and Taylor had needed him—then he had turned his back. When Harley waited for her to come forward and exonerate his name, self-pity had overpowered her responsibility as a Christian. She had allowed the door to be open for the devil, and he had slid right in. Now sure that Harley would soon expose her, not only her pride and reputation was at stake but also her worthiness as a mother. She could never let Taylor find out what she had done. That was why she had to come up with a foolproof plan that would propel Harley right out of town. He wouldn't be able to endure another charge of misappropriating funds.

Joan had been true to her word. She was inhaling her breakfast and gulping her coffee. Lilly returned to fill her cup, taking longer than usual. It was astounding how much one could hear when one really listened. Joan began encouraging Martha to finish and give her an answer.

Martha's green eyes narrowed as she looked up at Lilly and pasted a polite smile on her face. "Could I please have some more cream?" Lilly reached into her apron pocket and brought out a handful of creamers and laid them on the table, but she kept her concentration on Joan, watching as she yanked a small notebook from her purse and forced it between Martha's plate and coffee cup. "What's this?"

"Just read it, and tell me you'll help."

Lilly hurried back to the table with more coffee, all the while observing Martha's reaction to the contents of the notebook. The look on her face changed to one of horrific disbelief as comprehension dawned. Her voice was stern with no vestige of sympathy in its hardness. "You and I may be friends, but you're also one crazy bitch. Do you know that? What is wrong with you? I want nothing to do with this scheme. You're all on your own for this one." Without finishing her coffee, she swung her legs out from the booth; and in a lightning-fast motion, she was gone.

Joan kept her expression under stern restraint and continued drinking her coffee as if nothing had transpired between her and Martha. No one else in the diner had been observing the two women except Lilly, who wished desperately that she could have seen the contents of that little notebook. A cold, congested expression was settling on Joan's face, giving the impression that she was not happy with Martha's response. She reluctantly paid the bill at the register and walked out the door with the gait of a predator.

Lilly wasn't exactly sure what to do with the little bit of information that she overheard. Should she tell Harley or Mrs. Black? According to the listing of the deed in the local newspaper, Mrs. Black was no longer the owner, and she didn't know Ms. Weaver well enough to totally trust her. She might find her accusations a bit cavalier. Rumors were still flying around town, and questions were being asked as to why she would want to allow strangers in her private domain. A bed-and-breakfast seemed too invasive, given the lifestyle Mrs. Black was accustomed to. It was even alleged that the "poor ole soul" must be at the onset of dementia.

Lilly knew Mrs. Black well enough to know that, if this bit of gossip found its way to her ears, the person spreading the rumor would be unprepared for the scalding fury that could bury them in seconds. Mrs. Black was sweet as thick molasses covered in dark chocolate, but underneath, she was as strong as a mother bear protecting her cubs.

Chapter 39

But they who wait for the Lord shall renew their strength; they shall mount up with wings like eagles; they shall run and not be weary; they shall walk and not be faint.

—Isaiah 40:31

Mrs. Black was troubled by the thought that Joan was plotting some vindictive notion against Harley and that Summer Rain would be entangled with the conspiracy. She had tolerated Abby's decision to hire Joan, even though she had doubts about the woman's integrity. Shirley knew from the moment she saw the look of sympathy on Abby's face that the distraught lady would be on the payroll. Abby's mission was to help those in distress, and what better way to launch her inspirations than to improve the life of a desperate woman?

Shirley found the information from Lilly not only disturbing but also very sad. She knew that Abby's unfettered heart would overflow with emotion when she became aware of the intended plan. Finding herself vulnerable to a stranger in need came easy for Abby. Discovering that Joan was in the process of formulating a ruse against her would reinforce her doubts about her future, something that Shirley knew Abby's heart wasn't up to enduring.

Shirley's steps slowed as she pondered the best time to tell Abby of the situation. If there was a way to exonerate the allegations against Harley, she needed to come up with a plan to trap Joan. It seemed like the most logical thing to do, but would it be the most ethical? Being disingenuous went against everything that Summer Rain stood for, and hypocrisy was not part of the inn's vocabulary. Those same practices had fostered the accusation against Harley, allowing no room for honesty. The mission statement at Summer Rain was quite simple: "Our hearts and doors are always open. We provide shelter for those in need and rest for the weary."

Shirley knew that Abby would include Joan in her decree even when she found out

the truth. That was just the kind of person she was. Her commitment to her mission would overrule her insecurities. At any rate, they would have to have patience and proof. Right now, all they had was suspicion, and that was like a crow on a fence post—it always found a place to land. Shirley had to be sure that Lilly had not misunderstood the banter between Joan and her friend. She also knew that the accusation, if one was warranted, needed to be acknowledged and a solution to benefit everyone be found.

That evening before bedtime, Shirley called Abby into the sunroom and asked her to sit down. Abby flopped onto the sofa with a grateful sigh as a gentle breeze drifted past, carrying the subtle scent of roses. The serenity of this room still amazed her every time she walked into it. It was where she came to find comfort, but she could see that her mother was not in a very cheery mood. Her coolness was evidence that she was agitated about something. "Mom, what's wrong? Did something happen today with one of our guests?"

"It's not about our guests but one of our employees. Remember that hunch I told you about with Joan? Well, I heard some new hearsay today, and that's all it is until proven otherwise, but it does involve Summer Rain." Shirley proceeded to relate the conversation, as told to her by Lilly, and waited for Abby's response.

"I know I keep asking you the same question, but what do we do?"

"I think Mrs. Martin has underestimated her new employers. Please don't say anything to Harley. He has enough to deal with just knowing that she's here. I have a plan, but I need to work out the details. When I have it finalized, I will let you know. Until then, please go about your daily routine, keeping everything as usual." In a voice so serene that it surprised even her, Shirley said, "Harley deserves to be free of the weight on his shoulders. He's carried it long enough." A giant smile brought an immediate softening to her clenched jaw. "You know that gut feeling you had about Joan? You were right. She *is* going to make a difference here at Summer Rain."

Abby started to launch more questions, but her mother was already halfway down the hall. Abby found the thought of giving Harley his life back very satisfying. Seeing him every day at Summer Rain had brought an unwelcome surge of excitement. She was not ready for another man in her life, nor was there room for romance in her busy schedule. Jeff's name lingered too often on the edge of her mind and intruded many times during her day. She wanted the memories to stay, but that was all they were—memories. And truthfully, if she was with someone new, she wanted to do more than reminisce; she wanted to make new memories.

She found herself looking for reasons to go outside, and every time Harley's gaze met hers, her heart turned over in response. He radiated a vitality that pulled her closer to him. As much as she felt drawn to him, she doubted the feelings were mutual. He was very good at being self-sufficient, being detached. Even though there was an inherent strength in his face that whispered steadfast and serene peace, she wondered if his broad shoulders ever tired of the burden he carried.

She found him trimming the rose bushes in faded jeans that fit the man all too well. She watched from the stone path while his arms rippled with movement. She waited until he glanced over his shoulder and mopped the sweat from his forehead. Within seconds, she was offering him a large glass of iced tea. He held out his hand and accepted the drink. Abby could feel the animated connection that hummed between them.

"Harley, may I talk to you about something?"

"Yes ma'am—sorry, I promised not to call you that. Okay. Yes, Abby. Is there something that you would like me to do?"

"Well, I guess you could say that." She so desperately wanted to cross the chasm that separated them. "Could we please sit down and talk?"

"About what?"

"About what you want in life and why you're trimming rose bushes at a bed-and-breakfast. I'm sure you have other aspirations. Don't you miss your church?"

"That's a lot of questions. Do you want them answered all at once, or can I think about them?"

The intensity in his eyes made her stiffen. "I'm sorry for interrupting your work, Mr. Davidson. When you are done with the tea, you may leave the glass on the bench. I'll come out and get it later."

Harley let loose a breath that was half frustration, half disbelief. What did this woman want from him, and why did he always use a sarcastic tone with her? Was he purposefully trying to draw a negative response from her? Why did she continue with her attentive attitude toward him? Could it be possible that she was trying to initiate a friendship, maybe even more? He wasn't in the habit of making women cry, but he couldn't help notice that she blinked rapidly as if to chase off tears as she walked away. He assumed that she captivated the attention of every male around, so he wondered what she could possibly see in him—a backwoods country preacher who lived in a dilapidated camper. If she really wanted to get to know him, he was flattered, and he couldn't deny the spark of excitement at the prospect of a deeper relationship with Abby. He smiled as his thoughts filtered back to the day she had met him at the door when he showed up for the interview. He remembered the compassion and kindness she had shown him, even after the way he had lashed out at her in the parking lot.

Abby turned away, not waiting for an answer, as tears streamed from her eyes. A hot wave of embarrassment, unexpected and unwanted, washed over her, and frustrations spilled out in a fiery sigh. Just who did he think he was talking to? She was a human being—a human being who had given him a job and had overlooked the accusations against him. She even tried to be nice to him, but for some reason, he seemed so determined to keep her at a distance. She definitely did not understand his behavior toward her. Perhaps she had insulted him so badly that day in the parking lot that he just couldn't forgive her. However, he was a pastor, and shouldn't pastors be the first ones in line to show mercy? She realized that his pride had been seriously bruised by her conduct, but he shouldn't have been too quick to judge. Her intentions had been very sincere, just as they were now. But once again, the preacher couldn't seem to keep the venom from his voice; and again, she was offended. Despite his derogatory comments each time they faced each other, she sensed his vulnerability, and her compassionate spirit gave in to empathy toward him. But the intensity and immediacy of her attraction toward him mystified her. She never imagined that her heart would dance again with excitement for anyone but Jeff, yet she found herself extremely conscious of Harley Davidson.

CHAPTER 40

Those who think they know something do not yet know as they ought to know.

—1 Corinthians 8:2

Mrs. Black was offering information to Summer Rain's very first guests when Abby entered the foyer. It was a young couple who seemed very interested in staying for the weekend, but when the price list was laid before them, they looked totally wounded as if someone had just shot them in the foot.

Deep concern continued to spread over their faces as Mrs. Black asked if there was a problem. The husband spoke first, his low voice a little awkward, almost apologetic. "We were told that we could afford to come here for the weekend, but these rates are out of our price range." Abby saw the disappointment in his wife's eyes and stepped in to introduce herself. She offered to give them a tour of the gardens. They seemed hesitant at first, but they followed Abby outside as she guided them through the pines. Harley was hard at work, trimming more bushes, when he saw Abby coming down the path. She was wearing a floral dress with a snappy little jacket and dark sandals. She looked absolutely stunning. He looked away, hoping she hadn't seen him gawking.

Harley was bent over, trimming a low branch on a butterfly bush. He eyed Abby as she approached, and their gazes locked, triggering a moment of awareness. Abby's legs felt leaden as she moved on down the path, fighting the magnetism toward Harley. What was it about this man that kept eating away at her? Even though she had to admit that she was strangely flattered by his frequent stares, he seemed to be everywhere she went these days. She sensed a delicate slender thread beginning to form between them, binding their lives together subconsciously. She would not allow herself to be enticed by his good looks and charisma, yet the intensity of her attraction to him was a mystery.

Abby pulled herself back to reality and continued the tour. By the time they returned to the house, the couple was overcome with anticipation of their future visit. Abby too was amazed at their enthusiasm and offered them a complimentary night at Summer Rain. No newspaper ad would ever generate as much publicity as these two. She called for Shirley to show them to their room and give them the schedule of mealtimes. She turned as she entered the back door and found Harley watching her again. He seemed to be studying her very intently, so much so that he didn't realize she was staring back at him. She quickly closed her eyes and drew in a calming slow breath. She tried to force her confused emotions into order, but she knew she would not be able to find a solution without first conversing with Shirley. She went to the kitchen to put on a fresh pot of tea and waited for her mother.

When Shirley entered the kitchen, Abby was staring out the window, apparently unaware of the whistling sound coming from the teapot. Shirley quickly removed it from the burner and tapped Abby on the shoulder. Startled, she turned quickly and, seeing that it was Shirley, began crying and mumbling words that Shirley couldn't understand. Taking her by the arm, Shirley sat her down, allowed her to continue crying, and waited till she was quiet. "What on earth are you so upset about?"

"I just saw Harley."

"But you see Harley every day. Did he do something to offend you today?"

"I'm not sure. I just saw him looking at me, and I felt this need to run, only it wasn't to run away from him. It was to run toward him." She stirred uneasily in the chair, hoping that Shirley would have some constructive advice.

"Well, kiddo, the way I see it is the more you get to know the preacher, the more you like him. Why don't you quit trying to analyze everything and let the chips fall where they may."

"Oh, now we're using casino language? I was hoping for more than a cliché from you." Abby rolled her eyes and groaned. "And what makes you think I like this guy? I barely know him."

"Ah, but you do know him, and you wouldn't have hired him if you didn't like him. You saw something in him that allowed you not only to open the door to the house that day but also to open your heart." Shirley leaned against the counter and breathed deep. "He's a good man, Abby. Don't be so sure he is outside of God's plan for you."

Abby drew her legs up, placing her feet on the chair seat, burying her head in her knees. Shirley reached out and touched her shoulder with a gentle hand. "Remember that Harley is still a pastor, and he could help you with your grief and whatever else you're feeling. Why don't you give him a chance?"

When Abby lifted her head, she was alone in the room. Shirley had obviously slipped out quietly, allowing her some uninterrupted moments to reflect. Someone was ringing the doorbell, so she crawled down from her chair and hurried to the door. The technician from the security station was standing on the front porch, laden with equipment. Abby had scheduled installation for surveillance cameras on Joan's day off. If Shirley's plan was going to work, it had to be accomplished in secret. Hopefully, Harley was still trimming bushes on the far side of the property and would not notice the company truck in the driveway.

Shirley had consulted with several of her friends and business owners and devised a plan that could prove Harley's innocence. If what Lilly overheard at the diner was true, Joan was evolving her own plan for embezzling money from Summer Rain. So when she tried to pin the blame on Harley, Shirley and Abby would have video proof of her dishonesty. The plan wasn't foolproof, but it did seem feasible.

Joan had proven to be a good worker, and Abby hated the thought that she would have to go through the hiring process again if her suspicions were confirmed. Even though justice needed to prevail, she somehow wished she didn't have to be the one who provided the proof that Joan was the cause for Harley's current situation.

Installing the cameras seemed to be an easy enough job for the young technician, and within a few hours, he was packing up his equipment, leaving instructions and phone numbers in case of any problems. Abby felt a bit guilty as she watched him leave. After all, this was supposed to be a place of renewal and trust, not a dwelling filled with suspicion.

Abby found Shirley and gave her the information about the new system. As she handed her the papers, Shirley spoke with a quiet certainty in her voice that stopped Abby cold. "I can see by the look on your face that you're not really sure if we're doing the right thing. We really don't have a choice. We can't go around accusing someone of a crime because of hearsay, but we can try to find out the truth. Joan's poor judgment was to betray Harley, and if she decides to betray us, that will be her second and final mistake." Abby had come to know that Shirley was good at masking her real thoughts when it was necessary, but today she was sensing that these emotions were coming straight from the heart. A tight note in her voice also hinted at concern toward Abby. "I think you are having second thoughts about this camera device because you've come to like Joan, and you don't want to believe that behind her pleasant smile is an impulsive, agitated woman who is eaten up with grief and bitterness."

Shirley then shrugged, as if apologizing, but continued in a firm no-nonsense voice. "Look what she did for money. She deceived her pastor, a man who had given much of himself to help her. Look what she is doing for revenge now, using her job as a maid to hurt him again. Desperation is the number one motive."

Abby sat very still, her eyes narrow, jotting all of this down in her brain. She had to remember that the real mission they were trying to accomplish here was to return Harley to his congregation. Not that they deserved him, but he deserved to be set free from the shackles they had placed upon him.

"I realize what you are trying to make me understand, but it's so hard not to sympathize with Joan's situation. I can identify with the grief but not her financial state. Who's to say I wouldn't have done something similar in her place? If our hunches are right and she falls into our trap, what are we going to do?"

Shirley leaned back and closed her eyes as if praying. Without opening them, she declared, "We are doing this for Harley, so it will be his call. Watch and learn, Abby. It will be one life lesson that you'll never forget."

CHAPTER 41

So do not throw away your confidence; it will be richly rewarded.

—Hebrews 10:35

Harley began walking the two-mile trek back to his trailer, thinking about working for Ms. Weaver and how fortunate he felt to be able to say that he was now employed. He was at the edge of town, getting ready to head down Main Street, when he heard the church bell ringing. Every day at noon, the bell was set automatically to ring five times. It had started out being a very vital part of the town's everyday existence, but over the years, the bell had surrendered its resonance to many other sounds in town. A person now had to listen very carefully to capture the peals coming from the bell tower of the church. When Harley heard those clangs, no matter what part of town he was in, it reminded him that it was the very sound that had persuaded him to stay in New Hope. The sound of the bells ringing was the very sign that he had needed to convince him that he belonged there. When he first heard them, not knowing that it was a ritual for the bells to ring every day at noon, he had just finished saying a silent prayer, asking for a sign that would revive his doubts about his new position.

Fresh out of seminary and almost thirty years old, he had been offered a pastoral position at the Morning Son Bible Church. Finishing his studies in three years instead of the usual four, he was considered somewhat of a prodigy at the school. His mother had always called him "her little preacher man," but he had fought that title and the calling right through elementary, high school, and especially his college years. Public speaking class had been nothing short of a nightmare. He became so nervous at the podium that he had to take a Valium pill before he could even attempt to walk to the front of the class. Despite this struggle, none of his intellectual qualities fell on the side of the road that would lead to a pastoring job. Because of his stage fright, he kept telling himself that he could never be a pastor or anything affiliated with a church. His major had been in psychology, hoping to be a social worker, but he soon realized that God had other plans for him.

It was a testimony to God's grace that he became a preacher, what with his tough beginnings. After being abandoned by his biological mother at the age of two, he had been placed in a foster home. The Davidsons fell instantly in love with him and, after much paperwork, legally adopted him. Until he was about six years old, he didn't understand why people always laughed when he told them his name. He actually went through school with the nickname of "Cycle." At first, he cried and made every excuse not to go to school; but after hearing his mother explain why they kept his name Harley, he understood and became proud. She told him that Harley Davidson was a great name, and instead of reading a typical bedtime story, she would often come up with more reasons why he should be proud of his name. She told him about the man by the name of Harley and brothers by the name of Davidson, who had been childhood friends, and how they decided to build a motor bicycle. After years of experimenting and improving, the great Harley-Davidson motorcycle was born. The name Harley and the name Davidson were just meant to be together. She would tell him how it had been one of two major motorcycle companies to survive through the Great Depression. It was a name that everyone was familiar with, and as a company, it provided much help to many charitable organizations. She used to tell him that he too would someday do great things and would be remembered for his charity to those in need.

Many times, he had contemplated changing at least one of his names, but the pride in his mother's voice always became louder than the reaction that he got every time he introduced himself. He was always asked if he was an heir to the company's fortune. Sometimes he would just smile and say, "Yes, Arthur was my great-great-great-grandfather." Most people had no clue as to what year the Harley was manufactured, so knowing if the numbers added up just didn't seem to matter. They walked away feeling good because, in their minds, they had just met someone from a famous family that they could tell their friends about.

Thinking about the first time he came to town made his walk home seem shorter, but laying eyes on what he called home made him wish his walk was longer. His humble living space in a worn-out camper brought tears to his eyes every time he actually opened the door to go inside. He began to chuckle ruefully as he thought about what his mother used to say. She had been right about one thing. People in this town did remember his name and, oddly enough, seemed to associate it with money. But the money they linked him to was not a motorcycle fortune but stolen money—money that had been taken but not by him.

Even more difficult than being accused of such a crime was the fact that he knew who stole the money. His first instinct was to say, "I didn't do it, but I know who did." When Mr. Walker, the board chairman, and his posse stormed into Harley's office and Harley tried to state his case, a verse literally appeared in front of his eyes: "Turn the other cheek." He had no choice but to be quiet. He knew Joan, the office secretary, was the color of snow when she came into his office to announce Mr. Walker's presence. *Why hadn't I noticed the change in her after she found out that her son, Taylor, had not been the camp scholarship recipient?* He never dreamed that she would go so far as to steal church money. The atmosphere in the office for a few weeks after the announcement had been quite strained, but he thought that, if he gave her some time to get over the disappointment, everything would eventually get back to normal. He had no idea that she was so desperate. If only she would have confided in him about her financial needs.

Two years had passed since that earth-shattering day, and not one of those days had passed that Harley didn't relive that moment. He had no regrets. He felt that he had done the right thing by not revealing the real thief. His hope was that Joan's convictions would give her the courage to turn herself in, but so far, a darkness seemed to have folded over her that brought with it a plan of silence. Since the incident, he had only seen her twice, and she had done her best to dodge him. He wanted to approach her, but he had a gut feeling that he would be interfering with God's plan. He took an oath to shadow God's footsteps, and if his shoes became too big and stepped out of the imprint, he knew he would be on the wrong path. He needed to sit back and wait for God to amend this problem. But how long could he continue to live like a bum? How long could he go on allowing people to regard him as a thief? He thought about Job in the Bible, all the adversity God bestowed on him, and how his continued faith had eventually brought him peace.

Harley reached inside the picnic cooler, which was serving as a refrigerator, to retrieve a bottle of water and realized that he needed more ice. The owner of Ice Shed, a former parishioner who believed in his innocence, offered Harley a free bag of ice as often as he needed it. As soon as the sun went down, he would take his evening stroll. Before long, he would have to buy more jugs of water too. The few bottles that he kept refilling with tap water were so worn that the caps would no longer screw on tight.

He lay back on his bright orange and green woven lawn chair and reminisced about the past two years. Just how did a man with a four-year degree in psychology, a theology degree from a prominent seminary, and successful years as a pastor end up living in such conditions? Thank heavens for Mr. and Mrs. Smith, who were allowing him to reside in their ready-for-the-dump camper. Financially, they were not rich people; but like the woman in the Bible who gave all she owned, so had they. Not only was he thankful for the roof over his head but he also was so appreciative of their belief in him.

Harley's mind once again took him back a few years as he remembered the call that he received two weeks before graduating from Great Lakes Seminary in Central Ohio. A message had come from the president, asking him to stop by his office. Harley's mind had been instantly ravaged with questions and concerns of why Dr. Daniels would be calling him.

He had immediately changed his shirt and walked over to Old Main, one of the oldest and most beautiful buildings on campus. Since the president's office was on the third floor, Harley had taken the elevator so that he wouldn't be out of breath when he met Dr. Daniels. Just as he had his arm raised to knock on the office door, he felt a hand on his shoulder from behind, and a booming voice invited him to go in and have a seat.

As he turned around to see who the hand belonged to, Dr. Daniels had already moved toward the water cooler. Harley watched as he retrieved a glass of water and also noticed that he had dressed very casual today, no tie or jacket. He then left the water cooler and walked toward Harley. With a motion of his hand, he had directed him to a chair in front of the desk and said, "I guess you're wondering why I called you down here, Mr. Davidson."

Feeling a bit intimated by such an important man, Harley, without hesitation, took a seat, leaned back in the chair, sighed, and said, "Well, yes, sir, I am a bit apprehensive. I can't think of anything that I've done wrong."

Dr. Daniels had walked once more to the far side of the office and had already poured water into another glass and offered it to Harley. As he looked out over the top of his glasses, he spoke but not quite as loud this time. "We don't call people into this office only when they've done something wrong." He pushed his glasses back into the well-worn groove on his nose and continued. "We prefer to call them when they have done something right. And you, Mr. Davidson, for the past three years have been a model student. You've managed to maintain a 4.0 GPA, doing four years of classes in less than three. You've even worked part time in the campus library. It seems like you have befriended everyone who walks these halls. You are quite a phenomenon to those of us who have been here for many years."

Harley sat speechless. He knew he had worked hard these past years, but that was just his nature. He hadn't been born with a silver spoon in his mouth, so he had learned early that work was just a major part of life, and having a great attitude about it was just a bonus.

Dr. Daniels then stood up and looked out his office window as if he were watching someone. A few seconds later, he had turned to Harley and spoke as if his life depended on it. "I have a proposition for you, Mr. Davidson. Are you interested?"

Harley sat up straighter in the chair and again, without hesitation, answered, "Yes, sir, I am."

Dr. Daniels continued standing at the window as if the words he wanted to say would appear on the glass and speak for themselves. Harley tried to disguise his impatience by once again leaning back into his chair. The rich timbre of Dr. Daniels's voice brought Harley to the edge of his chair again. He must have misunderstood what he just heard. He sat silently, second-guessing his ears.

"Harley, did you hear what I said?"

"Well, sir, I don't think I heard everything exactly, but I thought you said that you want me to take over a church that is dying. You want me to bring it back to life? Could you tell me again because I must have misunderstood."

Dr. Daniels laughed in a deep, jovial way and, without taking a breath, began quoting a verse from the Old Testament. "It says in Joel chapter 2 verse 28 that 'your old men shall dream dreams; your young men shall see visions.' You're young, Harley. You have visions. I've read it in your compositions, and I've seen it in your daily pursuit of life. You have a viability about you that surpasses any other student that we have ever had. You have a tendency to take a situation, whether it's good or not so good, and treat it with merit and integrity. Do you know how rare it is to have both qualities in one person?"

Harley always knew that Dr. Daniels exuded an air of command, and now here he was, standing directly over him, obviously waiting for some kind of response. Not wanting to sound ungrateful, Harley had raised his head and looked directly into a set of intense brown eyes. "Thank you, sir, for saying all those nice things about me, but I have never thought of myself in that way. I've had a lot of adversity in my life, and honesty and hard work is just my mechanism for survival. I guess I feel like I need more information, so could you tell me more about this church?"

"Well, Mr. Davidson, we, the board and I, think you are the perfect candidate for a small church in New Hope, North Carolina. Are you familiar with the area?"

"No, sir. To be honest, I've never heard of the town, but I'm listening."

"Good. It's a congregation of about one hundred people—good solid Christian folks. The attendance has been getting less and less, and it needs some revival. The verse I just quoted applies to you because the current pastor is older and ready to retire. The church needs some young and creative inspiration. It needs some life. It's made up mostly of older parishioners, who, of course, we need, but a forest cannot survive without new saplings, and so it is with a church congregation. If this church isn't brought back to life in the near future, the conference will be forced to close the doors forever. It cannot financially stand on its own without some attendance growth. It won't be an easy transition for the congregation because, as I said, they are of the older generation and do not like change. For you, it will be a journey of patience, compassion, and most of all endurance."

There was an almost imperceptible note of pleading in his face as he said, "Harley, you're our only hope for the survival of this church. I'm sorry if I'm putting some pressure on you, but I and the board have discussed this in length, and we have no doubt that you are the man for the job. I have seen your passion to spread the gospel grow more intense each year that you have attended Great Lakes. Your compassion for mankind in general puts you on a plateau all of your own. Taking on a challenge of this magnitude may not be the normal path that we would send a 'new' pastor on, but you are the exception."

Without blinking an eye, he had reached for Harley's hand, shook it very firmly, and said, "We need your answer by tomorrow. I'll be in my office, so please call me. It's been a pleasure talking to you."

Knowing that this was his cue to leave, Harley had returned the handshake with a strong grip, mumbled a thank-you, and left the room. Outside the door, he had leaned against the wall to steady his shaking legs. He had just been offered the opportunity of a lifetime, but where in the world was New Hope, North Carolina? He used his foot to push himself away from the wall and began walking as fast as he could, without actually running to the library. Once he had found the atlas, he also found the location of his new home.

Telling Dr. Daniels his answer the next day was going to be easy. It was thinking about what lay before him that was hard. His experience with large groups of people, especially those with gray hair, was very limited. Being a theology major at Great Lakes had provided him with the opportunity to overcome his nervousness behind a podium, but it had done nothing to prepare him for what he was about to encounter. He smiled as he remembered his mother's nickname for him. When she called him her "little preacher man," he would cringe with embarrassment, now only to find that her intuition had been right. But this was something so different and so big. Being in charge of an entire congregation was going to be quite a responsibility.

Dr. Daniels seemed to think he was ready. But was he? In his heart, he knew that this was obviously God's plan for him, so he needed to put his trust in the one whom he was going to preach about.

After a sleepless night and a long hot shower, Harley decided to dress casually for his meeting with Dr. Daniels but no jeans. He found a pair of khakis in his closet that wasn't wrinkled and a dark brown polo shirt. He left a message on the answering machine that said he would be stopping by to give his answer, so he wasn't sure if any staff members would be present or not. He just knew that he wanted to present a good image.

When he had knocked on the office door, he was told to enter. As he opened the door, he had been greeted with a roomful of people waiting to wish him good luck. All his professors and dozens of students stood with glasses of Coke held high as a toast to his new position. They hadn't even known what his answer was going to be, and they were already celebrating. He accepted their well-wishes and their advice with graciousness and promised to keep in touch.

A strong arm came to rest on Harley's shoulders, and as he realized that it was Dr. Daniels's, he relaxed a bit. He still had not given him his final answer. "Well, Harley, my boy, you haven't made it official yet, but after a party like this, you can't say no."

The warmth of Harley's smile echoed in his voice as he spoke. "Even if there hadn't been a party, my answer was going to be yes. I need to follow where God is leading me."

Dr. Daniels removed his arm from Harley and shook his hand. "Wisest decision that you've ever made, Pastor Davidson."

Pastor Davidson—this would be his title for the rest of his life. He wished his mother were alive to know that her one dream had come true.

The next month had progressed slowly as Harley began the process of packing. He took only what fit into his Chevy Blazer, and the rest he either gave away or disposed of in the dumpster. Knowing that the church was providing a furnished house for him to live in was more than he could ever have asked for. He knew his salary wouldn't be the greatest at first, but the house more than made up for the lack of funds. Besides, he did it because he believed he was truly being called to be a minister of the gospel at this particular church. He didn't go there for financial gain.

Chapter 42

The way of the guilty is devious, but the conduct of the innocent is upright.

—Proverbs 21:8

Joan smiled as she maneuvered her car into the parking space behind the inn. Harley was coming around the corner of the house, arms laden with pumpkins. Obviously, he was beginning the decorating process for the fall season. She knew Abby wanted the inside decorated also, and she would want it finished by evening. This meant that Harley would be in and out of the house all day. If she were going to set him up, today might just be the day. Her smile faded a little when he stopped and watched her pull into the empty space. For an instant, wistfulness stole into his expression, but Joan only glared at him with burning, reproachful eyes. Realizing what she was doing, she quickly pasted on a disarming smile. Things were bad enough between them, and allowing him to believe she was mutinous would not be a good idea. To be honest, she wasn't exactly sure what she wanted or what she was doing. She did know that she was wrong, and what she was planning was even more unethical, but she had convinced herself that it was the only way out.

Harley was halfway to the shed by the time Joan stepped out of the car. She went inside and began her daily chores, all the while calculating Harley's movements as he carried pumpkins and corn shocks to and from the rented pickup. When he came in for lunch, Joan was going to ask him if he would help her move a desk so that she could clean behind it. She purposefully was going to leave her cleaning supplies in the pantry next to the kitchen so that it would take a few minutes to retrieve them, allowing Harley time alone in the room, where the open bank envelope would lay on the desk. She knew Harley would never touch it, but she planned to remove a substantial amount of money on her way to the bank, knowing that the bank teller would find a discrepancy in the monetary amount. She would have to return home with the news and replay her morning activities to Shirley and Abby, telling them, of course, how Harley had access to the money. She played out the plan many times in her head, the outcome always the same. They would be compelled to blame Harley. There was no one else who had access to that room. Joan knew it would be her word against Harley's, but she had convinced herself that Shirley and Abby would, without a doubt, believe her instead of Harley, given his past history with the church.

Joan had panicked the first day she saw Harley working at Summer Rain. It was a hard adjustment, knowing that he was just around any given corner. Paranoia took over some days, and Joan's ulcer generated a lot of pain. The discomfort was more of a nuisance when compared to the emotional pain she felt every time she saw her old friend. Had he confided in Shirley? Is that why they hired her? However, they had no way of knowing that she would even apply for the job. Each time she asked herself a question like this, she found herself coming up with a very rational answer to reassure herself—trust. Shirley and Abby trusted her. Why else would they have given her not only the job but also the custody of their money? Even though Shirley believed in Harley, she had no concrete proof that he was innocent. Neither woman had any reason to suspect Joan for the theft at the church, allowing her to assume that Shirley would have to reconsider her opinion of the pastor.

Each time Joan's plan came closer to fruition, she felt ill-equipped to undertake such a task, and the tight knot within her begged for release. Her deep sense of shame struggled intensely with her rebellious moods. In the end, her hurt and anger generated more reasons to continue on with her existing plan.

Joan executed her plan just as she had practiced. She had found Harley spreading mulch around some trees, and when he saw Joan approach him, he very methodically continued his raking.

"Harley would you please help me move a desk in the office so that I can clean behind it?"

With a certain tension in his attitude, he answered, "Sure, Joan. I'll be right there."

Joan smiled with satisfaction as she returned to the office to wait for him. He entered the room and immediately began pulling the desk away from the wall. "I'll be right back, Harley. I have to go get my cleaning supplies in the pantry."

Joan heard no verbal acknowledgement from him, but she really didn't care. She continued smiling as she thought about the bittersweet ending of this day. So far, Harley was acting exactly as she hoped he would; and before long, he would be looking for new employment. When she returned to the room, Harley was no longer there. But in his rush to escape her return, he had forgotten his backpack. Hanging on the doorknob, it seemed to be beckoning her to open it and plunge the money into it. It was a detail she hadn't anticipated but would cast even higher suspicion on Harley—a definite plus. After stashing cash in the backpack, she quickly zipped the bank-issued money bag, found Abby, and let her know that she was leaving for the bank.

When she returned to Summer Rain, she found Abby and Shirley looking for some tax papers in the office. Shirley turned around when she heard the door open and spoke first. "Hello, Joan. How was the traffic in town today?"

"It was quite busy actually. That's why it took me a little longer. The bank was super busy too, so I had to wait in line. When I finally got to the window, there was a problem with the transaction."

"A problem? What could possibly have been wrong?"

"There was an issue with the amount of money in the bag. I counted the money and filled out the deposit slip, like I always do, but when Heather counted it, the amount was different. It was two hundred dollars short." Joan's lids came swiftly over her eyes, and tears glistened on her face. Her tear-smothered voice was fragile and shaking. "I'm so sorry, ladies. I thought about the whole situation on the way home, and as much as I don't want to say this, I don't know any other explanation."

"Well, spit it out, Joan. Did you leave the bag unattended somewhere? Don't be so upset. We've all done things like that before. We won't have to file bankruptcy because of two hundred dollars."

Joan looked Shirley straight in the eyes and said, "Yes, I did leave the bag unattended, but it was right here in this room."

"You're going to have to be more specific, Joan. We haven't had any visitors here this morning. There's only the four us of on the grounds." Shirley suddenly gasped, put her hands on her hips, and quietly said, "You don't think Harley would do something like that, do you?"

So confident of her plan, Joan quickly spoke in a low, disarming voice as more tears fell on her cheeks. "I know how you feel about Harley, but I don't know how else to explain it."

Shirley looked at Abby and said, "Would you please take Joan to the kitchen and make her a cup of tea since she seems to be in need of some delicate care?"

"Of course, Mom. Come with me, Joan, and we'll find some tissues."

Once out of sight, Shirley practically ran to the office and replayed the surveillance tape. Even though she found what she had expected, an odd twinge of disappointment and anger tore at her heart as she viewed the work of the real thief on the screen. She rewound the tape and went in search of Harley. She found him in the shed, staining one of the wooden benches. He quickly laid down his paintbrush, wiped his hands on the towel hanging out of his pocket, and extended his hand in greeting. "Hello, Shirley. What brings you out to the shed today?"

"Well, Harley, I would like to say that I'm just out here to smell the roses, but the truth is I need you to come inside. I need to show you something."

"Do you need me to fix something? I'll be done here in about thirty minutes, if it can wait."

"No, Harley, this can't wait. What I have to show you is much more important than an unpainted bench. Can you please come with me now?"

Without another word, Harley followed Shirley into the house. "Abby needs to see this too, so wait here, and we'll be right back."

Harley couldn't imagine what was so urgent that Shirley interrupted his work, but she was the boss, and he never questioned her. Within minutes, Shirley, Abby, and Joan entered the room. Harley saw a satisfied light come into Joan's eyes as she shot him a withering glance. Why were they all here together in this room, and why did he have the sudden urge to wipe that smug expression off Joan's face? Looking at her now, the light he thought he saw in her eyes was more like a wicked gleam.

Shirley asked them to all please sit down. There was something that needed to be discussed. Silence as thick as mud oozed between the four. Harley gnawed on a ragged thumbnail. Joan fought the urge to turn and bolt but sat and watched silently, anxiously waiting to see her triumphant finale. Once the money was found in the backpack, she was sure there would be no explanation good enough to satisfy Shirley and Abby. They would have to grasp the fact that, indeed, the preacher was corrupt.

Shirley stood in front of two people, both of whom she had come to be grateful for, ready to convict one and eager to free the other. She had tried never to judge, but now it had gone beyond that. Harley had taken the punishment for Joan's behavior, allowing her freedom, while he barely existed. Not exactly sure how to begin, she expressed her gratitude for both of their services. Joan flattened her palms against her slacks as if she would soon be standing and returning to her duties. Harley lowered his head as if studying the scuffed toes of his boots. The look on Shirley's face suggested something very earth-shattering was about to take place.

"I'm sure you two are wondering why we've called you here." Raw hurt glittered in Shirley's eyes as she spoke directly to Joan. "Joan is familiar with the reason. In fact, Joan *is* the reason we are here." Shirley turned toward Harley and asked, "Do you have any idea why we are here? I want to give you the opportunity to speak if you need to."

Harley was momentarily speechless with surprise. When he found his voice, it had an infinitely compassionate tone even as he offered an impatient shrug. "I really have no clue as to why we're sitting here. Should I?"

"I'm not going to beat around the bush concerning this situation with the two of you, so I'm here to tell you that it will be settled today, one way or another." She watched Joan's eyes widen with concern when she asked her to tell the group exactly what had happened.

Ice began spreading through Joan's stomach. Terrible regrets began assailing her, and she stiffened at the confrontation. Yet somehow, she found a perverse pleasure in accepting this challenge. How could she charge an innocent man with such accusations while looking him in the eyes? Regarding Harley with impassive coldness, she gathered her defenses with several deep breaths and began once again to describe the events of the day. Her conclusion ended with downcast eyes spilling tears over her cheeks.

Harley was so shocked by her story that he gave no thought to object. It just seemed so preposterous. He hooked an ankle over his knee and looked toward Shirley and Abby. They were standing beside each other, neither looking surprised but with an uncanny look of relief on their faces. Frustration and curiosity danced dangerously inside Harley's chest, and he braced himself for what he might do. He stood and moved closer to his backpack, looking inside. It was just as Joan said. Now his frustration was turning into anger. His voice, vibrating with desperation, addressed only Shirley and Abby, declaring his innocence. "I don't know how to explain what just happened, but I have never touched that money. I know this sounds like a real cliché, but I really don't know how it got into my backpack."

Joan could hardly contain her anticipation as she waited for Shirley and Abby to lecture Harley on the hurts and disillusionments of betrayal. But instead, Shirley said, "Joan, I want you to take a seat next to Harley. There is something that you both need to see." She walked to the desk and wasted no time turning on the video.

Joan was appalled by the fact that her actions had been recorded. Almost choking with fury, she gasped for air and flaunted a hostile glare toward Harley. "You set me up." She tilted her head toward Shirley and Abby. "Is this why they gave you a job? Did they hire you to install these cameras? We used to be good friends, Harley. Why are you so against me?"

Harley hung his head, trying to stay civil. What was he supposed to say? Hadn't he been silent long enough? Should he blurt out the truth right now to Shirley and Abby or keep his silence? But how could he? The proof was on the screen in front of them. How did Joan think she was going to get out of this one? He raised his head, and as respectful as he could sound, he asked, "You think I'm against *you*?" Joan said nothing.

On the edge of impatience but still oozing that southern charm, Shirley's voice broke the silence. "I don't think honestly I have to tell you, Joan, just how disappointed we all are. You were doing such a fine job here—until today. It's too bad that we had to rely on a machine in order to get to know the real *you. Is* that the real you, Joan, or have you allowed this black rage to bubble in your blood for so long that you think it's normal? Don't forget, Joan, that Harley and I knew you before your husband died and before your world fell apart. We're not here to make your life miserable. We are not here to judge. We are here to help, if you want it."

Joan wasn't exactly sure what to do. She paled at the enormity of her circumstances. She sat speechless, feeling humiliated and deflated. She wasn't ready for this conflict to be over. Feeling bitter toward the world was not just a battlefield for her but it had become a way of life as well. She had come to rely on the shadows that covered her heart, like that of a tent providing shelter from the rain.

The silence lengthened between them, and she knew they were waiting for her to speak. She tried to smile, but it fell flat. She cast her eyes downward, hoping for another minute to compose herself. Gradually, she began blurting out words that no longer seemed convincing or accurate, only worn and hollow. She was speaking without inflection as if she had rehearsed the entire scene a hundred times before, only this was the final performance. For the past few years, she had taught herself not to need anyone and not to depend on anyone; yet at this very moment, her future was contingent on these three people.

Shirley was grateful that she didn't have to beg Joan to confirm her dishonesty. It was the first detail that she had addressed. The tears were still trembling on Joan's eyelids as she finished talking, and they appeared to be coming from the heart this time, and even though there was no illustration of any genuine apology, Shirley could physically see Joan's face soften, her anger beginning to fade.

Joan continued her silence. Could she really completely overcome the bitterness and resentfulness that she felt toward Harley? Could she ever look at him and not feel shame? The spark of hope quickly extinguished as Harley stood up, revealed the scowl on his face, and strode to the door. Joan felt, rather than saw, his shocked movement and was silenced by his angry expression.

Shirley and Abby watched Harley as he hurried out the door. He would need some time to digest all of this, but Shirley was positive that he would recover and would also be the main influence toward the salvage of Joan. How he was going to do that she didn't know, but she believed in the power of God, and she had felt his presence among them today.

Joan stood to her feet and spoke with a ring of resignation. "I'll gather up my things and wait while you call the police."

Until now, Abby had been silent; but shifting restlessly, her only sound was the faint whisper of her pink silk blouse against cotton slacks. Now that Harley was gone, she wanted Joan to sit back down and answer the many questions that were burning in her mind. "Start from the beginning, Joan, and tell me how you launched such malicious plans. Shirley tells me that you used to be a very kind and helpful woman, a great asset to the church." Abby sighed and then patiently waited.

Joan watched Abby sit back and relax, aware that she was not going anywhere until Joan spilled her guts. Joan cleared her throat and settled her body into the hard-back chair. "Life was pretty good before my husband died. We never talked about life insurance. I mean, who does that? We were young and healthy, and we had so many other expenses. When he was diagnosed with cancer, well, it was too late for an insurance policy. He had an aggressive form of the disease, and we were told there was no hope. That rocked my world. It was a little too late, but it was then that we reacted to our financial situation. That recognition was also too late." Joan reached for the pillow on the recliner and stuffed it behind her back and then continued. "One thing that was important to my husband and me was making sure that Taylor went to college. Rod died two months before Taylor's high school graduation. Tuition for the first college semester was based on the previous year's income, when we had been better-off. Therefore, we weren't eligible for any grants. I just didn't know how I was going to get Taylor enrolled with no tuition money. When the camp scholarship came available, I was ecstatic. Knowing that Pastor Davidson was camp chairman, I thought Taylor was a shoo-in. He met all the scholarship criteria, and it seemed most appropriate for him to be given the grant, since his father had just died." She dabbed her eyes and went on. "I cried for days when Pastor Davidson came to me and informed me that he had given the grant to another student. I was so hurt that I physically became ill. My friend Martha helped pull me out of my depression, but I was still facing the same issue. I wasn't real familiar with the benevolence fund at the church, but I knew it existed. One day, while organizing the pastor's files, I came across a number that looked like a combination for a lock; and being that there was only one lock in the office, I had to assume it opened the safe. I took the liberty to open the chest and count the money. It's more than enough for what I needed. I went home that night and began putting together a plan. I argued a lot with myself, but in the end, my desperate side won."

Abby was near tears. Life as Joan had seen it was becoming more transparent to her. She could almost see the battle going on inside of this forsaken woman.

Joan continued recounting the horror of the day when the group from the church board arrived to accuse Harley of being a thief. "I tried to speak and tell the truth, but Harley never gave me a chance. He just took the hit. At first, I was grateful for what he did; but when I tried to identify with that kind of selflessness, I drifted off course and became tangled with an invasion of bitterness and resentment. I found myself feeling remorse one minute and then absorbed with resentment the next. Witnessing Harley's chivalry as a martyr became offensive to me. I couldn't move forward, and I didn't want to stay where I was. In some twisted part of my mind, I became convinced that the pastor was wrong, and he should be punished for the sacrifice he made for me. Pretty stupid, huh?" She shifted the pillow again as if adjusting it would also change the outcome of her story.

"I expected Harley to save himself when questioned by the elders, but he chose to save me instead. It put me in a most unnerving dilemma. When the devil stepped in and took over my values, I was no match for his power." Her voice faded to a hushed stillness.

Grief and despair tore at Abby's heart. Who would have known that Joan was such a fragile, needy woman who hadn't been able to take care of herself and had given in to the whispers of temptation? A soft and loving curve touched Abby's lips as she said firmly, "Joan, I haven't known you very long, but during that time, I have come to respect you for your loyalty and your hard work. I guess that's why I'm having such a hard time believing all of this. I don't think this is truly who you are. We all yield to the lure of the devil at some time in our life and make major mistakes. I must admit, yours was a whopper. I am not condoning what you did, but I am trying to understand. Unfortunately, choices such as this demand consequences. And I think you know that." With renewed humiliation, Joan looked away.

Shirley jumped into the conversation and spoke softly, hoping to dispense hope and healing with her words. "Joan, I'm not exactly sure what's going to happen, but I want you to know that I truly believe there was some divine intervention going on here. Just think about everything that has happened. We set a trap. You walked right into it." Joan raised her head and was looking at Shirley as if she had lost her mind.

"As much as you're angry about getting caught and scared about what your punishment will be, I think you're glad it's over. I also think you're mortified by what you have done and are totally embarrassed. If I'm wrong, please tell me now."

Shirley waited, hoping for silence. Joan wrinkled her nose and shook her head, indicating that she had nothing to say. It was enough for Shirley to continue. "Joan, I'm sure you know the meaning of the word *pride*, but I want you to listen as I refresh your memory." Joan nodded her head, indicating that she would pay attention.

"Good. So listen very carefully. *Pride* is one of those words that can mean two completely different things. You can have pride in your accomplishments, and you can have pride that will block your way in life. Some people think of pride as a virtue, something that's great. It also can be defined as a disagreement with the truth. I think you managed to achieve full capacity on both ends. Your endurance for discretion became your virtue, and your disagreement with the truth became your redeemer. You really thought you would find peace. You never imagined that you could not only hold a grudge for so long but maintain it as well. And by that, I mean reestablishing its worth every chance you could. It was becoming a full-time assignment for you, wasn't it?"

Joan wiped her cheeks with the back of her hand and remained silent. Shirley continued. "I bet you've never done anything so desperate before. If only you would have had enough faith to ask for help. If only you would have explained to Harley about the scholarship, I'm sure he would have found a way to help your son. We live in an iffy world, Joan, and that can create a lot of regrets. 'If only' are two powerful words. You know you never want to regret what you've done—only what you haven't done. And right now, I'm guessing you're regretting almost everything you've done in the past few years. Am I right?"

Joan closed her eyes and tried to ignore the ache that had settled just behind her heart. Shirley had just laid out the undeniable and dreadful facts in front of her and was waiting for some kind of response. Feeling like a woman on trial, she didn't know what to say except that she was sorry.

Shirley retained her affability, but Joan detected a hint of censure in her tone. "I think you should go home and think long and hard about what you've done and all the people you have hurt in your pursuit for revenge. You might want to become familiar with the meaning of forgiveness and figure out a way to resolve your issues. I don't want to sound judgmental, as the Lord knows I've made more mistakes in life than I care to admit. But there was always some form of consequence to pay, even if it was just to say 'I'm sorry.' This battle is between you and Harley. I think God just used Abby and me as tools to bring Harley back to his people and for you to find peace. You have to decide if you can right this wrong." At these words, Shirley touched Joan's shoulder in a positive gesture, and then she and Abby left her alone in the room with the camera.

CHAPTER 43

Call to me and I will answer you and will tell you great and hidden things that you have not known.

—Jeremiah 33:3

Harley found himself following the path to the shed. He opened the door and sat down on an overturned bucket. His mind was racing faster than a NASCAR. What had just happened in there with Joan? Did she hate him so much that she was willing to hustle him into yet another scenario that involved his two best advocates and allow him to hang again, hoping for a similar result? Luckily, this time, his allies had cut the rope before it became a noose.

As he raised himself from the bucket, he fell instantly onto his knees. It was almost beyond his comprehension how someone could have such hostility toward him. This was something he couldn't deal with on his own. He was giving this one to the Lord on a silver platter. As a pastor, he knew forgiveness should be the main course on his menu; but as a wounded human being, he could taste the contempt on his tongue. It couldn't have hurt worse if Joan had taken a gun and shot him. At least then he could see the reason for the pain.

He remained on his knees for the better part of an hour, straightened, and then absently flexed cramped muscles in his legs as he limped slowly toward the house. His physical body may be aching, but his heart was now ablaze with the assurance of new hope. He felt the hand of God pulling him in the direction of the back door. As his hand reached the handle, his fingers gripped it in apprehensive anticipation. What was going to happen when he walked inside? Were Shirley and Abby expecting him to call the police, or were they anticipating him to do what a man of God should do? Which was exactly what? Only a handful of people in this town still respected him enough to call him Pastor. Should he act like a clergyman now and be all about forgiveness, or should he treat Joan like the thief that she was and hand her over to the authorities? For two years, he had waited patiently for Joan to contradict the board's decision to remove him from his pastoral duties, but she had never stepped forward. Now that she had been caught red-handed, his reaction to the aberrant situation would be scrutinized very carefully. He wanted to shout "O ye of little faith!" to the people in his congregation, and he wanted to hear apologies from each and every one of them, especially the board members. He wanted to see each one of them on their knees, begging for his forgiveness, asking him to return to the pulpit. Right now, his wounded ego seemed to be goading these thoughts. He realized just how satisfying it would feel to have all of that happen, but the real desire in his heart was not for recognition of trustworthiness but gratitude for forgiveness. The strength of his character was definitely being tested.

He removed his hand from the door. Hadn't he just emerged from prayer—prayer that begged God to allow his heart to forgive, to cover this hurt with compassion? He sensed God's touch, sanctioning his request, yet here he stood, hesitant about facing the three women waiting for him inside. He could understand Joan's hurt and why she did what she did, but for his congregation to be so cynical left him feeling susceptible to their judgments. If he could forgive Joan, then he must also pardon those in the flock, even the wolves in sheep's clothing. That was a tougher task.

The longer he stood at the door, the more uncomfortable he felt. He hated confrontation. It was one reason he didn't fight harder to keep his job. It was why he never acknowledged the fact that he suspected Joan as the thief. Coming to North Carolina was God's plan, not his, and however the idea played out, he would have to accept it. He grabbed the doorknob once again, and with no further thoughts, he stepped inside.

Joan, arms folded in defense, was slouched in the chair. She looked up to see Harley pause just inside the door. She noted his set face, his clamped mouth. Even as he stared at her, she could see the fierce power of a good, honest man. He was trying so hard to make his face a stoic marble effigy, but the eyes that were probing into her very soul exposed a different image. She detected a slight hint of empathy, and tears welled up in her eyes unexpectedly, her strength flowing away like water down a drain. She bent her head and studied her hands, waiting for him to speak. But he said nothing. He only shifted his feet, awkward and ill at ease. He was waiting, looking at her with those intense blue eyes, giving her another chance to apologize. What could she possibly say? *I'm sorry*? How ludicrous was that. A man lost two years of his life and his eminent reputation. *Sorry* just didn't sound gracious enough. Actually, Joan had no idea what would proclaim her remorsefulness. Besides, would Harley believe her? In fact, was anyone ever going to believe her again?

Obviously, he was going to wait her out, so she had to say something. She raised her chin and was impaled by his steady gaze. With all the dignity she could muster, she brought her eyes up to meet his and said, "Harley, I'm not quite sure where to begin. I am so sorry. I'm even embarrassed to say that because it's definitely not enough. I have so much more to say, but I'm not sure you really want to hear anything that comes out of my mouth."

The tension between them increased with frightening intensity, but she continued. "As many times as I listened to you speak about not allowing the devil even a little fraction of your heart, I still yielded to his irritating badgering and allowed him to slither in. I knew he was there and knew I didn't want him there, yet I tolerated his evil advice. He found a lot of ways for me to justify what I had done and what I was continuing to do. The past two years turned me into a resentful and cynical woman, a woman who couldn't even look into her son's eyes for fear he would see the shame, a woman who couldn't sleep at night, a woman who missed her work at the church and, most importantly, her friend. I've really missed you, Harley." Her lids slipped down over her eyes as she continued. "I can't expect you to forgive me, but deep in my heart, I know you already have. Your devotion and love for people, even those of us who have disappointed you, is a powerful characteristic." Hoping to draw a response, she met his steady gaze and then quickly looked away.

Harley allowed himself a moment of humble reflection, and then his hoarse whisper broke the silence. "Joan, I have waited a long time to hear you say that you're sorry. I know those words were hard for you to say, but I also recognize that they came from the heart of the Joan I used to know. I've prayed every day for you. I've prayed that you could forgive yourself and come back to the Lord."

Sweat broke out on his brow as his tone became gentler and resigned as though beaten down by sudden fatigue. "You're right about my forgiving you, although I must confess that only with the help of the Lord was I able to absolve my feelings toward you. You totally blew me away with your actions. It was one thing to steal from the church, even though you had every intention to repay the debt, but when you threw me under the bus, I was completely sickened by your behavior. Just today you once again tried to set me up for another plunge into the world of deception. I don't quite understand your animosity toward me. I was very fond of your son, Joan, and I had every intention of personally helping him, but before I could set something in motion, you not only stole the money from the church but you also robbed your son of a wonderful opportunity provided by our local college. There was an internship available, and Taylor had a very good chance of receiving it based on my recommendations. Being relieved of my duties as a pastor dismissed any legitimacy in my approval of Taylor. What happened to your trust in God, Joan? What about your trust in me as your pastor?"

Harley's scrutiny made Joan uncomfortable. He was asking her questions that she couldn't answer. She honestly didn't know how her faith had gotten so distorted, causing her to meander from her beliefs. It was a humiliating, deflated feeling. She raised her eyes again to find him watching her. A wry but indulgent look appeared in his eyes, and she met them without flinching. "I don't know how to answer your questions, Harley. When you announced that Taylor was not the recipient of the scholarship, something began gnawing away at my senses. Every time I looked in the mirror, I saw the same physical body that I was used to seeing, but my philosophies had totally changed. I felt trapped. I no longer had you as an ally. You became my enemy. When you decided to carry the burden for my weakness, I became even more offended. By playing the victim, I thought you were trying to set yourself up as Jesus, betrayed by his followers. For some reason, that made me even more outraged. Quite foolish of me, right?"

Rubbing the back of his neck with one hand, he replied, "Yes, Joan, that was ridiculous. I would like to think that I do follow Jesus as much as humanly possible, but in no way do I pretend to be him. I understand that financial issues cause a lot of anxiety, but you allowed yourself to be dependent on something other than the Lord. This was a hard lesson for you, Joan, but it has turned out to be a valuable one for me. You're not the only one at fault here. I should have been more in tune with my congregation. I should have recognized your need and sensed your pain."

He extended his hand and said, "You've awakened me again to the importance of paying attention to my congregation's needs."

Taking half a step back, Joan stared at him, her eyes wide with shock, her lips trembling. Tears were burning the back of her throat. She wondered if she should feel some guilt for the relief she was beginning to feel. "You're really willing to forgive me for all the pain I've caused you? For taking away two years of your life and ruining your reputation?"

Joan's genuine sincerity beckoned Harley like a glimmer of light beneath a lifting fog to a point of no return for him. A warm, friendly, country-boy grin tugged at his lips as he spoke. "Joan, I've had a lot of time to think about this situation, and although I wasn't sure this day would ever come to fruition, I knew God was involved. Patience is a difficult virtue to own, and I am guilty of the challenge. I was becoming more exasperated as each day passed, but in Isaiah, we find a promise that reads, 'Yet the Lord longs to be gracious to you; he rises to show you compassion. For the Lord is a God of justice. Blessed are all who wait for him.'" As sure as he had been that she needed to pay restitution for her sins, he now stood ready to help restore this tenuous woman.

Drawing in a slow, steady smile of happiness, Joan held out her hand, offering yet another apology. Acknowledging her guilt offered her spirits the chance to smile with shameless delight. It was so invigorating to her soul to be released from the sufferings of self-indulgence.

Chapter 44

For if you forgive other people when they sin against you, your heavenly Father will also forgive you.

—Matthew 6:14

Shirley and Abby were seated on the window bench, waiting for Harley to call for them. They knew he was in the back room with Joan, but they didn't know what was happening. Shirley held Abby's hand as she offered a prayer for Joan and Harley. Putting the situation into God's hands was the only thing she knew to do. Shirley rose from her chair and headed toward the kitchen to brew another pot of tea. While waiting for the water to boil, she asked God for guidance for everyone involved. She knew in her heart that Harley would forgive Joan, but she wasn't convinced that Joan would want or ever accept such a gift from a man she obviously loathed.

It was hard for Shirley to imagine anyone not liking Harley. She smiled ruefully as she remembered the "wolves" at the Morning Son Church when the first "den" meeting was called to order. Those old ladies fell instantly in love with the handsome preacher. They couldn't offer their cooking and baking services to him fast enough. They adored him—until a different kind of "dough" became the issue. They turned on him like a bulldog on a calico cat. Shirley had tried to encourage each lady to recognize Harley's good works and the new life that he brought back to the church instead of assuming he was a thief. But no matter how Shirley presented his attributes, the ladies would not listen. By noon the next day, he was no longer a pastor in the town of New Hope.

Startled by Harley's entrance to the kitchen and request for a glass of water, Shirley bumped the kettle against Abby's favorite blue and yellow primrose teacup and caused a hairline crack near the handle. A cry of distress broke from Abby's lips as tea seeped from the small fracture.

She quickly bit her lip and apologized for her outcry. Harley made no attempt to hide the fact that he was watching her as she carried the cup to the sink. His gaze was riveted on her face and then moved over her body. She looked up, and her heart lurched madly. What was it about this man? He was looking at her as if nothing else in the world mattered. What about Joan? She was just on the other side of the wall. He had just been accused of stealing, yet he was standing here as if everything was all right with the world.

Abby felt his eyes warming her, making her body tingle in a foreign and exotic way. Not even with Jeff did she remember this incredible rush of emotions that she was feeling at this moment. What exactly was she to do? She tried to speak, but her mouth felt full of cotton and painfully thirsty. She turned to the sink and began filling a glass with water. When she turned around, he was gone, his footsteps thundering down the hall toward Joan, with Shirley close on his heels. Abby took one swallow of water, set the glass on the counter, and quickly marched toward the sound of voices.

One look at Joan, and it was easy to tell that she was concerned about the outcome of her sentencing from Harley, but silence fell as he stuck his hands in his pockets and said nothing. In Shirley's eyes and voice lay the wisdom of age, and she could contain her opinion no longer. What she was seeing was a man in love with a woman who was afraid to love again and another woman who should be on trial for embezzlement but instead was on the threshold of a collapse. She began to speak, but her voice woke Harley suddenly from his stupor. He held up one hand like a traffic cop, and she immediately stopped talking. Harley finally began speaking freely about what he was thinking. "Joan, I think you know that what you did is jail worthy. Do you understand that? One call to the sheriff's department, and you'll be riding to town in a squad car."

Joan's jaw dropped open in surprise. Her face went dead white. Would Harley really turn her over to the authorities? She stiffened in automatic defense, his words stinging like needles. As she paused to catch her breath, her fears became stronger than ever. She never in a million years thought she would be the one facing jail time. Harley was the one she had envisioned behind bars. However, she *had* walked into a trap initiated by her own lies. Being caught on camera was more lethal than a confession.

Trying to sound sympathetic, he asked, "Joan, do you hear me? Do you understand what I'm saying to you? I can see that facing jail time is not in your plans, but what would you suggest I do?" Even though she had committed a crime, he still felt an urge to protect her from anymore adversity.

A flash of wild grief ripped through Joan, reminding her of why she was in this situation. She felt guilty and selfish, ashamed of what she had done, and ready to take responsibility for her actions but not ready to go to jail. She slowly spoke, her voice fragile and shaky. "Harley, please don't send me to jail. I've already told you how sorry I am for what I have done to you. You know I can't return the past two years to you, but surely, there is some way that I can make it up to you and Mrs. Black and Ms. Weaver. I was desperate, Harley, and desperation makes a person do crazy things."

Shirley and Abby were sitting quietly on the couch, listening to the bridled anger laced with some empathy in Harley's voice as he admonished Joan. Fear, stark and vivid, glittered in her eyes. She was definitely deserving of Harley's resentment, but as she said, desperation gave her strength to do inconceivable acts. Both ladies remained silent, giving Harley the chance to work through this exasperating matter.

Harley wiped his damp palms on the thighs of his jeans as if that action would wipe away his troubles. He was trying desperately to lighten his mood and thaw the coldness in his tone. "Joan, I am a man of God, and I have been given the gift of forgiveness. I have forgiven you for what you have done, but only you can forgive yourself. You also need God's forgiveness, and the only way to obtain that is to ask. I want you to judge yourself and advise me as to what your punishment should be. I trust that you will be able to recognize the severity of your wrongdoings and discern your penance. When you have that figured out, please contact me with your verdict."

With that being said, Harley held out an open hand and pulled Joan to her feet, all the while looking directly at Abby, his gaze locking with hers, causing an involuntary tightening low in his gut. She made the mistake of meeting his eyes and feeling the burn of heat in their shadowed depths. It seemed like the force of his presence struck her anew every time they encountered each other, and today was no exception. Shirley cleared her throat, loud enough for the neighbors to hear, pretending not to notice the electricity between the two of them but signaling for Harley to detach himself from his daydreams and return to the present matter.

Harley turned Joan over to Abby and Shirley. "Ladies, I have a lot of work to do outside, so I will leave the three of you to resolve Joan's predicament. I appreciate the patience that you have shown me today." He turned and strode away, his form moving with perfect grace.

Joan's legs were trembling so badly that she was afraid they wouldn't hold her, so she sat down on the nearest chair and waited to hear the terms of her dismissal from Summer Rain. Abby regarded Shirley with just as much authority as herself when it came to any decisions concerning the B&B, so when she saw Joan sink into the chair, she waited for Shirley to begin the process of removing Joan from the payroll.

Shirley began by asking Joan if she felt any resentment toward her or Abby because of the little "sting" they had set up. With little hesitation, Joan began talking, noticing how strange the words sounded on her tongue. This time, the lyrics were apologetic and very remorseful, a far cry from her earlier flamboyant attitude. She chose her words carefully as she continued to make an attempt to convince Shirley and Abby that, with every fiber in her body, she was sincere about her request for forgiveness. She soon had no more words left to say as tears flowed hot and humiliating.

Shirley and Abby wanted to pick up where they had left off what seemed like a lifetime ago, but today that didn't seem possible. Shirley spoke matter-of-factly when she reacted to Joan's response. "Everything must be out in the open and laid out for everyone to see. The indisputable and offensive facts must be dealt with and then forgotten. We know that Harley said you must choose your own atonement, and we are in full support of that, but he also left you under our care, and we believe that you must make restitution for your actions, and the first element for amnesty will be for you to go to the board at the church and admit the truth graciously. You need to ask for Harley's reinstatement as pastor. You need to request that you set up a payment plan so that you may pay the entirety of the stolen funds in a reasonable amount of time. Last but not least, you need to ask forgiveness from all those whom you involved in your scheme."

Shirley peered over the top of her glasses as if waiting for an answer but continued with the conversation. "If Abby agrees with me, you could continue working here at Summer Rain. You will be closely monitored, and you will no longer be taking care of the banking. We would like you to take the rest of the day off, go home, and think long and hard about this offer. We need your decision by tomorrow. Oh, one more thing, you will treat Harley with great respect. If it weren't for him, you would be unemployed."

A cry of relief broke from Joan's lips as she flung herself against Shirley and then Abby. Between sobs, she managed to say thank you to both ladies. She moved toward the door with a feeling of newfound freedom, triggering a smile, melting away her defenses.

Abby wanted to go outside to look for Harley, but Shirley vetoed the idea. A smile curved her mouth as she said, "Give him some time for all of this to settle before we go out there and interrupt his meditation. When he's ready, he'll reach out to us. He knows how much we care."

Abby agreed, waiting for Shirley to continue, but instead, her mother's sheepish smile turned to a chuckle. Two dimples appeared as if loving fingers had squeezed her cheeks.

Abby smiled tentatively as she asked, "Did I miss something?"

"No, dear, it's just that this day turned out much better than I had anticipated. What happens next with Harley and Joan is entirely in God's hands." Shirley walked down the hall and into the kitchen, not waiting for an answer.

CHAPTER 45

The end of the matter; all has been heard. Fear God and keep his commandments, for this is the whole duty of man.

—Ecclesiastes 12:13

The green folder was once more on Chief McDonald's desk with a blue sticker, coded as a cold case. How much longer he could continue to see it laying on his desk he wasn't sure, but he also knew it wasn't going away. Stacey insisted she was getting closer to the truth, so he was heavily relying on her details. She had already located Warren Wright and had scheduled a meeting with him for this morning. If this turned out to be a case of mistaken identity, Stacey would be back at the drawing board. She was so sure that this encounter with Mr. Wright was going to be so significant that the file could be put away soon. She even managed to get Tim to agree to a bet. If she were right, he would go to dinner and a movie with her; and if she were wrong, she would never ask him again. He reluctantly agreed, even though deep down he hoped she was right.

Warren had received the strangest call from the Carroll County Police Department. After providing his name, address, and time served in the army, he was asked to come down to the station to answer a few more questions. The lady on the phone would give him no more information but alluded to the fact that, if he didn't show up, a police officer would arrive at his office and escort him to the station downtown.

Warren pulled into the only parking space left at the police station. Ever since the phone call, his nerves had been playing games with his emotional stability. For some reason, he had been asked about his army stint. Did this have something to do with that era of his life? But that was so long ago. What could possibly be so important after all this time? He really didn't want to face any more memories of pain, terror, or death. He had put all of that behind him and tried to keep it locked away in his memory box. He thought it sounded silly when some of his buddies told him how they handled their memories. So he had worked long and hard at finding a way to forget. Just the mere mention of his army years was already bringing unwanted visions.

His nervousness touched him bone-deep as he crawled slowly out of the car. He pulled open one side of the double doors and walked to the receptionist's desk. The young lady, with hair the color of corn silk, was talking on the phone. She pointed to the chair and raised a brightly colored manicured finger in the air, motioning that it would only be a minute.

"Mr. Wright?"

Warren stood as ruthless and proud as his reputation. "Yes, that's me. I'm really anxious to know what this is about."

Stacey smiled, but the curve of her mouth had nothing to do with humor. "Mr. Wright, Chief McDonald will be with you shortly. Would you like a cup of coffee?"

"No thank you. My stomach seems to be doing cartwheels right now."

"I do have some ginger ale, if you think that would help."

"Thank you. I would like some please."

While Stacey retrieved the soda, the chief appeared in the doorway. After introducing himself, he invited Warren into his office. Stacey returned with the ginger ale and her notebook. Warren sat opposite the chief and waited.

Tim spoke with cool authority. "Mr. Wright, could you tell us your rank and serial number that could identify you in the army? And I need the years that you served also."

Warren's voice, cold and steady as stone, seemed to be teetering on the edge of impatience. He began reciting the information as if it were written on paper in front of him. Tim, impressed with Warren's memory, hoped this might be easier than he had anticipated. "Mr. Wright, did you know a fellow soldier by the name of Jeff Weaver?"

Warren's brows drew downward in a frown, his mouth twisted wryly. He replied without inflection, "Yes, sir, I did."

Tim could sense that Warren was not going to cooperate with any dimension to his answers. It just might be a long morning after all. "Do you remember your rank and the time span that you served together?"

Warren shifted to the edge of his chair. "May I ask what this is regarding? Did something happen that I don't know about?"

"Well, Mr. Wright, Jeff Weaver was killed in a car accident almost a year ago, and we've been investigating the accident ever since."

"What does that have to do with me?"

"We are trying to find someone who might have had a vendetta against the man. His brake lines were cut on his car, and he ran into the side of an oil tanker. We're interviewing everyone who has ever worked with him and in your case was in the army with him. When was the last time you saw him or had any contact with him?"

Warren leaned back and rubbed his chin as if he had fleas. There was a bitter edge of cynicism in his voice as he spoke. "I remember Jeff Weaver. We weren't exactly pals. I was his warrant officer, and he sometimes copiloted the planes with me. He thought he was better than I was by always telling me how to fly. He hobnobbed with the other officers and did a lot of complaining about me. I was a well-trained pilot, and I knew what I was doing. I took out a lot of the enemy and saved a lot of GIs." He nodded, not trusting himself to speak.

Recovering, he said lightly, "When I was a soldier, I saw enough death to last me a lifetime. I'm not sure what makes you think I had anything to do with Jeff's death, but I can assure you that I'm the last person on earth that wants to hurt anyone. I recently almost died myself, and I wouldn't wish it on anyone. Why have you connected me with his death?"

Tim chose his words carefully. "We have, as I said, interviewed many people and cannot find anyone to say an unkind word about Jeff. He never even had a parking ticket. We found your signature on the bottom of a potential army court-martial petition against Mr. Weaver. Even though a trial was never fully executed, it is on record. We know it was because of a physical altercation between the two of you that you claimed was started by Mr. Weaver, although his version was a bit different. He accused you of the initial push, stating that you were intoxicated. Whoever started it and for whatever reason is not my concern now. I really don't care. But what I *do* care about is finding the person who cut Mr. Weaver's brake line. You're the only person we can find that may have had ill feelings toward him."

Warren's thoughts pulled him back to a faded but never-forgotten memory of Jeff Weaver. That boy had so much confidence that it seemed to spill out his ears. He was liked by everyone in his platoon, but he just rubbed Warren the wrong way. He was a very intelligent young man and always had the right answers, even to questions that Warren didn't know. An officer should have been able to outsmart an enlisted man, but Jeff always overshadowed Warren's ideas. He hadn't thought about this man in over a decade. And now the police wanted him to remember and admit to cutting brake lines on a car. Just because he didn't like the guy was no reason to accuse him of murder.

Stacey was sitting quietly with her pen and notebook, waiting for Warren to continue. Tim cleared his throat, hoping the sound would bring Warren back to reality. Warren wanted to turn and walk out, but he knew that would make him look guilty, so he looked Chief McDonald in the eye and said, "I had nothing to do with Jeff's death. I wouldn't even know where the brake lines are at on a car. I always take my car back to the dealer, or I have my janitor, Hoafie, fix it, if it's not a real big job. He's an excellent mechanic. A little on the slow side, but he knows what he's doing. And he's real cheap."

Tim stood up, held out his hand to Warren, and thanked him for coming in and talking with them. If he was needed for anything else, Stacey would give him a call.

Warren unlocked his car, collapsed into his seat, and buckled the seat belt. His head was spinning with not only the questions but also the shrunken memories that the chief had evoked. His stomach was still reeling from the shock of the accusation from the police. He couldn't believe that they would try to charge him with a homicide. He was not a man out for revenge. Those days were long past, and he had no reason for hard feelings toward anyone. He considered himself a lucky man. He lived a nice life, and since his near-death experience, he felt blessed just to be alive. Plus, Lilly was now in his life, and he couldn't be happier. The incident with Jeff Weaver had happened a long time ago and was no longer important to him. He hoped the police could find the person responsible, but he knew it wasn't him.

CHAPTER 46

Blessed are the meek, for they shall inherit the earth.

—Matthew 5:5

Chief McDonald pulled the squad car into the only available parking space and cursed under his breath. When was the county going to enlarge the parking lot and allow him a marked spot? He was the chief of police, yet he had no designated space. Today, though, he had more important things on his mind. The green folder seemed to be overriding his regularly scheduled work. It was even haunting him in his sleep. The smell of coffee reached his nostrils just as he opened the door to his office. Obviously, Stacey had arrived early and was already piling files on his desk. Without looking, he knew the top one would be the color of grass. Even though its edges were getting a bit tattered, the green monster never weakened in its determination to discover the truth.

"Good morning, Stacey. You're here early."

In spite of her reserve, a tinge of exasperation came into her voice. "I came in early because I have something that I need to go over with you. It really seems like a far-fetched idea, but I can't get it out of my head, and I think we should at least check it out. We've exhausted every other lead."

"And am I to assume that you're talking about the green folder? The one that we can't seem to get away from?"

"Yes. When you're ready, I'll share my thought with you."

"Pull up that chair, and share them now. I'm willing to look at anything if it could help in any way."

Stacey sank into the chair and nodded dubiously. "Okay, when we interviewed Mr. Wright, he mentioned his janitor, Hoafie. Do you remember?"

Tim looked at her enigmatically and, without humor, asked, "Who and what is a Hoafie?"

"It's not a what. He's a who."

"Speak English please."

"Hoafie is Mr. Wright's janitor. He talked about his knowledge of cars. Said he's the best mechanic ever. I did some checking with a friend of mine who works part time at Mr. Wright's real estate office. He said Hoafie is about ten slices short of a full loaf of bread, but he's the nicest guy you'd ever want to meet. He does exactly what someone tells him to do." Stacey then echoed the fresh-water-commode story to Tim. He smiled, visioning the prank.

"Okay, what's this got to do with Jeff Weaver's car?"

"I haven't quite got that figured out yet, but I know it has something to do with this case. I've been trying to come up with the most outrageous scenarios because I think, when we do solve this case, it's going to be so bizarre that even we won't believe it."

"So you think this Hoafie character has something to do with the car brakes?"

"Yes, I do. If he's the car expert that Mr. Wright claims he is, then he would know exactly how to cut the line. What I don't understand is why would he do it? Everyone I've talked to describes him as a gentle giant." She bit down hard on her lower lip as she continued. "But he could be the link between Jeff Weaver and Warren Wright. It may have been many years ago, but Warren did have a vendetta against Jeff. Warren was also well-known at the local bars. It seems he had an every-night affair with a bar stool—until he was diagnosed with diabetes. Word has it that he was a talker when he drank. I'm really grasping at straws here, but what if, while he was intoxicated, he talked about Vietnam to Hoafie. The word also is that, once he had a few drinks under his belt, no one would sit near him because he never shut up. But Hoafie is a very loyal employee. He would never leave Warren's side if he was told to stay there. He listens to every word, and he takes everything literally."

Tim was looking at her as if she had lost her mind. "So what do you propose we do?"

"I want to ask him to look at the brakes on my car, and then I'll start asking questions. If he's short a few slices, then he won't put two and two together and figure out what I'm doing. But I need your permission, sir."

Tim ejected himself from his chair and gave her a smile that sent her pulses racing. "You don't know how much I appreciate your help with this case. You're right. It does sound harebrained, but crazier things have been known to happen. We can't let any rock go unturned, so you have my blessing. If you need my help with anything, just let me know."

Stacey rose from her chair, gave the thumbs-up sign, and walked out the door with powerful grace and beauty, which surprisingly did not go unnoticed by Tim.

CHAPTER 47

So do not be afraid of them. There is nothing concealed that will not be disclosed, or hidden that will not be made known.

—Matthew 10:26

Dark smudges of exhaustion lay under Stacey's eyes when she showed up for work Monday morning. The weekend had not provided many hours of sleep. She had taken the green folder home with her and had pored over it time and time again, hoping to find some small clue that would lead her to Hoafie. Woman's intuition and a good old-fashioned gut feeling told her that Hoafie had somehow contributed to the accident. Her biggest question was why. And how did he get to Jeff's car? He could only have known Jeff through Warren. But why would Warren want to hurt Jeff after all these years? And Warren said he hadn't even seen Jeff in over a decade.

Stacey was determined to earn her dinner with Tim, so she wasn't giving up on this case. One way or another, she was going to solve the mystery. She needed to talk to Hoafie alone. *If he's as honest as everyone claims him to be, then he had to be the starting point.* She parked her car across the street from the WOW Real Estate office and waited until she saw Warren leave. As soon as she stepped inside the front door, she recognized Hoafie from the description Tim had given her. He had the front section of the vending machine lying on the floor and was tightening up some screws on the inside. He lifted his head alertly when he heard the bell on the door and smiled from ear to ear.

She strolled forward and extended her hand. "Hi, Hoafie. My name is Stacey. I'm a friend of your boss, Mr. Wright. How are you today?"

Hoafie offered a sudden smile and an immediate handshake. She was halted by such an iron grip. In a desperate attempt to befriend him, she had brought with her a bag of Tootsie Rolls. As soon as he saw the familiar-looking bag, his eyebrows rose and fell with more expression than he could ever have voiced, and he dropped her hand.

"I heard that you like these, Hoafie, and I wanted you to have some extras." Hoafie took the bag and instantly began tearing a hole in the top.

"While you are eating those, do you think you could look at my car? Mr. Wright said that you are the best mechanic around."

Hoafie, smiling while chewing the candy, began shaking his head no. "I can't leave my job. I have to fix that machine. People have to eat."

"I'm sure they do, Hoafie, but I checked with Mr. Wright, and he said it was okay for you to do this little favor for me. My car is in the parking lot, and I just wondered if you could take a quick look at it for me. It will only take five minutes."

Hoafie looked around as if he were going to ask permission, but seeing no one at the front desk, he shrugged his broad shoulders and started walking toward the door. Stacey followed on his heels.

Once in the parking lot, she pointed out her red Mustang. Hoafie strolled to the car and stopped. He turned to look at Stacey and asked, "What's wrong?"

"It's my brakes. I've been having trouble stopping. They don't seem to be working right. I guess you know everything about brakes, right?"

"Yeah, I know everything about a car. My boss says I'm the best. It will take me a minute, but I'll be able to tell if there is something wrong." Within seconds, Hoafie had somehow glided his huge body underneath the Mustang, and Stacey couldn't resist a chuckle. *How did he do that?* Maybe he did have some sort of magic in his pockets.

Stacey stooped over so that he could hear her next question. "Do you fix a lot of cars, Hoafie?"

"No. Sometimes the people in the office ask me to fix their cars. I used to work at a garage that my neighbor owned, but he died, and Mr. Wright was real kind and gave me a job. He's a real good boss."

"I'm sure he is, Hoafie, and you would do anything for him, wouldn't you?"

"Yeah, he likes me too."

"Well, I can see why. You're pretty special."

With that, he came out from under the car as if being shot from a cannon. "Your brake lines look pretty new. Maybe you should take some driving lessons."

Stacey laughed so hard that she ended up snorting in an unladylike fashion. "You do have a way with words, Hoafie. Let's talk about your boss. Do you ever fix his car or any of his buddies'?"

"No, but I broke one for him."

"What do you mean you broke one?"

"Well, one time, I cut one of these lines on one of his old army pal's car. It was a real nice shiny Lincoln. He didn't like this guy. Said they had a fight, and his buddy won. He wished he could do something to pay him back, so I thought I would help him. Guys really like cars, ya know, and I thought this guy would be mad if he wrecked his car. Mr. Warren laughed, so I thought it was just a joke. People are always pullin' jokes on me, so I thought it would be funny if I helped my boss. He didn't know it, though. I thought he would give me a raise if I did extra stuff for him."

"Did you get a raise, Hoafie?"

"No, the boss got sick and didn't come to work for a while, and then I just forgot about it."

Stacey knew without a doubt that this big teddy bear of a man was not a deliberate killer. She thanked Hoafie and walked with him back into the office just to be sure that no one would be asking about his whereabouts.

Stacey didn't even knock on Tim's door when she returned to the office. Bursting at the seams to divulge her new discovery, she nearly fell over the chair in front of Tim's desk. She had run the whole way from the parking lot and was out of breath.

"Who in the world is chasing you?" barked Tim. "You almost made me spill my coffee."

"It won't matter when I tell you what I just found out."

"Well, don't keep me waiting. I hope it's about the Weaver case."

"It is, and I was right. It was Hoafie."

Tim stood up and walked to the door, pushing it shut. "Okay, tell me the whole story."

As Stacey relayed her detective accomplishment to Tim, his mouth dropped open, and he seemed too surprised to do anything but nod. Her voice broke off in midsentence as she realized that he hadn't even tried to speak but was only grinning with a distinctly male satisfaction.

"Why aren't you saying anything? Don't you believe me? I told you this was going to be bizarre."

Tim held up his hand, motioning for her to stop. "Yes, I believe you, and I wasn't saying anything because you're right. It is very bizarre. I guess I'm at a loss for words except to say that you have done some exceptional investigative work with this case. I'm very proud of you."

CHAPTER 48

Think over what I say, for the Lord will give you understanding in everything.

—2 Timothy 2:7

Chief McDonald was having a hard time getting any work done. The Weaver case was just so strange that he couldn't get it off his mind. He also kept putting off calling Abby Weaver. How was he supposed to explain to a widow that her husband was most likely dead because of a misunderstood interpretation of one man's determination to please another? Hoafie seemed to be guilty, yet he was such an innocently simple man. He wondered how Abby would react to this theory. Would she press charges or recognize the circumstance as tragic and heartbreaking? His heart told him that she would at least ponder the latter. It was Marie Forester that he was worried about. This lady was much more combative than her niece. Remembering his promise to keep Ms. Forester up to date on the latest event caused him chest pains. He dialed her number, all the while praying that she wouldn't answer. He smiled as he left a message on her machine to please contact him.

He leaned forward in his chair and dialed the phone once more.

"Hello."

"Mrs. Weaver?"

"Yes, this is she speaking."

"This is Tim McDonald from the police department. How are you today?"

"I'm fine, Tim. And yourself?"

"I'm fine. I am calling to ask if you could possibly come into the police station sometime today. We have some new information on your husband's accident, and it's not something that can be discussed over the phone. I will be here until six o'clock, so you may come at your convenience."

"I will be there within the hour. Thank you."

A half hour or so later, Stacey knocked lightly on Tim's door and announced that Mrs. Weaver was there to see him. When he looked up, his eyes clung to hers, trying to analyze exactly what her reaction was going to be, but her eyes were misty and wistful. He pulled a chair up to her and asked her to sit. He walked around his desk, sat down, and shuffled through some papers as if he had lost his reason for calling her. "Mrs. Weaver, as I said on the phone, I have some news about your husband's accident. It's quite bizarre, so I'm glad you're sitting down. I think you know Warren Wright. He owns a real estate company over in Millersburg."

Hearing the name, Abby was suddenly on the edge of her seat, as an electrifying shudder reverberated through her. "What exactly does Mr. Wright have to do with my husband's accident?" she demanded.

"Please, Mrs. Weaver, please don't jump to conclusions. Sounds like he might not be one of your favorite people. In a roundabout way, he is involved, but we think we know exactly what happened. And if you will allow me, I will tell you, barring no details."

Abby leaned back against her chair again and remained still while Tim shared the latest information about her husband's collision. When he told her the very last element, he hesitated, not knowing exactly how to finish without sounding abrupt. The look on her face couldn't have been worse if he'd driven a knife through her heart. He broke off then with an apology as his hand came down over hers. Hastily, she drew it away and covered her face as if trying to hide from the truth. Within minutes, she rose from the chair and walked out of the police station without a thank-you or good-bye.

Tim was left speechless as he watched Abby get in her car and drive away. He wasn't sure if he should worry about her or be glad that she hadn't given him a quick karate chop to the back of his neck. He wasn't exactly sure about all the emotions she must be feeling right now, but he knew her face had paled with anger, and surely, her mind must be burning with memories of her husband. She must have questions too as to how something so unintended could turn into something so catastrophic. He realized she needed time to sort out the information that he had given her. He walked to the coffeepot and brewed the strongest cup of coffee that the pot would allow.

While stirring sugar into the muddy brew, his personal phone began ringing. "Hi, Chief McDonald. This is Bruce Smith. I'm Warren Wright and

Hoafie's attorney. I understand you would like us to come down there for an off-the-record meeting?"

"Yes, sir, if that's possible. I think it would clear up a lot of speculation that we all have about this case. It's very unusual, and it would be nice to at least get a handle on this before the media swoops in. If the three of you could come down this morning, that would be great."

"I think we can manage that."

"Great. I'll be waiting for you."

Before Tim finished his pot of coffee, the three men walked into his office. Mr. Smith—a pudgy balding, rumpled man in a wrinkled raincoat—took charge, directing each one to a seat. Hoafie was next to Warren but in front of the police chief. Mr. Smith stood next to the desk. After introductions, Mr. Smith began by asking Hoafie a few questions—how old he was, where he lived, if he had a telephone. Hoafie answered each one with precise facts.

The attorney's interest then shifted to Warren. He asked him questions about his business, his lifestyle, and, of course, Hoafie—how long Hoafie had worked for him and exactly what his duties were, how many times he had missed work, and how often they discussed the workings of cars. Question after question came flying at them faster than an automatic ball launcher. Mr. Smith explained it as a great way to find out the truth—no time to think, just answer the question.

When the meeting was finally over, Warren and Hoafie returned to the real estate office, while Mr. Smith stayed to talk to Tim. "I see what you mean, Tim, about Hoafie. Harmless as a kitten. He doesn't have a mean bone in his body. There is no way he did anything intentional. Have you talked to Mr. Weaver's widow yet?"

"Yes, I have, but I can't tell you her reaction. She bolted before I could determine her feelings. I think she just needs a little bit of time to let everything sink in, and then she'll come around."

Mr. Smith nodded perfunctorily and turned toward the door. "As soon as you hear from Ms. Weaver, please be sure to call my office. Even though Hoafie hasn't been detained and there is no warrant for his arrest, he will still have to appear before the magistrate, but I'll hold that off until I hear from you. So the minute Ms. Weaver contacts you, I need to know."

CHAPTER 49

Then you will know the truth, and the truth will set you free.

—John 8:32

Abby couldn't believe what she had just heard. Jeff's death was caused by a mentally challenged man who thought he was doing his boss a favor. And his boss, being drunk, had no idea that he had even talked about messing with Jeff's brakes. How was it that Mr. Wright was again involved in her life? Did he deliberately cause the accident so he could be the recipient of her husband's liver? Was he acquainted with a charlatan in the hospital that had access to the organ donor list? Was that even possible? Mr. Wright did have a reputation for being an astute salesman, but would he stoop so low as to use that shrewdness to end a man's life so that he could save his own? To have that much confidence in a self-centered conspiracy would take a lot of guts and a large amount of narcissistic brain waves. If it was true, how was she ever going to forgive this man?

The intensity of her headache forced Abby to lie down on the sofa, and soon she fell asleep. A repulsive monster by the name of Hoafie consumed her dreams, killing everyone in sight. He was plucking organs from unaware people and scavenging their hearts. His laughter sounded almost demonic, low and throaty. He had a list of victims, and like a devilish Santa Claus, he was checking it twice. Abby saw her name being rearranged so that it appeared at the top of the roster. She was next in line.

Bells began ringing. Was that an indication that her time had come? In her dream, she tried to run but instead fell off the sofa and woke with a thump on the hardwood floor. The landing brought her back to reality, and without warning, she began weeping, rocking back and forth, feeling intense fright and nausea. Desolation mixed with anger and rage seemed to sweep over her. She was relieved to know the truth, yet her relief altered instantly into suspicion. Could she really believe the story that Chief McDonald had told her? Surely, no one would make up such a tale. Maybe she was being a little skeptical, but that day had changed her life forever, and she needed to know the truth. The fact that Warren Wright was involved only made her more upset. Without another thought, she grabbed a tissue, dried her tears, and reached for the phone. When Chief McDonald answered, she asked him to set up a meeting with Hoafie.

CHAPTER 50

Blessed is the man whose sin the Lord does not count against him and in whose spirit is no deceit.

—Psalm 32:2

As Abby sat waiting for this man called Hoafie, she kept going over in her mind exactly what she would say to him. When he burst into the room and saw Abby, he slowed down and sauntered toward her, hands thrust in the pockets of his worn jeans. He reached up, took off his hat, and nodded a greeting. He swung his head around, peeking over his shoulder as if waiting for someone else to enter the room. Within seconds, Warren Wright made himself visible.

Abby felt as hollow as she knew her voice would sound if she spoke. What was this man doing here again? She had requested to be alone with Hoafie. Did Mr. Wright think he could intimidate her with his presence? If her voice echoed her feelings, well, so be it. She wanted him to know exactly how she felt. "Mr. Wright, I assume that you were the transportation for Hoafie today, but I really want to speak to him alone."

"I understand, Ms. Weaver. I have some errands to run near here, so I will leave you two alone."

"Hoafie, this is Ms. Abby Weaver. She wants to talk to you for a few minutes. I'll be back in a little while for you, and we'll go back to work, OK?"

Hoafie broke into an open smile and indicated by a motion of his head that he would obey. His big workman's hands promptly reached out, grabbed Abby's hand, and began shaking it intensely yet with extreme tenderness. Abby made no effort to disengage her hand while stealing a glance at his face, ruddy and ravaged by old acne scars. The expression in his black eyes seemed to be pleading for understanding. Obviously, Mr. Wright had explained the situation as best as possible to this trusting soul.

Abby found herself trying to overcome her reactions to this man, who appeared to be intellectually disabled yet so comfortable in his own skin. "How are you, Hoafie? It's so nice to meet you. I understand you're a great mechanic."

As soon as Abby mentioned the word *mechanic*, Hoafie's face lit up like a Christmas tree. "Yes, ma'am. Mr. Warren—he's my boss—well, he says I can fix anything on a car. He says I'm the best."

"I'm sure you are, Hoafie. May I ask you a few questions?"

He gave her a reluctant nod and a boyish grin that made her heart do an instant flip. She knew she could never accuse this timid man of any wrongdoing. Whatever he had done, it hadn't been achieved because of malice.

"Hoafie, I guess you really like working for Mr. Wright."

"Yes, ma'am. He's a real good boss. He even took me to Cherry's for a big piece of steak." He began licking his lips as if he had just finished a rib eye.

"Do you work on your boss's car?"

"Sometimes, but he always has a new car, so nothin' ever breaks."

"Does he ever ask you to work on someone else's car?"

"No, but once, I thought he wanted me to break someone's car, so I did."

His words chilled Abby to the bone. She began to shake as the visual images built in her mind. And this man, sitting in front of her, had no idea what devastation he had caused. Abby couldn't help but ask, "Hoafie, did your boss tell you exactly which car to break, or how did you know where to find the car?"

Hoafie seemed tormented by confusion. He spoke as if he knew he had done something wrong, yet he couldn't define exactly what it was. He began explaining to Abby about the night at Cherry's when Warren was talking about his friend Jeff and how he had been mad at Jeff all those years ago. He had wanted some kind of revenge but had never followed through. Hoafie remembered whispering to Warren about cutting the brake lines and how his boss had doubled over in laughter. Hoafie took that to mean it was a good idea, and he always did what his boss wanted. He couldn't remember how he found Jeff's car, but he did recall asking a secretary in the real estate office if she could find out any information on Jeff Weaver. Hoafie couldn't write very well, but he had a memory like an elephant. He memorized the make and model of the car and Jeff's place of employment. From there on out, it was like a game—find the car, cut the brakes, and make Warren happy. Hoafie admitted that he was hoping for a raise because of the great job he had done, but he had gotten distracted because of Warren's illness and never informed Warren of his actions.

Abby looked up as she heard the door open and realized that Warren had heard the last bit of Hoafie's conversation. She watched as his smile vanished, wiped away by astonishment. There was unmistakable regret in his tone as he spoke. "Hoafie, can you wait for me outside, and then I'll take you back to the office?"

Hoafie jumped at the sound of his voice, nodded half-heartedly, and walked out the door as quickly as he could.

Warren leaned against the wall and breathed deeply as if waiting for Abby to speak first. When she didn't, he spoke with a quiet strength that brought her eyes around to meet his. What she saw in those eyes were life, mixed with pain and substantial warmth. She heard it in his voice too. He was profusely apologizing for being under the influence and for dragging Hoafie into the whole mess. He was saying that if anyone was guilty, it would be him. His request for forgiveness caught her off guard, and before she had time to ponder the confession, she jumped to her feet and began accusing him of causing the accident intentionally.

He reacted angrily to the challenge in her voice. "I am not a vicious man. I made a stupid statement when I was intoxicated, I'll grant you that, but I did nothing premeditated. Hoafie thinks everything I say is gospel, and I guess I didn't take that seriously enough. What makes you think, after all these years, I would want to hurt Jeff? Alcohol causes people to do crazy things, and that's my only explanation. I am not a vengeful person."

She shot him a cold look and said, "You may not be a vicious man or even a vengeful one, but when it comes to saving your own life, motives can change a person's perspective real fast. When you found out you needed a new liver, your warped mind came up with a conspiracy."

Warren was now seething with mounting rage. Where in the world was this woman getting her ideas? "Ms. Weaver, please tell me where you got this information. You can't go around throwing out accusations without proof."

Abby spat out the words contemptuously. "Proof? You want proof? I can show you written proof. Tell me, Mr. Wright, is your attorney's name Gary Wentz?" Curses fell from his mouth as he told her that was none of her business. "You can say it any way you want, but it became my business the minute they removed your liver and replaced it with my husband's."

Warren felt as if he had been gut-punched and the wind knocked out of him. He had been given Jeff Weaver's liver? He had no idea. Soon after the transplant, his attorney had asked if he wanted a letter of gratitude sent to the donor's family; and within days, a copy had been placed on his desk, but he had somehow overlooked the donor's name. "Ms. Weaver,

I'm so sorry. I didn't mean to sound so smug, but I had no idea where my liver came from."

Abby's lips puckered with annoyance. How dare he act so sanctimonious? Where did he think he got his new liver, Kmart? A minute ago, he seemed so genuinely sorry, and now he was telling her that he didn't even know the name of his donor. "Mr. Wright, I find it hard to believe that you could be so insensitive about such a delicate issue. Because of my husband, you have been given another chance at life, yet you didn't have the guts to say thank you to me in person. I was giving you the benefit of the doubt, thinking that maybe it was another Warren Wright. Deep down, I think I knew it was you, but I couldn't figure out why you wouldn't have told me, especially since we know each other and have met several times since your transplant. I feel sorry for you, Mr. Wright, and I feel sorry for Hoafie too. Because of your actions, you have put that poor man in a very difficult situation."

Warren gritted his teeth together tightly, trying to keep his emotions under control as he spoke. "Ms. Weaver, I am well aware of the situation that I have put Hoafie and myself in, but right now, I thought we were talking about your husband and my transplant. As I told you before, I am very sorry for your loss, but I had no idea that the donor was your husband. My attorney did draw up the paperwork to include a thank-you letter, and I apologize for my disregard to that process, but I deal with stacks of papers every day, and it sometimes becomes so mundane that I fail to notice something out of the ordinary."

He felt the need to keep talking, to apologize, but the look on her face was anything but forgiving. For a brief moment, her intense eyes held him prisoner while he searched for the right words. When he spoke again, his voice was a husky whisper. "I am truly sorry, Ms. Weaver. If there was anything I could do to change what happened, I surely would. You need to know your husband's death was a tragic accident, and no one meant for any harm to come to him. Hoafie is still not quite sure what he did wrong nor of the heartache that it has caused you. I am willing to take whatever punishment the courts seem fitting, and I will assume Hoafie's penance too. I will live with this for the rest of my life. From the bottom of my heart, I am truly sorry." Without waiting for a response from Abby, he turned and walked out the door. He motioned for Hoafie to follow him, and together, they walked to Warren's car. His heart was spilling over with remorse, but he could find no more words to express his empathies to Ms. Weaver.

Warren returned Hoafie back to the office and watched as he walked through the front door and turned to wave at Warren. He broke into an open, friendly smile, unaware of the bleak future that he might be facing.

Chief McDonald informed Warren that a small-court hearing would be scheduled, and their fate would be in the hands of the judge. The only evidence they had was Hoafie's confession, and Warren wasn't sure how substantial that would be. Would the judge hold Hoafie accountable for his actions, or would he blame Warren? He assumed that Abby would have some influence over the contents of Chief McDonald's report. He also wanted to believe that she was a fair and compassionate person, but the fact that he had received her husband's liver put a different spin on the incident. He had no idea how this chapter of his life was going to end.

Abby couldn't deny the evidence any longer. Jeff had died for no reason. Technically, he had been murdered. The brakes had been cut cunningly yet with no intent to harm. She could blame Warren for getting drunk and talking to Hoafie, but that wasn't a crime. It was what Hoafie did with the information that was criminal. He had no idea that trying to please his boss would bring harm to another person. Had he been conscious of that, he never would have cut the Lincoln's brake line. How in the world was she going to handle this? There was no way to justify Jeff's death, yet there was no way to escape from the reality of it either. She was either going to hold a grudge for the rest of her life *or* going to learn to have to forgive—first Joan, now this.

Without diving deep into thought, Abby found herself dialing Harley's number. *He used to be a pastor. Maybe he can give me the right advice*, she thought. He answered the phone after the second ring, and at the sound of his voice, a pang of longing shot through her. Suddenly, she wanted him to hold her close, kiss her, and tell her it would be all right.

"Hello? Hello? Is anyone there?"

"Yes, it's Abby. I'm sorry to bother you, but would it be possible for us to talk? I could come by your place and pick you up, or if there is some quiet place nearby that we could meet, I would really appreciate it. I could use some advice."

"You're sure you want advice from me?"

"Yes, I'm in a bit of a quandary, and I could really use someone else's perspective. I was hoping you could give me some biblical insight."

Harley cleared his throat, pretending not to be affected by the sound of her voice that was vibrating with desperation. He couldn't believe that she was actually asking for his help. "I will meet you in the park by the big willow tree in thirty minutes."

"Thank you, Harley. I'll see you soon."

Chapter 51

Love bears all things, believes all things, hopes all things, endures all things.

—1 Corinthians 13:7

When Warren's alarm clock declared that it was six o'clock, he nearly somersaulted out of bed with excitement, brewed his first cup of coffee, and dialed his fiancée's number. Fiancée—that was such a foreign word to him. It was going to take some practice on his part in order to get used to the idea that he was getting married. When he saw Lilly tonight, he hoped they could set a date. Warren Wright getting married—that should make big headlines in the local paper. He wasn't known as the marrying kind. He didn't quite believe it himself. Would Lilly want a fancy wedding, or would she want to elope? He had become accustomed to upscale affairs, and now he could be in the limelight of his own event, but only if that was what Lilly wanted. She was not familiar with the finer things in life, but Warren was going to change that. She could have the wedding of her dreams, if that was what she wanted.

Lilly answered on the first ring, hoping it was Warren. "Hello. Hellooooo? Is anyone there?"

"Hi, Lilly. How are you? I'm sorry, I was lost in wedding thoughts."

"Really? That's all I've thought about all night long. I didn't get much sleep."

"Neither did I. What time is your shift over today?"

"I'll be done by five-thirty and home by six."

"Good, I'll be at your door by six-fifteen."

"You sound a little anxious. Is everything okay?"

"It's better than okay. I finally have something to live for. Can't wait to see you. Bye."

Lilly felt a warm glow flow through her as she laid down the phone. Her stomach was in knots. Her mind burned with the memory of Warren proposing to her on bended knee. She would never forget a single detail of his face as he asked her to marry him. She recalled the ecstasy of being held against his strong body, and even in remembrance, she felt the intimacy of his kisses. If she closed her eyes, his scent curled through her memory. Her whole being seemed to be filled with waiting as she calculated the hours until she would see him again. Anticipation thickened the air in her lungs. Was it going to be like this every day? How could she ever concentrate on her job?

The doorbell chimed, bringing Lilly back to reality. She grabbed her robe and rushed to the door. When she opened it, a young boy was holding the biggest bouquet of yellow roses that she had ever seen. She thanked him and carried them to the table. Her kitchen soon oozed with their sweet floral perfume. She gingerly fingered the note, curious of the sentiments inside. She flipped the switch on the Mr. Coffee machine and sat down.

Anxious to probe into the world of Warren, she opened the envelope slowly and pulled out the tiny business-size card. It simply said, in crude-looking cursive. "You make me happy. Can't wait to see you."

Lilly laughed with sheer joy. It was amazing how nine words could make her so happy. She poured her coffee and resumed her morning routine. Big George would be impatiently waiting for her at the diner.

Before she even had time to put on her sneakers, the doorbell rang for the second time that morning. Her hands were still shaking from the excitement of Warrens words, and she had trouble getting the dead bolt unlocked. When the door finally opened, there he stood. The muscles rippling under his white shirt, straining against the fabric, quickened her pulse. His boldly handsome face smiled warmly down at her right before he kissed her with a hunger that belied his outward calm. She quivered at the sweet tenderness of his touch. At last, reluctantly, they parted a few inches, and he touched her cheek in a wistful gesture.

Excitement throbbed in his voice as it slipped over her like crushed velvet. "Every time I see you, you're more beautiful." His smile faded a little when he quickly changed the subject. "I have something to tell you, and we'll need some privacy. I made a reservation at the new Italian restaurant over on Washington Boulevard. As bizarre as it will sound, it's also very heartbreaking. I hope you will hear me out and understand the position I'm in."

She was puzzled by his abrupt change in mood and asked, "Are you in some kind of trouble?"

"I'm not exactly sure. The police are involved, but there are no charges against me yet. Can we just go to the restaurant, find our table, and let me start at the beginning?"

Sheer black fright swept through Lilly. Her life finally had meaning. The man of her dreams proposed to her, and now he was saying he might be arrested. For what? The question was a stab in her heart. Was he not the man she thought he was? Was it possible that he was a con man? Suddenly, her bright future began to look vague and shadowy.

"I can tell by the look on your face, Lilly, that you're scared. I'm a little scared too." He squeezed her hand and walked her to the car.

After arriving that evening at the restaurant, they followed their waiter to a secluded table in the corner—the perfect place for a discreet conversation. Warren ordered a bottle of chardonnay, leaned back in his chair, and contemplated exactly how he was going to explain to Lilly his involvement in a heart-wrenching situation. He realized she was watching him and patiently awaiting his explanation.

He began his story by describing his childhood years, followed by his two tours of duty in Vietnam. He spoke of his acquaintance with Jeff Weaver and the illicit altercation. He disclosed his problem with alcohol and his battle with diabetes. He consistently sighed heavily, his voice filled with anguish as he continued uncovering intimacies about himself. He informed her of the genetic disease that almost claimed his life and how his near-death experience had altered his way of thinking. His final declaration was how his janitor, Hoafie, was involved in a tragic set of circumstances.

"What I'm about to tell you is so weird that you probably won't believe me, but I assure you, it's true." She was shocked when his eyes suddenly filled with tears, so she reached out and clutched at his hand. His eyes darkened with more emotion, but in the same cool tone, he continued. He was breaking Lilly's heart with the sincerity of his words. He was right; it was the most bizarre story she had ever heard.

Warren waited for Lilly to make a comment, but she merely stared, tongue-tied.

"Please say something, Lilly. I need to know what you're thinking. I know it's a lot to throw at you, but you needed to know, and I needed to be honest with you. I don't want any secrets between us."

"Warren, I'm not sure what to say. I can't believe something like that could happen. You know I will stand beside you no matter what comes of this, but who will stand beside Hoafie? The only thing he's guilty of is being loyal to you. Can someone like him be held accountable for his actions? How are you going to handle this?"

"I don't know, Lilly. I'm praying that the law can find some justice in this case without being too harsh with me or Hoafie. I will know more tomorrow. I have an appointment with Chief McDonald. I'm hoping he will have some answers for me."

Warren's touch was reassuring as his thumb made lazy slow circles on the back of Lilly's hand. Her heart seemed to rush to the spot he was caressing.

"Lilly, you don't know what it means to me to have your support. Knowing you'll be beside me is like handing me the keys to the kingdom."

CHAPTER 52

Consider it pure joy, my brothers, whenever you face trials of many kinds, because you know that the testing of your faith develops perseverance. Perseverance must finish its work so that you may be mature and complete, not lacking anything.

—James 1:2–4

Harley reached into his cooler to retrieve a bottle of water when he heard voices on the other side of his camper. Not sounding familiar, he retreated to his orange plastic beach chair, laid back, closed his eyes, and waited. If they were looking for him, he was quite accessible.

"Pastor Harley, may we have a word with you?"

Pastor Harley? No one had called him Pastor in over two years. Should he open his eyes or pretend to be asleep? Curiosity got the best of him, so he opened one eye, squinting against the sun's intense rays, and lo and behold, there stood Bill, the chairman of the board from Morning Son and his sidekick, Luke. Harley wasn't exactly sure what to do or what to say, but instinct kicked in, so he stood immediately and held out an open hand. Bill exuded a level of charismatic power, even though he had the look of a good old country boy. Sometimes his disposition resembled that of a rattlesnake with a sore tooth, but today his firm, steady grip felt sincere and natural, bringing back memories of the many handshakes on Sunday mornings.

"Good morning, Bill. How are you? It's been a long time. What can I do for you?"

"Well, to start with, let me say that I am very sorry." He shook his head in utter disbelief. "We all are very sorry. We've come to beg for forgiveness and to offer you your old job back at Morning Son. When Joan asked for a special board meeting, we had no idea what she wanted. The entire board was in total shock. What she did to you was appalling, but what we, as a church, did to you was no less inexcusable. No one really had the guts to face you after finding out how we'd wronged you, but I guess because of my reputation as an eccentric old man with a lot of intestinal fortitude, I got elected to help encourage you to return to us."

Blood pounded in Harley's temples as he absorbed the shocking news. He was too startled by the request to offer any immediate objection or approval. He needed a minute or two of careful deliberation before he responded to Bill. His mind was refusing to register the significance of the old man's words, and mixed feelings surged through him as he fought to control his swirling emotions. Of course, he wanted to return to the church. Morning Son had become his home—a home filled with family. But he also had some pride. He wasn't sure they really deserved to have him back. And he had other misgivings. He wanted to return more than anything, but if he did, would he always be suspicious of any conversation between parishioners? He had found out the hard way what Pastor George had meant when he warned Harley about the "wolves in sheep's clothing." If he went back, it had to be on his terms. He didn't want to be looking over his shoulder everywhere he went and be paranoid about his congregation.

Harley raised his eyes to find both men staring at him, their eyes pleading for an answer. He had prayed so hard for this day to transpire, and now that it was here, he wasn't quite sure what to do. He knew it had taken a lot for these two men to show up at his humble abode and seek his forgiveness. Their facial expressions were strained, giving the impression that going back to the church without success meant a figurative lynching for sure. Harley took a deep breath and tried to relax. Being flippant wasn't his style, but what harm could it do to stage a bit of a parody? He shrugged in mock resignation, shot Bill a good-natured smile, and clapped an arm around his shoulders. "I'll tell you what, my friend. I will come back to Morning Son this coming Sunday and preach a sermon, and then we'll discuss as to whether I stay or not."

Bill's thick gray eyebrows rose over the tops of his wire-rimmed glasses in genuine surprise. "You mean you won't give us an answer now?"

Harley couldn't help himself as his behavior became more animated. He had to deftly cover his laughter with a cough. "What do ya say, Bill? You want me to preach on Sunday or not?"

"Of course, we want you to preach, but . . ."

"But what? If you have to hesitate, there must be another problem."

Bill spoke his words in a breathy rush. "It's just that the vote to bring you back was majority ruled, and there were a few—I'm sure you know who they are—who were not happy with the end result. So it was agreed that you would be given one chance to return, and that chance is right now." His gaze lowered as did his voice. "I'm really sorry about everything that's happened to you, Pastor. I have never understood why you didn't leave town and find another church, knowing how the majority of people around here feel about you, but you did remain here, and now you've been proven innocent."

Harley interrupted and said, "Bill, I realize you are only the messenger, so because of that, I'm going to give you some correspondence to take back to your group of doubters. Please give them the report that I will be in the pulpit Sunday morning for worship service. That's all I want you to say. Please allow me to handle the rest of the story."

Harley pumped both men's hands with enthusiasm and dismissed them with "I'll see you Sunday morning .

CHAPTER 53

Be joyful in hope, patient in affliction, faithful in prayer.

—Romans 12:12

There was a message waiting for Abby when she returned home. Chief McDonald had called to say that the hearing for Warren and Hoafie was set for Friday morning at nine o'clock in Judge Green's courtroom. He sounded confident that having a private setting with only the judge, a police officer, and those involved in the crime could be a benefit for Warren and Hoafie.

After talking with Harley, Abby had a pretty good idea of what she was going to say if she was asked by the judge to give a statement. Harley had allowed her to speak freely about what she was thinking even as bitterness spilled over into her voice. Surprisingly, she found his voice to be mesmerizing and filled with promise. It sent vibrations deep into the core of her body. He was infinitely patient and encouraged her to speak honestly and openly. He gave her insight into what the Bible had to say about forgiveness, and she came away from the meeting feeling better than she had felt in a long time.

Harley walked home after his meeting with Abby and fell to his knees inside his little camper. He found it amazing how God was still working in his life day after day. For Abby to call and ask for his advice brought memories of his days as a pastor, how he used to love being able to talk to people and help them through hard times. The words that had fallen from his mouth during his and Abby's conversation had to have come from the Almighty himself, speaking not only to Abby but to himself as well. The counsel he provided to Abby was the exact guidance he needed for his situation with Joan. He just needed to pay attention to his own teachings. Spending time on his knees was a way to do that. The next few weeks were going to be very complex and heart-wrenching. People's character would be exposed for the world to see and to judge. Harley prayed for mercy on their souls and that the imprint of God's grace would be stamped on their hearts forever.

Harley was the first one to arrive at the courthouse Friday morning at the request of Abby. He allowed himself a moment of reflection before walking up the steps and through the big glass doors. How many families had been torn apart in this building because of divorce, and how many had been brought together because of someone's faith? The hallway was already filling up with families, and he found himself glancing uneasily over his shoulder, expecting arguments to break out.

He caught sight of Abby as she held the door open for an elderly lady but lost sight of her as she disappeared into the crowd. Without warning, a hand touched Harley's shoulder; and when he turned to see the source, he found himself looking directly into Abby's face. Even though her eyes were curtained with long curved lashes, he noticed a deeper calmness in them as if she had no worries or fears about what was to take place inside the courtroom. Her voice was music to Harley's ears. "Harley, thank you for coming today. I think we are all glad to have you here. I want you to meet Warren and Hoafie. I told them that I invited you, and they are so anxious to meet you."

"I'm honored to be here, and I hope I can be of some help. Let's find them. I think it's soon time to go in."

Abby clutched her purse hard against her chest and began waving with the other hand. From Abby's previous description of Hoafie, Harley knew she was waving to the wide-shouldered, bulky man as he shuffled toward him and Abby. His legs looked as firm as tree trunks, and his hands were big and square. His head was round as a pumpkin with darkly stubbled skin, and his chubby face was a map of faded scars. Yet with all his unkind features, his mouth appeared to have melted into a permanent buttery smile.

Hoafie began pumping Harley's hand even before Abby had finished introducing them, and they both found it impossible not to return his charismatic smile. Warren too had a repertoire of smiles for every occasion, but recently, his smile had shown some vulnerability. Today he needed to give the impression that smiling was easy.

The bailiff was calling all those involved in Weaver versus Wright and Snider to now enter Judge Green's courtroom. The cadence of Judge Green's low, whiskey-rough voice sent an odd jolt to the pit of everyone's belly. His voice rang with command as he ordered each one to stand and state their name and their purpose for being in his courtroom. After everyone was seated, he asked Hoafie to stand and, in his own words, tell his version of what happened. Hoafie was not used to speaking in front of people, and his voice shook with terror. He stared straight into the judge's eyes while he related the entire story, including his "piece of steak" from Cherry's. He was visibly shaken when the judge asked him why he cut the brake lines.

Hoafie stiffened at the question and looked to Warren as if he would help him with an answer. Judge Green spoke a little softer so as not to frighten Hoafie more. "Hoafie, I need you to look at me and tell me why you severed brake lines."

Hoafie looked even more puzzled. "Don't know what you mean, sir."

"I mean, why did you *cut* them?"

"Oh, I was just tryin' to get a raise. My friend told me that if I did everything my boss told me, I would get more money. He said bosses have lots of money, and if I always made my boss happy, I would get more money. I buy a lot of candy, ya know."

The judge's mouth turned into a grin that he couldn't control. Abby took note of several such expressions during Hoafie's rendition of the incident, and with a pulse-pounding certainty, she knew things were going to be all right. Judge Green had narrowed his eyes, gauging whether Hoafie was telling the truth, but then his dark brown eyes softened slowly, and she saw genuine compassion spill out.

Warren was called to the stand and gave his testimony. The first thing he expressed was his regret about the accident and how he never meant to hurt anyone. He became emotional during the remainder of his statement and collapsed into the chair as his knees buckled.

Lilly had slipped in quietly after everyone had been seated, but seeing Warren so vulnerable, she stood and, with feline grace, moved past the guard. He reached for her arm, but she shoved an elbow in his ribs. She managed to reach Warren before any other security stopped her and poured water from the pitcher on the table, forcing him to drink it. The judge called a short recess and motioned to the bailiff that Lilly be allowed to stay seated beside Warren.

When Judge Green returned to his bench, the only audible sound was his gavel striking the wood, calling the hearing back to order. As uncommon as it was for this judge to be silent, today he seemed to be at a loss for words. He retained his civility, but there was a distinct show of annoyance in his eyes. He looked intently at each person in the courtroom, making everyone wonder exactly when he was going to speak and what he was going to say. Known as a no-nonsense, very opinionated, high-profile judge, he was not exactly Warren's choice for vindication; but outside the courtroom, he was known as a humanitarian. Warren could only hope that he was feeling charitable today.

When Judge Green finally spoke, it was with great empathy toward Abby. He maintained the same manner of tone when speaking to Hoafie, but when he glanced at Warren, his vein pulsed at the base of his throat. His voice hardened ruthlessly. "I really have to wonder who the greater criminal here is, Warren or Hoafie. I have zero tolerance for people who drink excessively." There was no reprieve or mercy in his eyes.

Lilly was frantically holding on to a sliver of hope, but it seemed to be slipping fast. The judge was speaking again, his voice as sharp as a whip. "Warren Wright, real estate mogul, I did some research into your background, and I realize you worked hard to reach the top, and I also know you were an established barfly at the local pubs. I know you only quit drinking when you were diagnosed with diabetes, and your life was spared when you fell off the wagon, causing your blood sugar to skyrocket. If that wouldn't have happened, the doctors never would have discovered your diseased liver. I don't know if you're a believer, Mr. Wright, but for some reason, the good Lord decided to keep you in his favor. The death of Jeff Weaver happened because, when you were getting plastered, so to speak, and decided to condense four years of army woes into one, you caused Hoafie to feel obligated to support something that he thought was very important to you. He didn't understand the consequences that would follow." Judge Green had a hungry look in his eyes. Lilly began shaking, afraid that Warren's past life would become public. Could he really be held accountable for the words he said while drunk? She shuddered inwardly at the thought.

Judge Green's words hit Warren like body blows. He picked up his glass of water and swallowed, hoping he could wash away all the hurt he had carelessly caused. He couldn't bring himself to look at Lilly or anyone else for that matter. He hung his head in shame. How had he allowed such a primitive element to control his way of life. He was so much bigger and better than a bottle of beer. It was unbelievable to him now how incredibly stupid he had been. If only he could go back in time.

Lilly was tapping him on the shoulder to get his attention. The judge was waiting for a response from Warren. Warren's natural instincts told him to respond with fighting words, but considering the position he was in, showing his true emotions was a better idea—something he was just getting used to with Lilly. Today all walls that he had spent many years building were coming down.

When Warren lifted his head, a set of cold brown eyes was boring into him. He decided to start talking before the judge declared him guilty. "Judge Green, you're right. Jeff Weaver didn't deserve to die for any reason. I take full responsibility for what Hoafie did. He really didn't know he was doing something wrong. I took Hoafie in to work for me a long time ago. He looks to me for everything. Some of my employees pull jokes on him, and the night in question, that's what happened. When I found out, I felt so bad that I took him out to Cherry's and bought him the biggest steak on the menu. I couldn't believe how great it made me feel to see him so happy. I wasn't used to feeling so worthy. I hadn't had a drink in over two years, and seeing how much Hoafie was enjoying that steak, I convinced myself that it would be all right if I had a drink to celebrate my generous mood. I had no plans to become intoxicated, and I especially had no intentions of telling Hoafie about my army days. I did ask him the next day about our conversation, but he told me we only talked about cars. I never gave it another thought because that's what he wants to talk about all the time. I can't believe how hard he worked just to please me. No one has ever done that before. It took him a while before he found the parking garage with Jeff's car. I've been told since then that he just kept asking questions, and because of his personality, everyone just played along, thinking that he was harmless. He can't write, but he has memorized some words, obviously enough to get him to his destination. His job at the office is so routine that he doesn't need a lot of vocabulary. The name of Jeff Weaver hadn't crossed my mind in over ten years, and I didn't remember saying the name to Hoafie, but unfortunately, he *did* remember."

He turned to look at Abby and saw tears running down her cheeks. "I can't express my sympathy enough to Ms. Weaver. I can't even imagine how she feels after hearing all of this, but none of this was done maliciously. It's so bizarre that I can't even believe it happened. Please don't punish Hoafie. He is totally innocent of any heartless act. He has a heart the size of Texas." He then added, "And it's for real. I hope everyone can forgive him and reserve his penalty for me. I'm willing to take the hit for him. The Lord knows he's taken enough punches in his lifetime." Warren's voice broke miserably as he tried to finish his statement. "Your Honor, I can't change the past, but I'm working on changing my future. I've already done a lot of transforming in my life, even before I knew about the accident. I have a fiancée now, and she's giving me the chance to see things differently. If there's anything I can do to help Ms. Weaver, all she'll have to do is ask. I truly am sorry for the heartache I caused."

Exhausted, Warren leaned back, feeling Abby's eyes evaluating his words. Judge Green was once again silent as if he too were calculating Warren's remarks. When he finally spoke, it was only to say that court would resume on Monday morning at ten o'clock; and at that time, he would have his verdict and the sentencing. He went on to say that his reason for the delay was simply that he needed more time to review the case.

A questioning gaze passed between everyone who was anxiously awaiting the verdict. Why was Judge Green doing this? Was he trying to come up with a stiffer punishment? After all the testimonies, did he still believe it was a premeditated plan? Court was adjourned by the bailiff, and with sad hearts, everyone filed out of the room, bewildered and silent.

Outside the courthouse, Abby watched as everyone shook hands and assured Warren and Hoafie that they would be back on Monday morning to show their support. She noted how the young waitress seemed to be flaunting the big diamond as she clung to Warren. Hoafie shadowed Warren and Lilly, enjoying the attention he was getting from the pretty girl.

Harley followed Abby as she made her way to her car. "Excuse me, Abby, but do you think I could hitch a ride to Summer Rain with you? I have a lot of work to get done today, and I don't want to waste the time by walking."

"Of course, I'll give you a ride. Hop in."

Abby initiated the conversation by asking Harley if it were true that he was going to preach at Morning Son on Sunday. "Yes, I am. I hope you and Mrs. Black can attend. The service begins at ten o'clock. I am so excited to stand behind a pulpit again, but I'm also very nervous. Not everyone is happy about my return, and I'm not sure what their reaction will be. I have, however, placed it in the Lord's hands, so I really shouldn't be worrying."

"I'm sorry all of this happened to you, Harley. It seems so unfair. Hopefully, after Sunday, you'll have a better feel for your acceptance back into the congregation. I'm sure everyone will be happy to have you back. A church needs stability, just like a family."

His smile was boyishly affectionate. "Thanks, Abby. I appreciate your encouragement. Being treated like a thief for the past two years has been hard on my self-worth. Even though I knew I had taken the honorable approach to the situation, I still felt overwhelmed by my congregation's shortage of trust. They put my head on the chopping block before I had a chance to speak. After the initial shock, I realized that it was all part of God's plan. That's the only way I survived the fall."

Abby pulled into her parking spot at Summer Rain and turned off the engine. "Harley, before you get out of the car, can we be outspoken and honest with each other?"

"Sure. I'd like that. What's on your mind?"

"Us."

"Us?"

"Yes. I said I wanted to be outspoken, which is totally out of character for me, but every time we're near each other, I feel this draw toward you. It's very eerie. I want to run toward you, yet I always run away from you. These reactions are very unfamiliar to me. I've been conscious for weeks now of these feelings, and it scares me. Maybe I'm being very forward in telling you this, but I just needed to be honest. I don't mean to put you on the spot, and you don't need to respond." She hesitated a moment, watching him in profile and trying to make a quick appraisal of his reaction to her revelation. Her heart was hammering foolishly as she removed the keys from the ignition and commenced to open the car door.

He halted her escape with a firm hand on her arm. "Abby, wait. You've taken me a bit by surprise here, but don't get out of the car just yet. I don't know exactly what to say. I don't have a lot of experience with women. I too have felt the magnetism you mentioned, only I wasn't sure just what to call it *or* what to do about it. A lot of things have been happening rather fast lately, so I brushed my thoughts of that aside." Tenderly, his eyes melted into hers as he confessed. "I really thought you hated me, so I tried very hard to stay out of your way. You always seemed annoyed with me. I think I did apologize for my rudeness in the parking lot, but if I didn't, I'm really sorry."

Abby cast her eyes downward and smiled. "Apology accepted. Let's go tell Shirley about the hearing today. I'm sure she's anxious to know what happened."

CHAPTER 54

When you are brought before synagogues, rulers and authorities, do not worry about how you will defend yourselves or what you will say for the Holy Spirit will teach you at that time what you should say.

—Luke 12:11–12

Warren, Lilly, and Hoafie walked into the courthouse at exactly nine forty-five on Monday morning. The bailiff was calling for Weaver versus Wright and Snider. Warren flinched and moved away from the door. Lilly clutched his hand with both of hers and guided him in the direction of the designated room. Judge Green appeared from behind the closed door in the back and called the trial to order. The man who carried himself with a commanding air of self-confidence looked beaten down. The tense, drawn face that greeted them today showered doubt about any kind of pardon. Shadows had deepened under his eyes, evidence of sleep loss. His intense eyes held everyone prisoner until he spoke.

"As I said before, Mr. Wright, I have no tolerance for men who can't hold their liquor and end up hurting other people. I am not a happy man today because I lost a lot of valuable sleep over the weekend because of the decision I had to make." He turned to look at Hoafie and eased into a smile. "I found no information on Hoafie. He owns nothing, has no driver's license, and has never been in any kind of trouble. He maintains a job and is known by others as a very kind and gentle man." His smile faded as he addressed Warren again. "You, on the other hand, Mr. Wright, have a bit of a reputation, especially when it comes to the opposite sex. It is not a crime to be wealthy and charming, but as I understand it, you're a real heartbreaker, Mr. Wright. Still not a crime, but it makes me wonder if I will be able to trust you with my decision. It took me a long time to determine just what that should be. Then I did an extensive background check, and I found your military past to be quite impressive, giving me more confidence in my judgment. Your two tours in Vietnam yielded you as a decorated war hero. The incident with Jeff Weaver was obviously not considered serious enough to end up in court. Your medals for bravery were notably inspiring. I have never been a soldier, so I cannot imagine the fear and anarchy that a soldier must endure. I want to say I admire your service that you gave to our country."

He took a drink of water before he continued. "I have been a judge for twenty years, and I've seen a lot of happiness, and I've seen a lot of heartache in my courtroom. I have to say this case has definitely topped the charts for being the most difficult to present a verdict. Your lawyers asked for this to be a private trial because of the media's tendency to attract attention. I do hope we can all be discreet and alleviate a lot of press coverage."

He continued on. "With a few sleepless nights and a lot of soul-searching, I finally made a decision concerning this case. It is probably one of the hardest things I've ever done, and I did it with a heavy heart because I settled on a decision I'm still not convinced is accurate. I first based everything on facts and then determined the rest on your remorsefulness and the likelihood that something this unconventional would ever happen again on my watch."

There remained a certain tension in his attitude as he resumed his admonishment. "I don't want to sound redundant, Mr. Wright, but I can't say it enough times. For a man with health issues such as yours to be so irresponsible is beyond my comprehension. I understand you are engaged to be married, and having a good woman does change a man's life. Hopefully, for you, it will be for the good. I am not blind to the anxiety that this trial has caused you, but in the whole scheme of things, it is nothing compared to what Ms. Weaver has dealt with over the past year. I find it very ironic that you were given another chance at life because of the generosity of her husband. You were very fortunate to be a recipient of an organ donor. Not everyone is so lucky, and because of that, I found that it created a change in my thought process. I began to feel encouraged about helping you instead of trying to punish you. After a lot of arguing with myself and considering all the extenuating circumstances, I think I have come up with a way that will be a constant reminder of your actions yet allow you to be doing a community service."

Hoafie's eyes darted nervously back and forth from the judge to Warren, and then he lowered his gaze in confusion. Warren's eyes were bright with hope as he glanced at Lilly, her eyes already brimming with tears.

Judge Green's even no-nonsense voice rumbled out into the air, filling the courtroom with audible sighs of relief. "Most of the evidence in this case is circumstantial. No one saw Hoafie cut the lines. There were no fingerprints found and no other solid proof. *And* there was no criminal intent. Because of Hoafie's IQ and his intellectual background, this court of law finds him incapable of bearing witness in the Jeff Weaver tragedy."

Everyone in the courtroom, to include Abby, gloried briefly in the shared moment of Hoafie's freedom. He didn't understand why everyone was clapping, but he smiled and slapped his big hands together in delight.

"Mr. Wright, would you stand please. Instead of a substantial fine, I am ordering you to build a self-sufficient room onto your home where Hoafie can reside for the rest of his life. This will save the taxpayers a lot of money, yet he will be well taken care of. To punish this compliant man would do good for no one. You will have custody of him, as a child. You will be responsible for his care and his well-being. You do not have a choice in this matter, Mr. Wright, and there will be yearly evaluations. If you do not comply with these regulations, you will be held in contempt of this court. Do I make myself clear, Mr. Wright?"

"Yes, Your Honor, I understand. And may I say thank you for your concern for Hoafie and for Lilly's and my future? This is the second time my life has been given back to me, and it will never be taken for granted again. Thank you, Your Honor, for a great gift."

Joy bubbled in Lilly's laugh and shone in her eyes as Warren picked her up and swung her around. Harley and Abby stood nearby, smiling as they looked at each other. "You seem to be handling this quite well, Abby. I know this is a painful process for you, yet you're still relinquishing your misery and grief so that others can have a better life."

Abby, unaware of the captivating picture she made when she smiled, caused Harley to fight an overwhelming need to be close to her. "You are an inspiration to me, Abby. Your attitude today can only be seen as a demonstration of agape love. Do you know what that is, Abby?" She shook her head no without speaking.

"Most people don't know the definition of the word, but even fewer practice it. What I have witnessed through this entire ordeal is your unconditional love, your agape love toward Mrs. Black, allowing her to live with you so that she didn't have to move away from her home. You helped save a man who caused your husband to have a fatal accident and even came to terms with the man who is alive because of your generosity when you donated one of your husband's organs to him." Harley moved closer to her, and she could now feel the heat from his body. He cradled her chin in his hand and forced her to look up at him. "That's a pretty impressive description of mercy."

Abby felt a bottomless peace and satisfaction as part of her reveled in his open admiration of her. His praise made her feel all bubbly inside. She realized that he was easily pushing his way into her heart. And she now realized that she didn't want to stop him.

Walking out into the cool air showed evidence of an afternoon storm that was beginning to gather on the horizon with a lacy overlay of gray clouds. Even if it rained, nothing could dampen the spirits of the small group as they exited through the doors and down the wide marble steps. Warren was having trouble holding back tears, while Lilly's gentle laugh rippled through the air. In spite of himself, he chuckled; and when he laughed, he felt ten years younger.

Harley and Abby expressed their congratulations to Warren and Hoafie and disappeared to the parking lot.

CHAPTER 55

Stand up, plead your case before the mountains'
let the hills hear what you have to say.

—Micah 6:1

The minute when Harley and Abby walked together through the back door, Shirley knew something good had happened. The conversation between them seemed more significant than usual, and their smiles insinuated that some form of harmony was being nurtured. Shirley's face beamed with joy. It was about time these two owned up to their feelings.

Abby began brewing a pot of tea as she shared the day's events with Shirley. Her voice, vibrating with sadness when speaking of her late husband, turned strong throughout the remainder of her description of the trial. Harley relaxed as he sat at the kitchen table, watching that strength transfer to delicacy on her porcelain-smooth face when she began talking about Hoafie. He heard her express the impact the judge's comments had on her and how she had come to see another side of the entire process. "Judge Green had definitely impressed me with his ruling," she was saying. "I was amazed that a man of his eminence would allow his softer side to be observed in the courtroom." Harley nodded in agreement.

Shirley expressed her happiness and her eagerness to meet Warren and Hoafie. She suggested to Abby that they have a small party to celebrate the good news. Abby let out a squeal and a giggle, to the surprise of both Harley and Shirley. "How about next Friday night? We'll have a small dinner party here to celebrate not only Warren and Hoafie's freedom but also Harley's return to his rightful position as pastor of Morning Son Church."

Harley released a short laugh and shook his head. "Slow down, Abby. That may not happen. I won't know that until after Sunday's service. Even if things remain as they are, we have plenty to celebrate. Hoafie and Warren's freedom is more than enough reason to have a party."

Shirley stopped Harley in midsentence and increased the reason for a party by announcing Warren and Lilly's engagement. "Oh, Abby, let's get started on the menu. This will be our first social event here at Summer Rain, and it needs to be perfect. I can't wait."

Abby laughed as she watched Shirley walk down the hallway, still talking to herself about food and drink. She thanked Harley as he stood, ready to resume his duties outside. He came close, looked down at her intensely, smiled, and walked out the door.

Abby waited until her quickened pulse subsided before going in search of Shirley. She found her in the sunroom, searching through her recipe box. She looked up over her glasses, pressed a hand to her chest, and batted her lashes. With a peaches-and-cream Georgia accent, she teased, "Why, Miss. Scarlet, you look a little flushed. What, may I ask, did Mr. Butler say to you?"

"Very funny, Mom. Actually, he didn't *say* anything. It was just the way he looked at me. He always seems so serious, but today his anxiety seemed shadowed with some happiness. It was almost as if he wanted to say something intimate to me, but his fear outweighed his need."

"Give him some time, Abby. He'll come around. By the way, Tim McDonald, the chief of police, called earlier, and he would like you to call him."

"Thanks, Mom. I'll do it right now." Abby went to the telephone in the other room and dialed the police station's number.

"Hello, this is the Carroll County Police Department. Tim McDonald speaking. May I help you?"

"Chief McDonald, this is Abby Weaver. I'm returning your call."

"Hi, Abby, thanks for calling me back. I didn't get a chance to speak to you after the trial, and I just wanted to say thank you for all your patience during the last year. In my line of business, I don't often see the kind of compassion that you showed through this process." His voice was thick with emotion as he admitted knowing about her meeting with the judge. "It's unprecedented for the plaintiff to speak on behalf of the defendant, and I'm sure Judge Green was flabbergasted. I was happy to hear his ruling. It would have been a shame to incarcerate Hoafie for something so innocent." Tim hesitated, not wanting to ramble. "I don't mean to make your husband's death seem insignificant because, as we all know, it was a terrible tragedy. We can't change what happened, and we know Hoafie meant no harm. Your act of forgiveness is very inspiring."

"Thank you, Chief McDonald. I'm sorry that it was my husband who was the target of a horrible mistake, but I have to believe that people make errors and that accidents happen. I can't forget what happened, but I had to forgive. And when I met Hoafie, my perception changed of the man responsible for my husband's death. I found it almost impossible to feel any animosity toward such a compliant, simple man. I feel bad that I can't say the same about Mr. Wright. You know he was the one who sold Mrs. Black's house to me, and then even though he never meant any harm, he does accept responsibility for my husband's death. By some twist of fate, his life was spared when he became an organ recipient of my husband. For some reason, which I guess only God knows, that fateful day changed my life in ways I never imagined. It's not quite as easy as it is for Hoafie, but I'm working on forgiving him. Thank you for calling me and expressing your condolences. These past eighteen months have been quite a journey for me, and I'm glad to finally have some closure."

"I'm glad we were able to piece together the puzzle and help you with that closure. If there's anything I can ever help you with, please feel free to call."

"Thanks again, Chief McDonald, for all your help. Bye."

Tim returned the phone to its cradle and dropped into his chair. He felt better now that the green folder would no longer be showing up on his desk. Stacey could finally file it in the closed-case section in the file room.

With one elbow resting casually over the arm of the chair, Tim took a minute to reflect the past. As tragic as it was, the Weaver case had ultimately driven him to recognize and identify his feelings about Stacey. When he thought back to all the hints that she had thrown him, he couldn't believe he had been so blind and so insensitive. Yet somehow, she managed to still be in love with him. Women—he would never figure them out.

"Knock, knock. May I come in? Why do you look so serious? Did something happen?"

"Come in, Stacey. Truthfully, something has happened."

She was caught off guard with the sudden vibrancy of his voice, and a soft gasp escaped her. "What happened, Tim? Not another murder?"

Tim responded with a crooked smile that hinted at a wild side. Stacey was intrigued. Obviously, a murder had not been committed, but something was in disarray. Tim's shameless grin seemed full of anticipation as he looked into Stacey's face and winked. With a secret slow smile, she understood that her feelings were finally being reciprocated. The implication sent waves of excitement through her, and her heartbeat throbbed in her ears. She moved toward him, impelled involuntarily by her own passion. In one bold move, she was in his arms, clinging to him as if he were her lifeline. Her head fit perfectly in the hollow between his shoulder and neck, locking her into his embrace. His voice was low and tender as he whispered into her hair, "Stacey, I guess this has been a long time coming. I'm really sorry I was so blind and stupid. I've thought a lot about this, and it feels right." She felt his hand brush the hair from her neck, and she stepped back, allowing him to search her upturned face. "Isn't it amazing how the one thing you're searching for in life is right in front of you, and you can't see it? Do you know it's actually the believing that enables the seeing? When I convinced myself to believe that you had feelings for me, I was able to see you in a different setting. I tried to step into your shoes and look at it from your perspective. I would really like to learn to communicate better with you."

Stacey smiled, excited about Tim's confession. "Sometimes our eyes hide the things that our heart doesn't want to envision. It's not always our sight that we should rely on but our insight. When I admitted to you how I felt, it was like a veil being ripped from your eyes. You finally saw what you had been keeping from yourself. Am I right?"

Tim rubbed his chin and sighed. "You're right. All the signs were there, hidden in plain sight, but I couldn't believe that you would ever want me in your life outside of the office. I guess believing in something is very powerful. If you can't believe in it, you sure won't see it. So getting rid of our disbeliefs can open our eyes to new possibilities. Is that what you're saying?"

"You're a fast learner, Tim McDonald, and quite a handsome one at that."

"Could I interest you in a bottle of wine and a good, juicy steak at my house tonight? The grill is just waiting to be fired up." Not waiting for an answer, he continued. "I'll pick you up at six."

When she arrived at his house that evening, Stacey was very impressed with Tim's culinary abilities. Two brass candlesticks supporting white beeswax candles sat precisely in the middle of the sage green tablecloth that covered the patio table. Two plates of fine china displayed matching cloth napkins. Two lead crystal wine glasses, already occupied with a fruity red wine, completed the setting. The hint of black cherry and spice paired perfectly with the porterhouse cut of steak. Tim's presentation of the Caesar salad and the roasted potato was also very colorful and creative.

As darkness approached, Tim lit the candles and turned on the radio. A pale crescent moon slipped in and out of view. Stacey closed her eyes and leaned back in her chair, absorbed in the soft music. She knew how much thought and time Tim had put into making this the perfect evening, and she wanted him to know how much she appreciated it. When she opened her eyes, he was kneeling in front of her. She smiled to herself as he spoke. "Stacey, you tore away my defenses; you revealed my weaknesses, which one of them turns out to be you; and you brought me out of hiding. I never expected to fall in love again, but I guess that goes to show you that life is unpredictable. I want to say thank you for making me believe in myself again. I will always be indebted to you for that. I have a small token of appreciation, which I hope you will accept."

He reached deep in his pocket and pulled out a small package tied with a pink ribbon. Brushing away tears to see, she opened the box, her senses reeling as if short-circuited. A cry of pure ecstasy broke from her lips. Lightly taking her hand, Tim asked, "Stacey Evans, will you marry me? Will you spend the rest of your life with me?"

As though his words released her, she flung herself against him and cried, "Yes, yes, yes!"

He threw back his head and let out a great peal of laughter. "Well, young lady, I guess we have a wedding to plan."

Stacey was floating on cloud nine. She was going to marry Tim McDonald, chief of police—the man she loved, the man of her dreams.

CHAPTER 56

Well done, good and faithful servant.

—Matthew 25:21

Harley began walking faster as he neared the camper. What a day this had been. Warren and Hoafie's freedom was sufficient reason to party, but Abby's confession to him the day before about her feelings was still causing his mind to reel. It was just out of the blue that she admitted her sentiments. Falling in love was all new to him. Even in seminary, he never allowed himself time or put forth an effort toward a social life. He was so committed to his studies and finding ways to pay for them that he withdrew from the group scene. He wasn't antisocial, just reserved and somewhat disconnected from the partygoers. He couldn't afford to be distracted by romantic notions. Once he came to terms with the fact that God was choosing his path in life, he exchanged his interpretation of living for that of the church. He found life in New Hope to be all he needed. Amazingly enough, his former demands of existence slowly melted into mere requests.

For the past two years, his prayers always asked for one thing, that he be returned to the church—hopefully back to Morning Son, but he was willing to go where God led him. He could never explain why he never pursued another church in another town or why he felt compelled to live as a pauper, but he knew someday he would get an answer. This Sunday that premonition might come true.

He finally reached his "house" and settled his torso into the orange and green lawn chair. He picked up his sermon notes from the evening before and commenced to work on the conclusion. He had spoken on the subject of forgiveness before, but this time, it was a little nearer and dearer to his heart.

Harley woke Sunday morning to the sound of "This is the Day" on his radio. He smiled. Quite fitting for his return to the pulpit as an alleged fallen preacher. The Lord had definitely made this day happen, and Harley felt responsible to follow the call. New Hope was a small town, and he knew word had gotten around fast about today's sermon, so it was no surprise when the pews began filling up. It felt so good to be back where he knew he belonged.

The office was locked; obviously, a few were still finding perverse pleasure in keeping him out as long as possible. Maybe Pastor Wayne, who had served as interim pastor for the past two years, was not ready to relinquish his duties. Maybe, like Harley, he too had fallen in love with these people and didn't want to leave. So today he needed to not only prove his trustworthiness and his commitment to the people of this church but to also convince Pastor Wayne that they would be in good hands.

When he walked out onto the stage, he suddenly felt all the emotions he'd conditioned himself not to feel. The ferocity of his passion for these people was frightening, as well as exalting. He wanted to shout and make them understand how much he loved them and that he truly forgave them. He wanted them to know how much he needed them and how much he had missed them. He wanted to continue on as if nothing had happened, but instead, he bowed his head and asked for God to begin and end his sentences.

He slowly lifted his head and said, "Good morning. I see some new faces in the congregation, so for those of you whom I have not had the pleasure of meeting, my name is Pastor Davidson. And if you're wondering, my first name is Harley. I see a few smiles and a few folks who look like they couldn't care less." Harley's eyes shifted from one person to another. "I understand that. It's been a while since I've seen a lot of you, and since today, I'm speaking so deeply from my heart I want to say that I've missed you. The majority of you wrote me up as thief. Since the truth has come out, I hope you have unwritten that narrative. I hope you have forgiven me for what you thought I did."

Harley trod softly away from the pulpit, standing in the middle of the stage. "Today's sermon is simply titled 'Forgiveness.' And just so you know, you're going to hear that word a lot in the next half hour. I didn't have long to prepare for this morning, so what I have to say is truly how I feel and who I am."

His arms spread expansively as he spoke. "Everyone here needs forgiveness for something, whether it be for gossiping, for not telling the truth, for taking something that's not yours, or for assuming the worst in your neighbor. Whatever the reason, we *all* need forgiveness. Now if I'm stepping on your toes, I hope you can go get a new pair of shoes if you need them.

"I looked up the definition for the word *forgiveness*, and this is what I found: 'Forgiveness is the intentional and voluntary process by which a victim undergoes a change in feelings and attitude regarding an offense, lets go of negative emotions such as vengefulness, with an increased ability to wish the offender well.' So this is saying that not only should you have a change in attitude but you also should wish good tidings to the offender. How many of us can actually do that? Corrie ten Boom put it like this. 'Forgiveness is the key that unlocks the door of resentment and the handcuffs of hatred. It is a power that breaks the chains of bitterness and the shackles of selfishness.' When we forgive others, we find that we are free and no longer chained by our own anger. It is not something you do for someone else but something you do for yourself. When you forgive, you're not condoning your offender's actions. You are just refusing to feel bad about them. You have to pray for people who have wronged you and love them. Trust me, it won't just change their life. It'll also change yours. It's about *our* attitude, not *their* behavior. And our attitude is to be tenderhearted, meaning that we are willing to forgive all those who have sinned against us. It is this tenderhearted attitude that prevents bitterness and resentment. We, as Christians, as we sit in these pews, are called to have this gracious attitude so that we can offer pardon to everyone who offends us. Forgiving will take us from our selfish fantasies in to a superb reality. We all know the old saying that nothing is easy. Well, that's definitely true about forgiveness."

Harley scanned the congregation, gauging their attention. He saw many faces piqued with interest and continued on. "You might be asking what actually is 'forgiveness.' Is it a form of an emotion or just a feeling, a sense of duty, or what? Ephesians 4:32 says that we have to forgive as God in Christ forgave us. How did God forgive us in Christ? All we have to do is repent our sins and believe in Christ. By doing that, God removes our sin and promises to never hold it against us. This is possible because of Jesus's suffering. It's important to know that God's grace is free. His forgiveness is offered to us through sincere repentance and faith in Christ. In accepting the gift forgiveness extended to us, we are rescued from the burden of sin. Then he makes a great promise. He wipes our slate clean and never remembers what we did. That sounds wonderful, doesn't it?

"Well, I told you, nothing is easy. There's one more thing we need to recognize. If we ask to be forgiven and the request comes from our heart, God *will* forgive. But he doesn't always remove all the consequences from that sin. We all remember the story of King David—his sin with Bathsheba and the murder of her husband, Uriah. David *did* repent, and God forgave him, but he also left him with a consequence. He allowed his son to die. I'm sure you're wondering how God can say he's taking away your sin and then turn around and give you grievous consequences. Hebrews 12 explains, 'For those whom the Lord loves, He disciplines, and He scourges every son whom he receives.' He deals with us as sons and He disciplines us so that we may share His holiness. In other words, God disciplined David to bless him and draw him closer, and that's what he does for us. As a parent, you discipline your children, teaching them right from wrong, not because you *want* to punish them but because you love them and want their future to be blessed.

"For the past two years, I have felt a little bit like Joseph after his brothers sold him into captivity. But they did it not knowing who he was. I, on the other hand, have walked among you for years, supporting you, crying when you cried, laughing when you laughed. You knew me well, yet you betrayed me. There are a few out there this morning who stood beside me, and you know who you are, but the majority of you were very quick to judge. I did not nor would I steal money from you or anyone else. I never imagined the love I experienced in this town would ever turn into the plague. A doctor doesn't treat someone for leprosy until the test comes back positive. You never gave me a test—no X-rays, no questions. You just diagnosed me with assumption. Just like Joseph's brothers, they assumed he was dead. But he emerged out of that pit, forgave his brothers, and went on to make a big difference with his people. I want this incident to make a difference in this church and in our town. I want people to realize the power of forgiveness. Even among the many obstacles that can be a hindrance, as a Christian, you still have power. I'm standing before you to admit that, yes, I had my pride. I felt I was misunderstood, and some days, I just didn't feel like I even *wanted* to forgive. I guess that was the human side coming out in me. The more I rehearsed the situation in my mind, the more it restricted my communication with God. Some days, I felt some *partial* charity toward my offenders. But to tell the truth, that's really the same as no forgiveness at all. *Unforgiveness* is a poisonous form of slavery, and you can't be released from it until you have heartfelt absolution. Your lips can say, 'I forgive', but unless your heart is echoing your words, it means nothing. It's deliberately *refusing* to give up the resentment and the thought of 'getting even.'

"The Lord promises that forgiveness is possible, even when we think our hurt is too huge to repair. Sometimes the offender is struggling just as hard as we are, and we get so caught up in our own emotions that we can't see *their* pain. A person needs to be held accountable for their actions, but they also need patience from us. Matthew 18:26 quotes someone in need of forgiveness who says, 'Be patient with me.' Patience is a true act of compassion, and it is needed to help the offender work through the pain that needs forgiveness.

"If any of you visit the gym or exercise at home, you know that the more you work at strengthening your muscles, the stronger they become. And the same goes when you exercise courage, patience, and letting the Lord into the process of your forgiveness. The potential for forgiving will be much greater.

"When Bill approached me about coming back to Morning Son, I must admit I wanted to shout hallelujah, but I guess fear overtook my excitement, and I suddenly had doubts about my own ability to forgive. I knew I couldn't stand before you and preach about such a personal topic if I still had a few links holding me to the chain of unforgiveness. I needed time to be sure. Even though the prayer that I had prayed every day was now being answered, my insecurities overshadowed my certainties about who I am. That evening, I spent a lot of time on my knees. I asked for guidance and the strength to once again take the weight of the problem from my shoulders and lay it on the heart of Jesus, the one who has no load limit.

"The next morning, I witnessed an act of forgiveness that I will never forget. Forgiving someone for their active part in the loss of a loved one takes not only tremendous courage but also incredible passion for showing the true heart of a Christian. I saw how a true believer of Christ should act. I watched as a young lady had more compassion on a most unlovable fellow human being than a mother with a sick child. God so graciously humbled me, allowing me to see that the journey I'm on is not over and that His divine intervention is everywhere, if only we unclutter our eyes and give our hearts abundant space to actually acknowledge His presence. The last two years have been long and hard for me, but with what God has shown me in the last week, there's nothing I would change about the past. I truly have forgiven all of you, even the person who originally accused me and sent me on this path.

"As I look back, I can now appreciate God's agenda. He replaced heartache with a lot of healing. I've learned a lot through all of this—patience, understanding, compassion—learning that my life is God's will, not mine.

"I'm sure a lot of you are under the impression that, just because I'm a pastor, all these things I just mentioned are automatic in my life. When it was rumored that I was a thief, all those traditional measurements that you used to gauge the worth of a preacher turned out to be distorted. The pedestal crumbled right before your eyes." He smiled and joked, "I'm afraid of heights, and you never should have lifted me that high. It only allowed me a longer distance to the floor."

He continued as the congregation chuckled. "I wrestle every day with the same battles as you. I'm human. I need food and water to sustain my physical body, just like you. On paper, my occupation may be listed as clergyman, but my true vocation is servanthood. I'm a person working in the service of another. I am a subordinate, working under the commandments of the Lord, working sometimes in conditions that I don't always like or understand.

"I loved my position here as your pastor. I was devastated when you lost your trust in me. But since I'm human, I did exactly what you did. I assumed. I convinced myself that you had finally found a concrete reason to get rid of me. Maybe you had been trying for years, and I just missed the signals. I tried to recall all the meetings and visits from board members. I played conversations over and over in my mind, wondering if I was really that immature about my actions. If you couldn't trust me, your pastor, then somewhere and somehow, I felt I had failed to convey the message that I came to share. Why else would you accuse me of such a crime? Obviously, something was missing in my daily effort to minister to you. I saw myself as a failure. At one point, I was ready to give up my calling and leave New Hope, but God wanted me to stay. So here I am.

"Forgiveness—it's a long word. It's a hard word. It's a very unselfish act. It's power. It's freedom. It's all these things, and through Jesus Christ, we can have it. He died so that we can be forgiven. All we have to do is ask.

"What I'm asking *you* to do today is not just for me. It's for all of us. I want to walk the next part of my journey alongside all of you. I want us all to walk the narrow road and make room for our neighbors. We've all been given grace, and we all should give grace in return."

Harley ended the service with a prayer and walked back the aisle to receive the parishioners as they left the building. There were tears, handshakes, and a lot of hugs. Even the "wolves" were displaying tattered tissues as they shook Harley's hand. As they filed past him, one by one, Harley looked at each one with new discernment. They seemed relieved that today was over and happy, that he was back in their lives. With every hug came encouraging words and thank-yous for a most needed sermon and for Harley's testimony concerning forgiveness.

Warren and Lilly reiterated the words of those before them. They seemed comforted by the words of the sermon. Tears fell on Harley's shoulder as Lilly whispered, "Thank you. You opened up a new door for me today. I have a lot of thinking to do. We'll see you next Sunday."

Harley's face beamed with joy. He loved hearing those last five words. Shirley was next in line, and as she threw her arms around his neck, she whispered, "I knew you could do it. We love you, Harley."

He looked up just as Abby approached him, and his compelling eyes riveted her to the spot. Her cheeks colored under his gaze. "Good morning, Abby. I hope you were pleased with the service. May I call you later?"

She found it hard not to return his irresistible smile. "That would be fine, Harley. Looking forward to later." She walked out the door, not waiting for a reply.

The last person in line strolled forward and extended her visibly trembling hand. "Hi, Harley. It was a wonderful sermon. I appreciated the part about forgiving the offender and showing compassion for their pain. I've been blinded with anger for so long that, no matter what I looked at or who I conversed with, I couldn't see the reality." With the last trace of resistance vanishing, Joan continued. "*You* weren't to blame, Harley, but *I* was in no position to take the blame either. Admitting to myself that I was the one who should be held accountable would have only reinforced my feeling of worthlessness. And I was afraid—afraid to die and reluctant to live. I owe my life to Shirley and Abby. They challenged my insecurities and forced me to come clean."

Joan flashed a sweet smile and offered one last thought to Harley. "I guess I've come full circle with you, Harley. It's a bit ironic that I blamed you for my fall, and then you turn out to be the one who pulls me back up on my feet." She placed her hand on his forearm and simply said, "Thank you."

Harley leaned forward, gave her a hug, and opened the door for her to exit. After all the parishioners had filed out, he turned the dead bolt lock on the front door and turned toward the side door. He had liked to think of this as his private entrance, a quiet way to come and go. He leaned against the door to push it open and, to his surprise, was greeted with a sea of people, all clapping and shouting his name. He shaded his eyes against the brilliance of the sun and reached into his pocket for his sunglasses. Without the glare of the sun, he could now see the pavilion covered in yellow ribbons and a big banner with Welcome Home painted in bright red, hanging from the rafters. There seemed to be enough food to feed the entire town. Harley was stunned. It was more than he could ever have hoped for. He scanned the crowd, quickly looking for Abby. He wanted her by his side. None of this would be possible if she hadn't played such an important role in his return home.

Abby watched him laugh, as if sincerely amused, while his dark brown eyes softened at the sight of her. The smile seemed to add a touch of vulnerability to his face when he caught her eye and winked. His gaze returned to her again and again as he made his way through the crowd.

As the members of the congregation and their curious friends proceeded to leave, Harley noticed Abby lingering near the punch bowl. He walked slowly in her direction, pretending to need something more to drink. Her stare was bold and riveted on his face, a look reciprocated, looking at her as if he were photographing her with his eyes. She was determined not to reveal her joy at seeing him, but his prolonged stare sent a rush of desire twisting through her. Harley too was full to bursting with feelings for the woman standing before him.

"Hi, Abby. This was sure a surprise for me today. Did you know about the party?"

"No, I had no idea, but I'm sure Shirley had something to do with it. She's a big fan of yours. She was very proud of you today. So was I. It took a lot of courage to stand before those who persecuted you and proclaim your forgiveness. I really admire you, Harley."

"Admiration? Is that the only feeling you have for me, Abby?"

Abby frowned, her eyes level under drawn brows. "I'm not sure what you want me to say, Harley. I tried to tell you how I felt. Why do you always have this sarcastic tone to your voice? If you want me to stay out of your life, then please be as honest with me as you were with the congregation this morning. Really, I can handle it." Her exasperated tone concealed the mixed emotions she felt.

"Abby, I'm sorry," he said a little sheepishly. "I didn't mean to sound unkind. I want you around. I want us to get to know each other. I guess I'm just in shock that a beautiful woman like yourself would have any kind of romantic feelings for me. It's really hard for me to believe that you think I'm worthy of your affection."

"Let's get something straight, Harley Davidson. I find you to be a very attractive, compassionate, and dedicated man. I was attracted to you from the very first moment I saw you, even though you were the rudest man I had ever met. I even had dreams about you."

Suddenly, Harley stepped forward and clasped her body tightly. His warm breath fanned her face seconds before his lips touched hers. She quivered at the sweet tenderness of his kiss and locked herself into his embrace. At last, reluctantly, they parted a few inches. Harley lifted one hand and smoothed Abby's hair back from her face as he spoke. "I've wanted to do that for a long time. I guess by your response, I can assume you have too."

Abby tilted her back to better study his face. "Harley. Yes . . . much to my surprise." She watched as his eyebrows drew together in a scowl. "Please let me finish. Since that day in the grocery store parking lot, your existence has haunted me. As much as I tried to put you out of my mind, I couldn't. And then you showed up on my doorstep. When I realized that my feelings toward you were amorous, I was in total shock. I did everything I could to put you out of my mind, but soon my late husband's face became your face. I wasn't ready for that to happen. I was so afraid that I would stop remembering the past that I became afraid of the future. I was caught between memories and opportunities. I felt as if I was betraying him by thinking of you. Every time you appeared in my mind, I vowed to prove to myself that I had a strong immune system against you and that I could resist whatever it was that attracted me to you."

The warmth of his laugh sent shivers down her spine. "So you don't know why you're attracted to me? How flattering."

"Don't take it personally, Harley. I just wasn't ready to have feelings for anyone. There was something about you that weakened my willpower and caused me to remember how it feels to have my heart flutter. I thought I had bolstered myself enough to not feel those emotions, but in my mind, I kept seeing little snippets of the life I had yet to live and knew that I wanted to pursue those images. I thought Summer Rain would be enough to quench my needs, but I was wrong. I miss the company of a gentleman."

Harley offered his kindest smile and cradled her face with his hands. What he saw was a mixture of fear and honesty. "Abby, you don't know how much I appreciate your truthfulness. I couldn't have said it better myself."

As the new couple walked to the parking lot together, Abby asked if Harley would like to drive her home to Summer Rain. He stared at her and then burst out laughing. As he jumped behind the wheel, he shouted, "This is the best day ever!"

As they pulled into the garage at Summer Rain, Harley turned off the ignition of the car and turned toward Abby. The strength and confidence in his voice sounded louder than the bit of insecurity that Abby thought she heard as he spoke. "I feel like a complete man today. Even though God is first in my life, I have wondered what it would be like to have a remarkable woman by my side. I hope I'm about to find out."

Abby's smile broadened in approval as Harley continued. "I realize we haven't known each other all that long, but I feel God led me to this town so that you and I could meet. I feel like he has taken me on the scenic route, but in the end, it's the scenery that makes the trip worthwhile. And you have definitely enhanced my surroundings." He smiled as his eyes clung to hers, analyzing her reaction.

The tenderness in his voice amazed Abby and pulled at her heartstrings. He seemed to be waiting for a response, but she couldn't give him one. He took her hand and put it on his heart, where she felt the beat hard against her palm. As if knowing she couldn't express her feelings at the moment, he indicated with a nod of his head that he understood.

He continued speaking. "I also learned that no matter how hard it is or how impatient I become, I need to be still and let God show me the way. I am convinced that God sent me here so that I could absorb and understand more of his ways. You and I got off to a rocky start, I'll admit, but if God hadn't brought you to New Hope and put you in my path, I might still be sitting in the parking lot."

As tears welled in her eyes, Abby smiled. She didn't know exactly what was going to transpire in her life, but she knew that having Harley as a friend was the best thing that could ever have happened to her.